The Bodleian Sequence

The Bodleian Sequence

PETER GRANT

First published in the United Kingdom in 2022 by
The Choir Press

ISBN 978-1-78963-277-4

The water in a vessel is sparkling.
The water in the sea is dark.
The small truth has words which are clear.
The great truth has great silence.

~ Rabindranath Tagore

Prologue

What a confounded nuisance, thought Professor Clinton Westley who, despite being American, spoke, and thought, more like one of Dickens' characters than a native of San Antonio. The forecast had said nothing about fog and yet here it was, thick, dank, and impenetrable. He slowed his car to a crawl peering into the gloom.

Yet Westley was excitedly expectant. Only another few miles and he'd reach his destination and, he was certain, find the answer to a puzzle that had baffled the finest minds of the Western world for more than eight centuries.

'Damn!' This time Westley exclaimed out loud and more in keeping with his Texan heritage. He just managed to brake before the car hit the fallen tree. He turned off the engine and got out to inspect the blockage.

'Ahh, not too bad. Should be able to move that myself.' As he bent down to grasp a protruding branch, Westley suddenly became aware of something else in the road. At first, he thought it was just a pile of old clothes discarded by some unthinking fly-tipper. But then it began to move. 'What the!' he exclaimed, just as an even thicker bank of fog swept over the road. The murk concealed whatever it was, but Westley was overcome by a creeping sense of unease. He let go of the branch and stepped back a few paces.

It was only at the last second that he turned slightly and saw, emerging from the fog, an arm. The arm was clothed in a loose, black garment. The last thing of which Westley was aware was a thin, wiry hand grasping for his collar, with long, pale fingers on which the veins unnaturally stood out. He tried to run but tripped on the branch and, as he fell, the hand tightly gripped his tweed waistcoat.

His last thought was of a sudden, immense coldness, but it was a coldness spreading from inside. He was unaware that a long, thin knife had been thrust deep into his heart.

*

Cecil Arbuthnot was looking forward to his dinner. *Should be steak and kidney tonight*, he hoped. His wife was sure to make his favourite so close to his retirement. He glanced up at the clock mounted on the dark wood panelling opposite his desk. Nine-thirty, only another half hour to closing. Approaching his sixty-fifth year Arbuthnot had worked at the Bodleian for more than twenty-five years, ever since BMW took over the old Rover car company. *Bit of a change from the assembly line*, thought Cecil looking round the library's Lower Reading Room.

Still, haven't done too badly, he thought. He'd been worried about finding another job back in ninety-four but had been fortunate to be offered a post as a junior security officer. He was now one of the most senior of the Bodleian's security staff, a position of huge responsibility, given the treasures the library contained. It was Arbuthnot who, in 2004, had unmasked Gerald Gadsby, the 'Manuscript Cutter' as the press had dubbed him. For seven years Gadsby had stalked the great libraries of Europe removing hundreds of pages from priceless manuscripts, cutting them from their bindings using a blade concealed in his wristwatch strap. *Commended by the chancellor himself*, mused Cecil. *Called me a master sleuth, no less! But I'd always had my suspicions. If Gadsby was a fellow of All Souls, then I'm a Dutchman!*

Cecil looked up again. 'Nine forty-five, a bit early but should do a last lap round the building. Don't want anything going wrong in my last week.' He made his way through the theology and philosophy sections to the south staircase and Duke Humfrey's Library, the oldest part of the Bodleian, whose earliest section dates from 1487. It closes three hours earlier than the main library, but Cecil Arbuthnot was a thorough man. He'd once found a weeping undergraduate in Duke Humfrey's who had been locked in for over two hours.

All seemed in order and Arbuthnot was about to return to the main building when, *'S'funny*, he thought. *Was that a shadow moving in the stacks? Probably just a trick of the light. I'd better make sure.* He walked towards the arched windows at the far end of the library but, as he did so, a figure emerged from behind him moving swiftly toward the door Cecil had just entered by. 'Oi! What d'ye think you're up to?' demanded Cecil as he strode purposefully toward the figure. Cecil had been meticulous and had locked the door behind him.

The figure turned and Cecil was so taken aback, he halted in his tracks. It was much taller than him, perhaps six feet four, and dressed in a loose-fitting, black, hooded garment. At first Cecil thought the hood marked the intruder as a youthful, opportunist thief, but he was entirely mistaken. From the little Cecil could see of the face it was a man nearly as old as himself with a prominent, aquiline nose. Both the face, what he could see of it, and the figure's right hand, which was grasping the doorknob, were very pale, almost translucent.

The figure calmly released its grip on the door. Cecil was unsure how to react. His initial unease at seeing the black-clad intruder began to transform into something far worse. His mind told him to flee but his body wouldn't respond. In a movement far more rapid than seemed possible for a man of his probable age, the figure sprang at Cecil, grasping for his neck. As it reached him time, for Cecil, seemed to slow down and he was acutely aware of the knife and then its icy embrace.

Mrs Arbuthnot waited in vain at home with the steak and kidney pie her husband would never eat.

Chapter 1

The fist caught her a glancing blow to her mouth. *She's good. I must concentrate in defence but let instinct guide my attacks. It has to be a kick*, thought Anna. Her right hand was throbbing with pain from her earlier, mistimed punch, it was either badly bruised or she'd broken something.

The blonde-haired woman tried her own side kick, but Anna parried it. Her opponent sprang quickly to her left, but not quickly enough. Anna anticipated her move and countered it by swivelling to her right. As she did so her body left the ground and her right foot smashed into the other woman's blue head guard. The blonde woman crashed to the ground, dazed and defeated. As her opponent struggled to her feet Anna felt exhilarated, but etiquette demanded she suppress her emotions and bow to her opponent, the referee and the three judges. *Courtesy, integrity, perseverance, self-control and indomitable spirit*, she told herself. Her teammates rushed onto the dojang as the tannoy announced: 'Winner in the fifty-three-kilogram category for women, Anna Carr, Oxford University. The result, Oxford University five, Cambridge University four.'

As Anna was embraced by her colleagues, she felt a not-unusual detachment. Her emotions were not those usually felt by athletes, which explained why, despite her outstanding talent for martial arts, she had never sought higher competitive levels. Her sabom, Saseong Alvarez, often told her she had the skill and mental toughness to make the British Olympic team, but Anna's goals were more personal. Sure, she enjoyed helping her team win but she never revelled in individual glory. The elation she felt was about the perfection of her final move. She hadn't executed the jump spin hook kick so flawlessly before, even in practice.

Back in the changing rooms Anna removed her head guard and examined her mouth. A small trickle of blood had stained her teeth, but it was minor. It was more difficult to take off her right half-finger protector. The hand was swollen, and it hurt. *Better see what it's like tomorrow*, thought Anna. *Not worth hours in A and E if it's just bruised.*

She stripped off the rest of her clothes and stood in front of the full-length mirror to check for any other injuries. She ran her fingers through her short, lilac-dyed hair, which stood up in sweat-soaked spikes. Circling her left bicep was an inscription in a flowing script: 'the great truth has great silence'. A girl she'd taken to bed last term had puzzled over the motto, despite being an English literature student. *Mind you she also said my arse looked like a boy's.*

Anna was a lithe five-feet-four tall, and her distaste of the feminine beauty ideal was obvious. Her pale skin had never been near a tanning studio, and she didn't shave her body hair. Anna's view of depilation was that it was a male-imposed cultural device. Removing pubic hair had particularly dubious connotations. 'It makes women look like children,' she'd told her friend Nikki. 'Basically, it suggests that men are closet paedophiles.'

'Isn't that a bit extreme?'

'I'm an extreme person,' Anna had replied. 'The body hair thing goes back through the entire history of Western art.'

Anna opened her locker and found her pendant, a silver triskelion in a circle on a black choker. It represented the three realms of material existence in Celtic thought: earth, water, and sky, but also evoked Norse mythology, which speaks of the three states of matter before creation, the three goddesses of destiny, and the three deities – Odin, Vili and Ve – who created humankind.

She put on her clothes, all of them black. She checked her shoulder bag, also black with a skull and a raven embossed on it. Finally, she pulled a black hoodie over her head. On the front was a pentagram, the figure 666 and the logo 'Satan Loves Me'. As she walked out of the doors of the sports centre a thin drizzle had begun, and the pavement was shining in the streetlights of early evening. Anna took her phone out of her bag, plugged in her ear buds, and pulled her hood over her head. In a cacophony of echo, noise, and feedback a female voice could be heard speaking, before guttural male vocals cut in. It was the opening of one of Anna's favourite albums, *God Hates Us All* by Slayer. Her phone interrupted the song.

'Anna? It's Magnus. Do you think you could pop over to my study this evening? I may have something that would interest you.'

'Sure,' was the terse reply. 'Be about half an hour.'

'Great. See you soon. Bye.'

Anna considered what her former tutor might want. Since completing her PhD that summer she had received many offers of post-doctoral scholarships, but nothing sufficiently intellectually challenging. She was annoyed that her usual decisiveness seemed to have taken a holiday but remained positive something would turn up. Perhaps this was it.

Chapter 2

Magnus Strachan (he pronounced it to rhyme with 'brawn'), Merton professor of Old English studies, never regretted taking Anna Carr as one of his postgraduate students, despite warnings from some colleagues that she was 'difficult', 'surly', or worse. Waiting for her to arrive Magnus thought back over the six years he had known this rather extraordinary young woman.

He first encountered Anna at her entrance interview. From her application he knew she'd attended a North London comprehensive, well-known for having the most culturally diverse mix of any school in Britain. There was nothing about her family background, but the academic reference from her history teacher, Eleanor Smallbone, was both fulsome and intriguing. 'Please do not be prejudiced by her appearance,' was one comment.

Her sample written work, arguing that the term Viking had been descriptive of an activity rather than a geographic nation, and her History Aptitude Test were exemplary. Most extraordinary was the handwriting in the HAT, a beautiful and fluent calligraphy Magnus thought had disappeared before World War Two.

His colleagues for the interview were Priscilla Edgeley, a classical specialist, and Hugo Finch, a rather pedantic scholar of the Italian Renaissance. They didn't quite know what to expect. Did she have some form of disability that wasn't allowed to be declared? It was mid-afternoon and they'd already seen some exceptional candidates, as well as a few obvious rejects.

There was a knock on the door. 'Come in.' Strachan was chairing the panel.

At the time of the interview Anna was in what she called her 'ultra-goth' phase. That day her hair was cut short and gelled so that it stuck to her scalp, with wisps all round her head. She was wearing black jeans, ripped at the knees, Doc Marten Pascal boots, and a battered leather jacket over a tee-shirt. She had far more piercings in those days too. Six in her left ear, two in the right plus, of the others that were visible, a nose and a tongue piercing. Since she'd taken up martial arts, she'd cut down on them for safety. Anna looked intently at each of the panel members in turn. She decided Magnus looked crumpled, a typical Oxford don, trying to look old before his time. *He'll be a bit scared of me*, she thought, *but he'll probably be open minded.* Eleanor seemed very similar to a teacher Anna had liked at school, tweed skirt and jacket and a slight whiff of moth balls. *Probably a closet lesbian and likely to be fair*, she thought. Finch she took an instant dislike to. It wasn't just his red bow tie, but that didn't help. He was sitting back in his chair with his hands behind his head. *He's looking down his nose at me*, she thought. *He won't want me in, so I need to fight him.*

The tee-shirt under her jacket had indecipherable writing, so after sitting her down Magnus thought he'd break the ice with: 'What does your shirt say?'

'Rotting Christ,' Anna replied and then, in case they needed enlightening, which they did, added, 'They're a black metal band from Greece.'

'Oh, arr, well.' Strachan was stumbling with the reply then, for the first time, noticed her eyes. They were green and the intensity of her look was unsettling.

They got down to questions. Anna was right that Finch had taken against her and was going to be awkward. His first was, 'How would you poison someone without the police finding out?'

Anna treated the question as if he'd merely asked her the time of day. 'Let us say that I wanted to poison *you*. I would synthesise the poison from a natural source, belladonna, or monkshood, for example. I would then visit you in your rooms having told you in advance that I was madly in love with you. You would obviously be very careful not to disclose this to anyone and then, after we'd had sex, and your guard was down, I would make you a nice cup of tea.'

Finch was so taken aback he couldn't respond. Priscilla Edgeley tried unsuccessfully to suppress a chortle. Magnus thought that asking some actual history questions would be a better tactic, if only not to embarrass Finch further. He asked:

'Do you think Suffragettes should be given a pardon for the offences they were convicted for?'

Anna's answer was revealing. 'No, they shouldn't be pardoned. There're two reasons. The first is this would be imposing hindsight on historical decisions. Take the "shot at dawn campaign" for First World War deserters. The argument wasn't that they hadn't deserted but that their treatment was too harsh by today's standards. On that basis you might as well waste all your time correcting miscarriages of justice from the past. I'd start with those condemned as witches. At least we know they were innocent.'

'Is that true in all historic cases?' Priscilla asked.

'No, there are some that are different, especially when they're part of a genuine reconciliation process, like in South Africa after apartheid, or where a colonial power is correcting historic injustices.'

Other candidates had given similar answers but her second reason was unique. 'There's also the question of honour,' she said. Magnus looked at her questioningly. 'These women deliberately broke the law to draw attention to their cause. If their so-called crimes were pardoned it would dishonour their memory by belittling their actions.'

The last question was to be asked by Finch. Anna had noted in her application that music was one of her interests and they'd agreed to ask: 'Imagine we had no records about the past at all, except everything to do with music – how much of the past could we find out about?' Finch, however, was feeling malicious because he substituted cricket for music. But his tactic backfired. Cricket rather fascinated Anna. Even though she didn't play herself, it's complexity and the time it took were worthy of study. She'd also had a short affair with an Australian woman cricketer who had got her into watching the sport.

'It's a very good choice,' said Anna, smiling at Finch while giving him an icy glare at the same time. 'The history of cricket can tell you everything you need. There's its relationship to issues such as colonialism and racism, the way it spread round the British Empire as part of the Imperial hegemony. You only have to read the work of CLR James or look at John Arlott's crusade against apartheid to see that. Another example is the growth of nineteenth-century club and village cricket which mirrored the industrial revolution and working men's enfranchisement.'

'I wonder could you explain that rather more?' Finch said condescendingly.

'Let's take the Reform Act of 1867. After extending the vote you needed to ensure working men *felt* enfranchised and integrated into society. One way was through leisure activities that brought the classes together, and cricket was the perfect model. A town or village cricket club which, for the first time, had a constitution, officers, and subscriptions that skilled working men could afford, and where they could occupy at least some of those positions themselves, was perfect. A Marxist would call it an example of social control though my view is that it was more complex than that.'

'You've mentioned James and Arlott, what other writers would you recommend on the topic?' Finch was trying to trap her, thinking her knowledge was only superficial.

'I'd start with Derek Birley's *A Social History of English Cricket*, the best and most serious analysis by a real historian,' again she gave Finch a glare that said, 'Unlike you, mate!' 'Then JA Mangan's work, especially *Athleticism in the Victorian and Edwardian Public School* and *The Games Ethic and Imperialism*.'

'Ahh. Well, yes,' it was clear Finch hadn't read any of them.

The final part of the test was to comment on an historical artefact. In Anna's case, given that she was intending to specialise in Anglo-Saxon and Norse history, the object was a spindle-whorl, and she was asked what the object could tell us about life in Anglo-Saxon England. It wasn't the content of Anna's explanation that startled the three professors but how she answered. She asked if they minded her continuing in Old English, the language of Anglo-Saxon England. 'It gives the opportunity to really understand women's domestic roles,' she explained. She mentioned that she had been learning the language, out of school time, even though the entrance qualifications didn't require any prior knowledge of the period or its languages. This was more than impressive, even to Finch, and they also learned that she could speak and write both

Swedish, and Icelandic, which is a close relative of Old Norse.

Anna left the interview not knowing if she'd helped or hindered her chances. Did she really care? Though she wanted to be a historian who weighed all the evidence before reaching a conclusion, she knew she was more impulsive. *I liked Magnus Strachan*, she thought, *and I really* do *want to study here.* She clamped her ear buds in and turned on 'Rebel Girl' by Bikini Kill, which always calmed her down.

After she'd gone Magnus leaned back in his chair and blew out a long breath. 'Well, that was one of the more interesting interviews I've had!'

'You can say that again' replied Edgeley, 'I'm not sure if I'm distraught that because of my retirement I won't be able to teach her or whether I'll have had a lucky escape! Either way she is top of my list.'

Finch said very little, but couldn't muster sufficient counter arguments and, consequently, Anna received her open offer of a place.

*

Strachan next encountered Anna as an undergraduate in his lectures on the Anglo-Saxon sagas, which confirmed that she possessed a brilliant mind, but also required careful handling. At first, she was rather quiet in tutorials, unlike the boys from the better public schools who were keen to impress with their rather superficial knowledge. He wondered if she was out of her depth socially, or at least felt so. Perhaps she would drop out, as more than one brilliant student from an ordinary comprehensive had done. But he needn't have worried. She was just thinking about the topics before expressing her own ideas. In the middle of her first term Anna arrived with some notes written on what looked like café napkins, but still in her elegant hand. She came out with a devastating analysis in support of Katherine Scarfe Beckett's ideas on representations of the Islamic world in Anglo-Saxon England.

Subsequently she could be extremely abrupt in tutorials if another student failed to prepare adequately or made a facetious comment. But she remained an enigma. Even after knowing her for more than six years Strachan knew little about her background. Other than through her interest in martial arts, she didn't have any group of close friends, and she'd had no longstanding romantic relationships he knew of. Nevertheless, Strachan had absolute faith in Anna both as a historian and as a person. She had an exceptionally strong sense of justice and was unshakable in her opinions, but she often hid her feelings behind a mask of stroppy indifference. There was also a story circulating that she had taken in a homeless person for an entire term, hiding them from the college porters. Strachan knew the truth, but Anna had firmly told him not to mention it to anyone else. Then there was Garm.

One of Anna's traits, he hesitated to say obsessions, was punctuality. She was always on time to every lecture and tutorial, and quick to criticise anyone who wasn't. 'It's like quoting out of context,' she argued. 'If you don't hear everything someone has to say, how can you claim the right to criticise it?'

One day she wasn't there for a tutorial, hadn't sent apologies nor said she was sick. Magnus was understandably concerned, so as soon as the class finished, he went over to her room. He knocked a couple of times and then heard shuffling footsteps. The door opened a crack. The first thing he saw was her face. One eye was shut and there was a large bruise forming around it. Her bottom lip was cut as well. Her left arm was hanging limply with the hand bound up with a torn tee-shirt.

'Good God, Anna! What on earth has happened?'

'Nothing. I'm fine,' she replied and tried to shut the door.

'No. You must let me in. It looks like you ought to be in hospital.' Reluctantly she let him in. Magnus noticed her discarded clothes which were also bloodstained. 'Let me have a better look, Anna,' he insisted as she sat down on the bed.

It was at this point he realised they were not alone as, from under the bed, came a low, menacing growl. 'Garm,' said Anna, 'It's okay, boy, he's a friend.'

She reached under the bed and patted whatever it was under there. The 'it' stopped growling, then the black head of a mid-sized Staffordshire terrier crossbreed poked out. The dog looked almost as battered as Anna. It had several deep cuts on its face and one ear was half chewed off. A series of thoughts flashed through Magnus's mind. Surely, she hadn't been attacked by the dog. Or maybe she'd been beaten up by a lover? Neither idea appealed. He tried to question Anna as to how she'd received her injuries and how she'd suddenly acquired a dog which, by the way, were banned from college accommodation.

As she wouldn't explain he concentrated instead on checking how badly hurt she was. Fortunately, none of the external injuries seemed too serious, though the hand appeared to have defence wounds caused by a knife. Nothing was obviously broken, though she could have a cracked rib as it was hurting her to breath. She insisted she wasn't going near a hospital.

'And the dog?'

She was just as evasive about Garm, who was now sitting on the floor licking her feet. 'I suppose I'll have to find him a home.'

Impulsively Magnus replied, 'Well, I've always liked dogs, I could look after him for a while.' Magnus wasn't married and lived in a spacious Edwardian house on Woodstock Road. After making friends with his new canine housemate, Strachan did a little sleuthing. He didn't say anything to Anna but made discreet enquires about any incidents that had taken place the day Anna got injured. Though he couldn't prove it, he was certain it was linked to a dog-fighting gang the RSPCA and police had been monitoring. They were supposed to meet at various locations near the city, where large sums of money changed hands in bets, and fighting dogs were bred and brutalised for their so-called 'sport'. The day of the incident three men, thought to be connected with the gang, had been admitted to what he still called the Radcliffe Infirmary. One had concussion, one a collapsed lung and the third had had a knife driven through his hand. It was not surprising that rumours about Anna Carr abounded. She became someone other students would point out to freshers, advising them to take care.

Though he wondered if Anna would complete her degrees she had stayed and proved Strachan right regarding her intellectual brilliance. After a first at undergraduate level, she was successful in securing several bursaries to help fund her doctoral studies. In everything academic she was a star, at both history and early European languages, and he felt sure she could become a scholar of international standing. Whether she could ever become a great teacher was another matter, but as a researcher and writer he had never seen anyone to rival her.

As time passed the fonder of Anna he became. He didn't have children of his own and secretly began to think of Anna as the daughter he never had. He was careful never to suggest anything like this to Anna herself, as he felt sure that if he hinted at his affection, she would disappear from his life immediately. This was why he wanted to help her find the right job. It was clear that a run-of-the-mill post doc would never be sufficiently challenging, even at a top American institution like Harvard or Berkeley. That was why this possibility seemed so intriguing. It was out of the ordinary and might whet the appetite of Dr Anna Carr.

Chapter 3

Anna climbed the stair to Magnus Strachan's study on the first floor overlooking Fellows Quad. She walked straight in, getting his invariable response. 'Don't you ever knock, Anna?'

'Well, if you'd been watching porn, you'd have locked the door.' She slumped into the elderly armchair by the window, glancing at the screen of his desktop. 'I wouldn't quote Fredericks on Irish Sea trade in the sixth century if I were you. You know his unreliability over the Jutish invasion of Kent.'

Strachan made an immediate mental note to check alternative sources. 'Always glad to accept your criticism, Anna.'

'Not criticism, just advice. Anyway, I know you'd have gone to the primary sources.' This was high praise from her, and Strachan was grateful. She wouldn't be so respectful of certain other members of the faculty.

'What's this "something" then?'

'You've heard of Oliver Cloote I assume?' Anna flashed him a withering glance. He called it her 'do you think I'm a total imbecile' look.

'I thought his book on the *Prose Edda* had some valid insights,' she replied in a more conciliatory tone.

'Don't let Compton-Yates hear you say that. He tried to get Cloote's books excluded from all reading lists in the country.'

'All the more reason to think he's a decent historian.'

Gregory Compton-Yeates had been Anna's most vehement critic during her years at Oxford, and Anna held him in equal contempt. Magnus chuckled. 'Just thinking about Compton-Yeates and your, err, disagreements with him. You know he tried to get you rusticated?'

'When?'

'In your second year.'

'He was always an opinionated pompous ass.'

Magnus didn't contradict her and explained that in Anna's sophomore year she took Compton-Yeates' module 'From

Paganism to Christianity'. One day there was a knock on Magnus's study door. 'Magnus I've come to see you about your little protégé.'

'Oh yes, Gregory, and who would that be?' replied Magnus, knowing full well who he meant.

'Anna Carr of course.'

'And what seems to be the problem?'

'Well, Magnus, it's her *attitude*.'

'I'm not sure what you mean, Gregory. Is she missing tutorials or not contributing to class discussion?'

'No, no, it's not that. It's ... she's ... it's the way she looks at one. And she's so disrespectful.'

'You mean she's rude?'

'Not exactly rude.'

'What then?'

'She doesn't have respect for my views.'

'You mean she argues? But does she put forward reasoned analyses that counteract yours?'

'Of course she does but *I* am a professor of the University of Oxford with four published monographs to my name and she's an, an ...'

'Undergraduate?' Compton-Yeates scowled at him. 'Gregory. It sounds to me you need to meet reasoned argument with reasoned argument. You should welcome well-founded critiques of your work.'

Compton-Yeates tried a different tack. 'Then there's her belligerence *and* the way she dresses.'

'Is it inappropriate? Does she not wear sub fusc for exams?'

'I don't know about inappropriate but some of her tee-shirts!'

'Yes?'

'Last week she was wearing one that said "Some People Are Lesbians, Get Over It".'

'Well, they are, and you should.'

This was too much for Compton-Yeates. 'If her attitude doesn't improve, I'll report her to the dean.'

'Feel free to do so, Gregory. And if Anna's marks appear in any way unrelated to her clearly outstanding academic ability, then I, as course director, may need to take the matter further.' Compton-Yeates spluttered some more but realised further discussion was futile.

'He gave me a first for that module,' Anna reflected.

'Of course he did. He may be an ass but not a complete one.'

'So why did you mention Oliver Cloote?'

'He's got a job on offer. Full-time research assistant. Must be able to read documents in Old English, Anglo-Norman, Old High German, Icelandic and Old Norse and be expert on both early monasticism and mythology in the Middle Ages. I thought of you.'

'Pretty specific, isn't he?'

'I'm sure I'm not the only person he emailed. There are still *some* academics who take his work seriously.'

'What's he offering?'

'He just says "generous terms for the right candidate". I'm sure they will be because you know he's independently wealthy. His family are Cloote's the Grocers, you know the shop in St James's Street? Shall I tell him you're interested?'

Intuition told Anna that this was going to be the 'something' she'd been waiting for. 'Okay,' she said.

'Right. I'll email him your CV.'

Chapter 4

Anna had her laptop open on the table attached to the seat in front of her. Fortunately, her hand had only been bruised and she could type, if a little stiffly. The train had just left Ipswich, so she had about thirty-five minutes before her stop. She'd been doing some research on Oliver Cloote.

Cloote had never held an academic post and his doctorate, from Uppsala, entitled 'Magic and the "Golden Thread" in Scandinavia 500–1000', argued that supernatural belief, and even actual magical powers, endured through the early Christian period. His later books claimed to discern patterns of belief and behaviour, inspired by paganism, throughout Northern Europe and beyond. The ideas intrigued Anna, though she didn't find all Cloote's arguments entirely convincing. One thing she couldn't find was a photograph of her potential employer.

When she got off the train in Saxmundham she was fortunate there was a taxi on the rank, as the clouds were looking threatening, and the wind was gaining strength. She gave the address. 'Alright love,' said the taxi driver. 'What brings you 'ere?' It seemed an innocuous enough question, but it elicited no verbal response, just a rather frosty look from what he thought of as the 'girl' in the back. Anyway the 'girl' was clearly a weirdo. She was small with spiky hair, wearing a studded leather jacket and heavy black boots. For the next twenty minutes she said nothing while he mused about what he'd like to do to her, even if she did look like a frigid dyke.

The cab turned sharp right onto the wide high street in Aldeburgh that, even at this time of year, was busy with both locals and tourists. Cloote didn't live in one of the highly sought-after properties facing the sea, instead they turned right at the end of the high street. After a short distance they passed brick gateposts with a sign that informed drivers that: 'This gate will be closed every weekend between 1 May and 30 September'.

A few yards further on the cab turned left onto an unmade-up road and stopped beside a high wall. 'S'it,' said the driver, making the announcement 'this is it' sound as close to 'shit' as he could. He didn't get a tip.

Anna walked a few paces to a set of high wooden gates with a smaller side gate set into the wall to their left. Both were painted a tone of sky-blue Anna couldn't remember having seen before. Between them was an intercom with a small lens set above it. She pressed the button.

'Yees?' The enquiry was slightly drawn out, the voice quite high pitched and refined.

'Anna Carr for Oliver Cloote.'

'Ah yes, Dr Carr. Please come through. I'll be waiting at the front door,' his tone significantly improved in warmth.

There was a buzzing noise and Anna pushed the gate inwards. It swung easily and she found herself on a gravel driveway. Ahead of her was a large, red-brick building of three floors in the style of the Victorian High Gothic. The windows had multiple arches with stone mullions and, at the far end, a round tower, rising to four storeys, was capped with a conical roof. It was, thought Anna, the most beautiful house she had ever seen.

As she approached the arched oak front door it was flung open. Anna was not disappointed by Oliver Cloote's appearance. It was difficult to pinpoint his age but somewhere in his fifties she reckoned. He was of average height with shoulder length, greying hair and wore a pair of antique looking half-moon glasses, positioned well down his nose, attached to a gold chain. He was wearing a loose-fitting suit of dark green velvet with a colourful waistcoat of a checked design, a white string-tie shirt, whose wide cuffs protruded from his jacket, and a cravat of a similar shade of blue to his gates. Anna thought he looked as if he'd stepped straight out of the pages of a Conan Doyle or HG Wells novel.

Cloote extended his hand to her, which she shook, a light delicate touch. 'Dr Carr I am *so* delighted you were able to come. I do hope I have not inconvenienced you at all?' *Very polite*, thought Anna, and *he uses my title, no over-familiarity there*. And he hadn't batted an eyelid at her appearance, so two brownie points for Dr Oliver Cloote. Anna assured him it was no inconvenience and remarked on the beauty of his house.

'I am so pleased you think so. It was designed by the great architect William Burges, one of only four domestic buildings he completed. You will have heard of him no doubt?'

Anna said she had indeed heard of Burges and had visited both Cardiff Castle and Castell Coch, admired his work at Worcester College and stared several times at the Tower House in Holland Park, hoping Jimmy Page would pass by and invite her in for a closer look. 'I had no idea he'd designed a house in Aldeburgh.'

'Very few people do. It has been in my family since it was built, and we like to keep it a bit of a secret. But do come inside, the weather looks as if it may soon turn most unpleasant.'

He ushered Anna into the central hall. It was extraordinary, decorated with life-size frescoes and magnificent stained glass depicting four female figures. 'The hall's theme is "Time", do you see? The frescoes depict the sun and moon, and the windows symbolise Dawn, Noon, Twilight and Night. The ceiling shows the position of the constellations at the exact time my great-grandfather moved in. You'll see it at its best if you stand *here*,' he guided Anna to a spot where the light from the main windows seemed to be focused. She looked up. As well as the stars and astrological signs, the ceiling depicted birds in flight against a background of an incandescent blue, there was the same colour again. There was also a quotation:

See yonder, lo, the Galaxye
Which men clepeth the Milky Wey,
For hit is whyt.

It was Middle English, so Anna pointed to it and suggested, 'Chaucer?'

'Yes indeed. A quotation from *The House of Fame*, and the earliest use of both "galaxy" and "Milky Way" in the English language.' Anna thought it interesting that, while she was perusing the ceiling, Cloote's gaze hadn't followed hers, as one would expect, but instead remained firmly on her face. 'But you must be fatigued after your journey, Dr Carr,' Cloote resumed.

'Can I offer you some refreshment? Some tea perhaps? Or would you care for something a little stronger?'

'Thank you, I don't often drink. Tea would be, er, very nice.'

'Of course. Gordon!' Cloote slightly raised his voice and from the room to the right a tall black man, perhaps in his late thirties, emerged. His attire was a complete contrast to Cloote's, a slate grey cashmere polo neck and black chinos. There was a glint of gold from something round his neck and he was carrying a copy of Djuna Barnes' *Nightwood*.

'Good afternoon, Dr Carr, welcome to Summerland. I'm Gordon Rees.' Anna couldn't quite place his accent but thought it was probably a refined North American. She mumbled a greeting as Cloote asked Gordon if he could make some tea. 'Earl Grey, Orange Pekoe or Darjeeling?'

'Oh, not Earl Grey thank you. Orange Pekoe?'

'Excellent. Shall we take it in the library?'

'Would you like something to eat, Dr Carr?' Rees asked, as Anna considered the nature of his and Cloote's relationship. She declined and followed Cloote through the hall to the rear of the house.

Every time Anna glanced at him his gaze moved away. He was trying not to make it obvious, but Cloote was clearly studying her, which was slightly discomforting. 'Just a prospective employer trying to sum up the interviewee,' Anna wondered, 'or something more?'

The library was, if anything, even more impressive than the hallway. The walls were lined with richly painted bookcases but the first thing that struck Anna were the windows. There were two large bays running from floor to ceiling, again with stained glass panels, this time depicting the arts and sciences. They looked out over a stretch of formal gardens and lawns, sloping away, and giving magnificent views over the Alde River and the desolate looking marshes on its banks. 'The ceiling depicts the six founders of law and philosophy according to my great-grandfather and his architect,' Cloote explained. 'Might you recognise them?'

Anna had no difficulty identifying Moses, St Paul, Martin Luther, Muhammad, Aristotle, and Justinian. 'But there's a seventh figure,' she said.

'Ah yes. Another Roman Emperor. The one who tried to, shall I say, stem the tide?'

Anna immediately understood. 'Julian the Apostate who rejected Christianity and promoted Neoplatonic Hellenism?'

'Indeed. Magnus told me I would be impressed.'

Anna immediately felt defensive. 'What did he say about me?' she said, flashing one of her sharper looks.

Cloote held up his hand in a placatory gesture. 'Very little I assure you, Dr Carr. Please sit down.' He indicated one of the window seats. Anna sat in the nearer bay. Cloote placed himself opposite.

Gordon Rees entered with a tray containing gold decorated porcelain cups and saucers and a silver teapot, milk jug, and sugar bowl. He bent over Cloote and gave him a quick kiss on the top of the head, confirming Anna's earlier thoughts. He smiled at Anna as he left. 'Shall I pour?' asked Cloote, not waiting for a reply; it was part of his exaggerated politeness. 'As you know I am in need of an assistant with somewhat specific skills.' He looked at Anna but as she said nothing continued. 'I am undertaking some extremely complex and, umm, delicate research. It may lead nowhere, a dead end. On the other hand,' Cloote paused and looked penetratingly at Anna, his blue-grey eyes sparkled with enthusiasm, 'if I am right. Then they will result in not just my apotheosis but one of the greatest achievements in modern scholarship.' Cloote sat back in his seat. Anna was intrigued.

'Can you tell me more about the nature of the research?' Cloote noticed how she avoided using people's names. Just a quirk, or something deeply seated in her personality, he wondered.

'I'm afraid not Dr Carr. Unless,' he paused, 'you agree to take the post.'

'But what about the other applicants?'

'Oh, there are *no* other applicants. Only yourself. I have been most thorough in my research about *you*, Dr Carr. No one else would fit the role.' Anna wasn't sure whether to be flattered or worried. She was naturally wary, especially with men. Should she trust Cloote and his partner? She decided to put faith in her instincts. 'I know we've only just met,' Cloote continued, 'but I can only ask that you trust me a little. If it doesn't work out, you can simply leave. My terms are, I hope you will agree, most generous.'

'And they are?'

'Five thousand pounds a month, accommodation provided here, transport provided. Do you drive?'

'Yes, but I prefer motorbikes.'

'That would be perfectly fine. I assume you have a student loan outstanding?'

'Err, yes.' Even with her bursaries Anna's loan was approaching fifty thousand.

'As a token of my faith in you, Dr Carr, I am happy to pay it off for you. You won't owe me anything, even if you hate me and leave after a week.'

Is this just too good to be true? thought Anna, but something about Oliver Cloote and his lover convinced her. *I think it was probably* Nightwood, she thought later.

'Okay. I accept. What next?'

'Before you do, Dr Carr, I feel I should just add one further point.' Rain was now lashing the windows as Anna looked at him enquiringly. Cloote slightly lowered his head and his voice. 'I understand you are an extremely accomplished taekwondo sun soo?' He pronounced it perfectly, if a little pedantically.

'Why do you ask?'

'It shows you can look after yourself, Dr Carr. It's just that there may be, err, a certain element of danger associated with this task.'

Chapter 5

Two days later Anna was sitting next to Gordon Rees motoring from Oxford to Aldeburgh, with her few necessary possessions stashed in the back of an extremely smart, green, metallic sports car. Rees had asked her what she thought of the car.

'Very nice. What is it?' Anna replied in a voice that suggested she really couldn't give a damn.

Nevertheless, Rees was obviously keen to tell her more, so she tried to look attentive as he explained that it was a Porsche Taycan Turbo. 'It's been called the world's best electric car,' he said proudly.

Anna hadn't realised the thing was electric until Gordon told her, as it certainly made a noise like other V6 sports cars. Rees explained this was an optional extra, 'But it also makes it safer for pedestrians.' Anna doubted that was the real reason he'd had it installed. *Boys and their toys*, she thought.

'I still prefer a bike,' she said. 'And not an electric one. Not even the Harley Livewire.'

'Great bike' he replied, 'I used to have a Bad Boy over twenty years ago back in Boston.' Now he'd got Anna's attention he told her some more about himself. He'd been brought up by his mother, who'd worked extra shifts at Iron Mountain to pay Rees's way through college. He'd studied mathematics at Columbia, then after a post-grad in e-business and digital marketing at Carnegie Mellon in Pittsburgh, attended MIT for a course on cyber security.

'It must have been hard for your mum,' Anna said.

'It was. My dad left when I was three and I have two older sisters.'

'But she must be proud of you.'

'She is. How about your parents – what do they do?'

'They don't,' Anna replied stonily. 'They're dead.'

'Oh I'm …' Rees was about to express his condolences but realised this wasn't a conversation Anna wanted to have. Instead, he asked, 'Where are you from? London?'

'Sort of.'

Oh God, thought Rees, *this could be a long journey*. He tried another tack. 'Um, that didn't go well, did it?' He shot her a glance.

Anna was a good enough judge of character to realise he meant well and was just trying to make friends as they'd be working together. 'I'm sorry,' she said, 'I don't like talking about ... those things. I'm a different person now.'

Despite this setback, Rees proved an entertaining conversationalist and Anna found herself, somewhat unusually, chatting freely with him. 'How did you and Oliver meet?' she asked as they were approaching Bedford. Rees had asked her what route she wanted to take, and she said she'd prefer to miss the motorways, especially the M25.

'It was in New York. A friend of mine was directing a play based on the *Satyricon*. I was handling the publicity and Oliver was one of its angels, its financial backers. Mind you it was more influenced by the Fellini film than Petronius's original.'

'Sounds fun,' Anna replied, Fellini was one of her favourite film directors.

'That was six years ago. He was over giving some lectures to his fans.'

'He has fans?' enquired Anna.

'Oh yes. His books are very popular in the States, though I find some of them a bit intense. Now I run his online site, he's not exactly tech savvy. It's patrons only but he has a devoted following.'

In Bury-St-Edmunds they stopped at The One Bull for something to eat. Rees took the opportunity to recharge the car, even though it could do around two hundred miles on a single charge. Anna liked the story of St Edmund more than she admired the town named after him. Edmund the Martyr, later St Edmund, was the co-patron saint of England until Edward III adopted George. Edmund was king of East Anglia from about 855 until 869. By tradition he met his death at a place known as Haegelisdun, after he refused the Danes' demand that he renounce Christ. On the orders of Ivar the Boneless and his brother Ubba his enemies beat him, shot him with arrows and then beheaded him. According to legend, his head was then thrown into the forest, but was found safe by searchers who followed the cries of a ghostly wolf that called out in Latin, 'Hic, hic, hic' – 'Here, here, here.' Anna had always wondered why the wolf didn't speak in Old English. Magnus claimed it was probably a lay brother, which he thought a great joke though his students didn't.

By the time they reached Aldeburgh the sun was setting, and the night promised to be clear, though cold. Rees used a small remote unit to open the gates, but Anna noticed that, before he did, he looked carefully up and down the road, which seemed excessive care to take in such a quiet spot. Cloote welcomed them.

'I've put you in the Butterfly Room. I hope you like it.'

The Butterfly Room was on the third floor, up the spiral staircase of the tower. The windows of the tower represented 'The Storming of the Castle of Love' while the room itself was a blaze of golds and reds, with a heavily decorated ceiling of butterflies and a frieze of plants and flowers. Anna did like it even though she thought it a bit 'girly'. It occupied the whole of the third floor of the tower, with the modern addition of an en-suite bathroom, and had windows looking out on three sides. In one direction were the river and marshes she had seen from the library. In the next she could see the town of Aldeburgh itself and in the last the yacht club, the Martello Tower and, more distant, the disused communication masts on Orford Ness that had been part of Britain's Cold War defences.

Rees brought up her bags, despite her protest that she could manage them herself. 'Oliver suggests you get settled in and then join us for supper in the dining room.'

Before she could ask which the dining room was, he'd gone. It turned out to be the room to the right of the hallway. The decoration was devoted to 'The House of Fame' and the art of storytelling, including depictions of women in Greek mythology who were betrayed by their lovers. Cloote explained they were 'Phyllis, Breseyda, Aenone, Hypsipyle, Dyanira and Ariadne. Wronged women were something of a theme for Chaucer, and tall stories are part of the dining room rite.' He suggested that one day they might try a repeat of the famous storytelling at the Villa Diodati.

Anna replied that she didn't think her imagination could remotely match Mary Shelley's, which made both men laugh. 'This is already a *very* unusual experience,' she mused.

Above the fireplace was a bronze figure representing the goddess of Fame; its hands and face made of ivory. Anna walked over to inspect it. 'Yes, the eyes are real sapphires,' explained Cloote. 'Though not especially valuable ones. Otherwise, I think someone might have stolen them before now.'

Large sections of the walls were covered with decorative tiles that depicted some of the Grimm Brothers' darker fairy stories, including 'The Juniper Tree', 'Rumpelstiltskin' and, aptly, 'The Strange Feast'. 'I'm not sure I would have chosen such disturbing stories to decorate my room,' Anna said.

'No? Well at least the liver sausage escaped the knife. I think my great-grandfather had a rather morbid sense of humour.'

Anna enjoyed a pleasant meal, which included local smoked mackerel and cheeses, though she refused the offer of a rather fine white Burgundy. They took coffee in the library and Anna started wondering when Cloote would tell her more about her new job. Rees picked up *Nightwood* and sat back in a chair by the fireplace, which was clearly a sign that he expected her and Cloote to have a conversation. 'Perhaps I should explain a little more about my research and how I think you can help?' Cloote eventually said. His index finger pushed the bridge of his glasses up his nose, which Anna had already noticed he did when he was about to say something more important. 'For some time, I have been exploring the connections between the mythical tales of Northern Europe. You are familiar with my ideas on the exaggerated differences between myth and so-called facts?'

'I've read *Dark Kingdoms*,' said Anna. 'I find the ideas intriguing.'

'But not convincing? I have no problem with that, Dr Carr. I don't expect you to share my conclusions. Well, just over five months ago I received an unexpected communication. You know I studied at Uppsala?'

Anna nodded.

'Then you may also know about the *Codex Argenteus*?'

'The Gothic text in the Carolina Rediviva library. The largest surviving document in the Gothic language.'

'Quite so. It was part of the *Silver Bible* written for Theodoric the Great. Though we have very few substantiated Gothic texts I became perhaps the leading authority on the Gothic language whilst I was at Uppsala. Over the years I've been contacted several times by people claiming to have discovered new Gothic writings, but they have invariably been forgeries or not in Gothic at all. Then in June I received an email from a Professor Clinton Westley, saying he had found a hitherto unknown Gothic manuscript.'

Rees had finished his book. He walked over to the fireplace and put another log on the fire. Cloote continued. 'I knew something of Westley's work on early medieval manuscripts of Central Europe, so didn't dismiss the idea out of hand. I asked him for more details, but he wouldn't give them to me until after we had spoken by encrypted video link.'

'I had to set all that up,' interrupted Gordon, who had come over to sit on the arm of Cloote's chair. Cloote put his hand on Gordon's knee.

'Yes, I'm afraid that kind of thing is entirely beyond me. Anyway, when I spoke to Westley, I was sufficiently convinced that what he'd found could well be genuine.'

'Why was that?' asked Anna.

'He showed me the document itself and explained where he had found it. It was amongst some mis-catalogued monastic documents in the Herzog August Library in Wolfenbüttel.'

'But how had he acquired the document? Surely such a discovery would have been reported?'

'Oh, he stole it of course.' Cloote was offhand about it. 'He also sent me his transcription. It appeared to be a fragment of a chronicle, perhaps of a late Ostrogothic king. This was the key extract.' Cloote reached into the inside pocket of his jacket and handed Anna a sheet of paper. She unfolded it:

Airknastains Brisingamen bairgan Hildisvíni aikklesjo austra Aggils.

'How would you translate it, Dr Carr?'

Anna sat forward in her chair. 'I think a rough translation would be "The jewel Brisingamen is kept by Hildisvíni at the church of the East Angles." But this is extraordinary,' she exclaimed. 'It would link the Goths to England and the Norse sagas.'

'Exactly,' said Cloote a slight smile on his lips. Anna noticed he exchanged a quick glance with Rees.

In Scandinavian myth Brisingamen was a beautiful torque or golden necklace made by the four dwarves Alfrigg, Berling, Dvalin, and Grerr and given to the goddess Freyja. Hildisvíni, which means 'Battle-boar', had golden bristles, and was owned by the goddess. At the end of the Eddic poem Hyndluljó? it is revealed that the boar is in fact Freyja's human lover Óttar.

'Of course,' Cloote added, 'Brisingamen could be a euphemism for an earthly treasure of some kind, or simply a way of referring to the wealth of the church.'

'It doesn't say which church,' queried Anna. 'Do you know which one it refers to?'

'No, it's one of the things we hope you might assist with. After all there are well over two hundred known monastic houses in Essex, Suffolk, and Norfolk alone, though it seems likely to refer to one of the larger ones, possibly an abbey.'

'You must have been pretty amazed.'

'I most certainly was. The evidence was strong, and I told Westley I would need to see the original to verify its authenticity. I *didn't* say that I would also try to persuade him to return it to its rightful owner. He told me he would be coming directly to England and said he'd contact me again when he arrived.'

'And did he?'

'Ah no, unfortunately not. He did get here. In early July he checked into a hotel in Thetford. But then he just disappeared.'

'What. Weren't the police involved?'

Rees took up the story. 'They were. He's got no close relatives, but the hotel informed the police when Westley didn't return. Oliver's details were on a notepad, and they contacted us. They also found his car abandoned between Thetford and King's Lynn, but of him not a trace.'

'Is this why you warned me about possible danger?'

'Not entirely,' Cloote said and fiddled with his glasses again. 'I don't know for sure what happened to Westley, but I *do* know what happened a few weeks later to Cecil Arbuthnot.'

Anna knew she'd heard the name recently, then remembered.

'The security guard at the Bodleian who was murdered. But how is that connected?'

Cloote looked at Gordon. 'We can't be sure,' he replied, 'but there seems to be a possible connection. You see a part of the *Codex Johannem Regem* is missing.' Anna knew this was a group of manuscripts collected by King John and his son Henry III which covered a wide range of subjects. 'The missing pages are in the section added by Henry that cover the Old Norse myths. There is specific reference to the necklace of Brisingamen.'

'I thought the police suspected the guard had been killed by a petty thief he disturbed?'

'Yes, no one has connected the murder to the missing manuscript. The fact that pages had been stolen wasn't discovered until several weeks later.'

'But you think there must be a connection and if murder is involved then there's danger?'

'I'm not entirely sure, Dr Carr, but there may be. So, I will ask you again. Are you sure you want this job?'

Anna gave Cloote a half-strength withering look. 'If I make a decision, it means I'm certain,' she replied.

'Good. I looked very carefully for the person who could help me solve this puzzle. There are many young academics whose knowledge could meet my requirements, but several things drew me to yourself. The first was your decisiveness. I judged you would be resolute in pursuit of our goals, should you share them.'

'And the others?'

'Well, Dr Carr, you see connections no one else does.'

Chapter 6

Anna woke at seven. She went through her workout routine in the bedroom. Not having to move furniture, as she had to in her cramped bedsit, was a joy. She put on her running gear and headed downstairs. Gordon Rees was already up and about. 'What do you eat for breakfast?' he asked.

Anna gave him a quick list: 'Avocadoes, fruit, Greek yoghurt, wholemeal bread, porridge. But not all in one go,' she added. 'No coffee or breakfast cereal. And I have my own protein shake, but I make it with unsweetened soya milk.'

'I think we have all those,' replied Gordon. 'And more generally?'

'Eggs, spinach, and other green vegetables. Salmon or oily fish, occasionally chicken. No pasta or processed meat. Enough to be going on with?' Gordon said it was. 'Can you let me back in after my run?' Anna asked.

'Sure, just press the intercom. After breakfast I'll fill you in on the security system and explain your new laptop. There's a few bits of equipment you'll need.'

Anna was intrigued but simply replied, 'Okay.'

She turned left out of the gate to head away from the town. The road with Cloote's house re-joined the private metalled one after about four hundred yards. She jogged past a cottage hospital, surprised that a town as small as Aldeburgh still had one, given the NHS cuts of the last ten years. Eventually the private road joined the main one into the town close to a roundabout, some shops, and the library. Anna turned down a path to her left that led to playing fields and found they housed some recently installed outdoor gym equipment which she thought she'd test. She took off her hoodie, which boasted the logo: 'Why be racist, sexist, homophobic, or transphobic when you could just be quiet?' and sat on the pull down and chest press. As she moved onto the cross-country skier a bright red Kia Rio pulled up in the car park about fifty yards away. A woman of about Anna's height and build got out wearing rather garish Lycra leggings and a pale grey sweatshirt. She had long black hair tied in a ponytail. The woman glanced toward Anna and then began some slow and graceful movements that Anna thought might be one of the many variants of Kung Fu. As Anna finished and picked up her hoodie the woman came over to the exercise area. Their eyes met briefly, and Anna saw the woman notice her tee-shirt design and then her arm tattoo as she put on her hoodie. They didn't speak.

Tying the hoodie round her waist, Anna set off jogging again. On the far side of the field, she took another path with allotments to the right, beyond which were the marshes leading down to the river. The path ran behind the hospital, and then behind Cloote's house which was bordered by another high red-brick wall. A new gate was set into it that looked very secure, as its thick metal frame was cemented into the wall. She ran on until she passed a former pumping station. Here she turned right onto a muddier path leading towards the river. It terminated in some steps that took her up onto the high embankment constructed to prevent the river flooding. She could now see over the marshes to the masts on the Ness, as well as the estuary of the Alde which also housed the yacht club. Turning left onto the wide gravel road leading past the yacht club Anna came back to the town and the private road leading to Cloote's house. She pressed the intercom, and, after a few moments, Rees buzzed her in.

She jogged round the side of the house to the garden to do her warm down, passing between the house and, to her right, a large, much newer building. It had been expertly designed to be in keeping with the main house without being an inferior copy of its style. It was also partially sunken, the driveway dropping about three metres to reach its main door. On the lawn she could see the other side of the rear wall and gate. There was a shed close to the gate and, she was sure, several CCTV cameras discreetly situated in the trees. The kitchen was on this side and Gordon watched her as she did her stretches. When she'd finished, he opened a side door to let her back in.

'You're certainly much fitter than me, Dr Carr,' he said. 'I work out in our gym, which you're welcome to use. It's in the studio attached to the garage – you'll have seen the building as you came round the house.'

'Is it new?' asked Anna.

'There used to be stables there but they were badly damaged by fire in the 1950s. Oliver's father replaced them with a horrible garage that we had torn down four years ago. It's got the exercise studio, a music room, and a workshop as well as the garage.'

'You like music?'

'I'm something of a mainstream guy I'd say; it's Oliver who's into the more esoteric stuff. Is that a band on your shirt?' he added enquiringly.

Anna said it was. The shirt had the design of a pentagram and skulls and bore the logo 'Dimmu Borgir' and 'Anno MCMXIII'.

'What sort of music?' Rees asked.

'Symphonic black metal,' replied Anna. Rees looked somewhat baffled. 'I'll show you,' she said. She picked up his iPad. 'Can you let me into this?' He tapped in the password and Anna Googled the YouTube video she was looking for, Dimmu Borgir and the Norwegian Radio Orchestra. She selected 'Progenies of the Great Apocalypse'.

Gordon's brow furrowed as he listened. After a couple of minutes, he said, 'Goodness, not quite what I was expecting I don't think. They seem a little,' he paused, 'OTT?'

'They're meant to be. They like to tread the line between theatre and parody. There's a great irony in their performance.'

Rees looked slightly unconvinced. He changed the subject. 'I've done you some yoghurt with strawberries and some wholemeal toast. Okay?'

Anna said it was but added that she could make her own breakfast. Gordon didn't seem to mind the rebuke and instead showed her where the soya milk was in the fridge. Anna fetched her protein shake from her room and sat down with Gordon. 'Where's Dr Cloote?' she asked.

'Oh, Oliver isn't usually up before about ten,' he replied. 'I usually get most of my work done before he emerges,' he said with a smile. Anna decided she rather liked Gordon Rees. He admitted when he didn't know something, and he had a wry sense of humour. She wasn't sure the same applied to Oliver Cloote, especially the first bit.

*

After breakfast Gordon fetched her new laptop, a top-of-the-range Dell XPS 13. He explained that it was specially encrypted so that it didn't store anything on the hard drive. 'Everything is sent to a "cloud" which has six sites in six countries,' explained Rees. 'None of the data is readable unless you have all six components.'

'Isn't that a bit paranoid?' asked Anna, immediately regretting the question. She believed Cloote when he'd said there could be dangers in their research, so added, 'How secure is that? Wouldn't an expert hacker manage to break in anyway?'

'Theoretically it's possible,' replied Rees, 'but they'd need huge resources and, even then, they would only be able to reassemble documents and get the IP addresses of websites you'd visited. Keystrokes and individual pages are so fragmented they would be impossible to reconstruct.'

'Oh great. I can visit BDSM sites, and no one will know.'

Rees couldn't tell if this was a joke or not so instead continued, 'The laptop also helps to control the security system for the house. It needs a fingerprint and eye scan. It then links to your phone.' He unpacked a new iPhone and handed it to her. After they'd configured the phone, he went on, 'To enter the house, activate the app here,' he pointed to a key icon on the phone. 'Then look into the camera and the outside door will open. If you're in a car you can activate the app with a fingerprint while still inside. To disable the alarm the app will generate a new PIN every time you arm or disarm it. You then need to put that code into the pad inside the front door *and* look into the camera. If you were ever under duress, say a burglar had captured you …' Anna gave him a disapproving look. *No,* thought Rees, *a common-or-garden burglar would struggle to capture Dr Carr.* So he said, 'Well suppose a burglar captured *me.* Then I would simply blink three times while looking into the camera. The alarm would disarm itself, but the security company would be alerted, and they'd have someone here within ten to fifteen minutes.'

'Very impressive,' said Anna, picking up the phone. 'Can you actually make calls on the thing?' Rees began to answer but then realised she *was* making a joke, though her expression never changed, so he laughed.

At that point Oliver Cloote came down the stairs. He was wearing what, for him, obviously constituted casual wear. Oxford bags in a cream colour, a loose blue silk shirt and a colourful cardigan that appeared to be made from an oriental rug. 'Good morning, Dr Carr. I hope you slept well, and I see Gordon has made breakfast.' Anna agreed she'd slept well. 'Perhaps you'd join me later in the library?'

'I have to go into the town for a few things,' said Rees. 'I'll see you later. I've left your breakfast in the kitchen, Oliver,' he continued, giving him a quick kiss.

He's feeling more relaxed around me, thought Anna.

While Cloote ate his breakfast, Anna had a closer look at the contents of the library. There was a relatively small section that was obviously Rees's territory. It mainly comprised maths and IT textbooks, modern novels, and criticism, with a scattering of the classics of world literature. Most of the library indicated Cloote's passions. Hundreds of books on the medieval and earlier 'Dark Ages'. In one cabinet, fronted by a strong looking but elaborately designed metal screen, were some incredibly rare editions that were the equal of many specialist university collections, as well as bound medieval manuscripts. One surprising thing was the large number of books on magic and alchemy, with many again dating back several centuries. *He really takes this stuff seriously*, thought Anna, not quite knowing if this meant she should take him *less* seriously as a scholar.

Cloote then joined her. 'Can I change your mind?' he asked. 'It looks like a nice day; shall we take a stroll round the garden?' She was happy to do so and as they walked to the end wall Cloote told her more about his family. The grocery business had been founded by his great-great-great-grandfather. 'In great-grandfather Sebastian's time we became quite wealthy. There weren't just the big shops in St James's and Cheapside but a whole chain across the southeast. But then my grandfather was killed in the First World War, in the final hundred days campaign, near Cambrai. It was three months before father was born. Great-grandfather died soon afterwards. So, two lots of death duties. Father consolidated the business, but it is now just the two big shops and the brand. I was born when father was well into his fifties.'

'Who runs the business now?' asked Anna.

'Oh, I've no interest in groceries so it's my nephew. He'll inherit the whole thing when I'm gone.'

By now they'd walked round the garden, so Cloote unlocked the door on the side of the garage block. It too opened with a PIN on a keypad. The garage contained another car in addition to the one she'd already seen. A Jaguar I-Pace EV400 S, Cloote explained, the electric version of Jaguar's SUV range. It was painted the same Cloote family shade of blue.

Behind the garage were several rooms. The one furthest from the house was a workshop. It contained the usual things. Two workbenches, one against the wall, the other free standing, tools in racks and a gantry for lifting heavy objects like car engines. Adjoining this was a storeroom for paint, cleaning materials, bird food and other dry supplies. The middle room was an excellently equipped gymnasium with a treadmill, rowing machine, multi-gym, and exercise bike. On the far side it had a separate wet area with two showers. 'That's Gordon's preserve,' Cloote explained. 'My idea of vigorous exercise is a particularly challenging crossword.'

The room nearest the house was very different to these somewhat Spartan spaces. It was a superb music room with sound baffling and rack after rack of vinyl LPs. Most of these were Cloote's collection of classical recordings, many of which Anna didn't recognise. The sound system looked impressive too, though Anna was a child of the digital era. She spent her money on streaming services and downloads, not hardware. She did own a second-hand Bose Wave for plugging in her phone, but that was about it. Cloote was obviously very proud of the room, and he entirely lost Anna in an explanation of high-frequency transducers, 'O' rings supporting the sub-chassis and boron cantilevers. She did remember a couple of pieces of equipment as they sounded like something out of pre-history, the Bloodstone Platinum Moving Coil Cartridge and the rather handsome Martin Logan Neolith speakers which were a fetching shade of deep blue and stood taller than her.

'Let me give you a demonstration.' Cloote was clearly itching to do so, and Anna was happy to indulge him. 'You need to sit there,' Cloote indicated the middle reclining armchair in a row of three.

'Oh,' said Anna. 'Who's he?' she asked, pointing to a rather ancient looking Steiff teddy bear that was currently occupying the chair.

'That's Bradshaw,' said Cloote, as if introducing a significant member of the family. 'He's been with me since I was two and has visited over a hundred different countries. Hence the name.'

Anna carefully placed Bradshaw on another chair. Cloote went over to a section with hundreds of albums devoted to the works of Richard Wagner and selected a disc. It was George Szell and the Cleveland Orchestra's highlights from *The Ring* recorded in 1969. 'Siegfried's Funeral March' nearly blasted Anna out of her seat. It segued into the final scene of *Götterdämmerung*, 'Brunnhilde's Immolation' and the destruction of Valhalla. Anna couldn't remember having heard music in such extraordinary detail and clarity before.

'Wow!' she said.

'Impressive?'

'Yeh.'

'Are you a Wagner fan at all, Dr Carr?'

'Not really my thing, unless it's his influence on metal with things like Apocalyptica's *Wagner Reloaded*.'

'Ah yes, I listened to that. It was, what shall I say, innovative.' Cloote smiled. 'As you can see,' he said, indicating the records, 'I am something of an aficionado. His adaptation of the sagas and the *Nibelungenlied* were perfect for his exploration of the capitalist industrialism of his time, and his music remains astonishing. But I suppose we should begin work. Please feel free to use this room, or any other, whenever you wish. I want you to feel more than a guest or an employee. If we are going to succeed, we must work as a team.'

*

That afternoon they sat together in the library looking at Cloote's notes. 'So,' he began, 'what do we know thus far? We know Westley was a central European specialist. His discovery led him to England because of the reference to the East Angles. He needed someone to help him who was more skilled in the Gothic language and Norse history, which is why he turned to me. What I don't know is if I was the *only* person he contacted. There may have been others. But he knew some things he didn't tell me.'

'How do you know that?' Anna asked.

'I didn't mention this before but the first thing he did when he got to England was to visit Oxford. And guess what he did there?'

If Cloote wasn't simply asking a rhetorical question it must be something he'd already told her. 'Went to the Bodleian and consulted the *Codex Johannem Regem* ?'

'Very good, Anna!' In his excitement Cloote used her first name. 'You see, you make connections. Exactly.'

Anna ignored the condescension. 'So, he discovered something there and then went to Thetford?'

'No, not immediately. It was three weeks later. So, the fact he didn't make contact suggests he thought he didn't need my help.'

'The "something" would have to be clear even to someone who wasn't an expert on the period. Could Westley read Anglo-Norman? A lot of the *Codex* is written in it, but there's also plenty of Latin and even some Old Norse transcriptions.'

'I'm not certain, but I doubt he'd be able to quickly translate anything except the Latin.'

'But the fact that the security guard was killed, presumably for the part of the manuscript that's missing, suggests it was critical.' She thought for a short while. 'For all we know the guard could have been killed by Westley, who came back to secure the text.'

'That's certainly possible,' replied Cloote, 'but it could also be someone else we know nothing about. Westley may be a thief, but he didn't strike me as an assassin and, as I said, he may have shared his discovery with others.'

A train of inquiry was forming in Anna's mind. 'What did Westley look like? Do you have a picture?'

Cloote tried to search documents on the library's Apple iMac but was having some problems. 'Gordon!' Rees had returned earlier and had been working on his laptop.

A few quick keystrokes and 'Here you go,' he said.

Anna looked at the screen. The photos must have been taken at a conference and been enhanced. She saw a short, rather rotund man, with a dark beard and glasses. 'Thanks. Could you give me a copy?' Gordon sent copies to her phone and by email.

'Oliver and I have got as far as we think we can without another, more highly attuned brain,' said Rees, hoping Anna would take it as a compliment. 'We went to the Bodleian after the theft,' he added. 'Though we left it a couple of weeks as we didn't want to raise suspicion.'

'I had an inkling there could be a connection,' Cloote went on. 'As you know the *Codex* hadn't been digitised but the link with Brisingamen couldn't be coincidence.'

'While Oliver chatted to the archivist, I had a quick look at their database which showed who had requested the manuscript. Sure enough there was Westley, two weeks before he went missing. And we don't know where he went in those two weeks,' he added.

'I told the archivist much of the truth,' Cloote continued. 'They know my interests and I said I wanted to help reconstruct the missing pages. So, over the next few days Gordon and I checked off the catalogue entries for the *Codex*. We now know what *hasn't* been stolen.'

'I see,' said Anna. 'I assume there are at least partial copies of the *Codex* in other archives?'

'Yes, indeed Dr Carr.' Cloote had regained his composure. 'But no complete copy.'

'So, our first task is to check the other manuscripts to see if the missing material is copied there?'

'Exactly! Gordon, could you print off the list for Dr Carr?'

Rees did so and Anna studied it: Canterbury Cathedral; Durham University; Ely Cathedral; Exeter Cathedral; Lincoln Cathedral; Norwich Cathedral; Salisbury Cathedral; Trinity College Dublin; York Minster. 'We've already done the nearest, Norwich and Ely,' explained Rees. 'None of the missing material's there.'

'Do you have a preference as to which you visit, Dr Carr?'

'Could I cover Salisbury and Exeter?' asked Anna. This would fit with the plan she was beginning to think about.

'Excellent,' replied Cloote. 'If you do the nearest and furthest, Gordon, that's Canterbury and Dublin, I can visit Lincoln, York, and Durham. That's settled then.'

'You'll need your own transport,' Cloote told her. 'Please feel free to purchase whatever you wish.'

Anna knew exactly what she wanted. 'I need to go to Norwich for that,' she said then added, 'Of course there are two other lines of enquiry.'

'And they are?'

'Find what happened to Westley and find who murdered Cecil Arbuthnot.'

*

The next morning Rees drove Anna to Norwich. She was thinking over what Cloote had told her and was somewhat uncommunicative, though Rees didn't seem to mind. Was there a connection between the disappearance of one man and the murder of the other? If there was, why were the missing pages of the *Codex* important? Why couldn't the thief just have taken photographs, why did they need to physically possess them?

They parked in Rouen Road and walked the short distance to the motorbike saleroom in Ber Street. The discussion with the man at Harley-Davidson didn't get off on the right foot. The salesman immediately thought Gordon was the customer and ignored Anna entirely. 'How long have you been riding a bike?' he asked.

'I've never ridden a motorcycle in my life,' Gordon lied, smiling sweetly.

For a moment the man looked confused but finally noticed Anna. At least she looked a bit like a biker with her leather jacket. 'Oh. Ahh. My apologies. You're the one wanting a bike?'

'That's right,' she replied, coldly.

'And what did you have in mind?'

'The Low Rider S.'

'That's a big bike. Eighteen-hundred cc,' he said, meaning: 'You look too small to handle it.'

'I know. One hundred-and nineteen foot-pounds of torque at three thousand rpm. I believe your advertising concludes that:

"The Low Rider S is aimed at a rider who wears a confrontational personality proudly and wants a motorcycle ready and willing to support that belligerence." Well, I'm pretty fucking belligerent.'

'Oh, well, err. What colour were you thinking of?'

'Vivid black.' She didn't add 'you fucking moron', but her look implied it.

The man's next thought was to wonder if she could afford over £15,000 but her boyfriend, in his expensive camel hair coat, looked like he had money. The deal was quickly concluded. Despite the salesman claiming she'd have to wait several weeks; Anna had already done her homework and was able to inform him that there was one in stock in London. He checked his records. 'I'm afraid it's reserved for another customer.' He knew it was the wrong thing to say even while saying it.

This time Rees intervened. 'I'm sure an additional, shall we say, three thousand pounds would secure the bike?'

The salesman readily agreed, his cut would be at least six hundred of that, not bad for an hour's work. 'Of *course*. Sir, madam.'

The details were concluded. Anna couldn't quite believe that in three days she'd be the owner of the kind of bike she'd only dreamed of.

Back at Summerland she went online to purchase the other gear she'd need. It had been two years since she'd had to sell her old Royal Enfield Classic 500, and her biker clothes had been worn too often as everyday wear. She ordered a Lewis Leathers Super Monza Black Jacket, Urban Rider Armour Ready Edition; Daytona Lady Star GTX boots; Halvarssons Rider Pants and Furygan Elektra Gloves, plus a Dainesen-Assen one-piece suit. Her GDM DK-140-MB Duke Series helmet had to be ordered from the US but, with express delivery, would be with her by the time the bike arrived.

Chapter 7

The man got up from the bed. He walked towards the chair where he had discarded his clothes and paused to admire himself in the large mirrors on the wall. Despite his fifty-three years he was inordinately proud of his body. His tanned skin, the muscle definition of his stomach, the lack of wrinkles or flabbiness and his full, even luxuriant, head of black hair without a trace of grey. What he didn't dwell on was the extent to which this was not the result of careful diet and exercise alone. Hair transplants, cosmetic surgery and visits to an exclusive Swiss clinic had played more than a minor role.

He pulled on his handmade, silk boxer shorts and the trousers of his bespoke Savile Row suit, made from finest vicuna wool. He put on a West Indies Sea Island cotton shirt and reached over to the bedside table for his specially commissioned gold cuff links, with the letters 'E' and 'F' intertwined in Lombardic Majuscule script.

The girl still lay face down on the bed, a sheet casually tossed over her. The bottom sheet was stained with blood that appeared to come from somewhere near her waist. She was sobbing quietly with the occasional moan of pain. At least he had untied the restraints that had bound her to the bed's metal frame.

Her name was Irina Danilenko. She was sixteen years old. Her family had lived in the small Ukrainian city of Artemivsk. When she was eleven Artemivsk was taken over by forces of the Luhansk People's Republic, supported by 'volunteers' from the Russian Army. They were Ukrainians living in a Russian speaking area. One day her father disappeared. Her mother's mental health problems meant she had to be hospitalised. Irina had no one else to turn to so sought 'protection' from an LPR officer.

The first time she was raped was three days after her thirteenth birthday. When she was fifteen, she was told she would be moving to England where she would be happy and rich. But the only difference was that the men who abused her spoke a different language.

The man neither knew, nor would have cared, about any of this. He didn't even know her name. To him she was a disposable toy. He gave her no more thought than if she had been an inanimate sex doll. He walked into the dressing room and stabbed his twenty-four-carat gold mobile phone. 'Vladimir? You can clear up now.' He briefly contemplated adding that Vladimir could 'dispose' of the girl but decided she wasn't worth it. Anyway, she certainly couldn't harm someone like himself. 'Pay her and take her back to her minder,' he said instead. Picking up his jacket he glanced back at the figure on the bed. Blood was now evident on the sheet covering her that could only have come from wounds on her back, buttocks, and thighs. 'Wait here,' he barked.

Strolling down the corridor he entered the room that served as his home office, opulently furnished in Louis XIV style. The wall in front of him was entirely glass, displaying a magnificent view over the River Thames and the Houses of Parliament. To his left was his ostentatious Parnian desk and, on the opposite wall, a massive plasma TV, its screen taller than him. He tuned to Fox News. Just in time, Carrie Prentiss was appearing on the *Noah Cross Show* for the sixth time that month. She looked immaculate, but not overstated or slutty. That was important. 'Men should want to fuck you, women should want to be you, and children should want you to be their mother,' he'd once told her.

Cross turned directly to camera. 'Yesterday Senator Maria Lozano-White, the leading candidate for the Democratic nomination, stated that she would,' he looked at a piece of paper to indicate that he was, supposedly, quoting the senator's words verbatim. 'Reinstate the full intention of Roe v. Wade and legislate to prevent the intimidation of women seeking legitimate, legal abortion. Well, I'm very pleased to have with me Carrie Prentiss, president of the Alvin Testerwood Foundation, to respond to Senator Lozano's views.' The camera cut to Carrie giving one of her most sincere smiles. 'Carrie, welcome. Do you think the senator's comments are worrying?'

'I'm so glad you asked that, Noah,' Prentiss preened. She was good. Even though the entire interview had been carefully scripted and rehearsed, it seemed wonderfully spontaneous. But then Carrie was a consummate professional in self-presentation. From the age of five her parents had entered her in child beauty pageants, and later she had been a contestant in 'Miss Teen America'. 'Every one of the Democratic candidates is committed to the violation of the sanctity of life. But Maria Lozano-White is by far the most dangerous. She is a self-confessed socialist.' Carrie pronounced the last phrase in the same way she would have said 'self-confessed paedophile'. 'You heard what she said yesterday? "The Bible should never be used as the justification for modern laws." Well,' she sighed and, as the screen cut to a close-up emphasising the perfection of her dentition, again smiled sweetly. 'Our laws against murder and stealing are based on the Ten Commandments. Which one of these would she like to throw away?' Carrie emphasised her point with a backward flick of her left hand. 'The truth is that killing children in utero violates the *natural* law, not just Christian teaching. If something is true, it remains true, regardless of who agrees with it. Should we stop teaching times tables in school because the Church agrees with arithmetic?'

The man was pleased. He had trained her well and she was worth every penny of the three and a half million-dollar salary she was paid for heading the Alvin Testerwood Foundation. No one knew he bankrolled the foundation, it was all done through an anonymous donor-advised fund, like many of the 'philanthropic' causes he supported. The choice of name had been controversial, but it told people exactly where they stood, and warned them that they would never stoop to compromise.

In 1993, in Atlanta Georgia, Alvin Testerwood had killed a doctor who conducted legal abortions, his nurse, a receptionist, and a pregnant teenage girl with a suicide bomb. Testerwood considered the girl legitimate 'collateral damage', after all she was about to murder her own child. Though some anti-abortion organisations condemned such acts, the man had ensured the Alvin Testerwood Foundation was the lead body of the radical wing of the 'pro-life' movement. He mused that it was only a few years ago that the current policies of the Republican Party were considered anathema by American conservatives and was inordinately proud that his foundation had helped bring about their acceptance by the Republican mainstream.

The interview terminated with unctuous 'thank yous' on both sides. Tomorrow Prentiss would be in London to launch the next phase of the anti-abortion campaign here, though they would be using the less confrontational brand the 'Sanctity Foundation'. Prentiss would be lobbying politicians committed to their cause. Her charms were always so effective with male members of parliament and, where appropriate, could be augmented by discrete 'gifts' of various kinds.

Satisfied, the man opened his laptop. A quick check of the markets and the political news that could affect him. Then he turned his attention to more important matters. He again pressed a speed dial number on his phone. 'Nesfield? What news?' He listened intently to a lengthy explanation from the other party. Eventually he asked, 'And Cloote?' Another explanation ensued. 'I see. Who is this new assistant? A girl! All right, continue the surveillance and keep me informed of any developments.' At that moment there was a discreet knock at the door. 'Yes!' his irritation was clear.

The man called Vladimir cautiously peered in. 'I have done as you asked, sir. Everything is in order and the girl has been returned. When will you require the next,' he paused looking for the right word, 'delivery?'

'I'm not sure. I may be too busy over the next few days though we may need a supply for others.'

'I understand, sir. Are you going to the office?'

Elias Forth said he was.

*

Forth descended to the basement in his private lift. Vladimir had his car ready, a coach-built Rolls Royce Phantom EWB in Imperial Purple. Forth settled himself into the luxurious rear seats. They were made from the leather of crocodiles he and his associate, former big-game hunter Savile Nesfield, had shot on one of their killing sprees.

The car crossed Westminster Bridge and circled the east side of Parliament Square, turning up Broad Sanctuary towards Victoria. They turned north to pass the high wall of Buckingham Palace, circling the Wellington Arch. Vladimir navigated the car into Piccadilly and turned left into Old Park Lane. After passing the rear of the London Hilton they made a couple of sharp turns to head north on South Audley Street. A final left and right took them into Park Street where Vladimir drew up and opened the door for his boss.

The building was a fine example of the Beaux-Arts classicism of the early twentieth century, red brick with Portland stone masonry. The only indication of the occupant was a discreet brass plaque on the black gloss door, 'Elias Capital Investments', but gave no indication as to what kind of investments these were. Forth was a hedge fund manager, a term that covers a range of activities where someone invests on behalf of others. Hedge funds imply aggressive forms of finance and Forth specialised in one of the most rapacious: short selling. Short sellers borrow shares from their owners and sell them on, in the expectation that the price will fall. They make a profit if they buy the shares back at a cheaper price when they return them to their original owner.

Forth's successes had been many. He had made his initial fortune with deals around the aftermath of 9/11. The 'War on Terror' had been extremely profitable for Forth, and many others. Then, in 2016, following the Brexit Referendum, he massively increased his wealth, entering the ranks of the UK's billionaires.

CCTV told security Forth had arrived, and the black gloss door swung open as he reached it. He stepped into the discreet foyer onto the thick purple carpeting with the same interwoven initials born by his cuff links. Emily Talbot, ECI's receptionist, smiled in welcome. 'Good morning, Mr Forth. Miss Clifford has informed me that she has arranged the meeting with the new secretary of state and will be arriving shortly.'

'Thank you, Emily. Mr Morten should be arriving soon. Please send him directly to me.'

'Of course, Mr Forth.'

Forth congratulated himself on his choice of staff. Talbot was the youngest daughter of an Earl and it showed in her impeccable manners and slightly haughty demeanour, that invariably impressed his foreign clients. Gabriella Clifford was his personal assistant. She came from a background of poverty in the Teesside town of Redcar. By her own initiative she had won a scholarship to the LSE and then an MBA from Harvard. Her first job had been political advisor to a group of Conservative MEPs in the European Parliament, but her ambition soon led her to more lucrative opportunities.

Forth recognised both Gabriella's qualities and her flaws, and he exploited them to the full. Given the right rewards Gabriella Clifford could be relied on utterly, though certain elements of his life could not be made explicit to her. They never spoke about these aspects, and Forth had no way of knowing if Gabriella suspected anything about what was, ridiculously, considered criminal behaviour. In recognition of this Forth had never, and would never have suggested any sexual or other impropriety with Clifford. To her he was always the perfect gentleman.

The lift had now reached the top floor of the building and Forth opened the double doors to his office. The anteroom contained Gabriella's desk, luxurious armchairs and sofas for visitors, and a plasma screen on the wall, with the sound off and subtitles on, tuned to Bloomberg TV. Forth's own office was through a smoked glass door to the right. The whole wall between the offices was a reciprocal mirror, confusingly referred to as both a one-way and a two-way mirror, that allowed Forth to see his visitors but not for them to see into his private space.

The room contained the trappings of his success. Photographs depicted his meetings with world leaders. Framed personal letters of gratitude from both the UK prime minister and former US president for his 'invaluable advice', in the case of the former, and 'undying loyalty and friendship', from the latter. Two paintings hung on the wall opposite the window which looked out over Park Street. One was a Raphael portrait of a young woman painted in the early sixteenth century. The other was one of Gilbert and George's *Naked Shit* pictures. In some situations, this contrast would have indicated a pleasing eclecticism of artistic taste. Here it said two things. It was a narcissistic display of wealth and it revealed Forth's intention to shock and intimidate his visitors. He revelled in telling the story of the visit of a famous American Televangelist to whom he had described in detail the creation of the Gilbert and George work. A discreet buzz and Forth tapped a screen on his desk.

'Good morning, Mr Forth,' it was Gabriella. 'Would you like me to debrief you on my meeting with the secretary of state?'

'Yes of course.'

Unfailingly discreet and polite, thought Forth. Gabriella would never think of coming straight into a room she knew he occupied. Gabriella Clifford was thirty-five, five feet ten inches tall and wore a dark grey jacket and skirt. Her shoulder length blonde hair was immaculately styled and, as usual, her discreet makeup looked newly applied. Forth wondered if she ever sweated. If she did, she would be far too polite to mention it. Her boyfriend was an international banker who spent long periods abroad, which was how Gabriella liked it. Though she had had many other job offers, including enticements to become a Conservative MP, she had always turned them down. The salary Forth paid her far exceeded anything she could obtain elsewhere, even if her lifestyle was not extravagant. True, they had a lovely mews house in Kensington, but apart from clothes and holidays Gabriella had no hobbies and very few friends, certainly no close ones. She recalled in horror the time, a couple of years ago, when a girl from the Middlesbrough comprehensive she had attended recognised her in the street. Despite her protestations, the woman had persisted to the point where Gabriella viciously responded that she had never seen the woman before in her life and if she didn't leave her alone, she would call the police.

Her meeting had been with the new secretary of state for business, following the dramatic cabinet cull of the previous week. This had been yet another coup for Forth who, given intimate inside knowledge, had placed hundreds of bets on those who were to be removed, netting him a not insubstantial sum. 'I think he understands our position very well,' Gabriella explained. 'I stressed how concerned we were that the deregulation promised after Brexit should go through as rapidly as possible.'

'And he looked as if he was telling the truth?' Forth enquired.

He'd sent Gabriella for two reasons: first because he knew the new minister lusted after her and second, she was an excellent judge of when someone was lying, which is why he was very careful never to tell outright falsehoods to her.

'Yes, I believe he was. Of course, I can't be sure the prime minister shares his determination.'

'You can never be sure of anything with the prime minister, so I think that's as good as we'll get.'

'In that case shall I initiate our preferred plan?' Forth had formulated a series of moves intended to anticipate greater deregulation of UK market investments than most others were forecasting.

'Yes. You know exactly what to do, Gabriella. Let the team know.'

The screen buzzed again. This time it was Emily on the front desk. 'Mr Morten is here, Mr Forth.'

'Thank you, Emily. Send him straight up.'

Gabriella Clifford frowned. Forth's 'special projects manager', Morten, no one seemed to know his first name, was not a person she looked forward to meeting. She waited in Forth's office until Morten arrived, not wanting to be alone with him even for a few seconds.

'Ahh, Miss Clifford. Such a delight as always.' Morten smiled slightly and Gabriella wasn't certain what the delight was, his seeing her or something entirely different.

She had once described Morten to another ECI executive as 'menacingly oleaginous'. In addition to his unctuous attitude his physical appearance was unusual. He was thin, tall, somewhere around six foot four, and invariably wore loose-fitting clothes that seemed a couple of sizes too big. He had very short greying hair and a prominent aquiline nose. His eyes were very pale and almost dead. It was extremely difficult to estimate his age. Probably later forties, thought Gabriella, despite his seeming at first glance to be significantly older. Most disconcerting was the fact that his skin was unnaturally transparent, making his veins, in the areas one could see, hands and face, excessively prominent. Gabriella had wondered at this characteristic and had done some research into what condition may have been the cause. Her best solution was vitiligo, which affects around one percent of the world's population. With vitiligo, the cells responsible for skin colour, called melanocytes, are destroyed. The affected cells no longer produce melanin, and the affected areas lose colour or turn white. If it was vitiligo, then Morten had an acute version. There were various rumours about Morten's past from his being a former Benedictine monk to being a member of the Russian special forces. Any of them could be true. Gabriella quickly made her excuses and left.

'May I?' Morten exuded, managing to reach the door and open it before Gabriella could. Another of his creepy aspects, she thought. Instead of returning to her desk Gabriella decided a strong cup of coffee was in order.

Forth was glad his assistant didn't stay as he would be able to speak freely. 'Well?' he demanded.

'Mr Zinchenko is entirely content with how matters are proceeding.'

Forth was relieved. Oleg Zinchenko was his biggest investor and one of Russia's richest men, a friend of the president and a member of the State Duma. 'Good. That means you can return to overseeing the other project. Nesfield has been keeping an eye on things. There seems little to report though.'

Morten looked as if he had just sucked on a lemon. 'I mean no disrespect, Mr Forth, but Nesfield is a fool. If nuclear war had broken out, I doubt he would notice.'

'Nevertheless, he has his uses.'

'Indeed so, sir. If you want a defenceless animal slaughtered, I can think of no one more suitable.' Morten was the only person who dared be so contradictory to Forth.

'In that case the sooner you can discuss things with him the better.'

'And where would he be at present, sir?'

'Suffolk. A place called Aldeburgh.'

Chapter 8

Over the next three days, while she was waiting for her bike to arrive, Anna got down to serious study about the *Codex Johannem Regem*. Cloote and Rees had discovered where copies of parts of the *Codex* might be, but the problem was that it was a list of all potential locations, with the likelihood that only one or two, or maybe none, would have manuscripts that were relevant.

Most archives now have online catalogues, and many have digitised their most important holdings. However, we are still decades away from being able to do everything electronically and there will always be aspects of research, especially with very old manuscripts, that can only be done by physically inspecting the document. Exeter and Salisbury were typical in their online offerings. Items were well catalogued, dated and briefly described, but the actual content would have to be investigated first-hand.

Anna also sent three WhatsApp messages in preparation for her trip. The longest was to Magnus Strachan, the others to Nora Greenwood and Nikki McDonald. In each she promised to follow up with a phone call when her itinerary was clearer.

She then read Westley's most recently published academic papers. The impression she got was of a thorough and careful man, who stuck to the more obvious interpretation rather than posing alternative hypotheses. *He isn't someone who would jump to conclusions*, thought Anna. *But then again he might have missed something because it didn't appear to fit the facts.*

This stage of her research was straightforward and completed in a few hours. She moved on to check leads Cloote may have overlooked. She didn't try any links with Gothic texts, as Cloote's expertise was far greater than hers in this respect, but she did carry out multiple searches for anything on necklaces, Brisingamen, Hildisvíni, churches, and especially abbeys, in East Anglia. This took some time and, after a day and half that had turned up nothing that seemed remotely relevant, she decided to take a break.

The day was fine, so she wore just her old leather jacket over one of her less confrontational tee-shirts proclaiming: 'I'm a Girly Swot'. She strolled down the high street, which was full of rather chic shops and galleries, with a smattering of more practical places to buy necessities in rural Suffolk, and two excellent looking fish and chip shops. *Sort of Shoreditch-on-Sea*, thought Anna. She investigated a couple of galleries – lots of seascapes and sculptures of oyster catchers – thought about having a drink, but decided to wait, and picked up a brochure about forthcoming arts events.

She walked along Crag Path, beside the sea past the old Moot Hall, to its end behind the Wentworth Hotel, before turning back up Wentworth Road to the high street. On her right was a small cinema. *Another plus*, thought Anna. *Must have a look at what's on*. Virtually opposite the cinema was the Aldeburgh bookshop which she'd heard was one of the best in the country. She wasn't disappointed. The shop was wonderful. Crammed not just with the latest best sellers but with superb sections on local history, poetry, and music. The last was not surprising as Aldeburgh's most famous former resident was the composer Benjamin Britten, who was a customer when it first opened in 1949. It had a thriving children's section too, which had a gaggle of eager young readers sitting on the floor. A reading group and several author visits and other events were advertised, and many of the books had handwritten cards that described why you ought to consider buying them.

Anna had a good look round before going to the local section to pick out a copy of WG Sebald's *The Rings of Saturn*. It was one of those books she'd always meant to read, but never quite got round to. As she was now staying in the area where it was set, it seemed a good time to buy it. Her eye was then caught by the note for a book she'd not heard of, *Ghostland* by Edward Parnell. She picked up the book and started reading the quotes. They mentioned several things that grabbed her interest, writers like Sebald and MR James, the film *The Wickerman* and psychogeography. As she pondered purchasing it, she became aware of someone standing behind her.

'It's a wonderful book. One of the best things I've read in ages.'

Anna turned to see the woman she'd noticed at the exercise area. She looked perhaps in her late twenties. She was wearing loose blue trousers and a black jacket with gold buttons. She had a plastic identity card round her neck that Anna couldn't read. What she did notice were her eyes. They were large and quite round. They were possibly the most beautiful eyes Anna had ever seen. 'Thank you. I think I'll get it then,' she replied.

'You're the woman who exercises in the park aren't you? I've admired your fitness and the tattoo.' Anna always got defensive when people mentioned her tattoo, as it was often followed by comments such as, 'Why do you want to mutilate your body?' or, 'What does it mean?' Instead, the woman said, 'I've thought of you as the girl with the Tagore tattoo,' and laughed slightly nervously. In all the time Anna had had the tattoo no one had recognised the author of the quote.

'I'm impressed, he's not an author many people have heard of, at least not in Britain.'

'But in India, or Sri Lanka where I'm from, he is revered. And still the only winner of the Nobel Prize for Literature from the sub-continent.'

'Yeh, I think some his ideas are pretty cool. Like true religion being an acceptance of the unity of all people. And he was a polymath, not just a writer but a composer and then at sixty he took up painting. Amazing.'

'And then there were his views on education,' the other woman responded, 'with Santiniketan and Dartington Hall.'

They went over to the counter and, as Anna was paying for her books, the woman asked 'Would you be free for a coffee? It's not every day you find a fan of Rabindranath Tagore in Aldeburgh.'

'Sure.' Anna's natural suspicion had been short-circuited by this attractive and rather fascinating person.

They walked a short way back towards the main high street and introduced themselves. Her new acquaintance was called Anula Hathurusingha and she was a doctor. Anna told Anula she was a historical researcher working with a local author. They entered The Cragg Sisters Tearoom where Anna ordered

China tea and Anula a Moroccan mint tea. Anula told Anna far more about herself than Anna offered in return. She was thirty-two and an orthopaedic surgeon based in Ipswich. Many of her patients were sent to Aldeburgh Hospital following surgery, so she made frequent visits to the town. She herself lived in Woodbridge, which was convenient for both.

'You're in the right place then,' said Anna. 'Did you know Aldeburgh had the first female mayor in England? She was also the first female doctor and surgeon, Elizabeth Garrett Anderson.'

'No, I didn't,' Anula replied. 'They should make more of her.'

'A statue would be nice, like the one to her sister, Millicent Fawcett, opposite parliament.'

Anula told Anna that her parents lived in Colombo, that her mother was a lawyer and her father a doctor. She didn't press Anna when she offered absolutely no information about her own family. Instead, Anna told her about her PhD.

'Where I live you can see Sutton Hoo,' Anula told her. 'I find that period of British history fascinating. All those invasions, nearly as many as we had in Sri Lanka.'

Anna did some explaining about the complexities surrounding the so-called Viking invasions and the many myths, which Anula seemed to find interesting. They were enjoying each other's company and ordered more tea. Their talk got round to martial arts and Anna asked Anula what the moves were she'd seen her doing in the park. 'It's angampora,' Anula replied. Anna looked slightly puzzled, so Anula went on, 'It's the ancient martial art of Sri Lanka. Some people say its origins date back three thousand years.'

'Oh yes, I *have* heard something about it,' Anna remembered. 'Isn't it very complex?'

'Yes, it combines many techniques. Armed combat, self-defence, sport, exercise, and meditation. In the use of weapons for example, called elangampora, there are twenty-one main implements. I wouldn't call myself an expert and it takes a lifetime to master even a few of the main techniques. Perhaps we should try working out together sometime? I could show you some exercises and you could give me some tips on taekwondo.'

Anna was slightly dubious about getting more friendly but

kept glancing at Anula's eyes. 'Sure. Perhaps when the weather's a bit better.'

Anula looked a little disappointed and then brightened up. 'Would you like to come to the cinema perhaps? I'm usually free on Wednesdays after visiting my patients here, and they're running a series of foreign classics.'

'That sounds, um, nice. Do you know what's on? I have to make a trip to some archives but should be back by Wednesday next week.'

Anula checked her phone. 'Next week it's Ingmar Bergman's *Seventh Seal*. Have you seen it? I haven't.'

Anna told her she had never seen it, even though it was her former supervisor Magnus's favourite film. 'He's got a picture of the last scene on his study wall, the "Dance of Death."'

They finished their tea. Anula had her car parked just up the street and asked if she could give Anna a lift. She politely refused. She wasn't sure Cloote would want a stranger to know where Anna was staying, so they exchanged polite goodbyes and phone numbers.

'I'll let you know if I've got any problems,' said Anna.

Anula got into her small red Kia and drove off. Anna watched her go and wondered if their friendship might develop. She'd not met anyone with eyes like those before.

Chapter 9

Both the Harley and Anna's clothing arrived promptly. She'd not found anything more that might help their work, and both Cloote and Gordon were already away on their visits when the low-loader arrived. Anna supervised getting the bike off the lorry and the young lad driving explained it had half a tank of petrol and was ready to go. He was just being cheeky when he left saying: 'You're a lucky girl. Wish I could afford one. All the best with it and I'll look forward to seeing you flashing past!'

Anna was in a good mood and played along. 'It'll definitely be the only flashing you'll get!' He laughed and climbed into the cab.

Anna didn't need to read the owner's manual, which she'd checked online. Instead, she stripped off her ordinary clothes and put on her new gear. She started the bike, and a satisfying roar came from the engine as she opened the throttle. She headed down the sea road to the quaint Edwardian model resort of Thorpeness, turned inland through Leiston and then to the A12. Most of it was single carriageway in rural Suffolk but beyond Ipswich it widened to a dual carriageway. Between Ipswich and Colchester Anna revved the bike up beyond the speed limit but, not wanting to get stopped on her first trip, kept under a hundred. Before Colchester, she turned off to go back towards Ipswich on the minor road through Ardleigh and Lawford and, instead of retracing her route, headed through Woodbridge. She stopped for a drink at the café by the station and wandered onto the quay nearby, wondering where Anula's house or flat was. The small marina was a picturesque spot, with boats of many types, and a former tide mill at the end of the quay overlooking the River Deben. Across the river were the low mounds of the Saxon burials of Sutton Hoo.

Returning to her bike Anna rode back to Aldeburgh on the B road through Snape, passing the Maltings and the concert hall that was the hub for the annual music festival. She locked the bike in the garage and texted Cloote and Rees. Oliver was in York on his second day in the Minster archives while Gordon had just arrived in Dublin. She told them the bike had arrived and that she'd be off to Exeter in the morning.

That evening Anna looked through all the reports she could find about Cecil Arbuthnot's murder. They agreed that he had disturbed an intruder, who had secreted himself in the library before closing. As he'd been stabbed, and given the increases in knife crime, the reports surmised that the killer was a young thug looking for something to steal who'd panicked when confronted by the security guard. This appeared to be confirmed by a witness who had seen a hooded figure coming out of the Wren Door of the Divinity School around the time of the murder.

Anna got up at six, completed her exercises, showered, and had a light breakfast. Just after seven she strapped her rucksack to the luggage rack, carefully set the alarm system, checking no one was around, started the bike and headed down the back lane out of the town past the hospital. She negotiated the roundabout and roared off towards the A12. In the car park of the Tesco Express by the roundabout a man got out his mobile phone. 'Savile? The girl just left the town on that new bike … Yes, they're all away now … She had a bag on the back. Looks like she may be gone overnight … Okay. I'll meet you there in half an hour.'

Anna hated motorways so, though it was further, retraced the route she'd taken with Rees back to Oxford via Cambridge and Bedford. After bypassing Oxford, she joined the A303 to cross Salisbury Plain past Stonehenge. Even at this time of year traffic was heavy but the Harley was such a joy to ride Anna didn't care about weaving in between the HGVs and erratically driven white vans.

It was now after midday, so she decided to stop for lunch. She headed for Café Newt in the Moto Corsa motorcycle dealership in Gillingham. She ate a vegetarian breakfast before visiting the shop where she picked up two pairs of stretch denim Kevlar jeans, a pair of Spada Pilgrim Grande boots, a retro-style Redbike Classic RB-500 Jet Helmet and goggles. She paid, getting the shop to mail the bulkier gear to Aldeburgh. As she did so a huge biker with a straggly ginger beard and a tattered denim jacket covered in patches bent over her.

'That your Low Rider?'

'Yeh.'

'Fuckin' cool bike.'

'Which is yours?'

He beckoned her over to the window and pointed out a heavily customised Tri Glide Ultra. It wouldn't have looked out of place at Woodstock or in *Easy Rider*. 'Even fucking cooler,' Anna retorted.

The biker responded with a raised right fist which Anna mirrored before they high fived. 'Take care on the road, sister,' he said as Anna left.

The remainder of the trip was uneventful and by two Anna was pulling into the car park of her hotel on the river in Exeter.

It wasn't the hotel's fault. In fact, it was a very nice hotel. Anna was grateful she could now stay somewhere she might get a good night's sleep and not be kept awake by TVs blaring through paper-thin walls. It was just bad luck that Anna's visit coincided with a convention of the online betting giant SmashBet! As Anna was checking in, a man was trying it on with two women who clearly weren't welcoming his attentions. Fortunately, the women seemed capable of dealing with 'Steve from marketing'.

'Will you be dining in tonight, Dr Carr?' the receptionist was asking.

'Err. No. Thank you.' It wasn't a hard decision.

Anna enjoyed a pleasant meal at a small vegetarian restaurant near the cathedral that seemed unlikely to be frequented by the SmashBet! staff. The same couldn't be said of the hotel car park when she returned. 'Steve from marketing' was sharing a cigarette break with two male colleagues and Anna had to walk past them to the door. She didn't catch everything he said but distinctly heard the words 'rug muncher'. Deciding she was too tired to respond, and he wasn't worth it, she ignored the insult.

After a run along the river in the morning Anna walked the short distance to the cathedral precincts. The library and archives are housed in the west wing of the Bishop's Palace just south of the cathedral, and it was there that Anna arrived at 10 a.m. sharp. Their most prized possession is a tenth-century manuscript known as the Exeter Book, a collection of poems, including riddles, in Old English that was owned by Leofric, the first bishop of Exeter. Anna had visited the library a few years earlier to study it. The archivist she'd met on her previous visit was there to meet her.

'Good morning, Dr Carr. Good to see you again. I hope Professor Strachan is keeping well?' Anna assured him that Magnus was indeed well. 'I'm afraid that, as you suggested, your enquiry could refer to quite a few manuscripts. What I've done is arranged for the ones you've selected to be brought up in batches every hour.'

Anna thanked him and said that should work fine. *It shouldn't take long to ascertain if there's any reference to the* Codex *there*, she thought.

She worked through twelve documents by the time she took a lunch break and another ten before the archive closed at four. She used the next hour for a quick look at the cathedral itself before it closed. As she left the building, she once again admired the West Front Image Screen, one of the greatest architectural achievements of medieval England. The screen took a hundred and thirty years to complete and is covered in a wealth of carving, dominated by three rows of statues. These would originally have been brightly painted to give worshippers what they would have considered a convincing vision of heaven.

That's one thing films set in the Middle Ages never get right, thought Anna. 'Church walls and statues are never painted. I expect it's because we're so used to seeing the bare stone, filmmakers don't think audiences would accept it.'

As she again wanted to avoid the SmashBet! crew Anna took the bike and drove a few miles south to the former port of the city, Topsham. She'd been told the Bridge Inn was worth a visit, both for its beer and its history. A dwelling on the site is recorded in the Domesday Book and the stonemasons responsible for the construction of Exeter Cathedral may also have lodged there, though the present building dates from the sixteenth century. The pub was cosy and simple, with wheel back chairs and real ale. Anna ordered a beer for a change and ate a straightforward ploughman's. There was live folk music, which wasn't exactly to her taste, but at least nobody bothered her or remarked on her appearance. She got back to the hotel around ten. No sign of Steve and his mates, though she did hear some of them returning as she was dropping off to sleep, which may have accounted for her dream.

In it she was in a dark tunnel. She knew that at one end there was something evil and at the other safety, but she didn't know which. She had to decide and started running in one direction. The scene then changed, and she was in the hall of a Renaissance palace amid a masked ball. She was obviously looking for someone but didn't know who. She approached a figure dressed in black with its back towards her when suddenly several people with wolf masks rushed towards them both. Then she woke up.

Chapter 10

The next morning in the archive again proved fruitless, but early in the afternoon she consulted item D&C2092. These were letters patent from King Henry III to William, bishop of Exeter, granting him the chapel of Bosham in Sussex and various manors. It was dated 26 November 1243, at Westminster. The patents themselves were standard stuff but the king also informed William of the *Codex* he was having compiled of his father's papers. There was a partial listing which Anna spent most of the afternoon transcribing. The remaining documents added nothing further, and Anna sent a discreet message to Cloote and Rees letting them know of her find. Cloote responded saying he'd found nothing in York and would be heading to Durham in the morning. He also said Gordon had drawn a blank in Ireland and was on a flight home.

Anna returned to the vegetarian restaurant for an early dinner and was back at the hotel by seven. She spent three hours checking off the list she'd found against the remaining parts of the *Codex* to see if any of them referred to the missing pages. Disappointingly they didn't. All the items listed were still intact at the Bodleian and so hadn't been the target of the theft. 'Bugger,' she concluded.

She decided to take a walk along the river. She put on some music, selecting *Ategnatos* by the Swiss folk metal band Eluveitie. One of the things she liked about them was that many of their songs were in Gaulish, an ancient Celtic language spoken in parts of Europe at the time of the Roman Empire. Though extinct since the late sixth century, the band have enlisted the help of university linguists to reconstruct the language for use in their songs. Anna had been a bit sceptical about the latest album, as the band had made several personnel changes, but she was pleasantly surprised by it. All their trademark characteristics, incorporating melodic death metal with elements of Celtic music, and blending modern and traditional instruments, were there. A thin rain was beginning to fall so she pulled her hood up over her head and concentrated on the music. It was this, combined with the disappointment of the afternoon, that accounted for what happened next. She walked into the lobby not looking where she was going, straight into Steve from marketing. Her in-ear headphones were knocked out as Steve exclaimed, 'Whoa! If it isn't the little dyke girl,' and grabbed hold of both Anna's wrists.

Despite her anger Anna thought she'd try being polite. 'Please let go of me.'

'No, no, no. I think you owe me at least a kiss. Then maybe I can help you with your problem.'

'I don't have a problem. Please let go.'

'Oh, but you do,' he was now pressing his groin into Anna's, and she could smell the alcohol and cigarettes on his breath. She was weighing up what to do. There was no receptionist. Steve was big, about six-two and had a strong grip. He probably worked out. But he'd been drinking, and both his posture and balance told Anna he wasn't a trained fighter.

'You need my nice, big, thick . . .' was as far as Steve got.

When he thought about it later, which he tried not to, several things seemed to have happened simultaneously. The receptionist started to come through the door to the lobby, two of his colleagues emerged from the bar and it felt like a horse had kicked him in the balls. Anna's right knee came up sharply into his groin. Steve let go his grip. Instantly she had his left arm behind his back which, together with the pain from his balls, forced him to bend forward. She kicked his legs from under him and put her right arm round his neck while her left kept his arm in place. She forced his face into the carpet as she whispered in his ear. 'Now you try a little rug munching, shit head.' Steve could only gurgle in response, so she relaxed her grip and got to her feet.

'Are you okay, miss?' The receptionist asked.

'What do you mean? She attacked him,' one of Steve's colleagues retorted.

'I don't think so, sir. I saw exactly what happened on the CCTV and have it recorded.' The two SmashBet! employees didn't argue. Turning to Anna again he asked, 'Would you like me to call the police? He definitely assaulted you.'

'No, it's okay, please don't. And I'm fine.'

Steve's friends were helping him to his feet. He still couldn't speak. He then broke free and staggered to the outer door. It opened automatically and he was violently sick over the shoes of a man who was just entering with an elegantly dressed woman. 'Cash! What the f—'

'Sir Maurice,' he managed before throwing up again.

'I do not expect my employees to get drunk at company functions. You haven't heard the last of this. Come, my dear.' Sir Maurice stormed past them to the lift. Steve's friends, supporting both arms, carried the groaning man toward the stairs.

The receptionist turned to Anna a grin on his face. 'That was very impressive and no more than he deserved. I'm sorry but I have no respect for those people. My religion says that all gambling is wrong, we call it maisir. I don't want to stop people playing the lottery but this,' he gestured towards the SmashBet! advertising board. 'They make many people's lives a misery. And do you know how much that man Sir Maurice earned last year?' Anna admitted she didn't. 'Over three hundred million. And yesterday he tipped his chambermaid two pounds! Two pounds!'

Anna suggested they were all bastards but her new friend Hafeez told her she should be forgiving even to men like that. Anna left him by agreeing in theory, but not in practice.

While the commotion was going on no one paid any attention to a black Range Rover with tinted glass that turned into the car park. It stopped next to Anna's bike so that it was between the bike and the CCTV camera on the wall. A man got out, quickly unscrewed the bike's fuel cap, dropped something in, and replaced the cap.

*

Anna set off early next morning after a quick shower and exercises. She stopped again at Café Newt for breakfast and was in Salisbury by ten. She parked at her hotel, the historic Chapter House in St John's Street, letting reception know she'd arrived and leaving her rucksack.

To enter the Cathedral Close she only had to cross the road and pass through St Ann's Gate. The library is housed in a room over the east cloister up a spiral stone staircase. Its manuscript collection catalogue has not yet been digitised, but an updated pdf of the 1880 Catalogue by Sir Edward Maunde Thompson is available online, which Anna had consulted before her trip.

There was no obvious document that might contain a reference to the *Codex,* but Anna was now focusing her attention on papers from around 1240. She started from that year and worked forwards and backwards. Soon after lunch she struck lucky in a batch of indulgences. Indulgences depended on the fear of purgatory, where people were punished for sins committed during their life on earth. An indulgence would make the period there shorter. They were granted in return for prayers or other acts of penance, such as going on a pilgrimage, but the Church also sold indulgences to raise money. Sales were contracted out to commissioners, such as Chaucer's Pardoner, who kept a proportion of the takings for themselves. The abuse of indulgences became a serious problem for the Church, and they were a target of attacks by Martin Luther and other Protestant theologians. Though indulgences still exist, the Church outlawed their sale in 1567.

The batch Anna was examining were not the indulgences themselves. These would have been given to the person involved and were often highly decorated. Instead, she was looking at the cathedral's copies. Most of this batch, from between 1233 and 1240, were in the same hand and the monk responsible had often got bored and had done little drawings in the margins. On the back of one Anna was amused to discover a drawing of a naked nun apparently riding a flying penis. Medieval monks were not always otherworldly and chaste.

She turned to the next example, an indulgence issued by Edmund of Abingdon, archbishop of Canterbury, granting relaxation of forty days of penance to contributors to the fabric of Salisbury Cathedral. The actual text was straightforward but on the back the scribe had used it for another purpose. It was a partial list of the contents of the *Codex Johannem Regem.* But this was different, it said:

> *A Candela ad Corpus Christi in hoc ego laboravi.*
> *I worked on this from Candlemas to Corpus Christi.*

Candlemas is celebrated on 2 February, whereas Corpus Christi is a movable feast between 21 May and 24 June, so the monk worked on the *Codex* for at least ten weeks. The annoying thing was that Anna could not see any clue as to who the monk was, which was unsurprising as few left any signature. Nor was where the document had been written stated. It may have been Canterbury or Salisbury but that was far from certain. Even the date wasn't mentioned, other than being in the range between 1233 to 1240. Anna photographed the page and spent the rest of the day checking if there were any more links to the *Codex* but found nothing more.

She returned to the hotel, where Rees had booked a beautiful wood-panelled executive room that had a large work desk and a king-size bed. She hadn't quite got used to this. When she'd been on research trips for her PhD Anna had mainly used Premier Inns or Travel Lodges. She set up her laptop and messaged Cloote and Rees with the photo of her document. Rees was in Canterbury and said he would try to find anything that might identify either where her monk had been working or his name. Anna spent a couple more hours searching online for any leads, especially to monks fond of drawing animal pictures, but nothing turned up.

She was just thinking about dinner when Cloote called. 'Anna? That's an excellent find. I've not found anything in Durham, but your animal loving monk reminded me of something. I seem to remember seeing similar drawings when I was in Lincoln about ten years ago. That's my next port of call so let's hope I remembered correctly.' Anna agreed it sounded promising. 'How long will you be in Oxford?'

'Should only be one night. Two at most.'

'Then we should all be back at Summerland by Monday then.'

Anna didn't feel like going out for dinner, especially with no SmashBet! around, and so ate in the hotel's restaurant where some of the stone for the initial construction of the cathedral had been quarried eight hundred years ago. She had a vegan curry followed by bread-and-butter pudding, so she'd need a bit more exercise in the morning.

Chapter 11

When she got up Anna checked the weather. It didn't look good, though it wasn't raining yet. She pulled on her tee-shirt, hoodie, and track suit bottoms and went for a run through the Cathedral Close, over Crane Bridge, and along the river. By the time she'd done some exercises and showered it was raining heavily. She had breakfast and paid her bill. As she left Salisbury the rain was torrential, interspersed with periods of sleet. *This should test the bike*, she thought as she headed north. The rain was incessant, but the bike remained anchored to the road. Despite the weather she was back at her ground floor bedsit in St John Street in an hour and a half. She didn't see the black Range Rover cruising past, turning right into Pusey Street, and parking in St Giles.

After a change of clothes, the rain was stopping, and Anna only had a short walk to the Old Fire Station in George Street for the first of her meetings. Skylight, the Oxford branch of the homelessness charity Crisis, was gearing up for Christmas and was busier than usual. Anna was greeted by a couple of the volunteers she knew as she headed to the office.

Nora Greenwood was looking over the designs for the Christmas appeal. When she saw Anna, she rushed over and flung her arms round her neck. 'Oh my days! Anna Carr!'

'Hey Nora, good to see you.'

'Neat garms, sis.' Anna was wearing one of her newly acquired jackets.

Anna had met Nora not far from where they were now, soon after she started her post-grad course. She was one of many homeless people on the streets of Oxford and Anna stopped to admire the chalk drawings Nora was doing to make money. It was the style that surprised her. They weren't the usual realist views of the Radcliffe Camera or Hertford College Bridge. They were vibrant with unusual colours and distorted perspectives. They reminded Anna of the Canarian artist Alberto Manrique, one of whose watercolours was Anna's most valuable possession.

She got talking to Nora bit by bit over the next few weeks, despite neither of them being exactly loquacious. She was nineteen and came from North Wales. Both her parents had been addicts. She had been constantly bullied as the only mixed-race girl in her school. She started drinking and taking any drugs she could get hold of, usually by letting boys do what they wanted to her. She left home at fifteen. At first, like so many runaways, she went to London, but a year later, after she was raped for a second time, she came to Oxford. One result of her stay in London was that she'd entirely discarded whatever accent she originally had and now spoke her own take on MLE.

One day Anna found Nora in Broad Street, drunk and trying to cadge smokes from tourists. Anna made an immediate decision. 'Oh, Nora there you are. You must come home at once.' She grabbed Nora by the arm and, before she could protest, marched her back to St John Street. Over the next few days Anna started getting her off drugs and alcohol. She contacted the Amy Winehouse Foundation, and they found her a place in rehab and then recovery housing. But Nora still needed more help. She was an immensely promising artist, but Anna didn't have the money to pay for a college course. However, Magnus did. One morning a very serious looking Anna turned up at Strachan's lecture on the *Book of Kells*. Afterwards she took him aside.

'Magnus, I need some money.'

'How much, Anna? Are you in debt?'

She didn't answer the second part. 'Probably about thirty or forty thousand should be enough.'

Magnus wondered just what kind of debts Anna could have. Had she got a gambling problem? Was it drugs? Neither seemed likely. Anna explained about Nora and showed him some sketches. He was impressed and agreed to meet her. Anna had thought they would get along and she was right. Magnus and Nora hit it off immediately. They got Nora enrolled for a two-year HND in Art and Design. Magnus let her stay in his small garden house for no rent and now she was working part-time at Skylight and studying art at Oxford Brookes University.

Nora and Anna went to the cafeteria. Staff and volunteers were making up parcels and sorting bedding ready for the rush. Since 2010 the number of rough sleepers had more than doubled. The way Anna thought about it was that there were now more homeless people in England than the entire population of Iceland.

'How's Nils?'

'He's bangin. You know he's on *Esperanza*?'

'Yeh, you said. Where are they?'

'Down at Ushuaia. Them's doing tests on the ice sheets down there.' Nils was Nora's Norwegian boyfriend. He worked for Greenpeace and was currently a crew member on their largest ship. The pair rented a small flat in Iffley and Nora now used Magnus' garden house as her studio. After catching up on gossip Anna got round to seeking Nora's help.

'You know that security guard at the Bodleian who was murdered?' Nora knew. 'I wondered what the word about it was on the street?'

Nora did a sort of shrug and snort at the same time. 'Not what the popo think. The dude what done it weren't a roadman.'

'What was he then?'

'Dunno for sure, but after he dipped the guy, dem saw him cutting say he had no face.' She meant he was wearing a mask or face covering.

'And no one's heard anything more?'

'Nah. Him breeze off. But him real sticky I tink.' Anna agreed that the masked man certainly sounded dangerous, and it was clear the police theory, that it was a panicked reaction following a casual break-in was, as she'd suspected, wrong.

Anna thanked Nora for her help, asked her to keep her ear to the ground and let her know if she heard anything more. 'You got any of your new work here?' Nora had a portfolio of recent stuff in the office which she showed her. There were figure studies in pencil and crayon, mainly of Nils. 'Good you've now got a male model,' said Anna. In the early days Anna had sat for Nora.

'Yuh. Guy's yakmules is more difficult to draw man.' Anna laughed. The drawings were, as usual, both realistic and revealing, and not just because they were nudes. Anna had four of Nora's drawings on the wall of her bedsit, which she found useful if she had visitors she didn't want. When the agent who managed the house had called, he'd approached them with a breezy nonchalance. As he realised their anatomical detail, and then that they were of Anna, he went bright red, found words hard to form, made his excuses and left.

There were some sketches in what Anna thought of as Nora's surrealist style. She'd shown her Manrique's work and that of Paul Delvaux and others and Nora had assimilated some of their elements. These often had links to storytelling after Nora became a voracious reader, especially of modern fantasy writers such as Neil Gaiman and China Miéville. Finally, there were some newer works which utilised great blocks of colour and seemed reminiscent of the Vorticists. 'I's trying out some tings,' Nora explained. 'Not sure how dey'll work out. I's doing some sculptures too for de show.' Nora's graduation show would be in the summer. Anna really liked the new direction but said she'd be sorry if her old style disappeared totally. 'Whatever,' said Nora.

Chapter 12

Anna's next call was to Magnus. She walked the short distance to his study and, as usual, went straight in.

'Anna. How lovely to see you. How's life with Oliver Cloote?' Anna said it was good. She had agreed with Cloote what she could, and should not, tell Magnus. She explained that part of their research involved the stolen pages of the *Codex Johannem Regem*. They were trying to find out what they contained because they seemed linked to Norse and Viking myth, and its depiction in the twelfth and thirteenth centuries.

'Your best option on the *Codex* would be Gervase Penhaligon at Cambridge.' Anna knew Penhaligon was professor of Celtic and medieval studies and she'd read his work. She thought it highly erratic. There was the odd gem of insight among many run-of-the-mill publications. 'He did some research on the *Codex* a few years back because he stayed here at Merton.'

'Did he publish anything on it?' Anna asked.

'I think he did.' Magnus turned to his PC and accessed Penhaligon's academic page that listed his publications.

'There it is. *Journal of Norse and Scandinavian Studies*, 2010. Hang on I'll print it off for you. 'Fraid my printer's on the blink but we can collect it from Mob.' Mob is reputed to be the oldest continuously functioning academic library in the world, having been built between 1371 and 1378. It occupies the upper floors of the south and west ranges of the Mob Quadrangle and, since its refitting in the early seventeenth century, has been virtually unaltered. Merton's libraries also have the distinct advantage of being open nineteen hours a day from seven in the morning until 2 a.m.

Magnus retrieved the paper, and they gave it a quick scan. When he started to read through the bibliography Magnus exclaimed. 'Of course. No wonder I remembered this paper. It was the one where Penhaligon demolished the theories of old Inkpen.'

'Inkpen?'

'Roger Inkpen. You probably haven't come across him. He was a specialist in the early Christian Church in Britain and a student of Tolkien's. Retired in the late nineties, I think. Penhaligon was one of his students. Never said much against him while he was around, but really had a go once he'd left.'

'What did Inkpen think of that?'

'Oh, he said nothing. He'd retired somewhere remote I think and never responded. Not in print at least.'

'Sounds a bit mean spirited if he didn't give Inkpen the opportunity to defend his work.'

'Most people thought Inkpen's ideas were rather outdated and Penhaligon's paper and book on early Christianity made his name and got him his chair.'

The paper didn't say much about the *Codex*, just a few references, and nothing about the detail of its content, but it was highly dismissive of Inkpen's ideas on linkages between the Norse myths and Christian thought at the time of the Plantagenets. They then looked at Inkpen's publications and found more references to the *Codex* in material from the 1950s and 60s. The library wasn't busy, and the duty librarian looked over Magnus's shoulder.

'Goodness. Roger Inkpen. Haven't thought about him for years. What were you looking for?' Magnus explained about the *Codex*. 'You know we've got Inkpen's papers?'

'No, I didn't. What, here in Merton?'

'Yes, that's right.'

'Can we look at them now?' Anna interjected.

'Well, it's not usual practice as the archivist isn't here but I'm sure he'd agree to let Professor Strachan take a look if I asked him.'

'Well?' said Anna.

'Would you be so good as to ask him?' Magnus requested rather more politely.

'Of course, Professor.'

While he went off to phone, Magnus and Anna sat down to look in more detail at Inkpen's 'Continuity and Change in the Regency of Henry III', published in 1963. It mentioned that the *Codex* may have been compiled at Medmenham Abbey. 'Isn't that the Buckinghamshire abbey famous as the location of Francis Dashwood's Hellfire Club in the eighteenth century?' Anna suggested.

'Yes, but I can't remember its earlier history.' They looked it up. A Cistercian abbey had been founded at Medmenham in the twelfth century, though it didn't receive a royal charter until 1200, so it would have been quite new in the early thirteenth century.

'It could be where my doodling monk lived,' said Anna, and then explained more about the drawings she'd found in Salisbury.

The librarian returned and said the archivist was quite happy for them to look through Inkpen's papers. 'But I'm afraid they've never been catalogued,' he explained.

The papers were housed in one of the upper library's furthest recesses. Anna and Magnus got the boxes down and began to search through them. Though the overall collection wasn't indexed, Inkpen himself had inserted a page in each box, listing the contents. After an hour or so Magnus suddenly exclaimed 'Eureka!'

Anna came over to the desk he was working at. The box's contents included Inkpen's notes for the paper they'd read. It was dated 1961–3. The notes included things Inkpen hadn't referred to in the paper, most notably his description of some pages in the *Codex Johannem Regem* and his surmise that they had been compiled by a monk at Medmenham. But the real find was a box of Kodachrome 35mm slides. On the side of the box was written 'C. Joh. Reg. Sept. '62'. Magnus started getting the slides out of the box, trying to hold them up to the light, but the library was quite dark, and it wasn't easy to see. 'We'll need a slide projector' he said, starting to walk back towards the entrance. The librarian thought there might be a projector in a cupboard somewhere and went off to look.

'It was how we used to do lectures before the advent of PowerPoint,' Magnus explained. 'Ah the joys of the pre-digital era. How long did re-typing your thesis take after your viva?' he asked Anna.

'A few days I suppose.'

'I had to re-type mine three times from scratch. Each time it took two weeks, working sixteen hours a day. You young people really don't know how lucky you are!' He said the last sentence in a kind of cackle. Anna frowned. 'Albert Steptoe,' Magnus explained. Anna knew he was a character from an old sitcom she'd never seen. The librarian returned with two boxes, one larger than the first.

'Here you go. Thought they'd be there somewhere. Can't have been used for well over ten years. When we need to see slides, we just send them off to be digitised. Shall I do that with these?'

'Not just yet,' said Anna. 'We need to look at them urgently.' Then to Magnus, 'I'll put the boxes away. You photocopy Inkpen's notes. Make two copies and send an e-version to me as well.' While Magnus did as she asked, he persuaded the librarian to let them take the slides back to his study as long as they returned them quickly. In the meantime, the librarian would arrange for them to be digitised as a priority job.

Back in Magnus's room he set up the slide projector. The other box contained what he called a carousel, a circular plastic holder for the slides that fitted into the projector. Anna couldn't recall having seen one before. 'I think they went out of production when you were about ten,' Magnus told her. He took down his picture of *The Seventh Seal* so they could project the image onto the wall while Anna drew the curtains. As Magnus brought up each image Anna photographed them with her phone. The images wouldn't be great, but she could at least let Cloote see what they'd found.

The slides showed several pages from the *Codex*, including ones that were missing. At first sight there seemed nothing especially extraordinary about the text. They would need to study it in more detail when they had the digitised images. However, there was one aspect of the manuscript that was distinctive. Whoever had written it had also drawn many small images of beasts and animals in the margins. Some appeared to be real and others mythological, but there was no doubt that they had been drawn by the same person responsible for the Salisbury ones.

There was no more they could do that day, so Magnus called Gervase Penhaligon. He answered and said yes, he'd be in Cambridge next week and would be happy to meet Anna, who

Magnus described as one of his post-doctoral research assistants. They took the slides back to Mob and the librarian said the digitised images should be with them by Tuesday. Anna called Penhaligon back saying she'd see him on Wednesday before meeting Anula at the cinema.

'While you're in Cambridge you could look up Rasmus Kask,' Magnus said to her after Penhaligon hung up. Rasmus had been a fellow PhD student with Anna. He was Estonian and rather quiet and reserved. Anna had liked him and, at a conference in Reykjavik, defended his interpretation of some of the Livonian texts against concerted opposition from a group of Russian scholars. He was now a research fellow in the same department as Penhaligon.

'I'd forgotten he'd gone there. I think I'll do that,' she replied. She agreed to speak with Magnus again when they'd both had a chance to study the images.

Chapter 13

On the way to her bedsit Anna bought some food for dinner and breakfast. When she got in, she immediately felt something wasn't quite right. There was nothing missing or even obviously out of place, it was just a feeling. As she hadn't been there for some time there was a slight layer of dust covering the room. Angling the flashlight on her phone she could clearly see the dust. She moved some books. They were exactly where they'd been. So were other objects round the room. She went over to the pictures on the wall. The Manrique and Nora's drawings revealed nothing but, just above her reproduction of Carlos Schwabe's *Death and the Grave Digger,* there were some very slight scratches in the dust. Someone had moved it to look behind.

Anna opened her door, carefully gripping near the base of the knob, and went to the shared kitchen. She looked in the cupboards and took out a jar of ground white pepper. It wasn't great but it would do. Back in her room she wrapped a scarf round her face to prevent sneezing and gently blew some pepper onto the doorknob. She found what she expected, nothing. The knob had been wiped or gripped by a gloved hand. If no one else had been in the room, her hands would have left grease which the pepper dust would have revealed. *At least there was nothing to find*, she thought. Anna had her phone and laptop with her but wondered if the someone might try to mug her for them. She decided she needed to hide the laptop when she went out, even it was supposedly unhackable.

She'd had a couple of messages from Cloote while she'd been at Merton. They said he had indeed turned up something in Lincoln and that he and Rees were on their way back to Aldeburgh. She replied letting him know about the intruder and that she too had found something of interest. She sent him the photos of the slides and said she'd see him around lunchtime the following day.

Neither of the women she shared the house with, Em and Gaby, were in, so she went up to the top floor. Under the hot water tank in the airing cupboard was a loose board that could be prised up. She stashed her laptop there. Then she called Nikki McDonald again to check their meeting was still on. She cooked herself an omelette with spinach and cheese in the kitchen and left at seven to meet Nikki at the Castle pub in Paradise Street.

Anna had met Nikki through taekwondo. They had trained with the same sabom, though Nikki had less time to practice as her duties with Thames Valley Police intruded more into her spare time. Anna had three reasons for wanting to see Nikki. The first was to congratulate her on passing the assessment process for promotion to inspector. The second was to gently enquire if the police had got any further in investigating the Bodleian murder, and the third was just to let her hair down for the evening.

Unsurprisingly, Nikki was several minutes late but it gave Anna a chance to check out the clientele of one of the city's gay-friendly pubs. Not that long ago Nikki McDonald would have had to conceal her sexuality to have had any chance of progressing her career, but things were changing, and she was a prominent member of the Thames Valley LGBT+ Police Network and organised their participation in Oxford Pride in May.

'Hey, Tiger!' It was Nikki's name for Anna, mainly because of her fighting style at taekwondo. Nikki was a good five inches taller than Anna and more heavily built, though her hair was even shorter.

Anna gave her a hug and went to the bar for a pint of Nikki's usual Guinness. She got another Diet Coke for herself. For the next couple of hours, they caught up on Nikki's news. Other than saying she was working as a researcher for an independent scholar, Anna said little about what she was doing. Nikki was in Thames Valley's Major Crimes Unit and so was able to give Anna all the publicly available information about the Bodleian crime. 'We've got an open mind on the perp,' Nikki told her. 'There were no forensics to speak of and we had no credible witnesses who saw him.'

'The word on the street is that it wasn't just some kid,' Anna said.

'Oh, where'd you hear that?' Nikki asked, though she had a shrewd idea.

'Just around,' said Anna. 'What about motive?'

'Are you turning detective?' Anna didn't usually go in for chats about local crime.

'It's just where it happened really. Anyway, what about your love life. Anything to report?'

Nikki didn't press Anna further on her interest but stashed away her thoughts. She laughed. 'Don't get much time to devote to it, Tiger. You?'

'I'm like a monk, or should it be a nun? Celibate since St Albans Day.'

'When the fuck's that?'

'Twenty-second of June.'

'In that case we could both do with a fuck. Fancy coming to Plush?'

Plush is Oxford's gay nightclub and had recently moved to a new location tucked away off Cornmarket Street. Ironically Thames Valley Police had opposed its application for extended opening hours. Anna was up for it, and it was only five minutes away. Nikki greeted a couple of people including the door staff, one of whom saluted and said it was good to see Thames Valley were there to protect them. Inside the club Nikki bought some more drinks – she never pressed Anna into drinking alcohol – and they parked themselves by the bar. It was Bent Saturday, and the club was already busy at eleven o'clock.

After a while Nikki was keen for a dance, but Anna was a reluctant dancer and declined to join her. 'No problem,' said Nikki. 'You should check out the baby dyke over there. She's been eying you up for the last twenty minutes.'

Anna looked to the other side of the bar and saw a slim girl with dark, curly hair and glasses who immediately dropped her eyes when she looked in her direction. 'Thanks. I might just do that.'

Anna strolled round the bar. 'Hey. I don't think I've seen you here before. I'm Anna.'

Not the most original chat up line but perfectly workable.

The girl agreed she'd not been there before; in fact, it was obvious that she was in the process of coming out, Nikki had been right in her surmise. Anna bought her a drink. Like many trendy young people, she drank weird, flavoured gin. Anna didn't need to do much talking. Now she'd made the connection the girl was garrulous. Her name was Margot Pennington, and she was a first-year law student. A few gins later and Anna asked, 'Do you want to come back to my place?'

Margot blushed but it was clearly what she'd hoped she'd say. Anna went over to say her goodbyes to a beaming Nikki. 'Be gentle with her, Tiger,' was her parting remark.

Chapter 14

In the morning Anna and Margo were woken by the sound of talking in the communal kitchen. 'Probably Em and her new boyfriend,' explained Anna. 'Would you like breakfast?'

'I'd love a coffee. I've got a bit of a headache.' Anna jumped out of bed. 'Aren't you going to put something on?'

'Oh, you're right the floor's a bit cold,' Anna replied and put on a pair of short socks. Margot was a little shocked.

Over coffee for Margot, herb tea for Anna, Anna discovered that Margot was the daughter of a High Court judge and had been brought up a devout Christian. She'd always been more attracted to women than men but found it hard to reconcile her faith with her sexuality. Anna said there was no reason she couldn't keep her faith and be queer too. 'I once had a lover who was a vicar. One of the kinkiest people I've ever met.' The revelation didn't seem to set Margot's mind at rest. 'Look,' she continued, 'only you know what your real feelings are. Just keep exploring them and you'll get there.' That seemed to go down rather better, and Margot determined to follow Anna's advice, if not her actions.

They went for breakfast in Broad Street, near Margot's lodgings in Balliol, before Anna wished her good luck and returned to collect her bike and head off to Aldeburgh. Her journey was uneventful other than intermittent bouts of sleety rain.

'Sounds like you've had a rather more fruitful trip than me,' Gordon greeted her. 'I knew Oliver would give me the bum rap,' he smiled as Cloote joined them.

'Anna, my dear!' She let the mild sexism pass, Cloote was getting less formal but was somewhat agitated as he was playing with his glasses again. 'You had a visit from our err friends then. I was worried about you last night and thought we shouldn't have let you stay there alone.'

'It's okay, I wasn't alone.' Cloote didn't enquire further.

Gordon had transferred Anna's pictures to his laptop and projected them onto a portable screen in the library. 'The slides are an amazing find,' he said. 'It looks like we've got most of the missing text.'

'I wouldn't jump to conclusions,' she replied. 'Not until we get the higher quality versions. Magnus will send them first thing tomorrow.'

'In that case let's have a look at *my* find,' Cloote enthused. Rees drew the curtains and turned out the lights as Oliver brought up a page from a manuscript which he projected alongside Anna's photos. 'It was in a manorial roll. I was simply looking at documents from the period in question and found this.'

Anna studied the images on the screen. Most of the page described the rents owed to the cathedral by a series of tenants in the area near Boston. But around the margins were illustrated animals and birds. She looked closely. They depicted several of the same creatures in Inkpen's slides. 'They seem to be by the same person.'

'Yes,' Cloote responded, 'I'm sure it's the same hand. What do you say, Gordon?'

'I'm no expert but they certainly look very similar. This bird here, the basket is the same and it's holding it with both beak and foot. What is it?'

'A partridge,' Cloote replied.

'But you also said you might know the monk's name,' Anna reminded him.

'Ah yes. Look here,' he pointed to the bottom of the document. 'Just enlarge it will you Gordon?' Rees brought up another image and Anna could see there were faint marks on the vellum.

'Here's a transcription,' said Cloote and another image appeared in his neat handwriting:

XVXXIIXXIVXXXIVXXIIIXXXIIXVXIVXXIIIXIXXIIXLIIIXLIVXLIIIXIIIXIVXXXV

'I believe it's a coded colophon.'

'A what?' asked Rees.

'A colophon comes at the end of a book giving information about its author and printing,' explained Anna. 'In the Middle Ages colophons were the usual place for encrypted information. The Anglo-Saxons were great at this, probably because they were so fond of riddles, but many medieval scribes understood the basics of constructing text using ciphers that could only be decoded with a key.'

'It's likely the numbers correspond to letters,' Cloote continued. 'So, the first thing to do is divide the string into individual numbers.'

'I see,' Rees said. 'So, the first number could be ten and five or fifteen followed by two tens or twenty or twenty-one or twenty-two?'

'Exactly,' replied Cloote. 'Why don't we work out all the possible combinations to see what we've got?'

They each worked on the sequence. There were plenty of possibilities. Even the first few numbers could read any of the following:

10, 5, 10, 10, 1, 1
10, 5, 10, 10, 2
10, 5, 20, 1, 1
10, 5, 20, 2
15, 10, 10, 1, 1
15, 10, 10, 2
15, 20, 1, 1
15, 20, 2
15, 22

Once they'd finished the possible combinations, Anna grasped the pattern. 'I think it's a Polybius square,' she exclaimed.

'Yes, I see. That would explain it,' Gordon replied. 'Oliver said you could see patterns! At MIT we were told it was one of the world's first ciphers.'

'Sorry, you'll have to explain it for me,' said a perplexed Cloote.

'It was developed in the second century BCE by the Greek historian Polybius for signalling purposes,' said Anna. 'I'll show you. It's only a question of whether the compiler of this one was using Greek or Latin. Let's assume it's Latin.'

Anna got a sheet of paper and on it drew a six-by-six grid:

	1	2	3	4	5
1	A	B	C	D	E
2	F	G	H	I/J	K
3	L	M	N	O	P
4	Q	R	S	T	U
5	V	W	X	Y	Z

'Because twenty-six characters don't fit into twenty-five squares, two letters have to be combined. It's usually I and J, though C and K is an alternative. Polybius wouldn't have had this problem because the Greek alphabet only has twenty-four letters. If it *is* a Polybius square, then there's no number lower than eleven. so The sequence would be:

'XV, XXII, XXIV, XXXIV, XXIII, XXXII, XV, XIV, XXIII, XI, XXII, XLIII, XLIV, XLIII, XIII, XIV, XXXV

'And the letters are E G J O H M E D H A M S T S C R I P.'

'It's not exactly hard to break,' Rees mused.

'No, but most codes at this time weren't that sophisticated,' Anna explained. 'In medieval England, substitution ciphers were frequently used by scribes as a playful way to leave their signature or as the solution to a riddle. The ciphers tend to be fairly straightforward because they weren't designed to conceal important information though, sometimes, they deviate from the standard pattern, which adds complexity.'

'In that case we have: "Ego Johannes de Medeshamstede scripsit hoc,"' Cloote concluded.

'Looks right. "I, Johannes of Medeshamstede, wrote this." And that means Inkpen got the location wrong,' Anna said.

'Yes, not that surprising if he didn't think it especially important. Medhamstead makes more sense too. Nearer to Lincoln.'

'Where's Medhamstead?' asked Rees.

'It's the Anglo-Saxon name for Peterborough,' explained Anna.

'If the colophon contains a code, then maybe the drawings hold an alternative meaning as well,' Cloote said.

'I'd say that's entirely possible,' replied Anna. 'I think I need to swot up on medieval bestiaries unless you're more of an expert?'

'Not especially,' Cloote responded, 'I'll do the same until the higher quality photos arrive.'

'Could you fill me in on medieval bestiaries?' Rees asked.

'A bestiary is a collection of descriptions of both real and mythological creatures and, in the later twelfth and early thirteenth centuries, they were very popular in England,' Anna began. 'They're organised in different ways depending on the sources they used. It could be by animal groups, such as land and sea creatures, or be alphabetical. But the texts never make a distinction between real and imaginary beasts because they weren't meant to convey knowledge. They were about the Christian message that the world was the Word of God, and every living thing had its own special meaning. Medieval bestiaries are rich in symbolism and allegory, to teach moral lessons as well as be entertaining.'

'Thanks. I'm learning a lot. Do you fancy a decent run before getting down to research?' Anna said she did. She'd not been exercising properly in the last few days. They ran out of the town past the golf club before turning off on the Sailor's Path that took them to the village of Snape before retracing their route. The whole thing was about fifteen kilometres. Rees had trouble keeping up at times, as Anna was younger and fitter. She made him stop in the playing fields for a workout on the gym equipment. 'I'm glad I don't do this every day with you,' he admitted.

'You're not doing too bad for an old bloke,' said Anna.

For an instant Gordon thought she was being serious, but realised she was just teasing him and laughed. *She seems to be getting more relaxed with us*, he thought.

*

Back at the house Anna showered and settled down to her reading. That night and the following morning she consulted Florence McCulloch's *Medieval Latin and French Bestiaries*, the first modern English language study, published in 1962; Pamela Gravestock's *The Mark of the Beast*; Ron Baxter's more recent *Bestiaries and their Users in the Middle Ages* and David C Lindberg's 1992 classic study, *The Beginnings of Western Science*.

Around midday the digitised photographs arrived from Oxford. They were of exceptional quality. 'It was lucky he made them when he did,' Rees explained, 'Kodachrome II had just come in. A couple of years earlier and we'd only have had black and white.' They spent several hours poring over the images. They managed to identify all the animals and creatures portrayed. But none of them could see any obvious pattern or meaning other than their allegorical ones.

'They're certainly very similar to the famous bestiaries of the period,' Cloote said. 'The creator of our texts could even be one of the people who worked on them. The most significant bestiaries are digitised and should be easy to consult.'

'Are there that many?' asked Gordon.

'Fortunately not,' replied Cloote. 'I think the three key ones will probably be the *Worksop, Ashmole* and *Aberdeen* ones. The *Worksop* is now in the Morgan Library in New York. Then there's the *Ashmole Bestiary*, dating from the late twelfth century, made in Peterborough or Lincoln, and now in the Bodleian. The last is from about 1200 and is in Aberdeen University Library though there's some debate about where it was produced.'

'Before we decide our next move, I think I need to talk to Gervase Penhaligon,' said Anna.

Chapter 15

Savile Nesfield felt at peace with the world as he drove the Range Rover up the drive of Satterthwaite Hall. *If I was back home in South Africa, I'd be working for some fucking kaffir instead of one of the richest and most respected men in Europe*, he thought. In the apartheid era Nesfield's father had been a member of the Buro vir Staatsveiligheid, the Bureau for State Security, better known as BOSS. Despite moving to the ultra-conservative Afrikaner stronghold of Orania after the 1994 election, when Savile was in high school, he had never reconciled himself to majority rule. If anything, his son was even more extreme in his views. Nesfield believed in the innate superiority of the white Aryan race, a concept shared by his boss, though Forth was far more discreet about it.

Another passion they shared was hunting. Nesfield was one of the most skilled big-game hunters in Southern Africa leading shoots, both legal and illegal, during the early 2000s. It was on one of these that he met Elias Forth. Forth recognised Nesfield's resourcefulness and, more especially, his ruthlessness and offered him highly lucrative employment. They still went on big-game hunts together. Despite increasing restrictions, money could circumvent them. As they grew to admire, though never to trust, each other they also shared an obsession for cruelty. Several of the girls Forth abused were handed on to Nesfield for further humiliation and violence.

In other ways Nesfield considered himself entirely different. Though he would never mention it to his boss, Nesfield despised Forth's impotence in most sexual situations. He knew Forth could only achieve orgasm during extreme sexual violence or vicariously through scopophilia. In contrast Nesfield prided himself on his virility. He could achieve sexual arousal in any situation and had early practice. At the age of fourteen his father made him rape a young black girl in front of her mother, a known ANC agitator. Despite his theoretical detestation he retained a fetish for sex with non-white women, especially very young ones. His neurotic machismo also contrasted with that of Forth's other lieutenant. 'I don't think Morten has ever fucked anything,' Nesfield had said, 'not even a boy or a dog.'

The many towers, chimneys and finials of Satterthwaite Hall now came into sight. The house had been built by the industrialist Luther Satterthwaite in the 1850s. Satterthwaite was said to be the model for Dickens's Mr Gradgrind, and the house had been described by Pevsner as, 'An overblown copy of George Gilbert Scott's Midland Grand Hotel.' Nesfield preferred the description by the wife of one of Forth's investors, 'It's got too many twiddly bits.'

Inside the house Forth was confirming Nesfield's opinion. He was in a room adjoining the main guest bedroom. Between them was another reciprocal mirror but, in this case, it wouldn't have mattered if it had been clear glass, because both occupants of the bedroom knew he was watching. A woman was kneeling on the bed. She was wearing only a red corset that left her large breasts exposed. A naked man stood beside the bed fucking her from behind. The man was Forth's chauffeur and general factotum Vladimir. The woman was Carrie Prentiss. As Forth himself reached a climax he imagined the response if he released the video he was making on national television.

Forth watched Carrie as she slowly got dressed, exposing herself to him as she knew he wanted. Vladimir dressed quickly and left as Forth entered. 'Thank you, my dear. A perfect performance as usual.'

Carrie immediately switched into her professional role. 'I think the minister was sufficiently impressed. He did say we may have a problem with the prime minister's girlfriend. But they need the support of the right-wing members more than the PM's whore.'

Forth smiled. She had the right attitude. 'So, you think Ancaster's bill has a chance?' William Ancaster was sponsoring a bill to restrict abortion to the first eighteen weeks of pregnancy and give father's the right to oppose their partner's choice to have one.

'Yes. Even if it doesn't pass, we'll have gained a lot of publicity. The BBC got very worried when we threatened them with legal action over their unbalanced reporting. Our pro-life spokesmen have doubled their presence since the letter.'

'And the other work?'

'We have to be careful. There've been a couple of journalists sniffing around hoping to connect the demonstrations to the official campaign.' Forth had been clandestinely funding demonstrations to intimidate women, doctors, and staff at abortion clinics. These people had defied court orders and were now being threatened with contempt actions.

'Oh yes. Mizz O'Driscoll,' he emphasised the title derisively. 'My associates have been collecting information on her. You saw the photographs?'

'It certainly deflected the conversation.'

Forth had obtained compromising photographs from one of O'Driscoll's former boyfriends and they had been widely circulated on social media. Now, whenever she was interviewed, the conversation began with these rather than her investigative findings. O'Driscoll was, however, proving extremely persistent, with the leaked photos simply making her more determined. 'We may need to take further action regarding her.' He didn't elaborate on what that action might be and instead asked, 'And the work at universities?'

'Great progress. Many have lifted bans against anti-abortion groups because of our challenges over free speech. There are now fourteen official anti-abortion student societies across the UK, compared to eight this time last year.'

'Excellent. You'll be coming over again for Christmas?'

'Of course, Elias. I have some very special outfits I'm sure you'll like. But you must provide me with ah … a wider selection of partners than Vladimir. He has a lovely cock, but I need greater, um … stimulation?' Forth agreed and made a mental note to carefully select Carrie's next sexual partner. 'Have you heard anything about the knighthood?' Carrie asked.

'Sadly not,' replied Forth. 'I'm told it's too soon after the fake news stories about my Middle East investments. And I have a hunch, but nothing definite yet, that that whore O'Driscoll was behind those too,' he added. His phone buzzed with a message that Nesfield had arrived and was waiting to meet him in the basement.

*

The basement of Satterthwaite Hall had been relatively modest when Forth took possession: a wine cellar, and some storage rooms. But he had extended it considerably. It now boasted a small cinema, a large gallery, and some 'specialist' facilities that had been constructed using builders supplied from Russia by his friend Oleg Zinchenko.

Nesfield was waiting in the gallery. This contained some of the artworks Forth couldn't display more publicly. As with his other paintings the selection displayed the erratic taste of a man more impressed by monetary than artistic value. However, the focal point was an undoubted masterpiece of post-Impressionist art, Paul Cézanne's *View of Auvers-sur-Oise*. The reason the picture was hidden from view was because it was stolen. Under the cover of the New Year celebrations of 2000, a thief cut a hole in a skylight at the Ashmolean Museum in Oxford, dropped a rope down into the galleries, let off a smoke bomb to render the CCTV cameras ineffective, and took the picture out of its frame, smashing the frame on the floor. The police theory was that it was stolen to order. Their spokesman was quoted as saying, 'We think an unscrupulous art lover earmarked the painting for their collection and hired a professional art thief to steal it.' It was one of Forth's earliest criminal coups.

Another group of paintings emphasised Forth's interest in the supernatural, from the sixteenth century, via the symbolists to present-day Japanese horror comics. But the gallery also housed Forth's extensive collection of Third Reich memorabilia. This included the finest collection of swords and daggers anywhere in the world. Several of these had been personally owned by high-ranking members of the Nazi hierarchy including Hermann Goering, Reinhard Heydrich, and Heinrich Himmler.

At the far end of the gallery the wall was made entirely of darkened glass. At the press of a button a current made the screen transparent. Behind it lay the rooms Forth reserved for 'special guests'. Nesfield thought of it as his dungeon and smiled as he recalled witnessing a memorable scene a few months previously. Though Forth made very generous contributions to religious causes, especially to fundamentalist churches in the

US, Nesfield had never thought of him as being religious himself, which was why he'd been surprised when Forth began telling him about a Catholic saint. She was Eulalia of Barcelona who suffered martyrdom in the early fourth century under the Emperor Diocletian. Oleg Zinchenko had made Forth a gift. A thirteen-year-old girl, the same age as the saint, whose persecution Forth now re-enacted. Though she was spared the ultimate decapitation, Forth gleefully inflicted both the flogging and crucifixion. Nesfield had no idea if she had survived after Zinchenko's men had taken her away.

Nesfield got up as Forth entered. 'The girl is back in Aldeburgh, so they're all there. They've certainly made progress after their visits to Salisbury and Lincoln. Should I do more?'

'No need,' Forth replied. 'We can allow them to continue following the trail. Just keep me informed.' Forth was not at all worried by the activities of Cloote, and certainly not of a twenty-five-year-old female, which was why he'd left their surveillance to Nesfield rather than Morten. 'Thank you, Savile. I won't need you more today, I have to speak with Morten.'

Nesfield scowled at the mention of his name but knew not to comment. 'I'll just check on the preparations for the hunt.'

'Please do, I want everything to be perfect for Mr Zinchenko's visit.'

Nesfield left him and Forth rang Morten.

'Mister Forth. How pleasant to hear from you.'

'Any developments yet?'

'No, I have several people working on it, but nothing has yet emerged. I wonder if we should involve our Cambridge friend?'

'Not just yet. He is weak and likely to prove unreliable if he has too much information too soon. Should you perhaps utilise your other abilities?'

'Not at this stage, sir. They need to be used carefully and sparingly.'

'All right. Continue your investigations. Where will you be going next?'

'I believe it must be St Petersburg, Mr Forth. The National Library.'

'Very well. And you'll see Oleg while you're there?'

'Of course, I will appraise him of our work.'

'Don't say we are having … difficulties. Just say progress is slow and complex but we have the matter in hand.'

'Certainly, Mr Forth.'

As soon as he was off the line Morten rang Oleg Zinchenko's private number.

Chapter 16

Anna set off for Cambridge just after eight. It should take an hour and a half to do the seventy miles, but the A14 was always choked with lorries from the container ports, and she'd need to find somewhere to park the bike.

The department of Anglo-Saxon, Norse, and Celtic, ASNC, is located on the second floor of the modern Faculty of English building in West Road, which is where Penhaligon had his office. Gervase Penhaligon was a rather short, balding man in his early fifties. He had a ruddy complexion and greeted Anna with a broad smile.

'Dr Carr, Dr Carr. How nice to see you. Magnus has always said you were his brightest and best. I hope you are well, and that Magnus is too? How was your journey? I hope the traffic wasn't too bad. Would you like a coffee or tea?' Anna wasn't sure which question to answer first but said Magnus was well and she'd have a cup of tea. They adjourned to the senior common room, which was empty. 'Now what can I do for you?'

Anna had her story worked out. She was interested in writing more about Scandinavian mythology preserved in English legends of the thirteenth century. Obviously, Professor Penhaligon had consulted the *Codex Johannem Regem* which referred to some of these connections. 'But unfortunately, some pages of the *Codex* are missing.'

'Oh dear. How could that have happened?'

'I'm afraid they might have been stolen,' Anna replied.

Penhaligon sighed, 'I'm not surprised. There are so many unscrupulous people around. And the *Codex* would not have been thought an especially valuable item, so I suppose lax security was to blame?'

Anna avoided any more details but did want to find out Penhaligon's thoughts on the *Codex*. 'Do you remember there being illustrations in that part of the manuscript?' she asked.

'Yes, yes I do seem to remember there were some drawings or sketches. Animals I think?'

'That's right. What did you make of them?'

'Not a great deal I'm afraid. Bestiaries are not my subject; I was concentrating on the political aspects and the source of power in the early years of Henry's reign rather than that.'

'Do you recall your old tutor, Professor Inkpen, saying anything about them? I believe he studied the *Codex* at one time.'

For the first time Penhaligon appeared slightly agitated. 'Oh, Inkpen had all sorts of ideas. Though he was my tutor we didn't really see eye to eye on what constitutes sound research.'

'How do you mean?'

'Inkpen was always going off on some flight of fancy that had no substantive facts behind it. He'd then try to find things that fitted his ideas. Totally unscientific. A true scholar should carefully ascertain the facts and only then reach a tentative explanation.' Anna was about to put forward her own view that unless you had a hypothesis in the first place it would be difficult to know where to start. 'Methodical recording of data. That's the right approach,' Penhaligon added.

'And did you?'

'Sorry, did I what?'

'Methodically record the data in the *Codex*?'

'Oh, ah, no, well only those parts that concerned my topic, Dr Carr. One can't record everything, you know.' He tried a little laugh, but it didn't sound entirely convincing.

So, Anna thought, *here we have a highly methodical researcher who didn't record what he'd seen*. 'Would you know if Professor Inkpen is still alive?'

'Oh, I'm sure not,' replied Penhaligon. 'He retired over twenty-five years ago. If he was alive, he'd be well over ninety. I've certainly heard nothing of him since about 1995.'

They chatted on for a while, with Penhaligon plying Anna with questions about her own work. She gave away as little as possible and made it sound as if she was continuing the research she'd started for her thesis with a view to publishing a book. Finally, she thanked him for his time, and he saw her off. 'Well, very best of luck with your research, Dr Carr. I would certainly be interested in seeing a book on the topic. I might even adopt it for my course here.' As soon as Anna had left, he went to his office to make a call.

Anna moved her bike up the road in case Penhaligon wondered why she was still around. She then crossed the river to a small coffee bar, tucked away on St Edward's Passage, where she'd arranged to meet Rasmus Kask. Anna immediately spotted Kask's slim figure sitting by the window. His blonde hair was cut shorter than she remembered, and he had new, round, gold-rimmed glasses. As usual he looked nervous. *I really ought to tell him he shouldn't be,* thought Anna, *I know he's got respect for my intellect, but he's one of the people who finds me rather intimidating.* She gave him what she hoped was her warmest smile and he seemed glad she was clearly not in one of her scary moods. Rasmus visibly relaxed as Anna asked him lots of questions about his research and seemed genuinely interested in his replies. She then asked what he thought about Gervase Penhaligon.

'He is a very methodical scholar and always seems friendly,' Rasmus said.

Anna could immediately tell this was a defensive response. One reason she'd always liked Rasmus was that he was a sensitive person who understood what other people were thinking. He was also exceptionally observant. So, she said: 'But you think there's something else too?'

Rasmus didn't reply immediately, thinking carefully about his response. Eventually he said, 'Yes, yes I do. First I do not think he is an honest man.'

'Why do you say that?'

'We had a student called Lucy, Lucy Tindell. She was a very good researcher. She found some new material about Peter des Roches and his relationship with Henry III. But she also had some serious mental health problems and eventually had to withdraw from her PhD. A few months later Penhaligon published a paper on des Roches. I'd read Lucy's notes and Penhaligon had stolen her ideas and references. He hadn't even gone back to the archives to check what she'd found. He gave her no acknowledgement at all in his paper, which he gave at the Louvain Conference last year.'

The revelation didn't altogether surprise Anna. 'What was your other thought?'

'I think there's something troubling him that he doesn't want anyone to know about.'

'And do *you* know what it could be?'

'I think so. He isn't the most careful person when it comes to switching his PC to sleep mode or putting personal papers away. I think he's a gambler.'

'How do you know?'

'I've seen some of the websites he visits and, once, there was a letter from a debt collection agency sticking out of his folder.'

'That's very interesting. Has his mood changed at all recently?'

'I thought so. He suddenly seemed much brighter a few months ago, though his worries seem to have returned in the last couple of weeks.'

'Thanks, Rasmus, I always knew you were a good judge of character. But I want to ask you a very big favour. You can say no if you want to.' Anna explained a little of what she and Cloote were doing but left out the potential link to the killing of Arbuthnot. She asked if he'd be willing to keep an eye on Penhaligon. Not spy, just let her know if anything unusual happened. Rasmus said he would.

Before she left Anna said to him, 'You know you don't need to be scared of me. When I like someone, I will stick by them. It's if you decide to be a bastard that you need to watch out!' Rasmus gave her a smile and she gave him a quick peck on the cheek. He blushed bright red but was obviously very pleased to have been taken into her confidence.

Chapter 17

Anna was back in Aldeburgh by early afternoon and, with Cloote and Rees, spent several more hours studying the images. Some of the creatures were only shown once, others recurred several times. Most were quickly drawn but with a few the scribe had invested greater care and they were more detailed. These included the partridge, the beaver, the dolphin, the cricket, the nightingale, and the swan. 'They must be more important for some reason,' Rees suggested.

'Yes,' replied Cloote, 'but in what way? Any ideas, Anna?'

'Not at present,' she said. 'I've re-read the key stuff on bestiaries, and nothing immediately springs to mind.'

They decided they couldn't get any further. 'What's our next step then?' Anna asked.

'I think we need another field trip,' Cloote responded. 'We suspect there's a connection between the writer of this document and one or more of the well-known bestiaries of the period, so I think we need to study them more closely.' Anna agreed that it would do no harm to try, even if it just gave them more thinking time. 'I know the archivist at Aberdeen well,' Cloote continued. 'So that would be my obvious destination. I don't think you should cover the Ashmole one, Anna. If we're being watched, you going there would be rather too obvious. So, Gordon does Oxford which means that you will have to go to New York.' Anna readily agreed and Rees said he'd make all the arrangements. He knew New York well whereas Anna had only been there once for a conference.

'How much can I tell Magnus?' she asked.

'Tell him what we're doing and that we're trying to work out why someone would have stolen the *Codex*.'

Anna said she would and then checked the time. 'Going anywhere special?' Rees asked with a grin.

'Just to the cinema,' Anna replied. She'd told them about Anula to ensure they didn't think there'd be any breach of their security arrangements. Rees had done some checking and had reassured her that Anula really was an orthopaedic surgeon at Ipswich hospital.

'Well enjoy yourself,' said Cloote. 'All work and no play et cetera.'

*

Anula was on duty until six, so Anna had arranged to meet her at the cinema. It had a rather quaint mock Tudor frontage and had been in existence for a hundred years. Anula cut it quite fine but was there just in time for the start of the film. 'Sorry, awkward operation, overran a bit,' she explained.

The cinema was surprisingly full for a black and white foreign classic. When the film finished Anna could see why it was Magnus's favourite. There were films about the Middle Ages she loved including *The Lion in Winter* and even Olivier's *Henry V*, but *The Seventh Seal* was easily the best at making you feel you were back in the period. This was partly due to the visual sources Bergman used, several of which Anna recognised, but also its sheer artistic brilliance. The first appearance of Death was straight out of a fifteenth-century morality play and the ending was stunning.

Anula suggested a drink and they went to the cosy Cross Keys pub on Crabbe Street. Anula told Anna more about her family. Her mother was a well-known human rights lawyer and had even spoken at the UN. Despite being Sinhalese, she had defended several prominent Tamil radicals, which hadn't endeared her to some people in the government, including the current president and prime minister. She'd been the subject of several death threats over the years. 'And we take them very seriously,' explained Anula. 'Lawyers can easily get murdered in Sri Lanka,' and she told Anna about the death of Nadarajah Raviraj in 2006. 'One of the most prominent threats even came from a Buddhist priest.'

'I always thought Buddhism was about the least violent of religions,' Anna said.

'It probably is, but when you think a group of people are your natural enemies, even theoretical pacifism can go out of the window.'

'But you must be pleased that the civil war in Sri Lanka is over?'

'Of course. But it came at a cost. In the end there are only two ways to stop most forms of terrorism. Compromise or repression. In Northern Ireland you settled for compromise. In Sri Lanka I'm not so sure. And it's like stopping a pot of water boiling over. If you just put a lid on, it stops in the short term but ten, twenty or a hundred years later it will explode. The only long-term answer is to turn off the heat.'

'But surely compromise won't always work. There are some terrorists who won't compromise.'

'Yes, usually the ones whose oppression is a delusion. Neo-Nazis or religious fanatics. But even there it's the leaders who manipulate individuals who *are* oppressed or desperate.'

'So, the problem can't always be solved, there'll always be people so desperate they'll do anything?'

'Sure. But then we need to understand them, not react with repressive measures of our own. Instead, we tend to completely misunderstand and respond by locking them up or killing them.' It was clear this was an issue Anula cared deeply about.

'I'm sorry, I've been doing all the talking,' she apologised. 'Tell me about your own family.'

Anna ignored the question and instead assured Anula she wasn't offended in the slightest. What she did say was that she didn't talk much about her own past. Even that was more than she usually revealed to someone she'd just met. *I do think this is someone I might really trust*, thought Anna. *But not just yet.* Instead, she told Anula that she also felt passionately about similar causes. She mentioned abortion which was a topic where their views coincided.

'You're right,' said Anula. 'The so-called pro-life movement provides a way for men to oppress women in societies where women are demanding equality. Do you think that abortion would be illegal for a single second if suddenly men could become pregnant too?' She told Anna that she worked as a volunteer at Lighthouse Women's Aid in Ipswich, a centre and refuge providing support to women and children experiencing domestic abuse. Then their conversation moved on to lighter topics, where Anna was happier talking about herself. 'We should go to the cinema again; they show some great classics as well as new stuff,' said Anula.

'Yeh, they've got Spike Lee's *Do the Right Thing* on in a few weeks, that's always been one of my favourites.'

'Oh, me too, I've got the DVD. Then there's *Thelma and Louise* next month.'

'Overrated,' said Anna. 'Directed by a bloke and a cop-out ending.'

Anula decided to change the subject. 'Music's really important to you?'

'Yeh. It came pretty close to saving my life a couple of times.' Anna didn't elaborate and Anula didn't press her.

Instead, she asked 'What kind of music then?'

'I like extreme stuff that challenges convention and stands up for the oppressed, including oppressed music fans.'

'Sounds interesting. You'll have to play me some.' Anna was doubtful she'd like it.

Finally, Anula said how much she'd enjoyed the evening and asked Anna if she'd like to go out for a meal. 'Either here in Aldeburgh or in Woodbridge where I live.'

Anna said she'd like that, but she'd be away for around a week from Saturday. Anna could see that Anula looked a little disappointed. 'I wouldn't be able to make it before you go. I'm pretty busy the rest of this week but let me know when you'll be back, and we'll arrange something.'

Anna said she would and then remembered, 'Are you in Ipswich or here before then? You mentioned telling me more about angampora?'

Anula explained that angampora divides into angam, the use of the body in hand-to-hand fighting, and illangam, the use of weapons. 'Angam makes use of both striking and grappling techniques, and opponents fight until one is forced into a submission lock. And meditation also plays a key role,' she explained. 'Then there's another more secret element known as maya angam, using spells and incantations. It involves hitting pressure points in the body that can paralyze or kill an opponent or even cause them to die a few days later.'

'That sounds interesting,' Anna exclaimed, not entirely convinced it sounded realistic.

'There are also techniques for reversing the effect of the pressure point shots too. They're called beheth parawal, medicinal shots.'

'So, it's like a poison, but with only the angampora expert being able to administer the antidote?'

'That's right. It's one reason the British tried to outlaw it,' Anula continued. 'Anyone found practising angampora in the nineteenth century was crippled by being shot in the kneecap.'

'This is definitely something I should learn!' Anna said.

Anula laughed. 'I've been studying since I was a girl and I'm nowhere near an expert, so I don't think we'll have you killing people just yet.'

'Could we meet up for a lesson though?'

'I'll be visiting patients at the cottage hospital on Friday afternoon so I could see you before. How would eleven at the playing fields be?'

'Should be fine,' Anna replied. She also thought she'd ask Cloote to see if he minded them using the gym at Summerland.

The women kissed goodbye. Anna watched Anula walking back to her car as she turned up Park Road. She was strongly attracted to her new friend but also felt reluctant to admit the strength of her attraction. *This isn't quite like me*, she thought.

Back in the house she found Cloote in the library. 'Yes, Anna?'

'I wondered if you'd mind if my friend and I used the gym on Friday?'

Cloote looked at her carefully. 'You're confident about her?' he enquired.

'Yes,' said Anna firmly.

'In that case I'd be delighted for her to visit.'

Anna went up to her room and texted Anula to tell her the change of plan. A few minutes later her message was returned. 'How very kind. What are the directions?'

Anna told her and finished with, 'Just press the intercom by the front gate.'

*

Promptly at eleven on Friday the outside intercom buzzed, and Anna let Anula into the driveway. 'What an extraordinary house, I'd only glimpsed it from the path at the back before.'

As Anna and Anula walked round to the garage block, Cloote emerged from the garden where he had been doing some late-season pruning. He was wearing an apron and a large floppy hat. 'Hello, Dr Hathurusingha, welcome to Summerland. I'm Oliver Cloote.'

'Very pleased to meet you.'

'If you have time after your, err workout, I'd be very pleased to show you the house, and you must stay for lunch.' Anula thanked him and said it would have to just be a quick tour as her patients would be waiting.

In the gym Anula told Anna that preparation for an angampora training session was almost as important as the session itself. 'You're expected to meditate and then light three lamps before making a vow to use the technique solely for the purpose of self-defence or defence of your family or country.'

She showed Anna some basic warm-up exercises, before explaining that foot movement techniques were the cornerstone of this art of fighting. She showed her a foot exercise called mulla panina. With her taekwondo skills Anna had no problems in following Anula's lead. 'You're a fast learner, Anna. It usually takes people many weeks to get even this far. I think we could go on to something more advanced. The hand fighting technique called amaraya is the next step. You'll see some similarities with taekwondo, especially in the mental approach, because observing the weaknesses of your opponent, and attacking their vulnerabilities is vital.' Anna was an excellent student. She had the seriousness and concentration required and Anula was most impressed. 'Just how good are you at taekwondo?' she asked.

'Ah, pretty good. My teacher did ask if I'd be interested in joining the GB squad for training but that's not what I'm interested in. I see it as a personal thing, not something you do for praise or medals.'

'Gosh, I'm impressed. We should do more of this and perhaps one day you might come to Sri Lanka, and I could introduce you to Guru Karunapala himself. He was my teacher and is the greatest living exponent of the art.'

As they were warming down Anna asked how usual it was for women to practice angampora. 'Oh, not at all unusual. As with other martial arts when you have two skilled fighters size matters. So, in gataputtu, locks and grips, and to some extent in pora haramba, the strikes and blocks, men might have a physical advantage. But with some of the Illangampora weapons, like smaller swords or knives, women can be better by being more agile.'

'I really enjoyed that,' Anna said. 'I'd love to learn more if I can.'

'And I'd love to teach you,' replied Anula. 'I certainly haven't had such an expert novice before.'

They went to shower. As they undressed Anna couldn't help noticing that Anula had perfect skin and adopted the same approach to body hair as herself and, for the first time, Anula saw Anna had another tattoo. Her small breasts were augmented by a sunburst round her left nipple in red, yellow, and orange. 'I *really* love the tattoo. Do you have any more?' Anna blushed slightly, which was highly unusual, and said she didn't. 'Did it hurt to have that done there?'

It was such a common question and Anna would normally have been rather brusque with a reply such as, 'Of course it bloody did,' or, if she was feeling stroppy, 'Actually it was incredibly erotic and gave me an orgasm,' which had once shut up a guy on a beach. Instead, she said, 'Just a bit, more like a mild electric shock.'

'I'm not sure I'd have a tattoo,' Anula mused, 'though we're okay with them in Sri Lanka.'

After showering they dressed and walked over to the house. In the kitchen they met Rees, who introduced himself and asked if Anula would like something to eat. 'I wasn't sure if you're vegetarian, so I stuck with some veggie dips and onion bhajis.'

'I'm not totally vegetarian but that's very thoughtful. Thank you.' For the next hour Cloote and Rees chatted happily with Anula and Cloote gave her a quick tour of the house. Unlike Anna, Cloote had been to Sri Lanka and spoke of his visits to the ancient cities of Anuradhapura and Polonnaruwa.

Anna said little. She watched her friend intently and tried to make sense of her feelings for her. After a while she decided they were confused and told herself she'd think more about it when she returned from her trip. As Anna said goodbye Anula thanked her. 'It's an amazing house. You really must tell me more about your research when you get back.'

Partly to get off that subject Anna asked where they might go for their meal. 'I thought the Lighthouse here in Aldeburgh. You've seen it on the high street? It's quite good but not too fancy, and they do decent vegetarian options.' Anna had seen the rather gaily painted restaurant and agreed it would be fine.

They exchanged another quick kiss and Anula drove off the few hundred yards to the hospital. She too was trying to organise her thoughts about Anna. She was attracted by her air of mystery and intrigued by the barriers she put up. But Anula also admitted to herself that seeing Anna naked she'd been strongly sexually aroused as well.

Chapter 18

In the morning Anna set off with Rees in the Porsche. Her flight wasn't until twelve thirty from Heathrow, but she always allowed herself more time than necessary. Rees had checked the traffic and assured her they'd be there in plenty of time, but Anna had given him one of her looks and he'd quickly shut up.

'I hope you like the hotel I've booked,' he said. 'Oliver and I used it last time we were there. Where did you stay when you went?'

Anna explained it was in her first postgraduate year. 'It was the first paper I'd had accepted for an international conference. Magnus offered to pay for my trip, but I wouldn't let him. So, it was cheap, just off Eighth Avenue. It smelled of stale sweat and had cockroaches.' Gordon laughed and Anna told him a bit more about the trip. 'I was a bit worried about my presentation,' she said. Gordon thought this was the first time she'd admitted any kind of vulnerability.

'And did it go well?' he asked.

'Kind of. There were a couple of pedants who tried to pick holes in my arguments, but a professor from Bryn Mawr stuck up for me. It also meant I could leave the horrible hotel for the rest of the week.'

'How's that?' Gordon asked.

'Because I moved in with her of course. She was a specialist in the history of magic and great in bed.'

Gordon mused on how Anna was so matter of fact about her sex life but so secretive about other things. 'I expect Oliver knows her then.'

'Yeh, guess so. So, tell me more about yours.'

'My what?'

'Sex life. When did you come out?'

'I never really did. My mom was always open minded, and I grew up without having to explain myself at home. It was a bit different at school, but I was always good at sports, so that helped.'

'But boys are usually worse than girls at calling you names.'

'Yeh, there were some.'

'And you've always fancied older men?'

'Not always, I've had younger lovers too you know. What about you?'

Anna thought for a minute. 'I think the oldest was in her fifties but usually around my own age.'

'And you've had lots of them?'

'What's this? You'll be asking about my favourite sexual position next!'

'Okay,' Gordon grinned, 'what's your favourite sexual position?'

'Bastard!' Anna said, smiling.

They were approaching Heathrow. Anna was rather excited, as it would be the first time she'd flown business class, though Virgin Atlantic called it 'Upper Class', a combination of business and first. Rees dropped her off at the entrance to Virgin's Upper-Class wing in Terminal 3. She was greeted at the door by her title, which was refreshing, had her bags carried to check in, and was through security and into the Clubhouse in less than ten minutes. *Quite a change from economy!* she thought. She got a few looks from other passengers who probably thought she was a musician or an actress, with her boots and leather jacket. She liked the cabins on the Airbus A350. They had large leather seats that doubled as flat beds, though she didn't convert them for this flight. Best of all was the privacy. No screaming kids, no flatulent drunks to pester you.

Anna settled down to read. Not anything connected with the mystery they were trying to solve but the copy of *Ghostland* Anula had urged her to buy. By the time they landed at JFK, Anna had finished the book and was enchanted. She knew she'd like the psychogeography and references to books and films but was a bit wary of the autobiographical elements, especially about bereavement. But it turned out they were the best bits. She thought it must have been a very cathartic book to write and had certainly been cathartic to read. In the limo from the airport, she texted Anula to thank her for the recommendation.

She was booked into Chambers Hotel in Midtown Manhattan. It was close to Central Park, which was nice, and only a hundred yards from Trump Tower, which wasn't. It was very tastefully decorated and packed with artworks by modernists like John Waters, Bob and Roberta Smith, and Sheila Pepe. When she checked in, the receptionist guaranteed her, 'The best showers in New York City.' So as soon as she got to her room Anna stripped and made use of them. He wasn't wrong she thought. The shower head was enormous, and the jet could be turned up to fire hose pressure.

Later she went for a stroll though, at this time of year, it was too late to visit the park. The receptionist had recommended a few nearby restaurants and she settled for the one virtually opposite. It was a rather old-fashioned, but decidedly New York style, Italian. She had a spinach salad, some delicious gnocchi, and some extremely fattening profiteroles. She even enjoyed listening to the conversations around her. At a nearby table was a man who would not have been out of place in *The Godfather* or *Goodfellas*. He was with a woman who was obviously his mother.

'So, I sez to the guy, hey, waddya do that for? And you know what he said?'

'No tell me what he said,' replied the mother.

'I was gonna tell you what he said.'

'Well tell me then, tell me!'

Anna thought she could listen to this for hours. It was far more entertaining than the TV. But jet lag was catching up with her and she wanted to have a day exploring the city.

*

Sunday turned out to be a dry, bright day, though rather cold. The first thing Anna did was go for a run in Central Park. She hadn't quite realised how big it was, a full loop was over six miles. Feeling physically fitter than for some time Anna had planned her free day carefully, and spent most of it in the Met Museum, but got back to the hotel early enough to do some further research before her visit to the Morgan Library.

On Monday morning, after a larger breakfast than planned,

Anna was on time at nine-thirty to meet the curator of medieval and Renaissance manuscripts at the Morgan Library on Madison Avenue.

The most influential financier in his country's history, Pierpont Morgan commissioned the building in 1902. Its most impressive room is Morgan's personal library, thirty feet high and lined floor to ceiling with triple tiers of bookcases made of inlaid Circassian walnut. She took a quick look before proceeding to the reading room, which was in a separate building.

The *Worksop Bestiary* had been given to what is now Worksop Priory, in Nottinghamshire, by Canon Philip of Lincoln Cathedral in 1187. Its famous owners included the State of Prussia and William Morris before its purchase by Pierpont Morgan. It comprises a hundred and twenty pages with a hundred and six miniature illustrations. Though the *Bestiary* is one of the most studied of medieval books she hoped there would be something to discover that would link it with the Bodleian *Codex* and the possible treasure of Brisingamen.

The curator was extremely helpful and gave Anna access to many resources that were not available on the net. She was able to view the entire manuscript both physically and in ultra-high-definition photographs. She could also study photos shot with ultraviolet light. Because the collagen in parchment fluoresces under ultraviolet illumination, whereas the ink absorbs the light, ultraviolet can reveal faded or hidden writing. If a parchment has been reused by scraping away previous writing, which was common due to the high cost of vellum, the previous text can be revealed. The *Bestiary* had been photographed in this way more than once, including when it had been disassembled from its nineteenth-century binding.

Over the next three and a half days Anna pored over every millimetre of the *Bestiary* but nothing she saw seemed to be of any help. On Wednesday evening she got in touch with both Cloote and Rees. Neither of them had found anything, though Rees did have one piece of interesting news. He found that the last person to look at the *Ashmole Bestiary* had been none other than Gervase Penhaligon. 'That's odd,' Anna responded. 'He said nothing to me about having done any recent work on bestiaries. In fact, he made it sound like he had very little interest in them.' This gave Anna an idea.

On Thursday morning she casually asked the curator. 'I was wondering if either of my colleagues had looked at the *Bestiary* recently. Professors Westley and Penhaligon?'

Penhaligon's name seemed to mean nothing to him, but she hit the mark with Westley. 'Yes, indeed, Dr Carr. Professor Westley was with us in the summer. July, I think. Other than the Russian gentleman he was last to study it.'

'Russian?' asked Anna as innocently as possible.

'Yes, let me think. Oh yes, Professor Smertski, from St Petersburg.'

Anna felt a little tingle of excitement and rather doubted that the curator was familiar with the Russian language. 'Smertski' would translate as 'pertaining to death'.

'Oh yes, Professor Smertski. I believe I've met him, rather short man with red hair?'

'No, that wouldn't be him at all. He was rather tall and thin, and I think he may have some kind of skin condition.' Anna looked queryingly and so he continued, 'Very pale skin, almost transparent.'

'And did they examine anything other than the *Bestiary*?' Anna asked.

'Yes, they also looked at the associated documents M81a.'

'I haven't seen them.'

'No. I'm sorry they're not as well catalogued as most of our other works. I'll get them up for you.'

For the rest of the day Anna looked through the associated documents, which had been purchased at the same time as the *Worksop Bestiary*. Most were descriptions and catalogue entries compiled by previous owners but there were also a few faded manuscript pages that were sketches for the *Bestiary* itself. All hundred and six beasts were drawn at least once and Anna felt another frisson when she looked at these, because they demonstrated clear similarities to the drawings in the *Codex*. However, there seemed nothing else visible that might help her. Annoyingly they were just that, sketches, there was no writing on the pages.

At the end of the day, she asked the curator whether it would be possible to view the pages using the library's ultraviolet scanner. 'Certainly Dr Carr. I can arrange that in the morning.'

Anna asked if either Westley or the Russian had done this, but he replied in the negative. *But they could have brought a portable UV light with them*, thought Anna, as these are now readily available for researchers.

When she reported back to Cloote he was equally fascinated by the mysterious Russian. She'd already ascertained that, as expected, there was no such person either at St Petersburg State University or anywhere else.

The library's UV equipment was the best Anna had seen and was housed in a superb photographic lab in the Thaw Conservation Center on the fourth floor of the building. She began to look at the first page but could see nothing out of the ordinary and so moved on to the second. It was here she first noticed something. Above the sketch of a falcon was a tiny crown. On page three, five lion cubs were portrayed, and they too had small crowns. The pages containing these sketches had been drawn on recycled parchment and she could easily have missed the detail, thinking it was just a relic of the previous document. But when she came to recheck the other pages, she could see that the marks she was looking at were part of the sketchbook itself.

Twenty of the drawings had a tiny cross placed on the parchment before the sketch had been drawn on top. She wrote down what was depicted in each. She had a little trouble with the cricket and the swan, as she needed to substitute one of their lesser-known cognomens, but using their Latin names, they clearly made an alphabetical sequence:

A – Amphisbaena. A serpent with two heads, one at either end.

B – Bonnacon. A creature with the head of a bull with horns that curl in towards each other.

C – Cornix/Crow.

D – Delphine/Dolphin.

E – Echinus/Hedgehog.

F – Fenix/Phoenix. The bird that rises from the ashes of its funeral pyre.

G – Gryphes/Griffin. A beast with the body of a lion, and the wings and head of an eagle.

H – Halcyon/Kingfisher.
I – Ibis.
K – Krillum/Cricket.
L – Luscinia/Nightingale.
M – Manticora/Manticore. A beast with a man's face, a lion's body, and the sting of a scorpion.
N – Noctua/Owl.
O – Olor/Swan. The mute swan is Cygnus olor.
P – Pelicanus/Pelican.
R – Rana/Frog.
S – Sera/Mermaid.
T – Tigris/Tiger.
V – Vulpis/Fox.
Y – Yena/Hyaena.

She was sure she had cracked Johannes of Medhamstead's code.

Chapter 19

Anna sent a message to Cloote: 'Have found key. Will soon be able to enter church.' He replied that Rees had booked her return flight at eight o'clock the following evening. He ended it: 'Congratulations. Enjoy your evening.' Even though her elation was tempered by the suspicion that she may not be the first to discover the key to Johannes's code Anna decided to do exactly that.

Back at the hotel she went online. The LGBT dating site she was a member of in the UK allowed her membership of a sister site in the US. Anna entered some search details and messaged a couple of likely contacts. She then took a shower. She had thought the power setting might be useful and found that sitting in the right position on the built-in seat and tilting the shower head produced exactly the result she'd anticipated.

After she dried herself, she saw she'd had a response. The woman was called Tina. She was thirty-five and identified as soft butch. Though Anna's profile suggested she was a stem/switch she'd decided that, for tonight, she fancied a more submissive role. A few more messages and everything was arranged. The details of the roleplay they'd enact, what they would call each other, where to meet, limits they'd set, safe words and how the role play would end. Tina also suggested what Anna should wear and said she'd send a couple of items to the hotel. There was only one thing that Anna rejected. 'Sorry, not high heeled boots. I'll never be able to walk properly and likely fall over and look stupid.'

Anna had first become interested in BDSM as a teenager. She'd tentatively experimented with a couple of girlfriends and expanded her activities with more recent partners. She thought about her previous trip to New York. The Bryn Mawr professor had been a real expert. However, she wasn't a fan of more extreme practices and there were some things she wasn't keen on: dildos that anatomically mimic penises were one of those.

Overall, she said, 'It's like art, I know what I like, and I know what I don't.' One of the most used symbols of the BDSM community is a derivation of a triskelion shape within a circle. This was another reason Anna chose to wear her choker.

Anna took the subway from 57th Street to Broadway-Lafayette. At Schott's store on Elizabeth Street, she bought some Chelsea boots and a leather Moto jacket. It was then a short walk to Bloomingdale's on Broadway where she added a pair of Sylvanna skinny leather pants and some horn-rimmed sunglasses. It was easily the most she'd ever paid for clothes from her own money. Back at the hotel the package from Tina had arrived and, in her room, Anna dressed for the evening.

At nine-thirty she took a cab to the agreed rendezvous, the rooftop bar of a stylish hotel in the Meatpacking District. The bar counter had four sides, three of them inside with the fourth opening onto the rooftop pool area. Anna kept her shades on, and her jacket zipped up, as she took a seat on the side facing the entrance. She ordered a margarita as she surveyed the trendy clientele.

One man stood out, as he didn't look entirely at home in the arty New York company of the bar. He was in his late forties and wore an American flag pin on his conservative business suit. His companion was less than half his age. She wore an expensive looking, and very short, designer dress. *The venue was probably her choice*, Anna thought. He was doing all the talking and seemed to be known to other people in the bar, as a couple of them were pointing him out. Anna decided to ask the barman. 'Excuse me. Who's the man over there with the girl in the pink metallic dress. I think I recognise him.'

'That's Noah Cross,' he replied. 'You're from England, right?' Anna nodded. 'He's got a big show on Fox News.' He bent a little closer to Anna. 'And she's Judge McKinsey's daughter. The guy who got appointed to the Supreme Court a couple of years back.'

'Okay. Thanks.'

Anna sipped her cocktail very slowly. As she didn't drink much, she needed to ration herself. Dead on ten Tina entered the bar. She was a little taller than Anna with dark brown hair which was cut short with a fringe falling over her right eye. She wore black ankle boots and a black skirt, with a white shirt half unbuttoned under a black jacket. On the collar was a silver, diamond encrusted double-Venus symbol. She carried a tote bag with a picture of a butch looking woman astride a motor bike and the slogan 'lesbian biker'. She sat at the bar facing Anna. Noah Cross looked over, grimaced, and moved away from her in his seat. His companion looked at Tina with more interest. Tina snapped her fingers at the barman and ordered a large bourbon on the rocks. As arranged, the two of them spent a few minutes just looking at each other before Tina called across the bar in a loud voice.

'Hey, girl. Come over here and sit by me.' 'Girl' was the name they'd agreed she'd use for the evening. Anna got up obediently and walked slowly round the bar. Many heads followed her. As she got close Tina stood up. She put her right hand behind Anna's neck, pulled her up close and kissed her passionately, using her tongue for emphasis. Now everyone in the bar was looking. When Tina released her, Anna stood with her back to the bar and slowly unzipped her jacket, revealing a shocking pink tee-shirt that proclaimed, 'Tomboy Femme' and a similar-coloured studded dog collar round her neck. Noah Cross got up from his seat and steered his companion to a table near the door.

'Sit,' Tina commanded. 'Hey, barman. Bring the girl a drink.' The barman delivered a second margarita. 'You look pretty good. Love the pants.' She clinked glasses. 'I think this could be a fun evening.' Then she added. 'Let's call a time out for a bit.' This was the trigger to come out of role for a while. They exchanged some more background about each other. As usual Anna said less about herself. Tina ran an all-female motorcycle repair business in Brooklyn and was also training as a sex counsellor. Her parents came from Puerto Rico though she was New York born and bred. 'Okay, girl, time to go,' Tina indicated their role play had resumed.

She reached into the tote bag and extracted a dog leash that matched Anna's collar. She clipped it onto the collar and began leading Anna out of the bar. All eyes were on them, some smiling and approving, a few scowling, of whom Noah Cross was one. He was clearly having a serious issue with their display of blatant deviance. As they walked past, he said in a loud whisper, 'Fucking dykes.' Anna didn't react and, at first, thought Tina wasn't going to either. But then she raised her eyes and took a deep breath. She let go of the leash, put the tote bag down and took out a large cream-coloured silicone object Anna couldn't quite see properly.

She strode purposefully over to where Noah Cross was sitting and thrust the 'something' under his nose. Anna could now see it properly. It was a double-ended dildo of a kind she'd not seen before. One end was traditionally shaped but the other curved upwards and outwards with two rounded protuberances. This was clearly intended to be held in place by a woman's vaginal muscles leaving the other end free for fucking her lover. Noah Cross suddenly realised what it was and jerked backwards spilling his drink into his lap.

'Yes, Mr Cross,' said Tina, 'fucking a dyke is exactly what I'm going to be doing with *this*. And I'm sure this,' she stroked the other end, 'is twice the size of what you've got *there*,' she pointed to his groin, turned on her heel, picked up the bag and they left the bar.

This was not the evening Noah Cross had planned, especially when Virginia McKinsey said, 'I think I would like to go home now, Noah,' and gave him a look that indicated his chances of getting her into bed had declined to hell freezing over proportions.

*

Tina took Anna to Henrietta Hudson's, which was just a few blocks to the south. Henrietta's is the oldest, and probably most famous, lesbian nightspot in New York and Tina was well-known to many of its regulars. Anna wasn't a great clubber, but whether it was the two margaritas or whether her role-playing emphasised personality traits she already possessed, like not speaking unless spoken to, or was simply the anticipation of what was to come, she really enjoyed herself. At around two o'clock the denouement of what they'd planned came to pass. One of Tina's friends asked Anna to dance and, without asking Tina, she headed off. When she returned Tina had on a very angry face. 'Girl! How dare you enjoy yourself without my permission. Come here!' Anna obeyed and Tina took her under the chin and raised her head. 'You have been a very bad girl and you know what happens to bad girls?'

'Yes, Tina.'

'What is it?'

'They get punished.'

Tina had already called a cab from 'She Rides', a women-only taxi service. They crossed the Manhattan Bridge to Tina's home and workshop which was on Lexington Avenue in the Bedford–Stuyvesant neighbourhood, once notorious for its drug gangs but, since the millennium, much gentrified.

Above the workshop a sign proclaimed 'Alvarez Cycles' and to the left was the door to Tina's apartment. Both had been converted from a former warehouse, Tina explained. They climbed a flight of stairs to enter a huge room that had polished floorboards. To the left, the original wooden warehouse doors, used for goods entering and leaving, had been made into large windows. A metal staircase led to a mezzanine with main and guest bedrooms, a small sitting area, and the bathroom. The area beneath the mezzanine housed a well-equipped kitchen. The rest of the living room had sofas and chairs, rugs and bookcases, the TV and, near the left-hand wall, what looked like an oversized piano stool. It had a wooden frame supporting a sloping padded 'seat' about two feet square, and the angle of this padded area could be adjusted. Projecting from the rear, where the seat was higher, was another upholstered portion just under a foot wide. Anna had seen spanking benches like this before but had never actually used one.

Tina went to a wall cupboard. Inside was an extensive selection of paddles, belts, whips, and canes. She selected a wooden paddle and an elegant riding crop and sat cross legged on the sofa. 'Come here, girl, and strip to your underwear.' Anna did as she was told. Her underwear was black and see-through and had been purchased from Agent Provocateur. She stood in front of Tina. 'Hands behind your back. Legs apart. Don't look at me, look at the wall.'

Tina took the riding crop and touched Anna's ankle. Slowly she ran it up the inside of Anna's left leg, then down her right and back again up the left. Anna's anticipation was increasing by the second. Finally, Tina flicked the crop between Anna's legs. 'Take them off,' she indicated the bra as well. Anna did so. 'Now turn round … Right. Assume the position.' Anna knelt on the smaller padded area of the stool and stretched forward over the upper part. Her entire body felt tensed almost beyond what she'd thought possible.

*

When their session finished, they ended the role play. Anna curled up on the sofa next to Tina, who held her close and stroked her hair for a considerable time until Anna had relaxed her whole body and her mind recovered from the intensity of her 'ordeal'. She accepted a strong coffee as a stimulant, though Tina took a pill Anna suspected contained something rather stronger. 'Okay?' Tina asked.

'Umm, absolutely,' Anna replied. 'I feel great.'

'And horny?'

'Oh yes.'

'Then I think it's time for you to meet my little friend.' She took the dildo out of her bag. She told Anna it was called the Share double dildo. They went upstairs to the bedroom.

Later, she asked if Anna would like to switch to the top role and she took the dildo and inserted it. She found that it exercised her Kegel muscles at the same time as the nub in the middle stimulated her clit. 'That thing is great. I need to get one,' Anna said as they finally relaxed to listen to some music.

Tina's musical tastes weren't quite the same as Anna's. She favoured modern Latina pop and rap. Tina played her some Joseline Hernandez, but Anna wasn't very keen. Then she tried Princess Nokia. This was a different matter. Anna had heard of her before, as a lesbian rapper, but hadn't listened to much of her music. She loved it. 'Her music suits you, girl,' said Tina and walked over to a chest. 'Here,' she said, pulling out a tee-shirt, 'have this as a souvenir.' She tossed Anna the tee-shirt which had the slogan 'Don't You Fuck With My Energy', a line from Princess Nokia's song 'Brujas'.

Anna got up to look at the pictures on Tina's bedroom wall. One was a photograph of Tina astride a powerful motorbike shot from behind. She was wearing a biking jacket and boots but nothing else. She was looking over her shoulder with a defiant look on her face. 'That was taken by my friend Kirsty,' she explained. 'It was part of an exhibition organised by Dykes on Bikes a couple of years back.'

There were also two framed DVD covers on the wall. The first was called *Revenge of the Lipstick Killers*. The cover featured a tall woman with long black hair bending over a blonde girl who was lying naked on an altar. The film's strapline was: 'Some vampires bite your neck. She bites your pussy.'

'Is that you?' Anna asked pointing at the 'victim'.

'My misspent youth,' Tina replied. 'It's not just porn, there's politics too as we take revenge on the patriarchy. Lots of men end up dead!'

'Sounds great.' The other was *The Vixens of Wall Street* advertised as: 'While the men fucked the markets the girls fucked each other.' There was Tina alongside two other women dressed in business suits. 'Did you make many films?'

'No, just a few, mainly for and with friends. The director of those two was Penny Dreadful.'

'The punk singer from the seventies?'

'Yeh, she's an old friend. Runs her own production company now. Given your "performance" tonight you should try it some time.'

'I'm not sure it would help my academic career. I have enough trouble as it is.'

'Well, if you change your mind let me know. You're a steaming hot girl and you'd be a natural. Haven't you ever done anything like that?'

'Not *that* public,' Anna replied and told Tina about photo sessions she'd done and Nora's drawings.

'I do have a poem about my um oral skills.'

'Do tell.'

'An ex who's a published poet wrote it. It's called "Your eloquent tongue".'

'Is it?' Tina responded, squirming slightly in the bed. 'And would your eloquent tongue like to make some more poetry?' It would and it did.

Finally, Anna got up to pick some music of her own. She

selected St Vincent's first album, one of the few more mainstream artists she rated. She lay face down on the bed and kissed Tina. 'Thanks for an amazing evening.'

Annie Clark started singing 'Your Lips are Red' and Anna joined in, but instead of singing the actual words she sang:

> *'My ass is red,*
> *My ass is red,*
> *From your sweet whip.'*

*

They got a little sleep before Tina's co-workers arrived. At least it was a Saturday, and the shop didn't open until ten. Tina made Anna some breakfast. Muesli, rye toast and avocado, fresh orange juice and herb tea. Suitably refreshed they went down to the workshop where Tina introduced Anna to Marcie and Jax.

A couple of black male bikers came in and greeted Tina, shaking hands with Anna as well. 'Hey, Tina you been schutupping this little girl?'

'Vern Lander you brolic sack of shit, you keep your potty mouth shut or I'll make sure your bike never starts again!' she said, though her smile showed she wasn't really pissed at him.

'OK sista, I get it. Mea culpa.' He bowed in Anna's direction, who smiled back.

Vern described the sound his bike was making and asked if Tina could 'Give it a peep.' She went outside to listen to it.

'When did you last check your valve clearances?' Tina asked.

'You think that's it?'

'Yeh there's a ticking that drops off as the bike warms up but rises with the revs. It's not major but loose valves cost performance, and they'll eventually put too much strain on the top end. Do you want me to check it over?'

'Sure. Can I bring it back Toosday?' She said Toosday would be fine, and the satisfied men left.

Tina had several bikes of her own which, as a fellow enthusiast, she showed Anna. 'Round the city I usually ride the Zero DS electric, good for the planet. For long distance there's my Harley Electra Glide.' She took off a cover to reveal a gorgeous bike, custom painted in rainbow flag colours. 'Then for special occasions I've got this.' Tina pulled off another dust cover. Anna gasped. It was a Vincent Black Shadow. The Black Shadow was the world's first superbike, a machine so powerful that Hunter S Thompson once claimed, 'If you rode the Vincent Black Shadow at top speed for any length of time, you would almost certainly die.' They were produced at Vincent's Stevenage factory in England from 1948 until they went out of business in 1955. 'It's a series C from 1949,' Tina added.

Anna had never even seen one and was awestruck. 'How did you get it? It must have cost the earth.'

'Well, a decent Shadow will set you back around a hundred grand and the rarer ones have fetched close to a million. I inherited mine from a friend.'

'Must have been some friend!'

'He was. Guy called Motorcycle Mike. He was a legend in the New York biker scene, and I was his apprentice. Taught me everything I know. He died from leukaemia a few years back, soon after I'd set up on my own. That was just dumb lit of him.' Tina had forgotten not to use New York slang with Anna, but she got the gist.

'Want a ride back to your hotel on it?'

'Fuck me, yes!'

'I may hold you to that,' Tina laughed. She tossed a vintage helmet to Anna and started the bike. It needed a few priming kicks with the decompression lever pulled before a sharper kick start. The sound of the engine was nothing like a modern bike. You could hear the pistons, and the sound of the exhaust was less extreme and more heartbeat-like than today's high-powered machines.

'We'll take a scenic route.' Tina drove out through Queens before crossing the East River. She stopped at Randall's Island Park and asked if Anna would like to ride the bike herself. She needed no second bidding and they swopped places. 'Take the bridge back to the city. Go straight ahead until you get to Park and turn left.'

Anna gave the bike some revs. Her Harley had a smooth increase in power as you revved the engine. With the Vincent it felt like a sudden leap into the void. *If ever I win the lottery,* she thought, *I'd get one of these.* Anna never played the lottery.

At the hotel Anna hesitated as to how to say goodbye to Tina. Tina solved the problem. First, she hugged Anna and then deployed the left-handed 'Low S', the granddaddy of all biker greetings. Left hand down and out to the side, fingers spread open palm side out which Anna reciprocated. 'And remember girl. If you ever change your mind about becoming a movie star.' Before Anna could reply, Tina had driven off.

Anna retrieved her laptop from the hotel safe and went to her room to check her messages. Cloote said that he hadn't deciphered Johannes's message yet. As she'd made the breakthrough they'd wait for her return. She showered and changed and went for a meal at the nearby Bengal Tiger before her pre-ordered limo arrived to take her to JFK.

On the return flight she made full use of the reclining bed to catch up on the sleep she'd missed the previous night. In her dreams she was in a dark forest. She knew something was lurking but not sure what. She came to a clearing, in the centre of which was a well. She was suddenly very thirsty and started drinking from the well's bucket. A hand then grabbed her from behind before there was a blinding blue light.

She woke up with the pilot announcing they were making their final descent into Heathrow and the flight attendant politely asked her to raise her seat.

Chapter 20

Gordon was there to pick her up and she slept some more in the car, but not before texting Anula. Anna said she was back and asked when they might be able to have their meal. Anula said she'd be free on Wednesday, and they arranged to meet at the Lighthouse at seven.

They got to Summerland by eleven. Gordon had pre-prepared a light lunch they could eat in the library and Cloote had all the pictures and documents arranged. With Anna's alphabetic decoding of the animal drawings, their first task was to see whether turning the drawings into letters made any sense. It didn't. According to Anna's code the colophon would read:

> BFRUEFDSNVMNEQNDHFCVRUMNORLRNUERDICRCRU
> PHTNUHIIHERHMNAVCLRDMNIHRSSRVLHDENSSRRUG
> RLNDRTHENCERHAHCEN

'Obviously there's another cipher at work here,' Gordon concluded.

Anna didn't say that the other explanation was that she'd been wrong, and they were nowhere near solving the puzzle. Instead, she tried to apply her brain to the riddle. 'It's not a simple substitution code,' she said. 'But there are some repetitions.' She pointed out the combination 'MN' which occurred three times. 'It's likely this is a common word, so in Latin it could be "id" or "et" or "de."'

'In which case what we've got is probably a Caesar alphabet!' Rees said.

'A Caesar alphabet?' queried Cloote.

'It's one of the simplest encryption techniques,' explained Rees. 'It's a substitution cipher in which each letter in the actual text is replaced by a letter a fixed number of positions up or down the alphabet.'

'Obviously it's named after Julius Caesar, who used it to protect messages of military significance,' continued Anna. 'According to Suetonius, he used it with a shift of three; so, A becomes D.'

'How do we find out how many letters it's shifted here then?' asked Cloote.

'Well, we can just use the crude method of testing a few shifts,' Anna went on, 'or we can apply a scientific one. Why not try both?'

'Absolutely,' Rees replied. So, while Anna and Cloote tested a few obvious shifts, utilising Anna's earlier example, he used letter frequency. This is a method for breaking substitution codes based on the frequency of letters occurring in that language. If you have a cipher in English and, in the coded message, the letter D appears most frequently then D is likely to correspond to E, as E is the letter that occurs most frequently, and least likely to be Z. In Latin the relative frequency of letters is different. The most frequently used letter is I followed by E, and K is the least used. The only complication is that the alphabet here didn't contain J, K, W, X, Y, or Z, but after a relatively short time both had an answer.

The shift used was thirteen letters to the right, or seven to the left, and Gordon typed the following key:

A	B	C	D	E	F	G	H	I	L	M	N	O	P	Q	R	S	T	U	V
H	I	L	M	N	O	P	Q	R	S	T	U	V	A	B	C	D	E	F	G

The message now read:

QUINTUSLEODETHESAUROINDEFICIENTISBRISINGAMENA
BBATIADEPORCISDEBAILLIOCASTELLIINVICESIMATERTIAP
ARTE

Cloote was fiddling with his glasses more than usual because the first thing that stood out was the word 'Brisingamen'. After splitting the text into words, it read:

Quintus leo de thesauro indeficientis Brisingamen.
Abbatia de porcis.
De baillio castelli in vicesima tertia parte.

Or in English:

> *Treasure of Brisingamen of the fifth lion.*
> *Abbey of the Swine.*
> *From castle bailey at the twenty third point.*

'I might know a bit about ciphers, but you'll have to interpret this stuff,' said Gordon, but Anna and Oliver immediately started grasping the significance of the meaning of the riddle.

'Okay,' Cloote began, 'so the "treasure" belongs to the person he calls the "fifth lion". Who does that suggest from the period we know it was written?'

'King John,' Anna replied immediately. 'He was the fifth legitimate son of Henry II.'

'I thought Henry II only had three sons, Richard the Lionheart, Geoffrey and John?' Rees queried.

'He actually had eight legitimate children by Eleanor,' said Anna. 'Five sons: William, the Young Henry, Richard, Geoffrey, and John, and three daughters, Matilda, Eleanor, and Joan. William died at the age of three and Young Henry aged twenty-eight, six years before his father, leaving his brother Richard to become the next king.'

'Oh, right.'

'And of course, plenty of bastards too,' added Cloote. 'Including Geoffrey, the Bishop of York, and William Long Sword, Earl of Salisbury.'

'It has to be John because there's another clue,' went on Anna.

'Which is?'

'The falcon. John was well known for having a pet falcon called Gibbun.'

'So, the Abbey of the Swine. Has to be Swineshead?' said Cloote.

'Absolutely,' Anna replied.

Before Gordon interjected again, Cloote explained. 'King John visited Swineshead Abbey just before he died. And doesn't Swineshead fit with the Gothic text as well?'

'It seems to,' replied Anna, 'The reference to Hildisvíni would make sense. And shortly after visiting the abbey he supposedly lost the crown jewels of England in the Wash. That's the bay to the north of East Anglia,' she added, in case Gordon didn't know, which he did, and it was his turn to use the Anna Carr look on her.

'So, you're saying this is telling us where to find King John's crown jewels?'

'Looks like it,' replied Anna.

'Just fill me in on the story. I might know where the Wash is but what's the truth about the crown jewels going missing?' So Cloote told him.

'Every English child knows the story of wicked King John being forced to sign the Magna Carta by his rebellious barons. Well, John hadn't the slightest intention of keeping his word and his opponents remained justifiably suspicious. Early in 1216 John led his army, mainly made up of expensive mercenaries, against the Scots and, after some killing and pillaging in southern Scotland, went south to East Anglia to eliminate his enemies there. But in May the French Dauphin, Prince Louis, landed in Kent with an army to back John's opponents and claim the English throne. He marched on London, where he was welcomed by the people.'

'I had no idea the French invaded successfully after 1066,' said Gordon.

'The war was in the balance for months' continued Cloote, 'but in October 1216 John was back in East Anglia when, according to some chroniclers, he lost the crown jewels.'

'But are the stories true?' asked Gordon.

'Well, the jewels certainly disappeared about this time,' Cloote continued. 'According to contemporary reports, he was in Bishop's Lynn on October ninth. On the twelfth John left for Swineshead Abbey. He took a longer route via Wisbech but sent his baggage train along a causeway and ford, only usable at low tide, which crossed the mouth of the Wellstream. The wagons moved too slowly for the incoming tide, and many were lost.'

Anna added to the tale. 'But scholars have never agreed whether the king's jewels were actually in the baggage train or not. Roger of Wendover's is the most dramatic, and probably false, version. He claims the entire treasure disappeared in a bottomless whirlpool. But Ralph of Coggeshall says that not everything was lost, and there's some evidence that the treasure was intact after the journey. Some accounts even say John left the jewels in Lynn as security for a loan.'

'Yes, Ralph was not a noted embellisher,' Cloote resumed. 'He's the one who said John died of gluttony, rather than dysentery or poison. Anyway, whatever happened to the treasure, John was seriously ill. He was carried to Newark Castle, where he wrote to Pope Honorius asking for absolution. He died during a fearsome thunderstorm on the night of October eighteenth. Some of his few remaining supporters were with him, most notably William Marshal, Earl of Pembroke, who became regent for his young son, Henry. Marshal had all the attributes John lacked and saved the kingdom. He reissued Magna Carta and by skilful diplomacy gained acceptance of the boy-king. Marshal signed a treaty with Prince Louis who retired to France with a bribe. So, peace was restored.'

'And what about the jewels, surely there have been attempts to find them?' asked Gordon.

'Yes, many,' said Cloote. 'In the last hundred years there've been several, including one sponsored by a rich American, James Boone, which included the famous archaeologist Sir Mortimer Wheeler. Most recently Ben Robinson has been using a system called LIDAR, light detection and ranging, to map the geography of the area and trace the exact route of the baggage train.'

'But it's a huge search area,' said Anna. 'And there are several theories as to where the baggage was lost. The traditional view is that it travelled separately from the king along the western side of the Wash near Sutton Bridge, on the River Nene. Others suggest it stayed with John and was lost either somewhere between Wisbech and Walsoken, or between Walpole and Foul Anchor to the north of Wisbech. Finally, there are those who think that someone stole it after the king's death and spread rumours of its loss to hide the theft.'

Cloote interjected, 'Even so, after eight hundred years of searching by local people, academics, newspaper tycoons, Victorian antiquarians, and various eccentrics no trace of the jewels has ever been found.'

'Amazing,' said Gordon. 'If true, this would be one of the greatest finds of all time. Like Tutankhamen. What would this stuff be worth?'

'Very difficult to tell,' said Cloote, 'but a crude estimate of the value was made a few years ago which said it was at least fifty million.'

'But John didn't actually die at Swineshead?' Gordon said.

'No,' explained Anna. 'He was there for three days and there are tales that he was poisoned at the abbey by a monk called Brother Simon.'

'Yes, Shakespeare, William Caxton and *Foxe's Book of Martyrs* all mention the story,' Cloote added.

'So, let's see if I've got this right,' Gordon considered. 'If King John's treasure *is* hidden at Swineshead Abbey then the accepted story about it having been lost in the Wash is wrong?'

Cloote agreed. 'Either he kept it or, more likely, someone else stole it, spread the story about it being lost, and hid it.'

'Then why didn't they reclaim it?' Anna interjected.

'The question always gets asked where treasure is concerned. Usually because something happened to them to prevent it.'

'Does it matter?' said Gordon. 'It's either there or it isn't.' The others had to agree. 'What does this last bit mean then?' Gordon asked, '"From castle bailey at the twenty third point."'

Anna was already busily searching the internet. 'Here,' she said, and the others came over to look. 'I thought there was a motte-and-bailey castle near the site of the abbey.' Cloote and Rees looked at the screen. It was the website of Historic England, and the page was titled 'The Manwar Ings: remains of a motte-and-bailey castle.'

Motte-and-bailey castles are medieval fortifications introduced by the Normans. They comprised a large conical mound of earth, called the motte, surmounted by a palisade and a stone or timber tower. In most cases an embanked enclosure with additional buildings, known as the bailey, adjoined the motte. They acted as garrison forts during military operations, as strongholds, and, in many cases, as aristocratic residences and centres of local administration. Over six hundred motte or motte-and-bailey castles are recorded nationally. They read the entry:

Situated 1km to the northeast of the village of Swineshead, it is believed to have been constructed in the twelfth century by the de Gresley family, lords of the manor of Swineshead, who also founded Swineshead Abbey. The castle is referred to in documentary sources of the late twelfth and thirteenth centuries, and artefactual fragments suggest that it was occupied until at least the fourteenth century.

The remains take the form of a series of substantial earthworks and buried features, including a circular motte-and-bailey with inner and outer moats, now dry. The motte is represented by a raised circular platform, now largely level, standing to a height of nearly 2m above the surrounding fields. On this platform would have stood the domestic and service buildings of the castle. The motte is surrounded by a deep inner moat about 15m wide, in turn encircled by the bailey which varies between 7m and 15m in width.

Surrounding the bailey is an outer moat 7m–10m in width. It is crossed on the northwest side by a modern trackway, beneath which it is partly infilled.

Meanwhile, Anna had been doing some more research on her laptop. 'Apparently before the castle was built some people think it was the site of a Danish encampment during the reign of Cnut. The abbey was founded in 1134, so that all fits with our possible dates. If we are to believe Johannes's instructions the location of the treasure is somewhere in the castle's bailey.'

'And the twenty-third point?' asked Rees.

'I'd say it was a compass point,' Cloote said.

'Really?' Gordon sounded highly sceptical. 'I didn't think compasses were used until much later.'

'Not at all,' Cloote went on. 'The first compass was invented over two thousand years ago in China. And Alexander Neckam described them in Europe at the end of the twelfth century, so it's perfectly feasible. As far as I remember I think early compasses were divided into thirty-two segments numbered clockwise, but I'll need to check. So, the twenty-third point would be err ...'

'West south-west,' Anna helped him.

'Well, that's supposedly where it is. How do we find out if there's something there?' asked Gordon.

'We'll need to go and look,' Cloote replied.

'What, just turn up and start digging?'

'I think not,' Oliver said. 'It would be rather obvious and if we *did* find anything, we couldn't say a word if the dig wasn't legal.' Anna said nothing. She was worrying that if they'd cracked the code, either Westley or the killers of Arbuthnot were equally capable of doing so. 'We need to do it officially' he continued, 'and we need the equipment.'

'We're talking stuff to survey for buried features and disturbed ground?' asked Rees.

'Indeed. A high-quality magnetometer for archaeological use and ground penetrating radar.'

'Leave that to me to sort out,' said Rees.

'Meanwhile I'll look into how we can dig at the Manwar Ings,' said Cloote.

'Fine,' said Anna, 'I want to check a couple of things for myself. And I want to call Magnus. How much can I tell him?'

'I think you can be completely frank,' said Cloote. 'Explain that we think we've solved the riddle of the stolen Bodleian text and it supposedly gives the site of the lost crown jewels of King John. Ask him if he wants to join us for the dig.'

Anna went back to look over Gervase Penhaligon's online research. She thought she'd seen something but couldn't remember what. She quickly found what she was looking for. In 2010 there had been an archaeological survey of the remains of Swineshead Abbey, which is now the site of a farm and private house. The historical advisor on the dig had been none other than Gervase Penhaligon. She hurried back to the library where she found Cloote. 'I've been thinking,' she began. 'Westley contacted you because you're an expert in Gothic, which Westley wasn't. He also wasn't an expert on English monastic buildings. So, if he found out that Swineshead was critical who would he have contacted? An expert in that field. And who was the most obvious? The man who advised the most recent investigation of the abbey, Gervase Penhaligon.'

'Yet again, Anna, you repay my faith in your abilities. But I'm not sure it alters our plans?'

'Perhaps not, but it may mean we have *three* different antagonists, or maybe they're all in league together?'

'The only way to find out is once we get to Swineshead,' Oliver concluded.

Anna then phoned Magnus. She said she needed to speak more securely and re-contacted him via WhatsApp. 'Phew!' was his immediate response. Once he'd got over his initial surprise he picked up on Anna's scepticism. 'But you're not convinced?' he asked.

'I'm not sure. The trail looks convincing. It took a great deal of working out. But,' she went on, 'John's treasure has remained undiscovered for eight hundred years and, even if it's real, it looks as if at least three lots of people could have got there first.'

'But surely,' Magnus pondered, 'if they had we'd have heard something? This would be one of the greatest archaeological finds of all time, how could it be kept secret?'

'A good point, and maybe I'm being over cautious. Do you want to be in on the dig?'

'Very much so. Just let me know when and I'll be there.'

Oliver had done his homework. The 2010 dig was a joint project between Cambridge and Southampton Universities. Since then, the latter had continued investigating sites in the vicinity and held a licence for digging both the abbey and castle sites. Bernard Strong was professor of archaeology there and, fortuitously, one of Oliver's keenest academic supporters. An email secured his permission for Cloote to dig some 'test pits' at the Manwar Ings to investigate the idea that the site may have had Danish origins.

Anna told him that Magnus would join them, and Gordon came back with the news that the equipment they'd need would be delivered on Friday.

'I think Sunday would be best,' Cloote considered, 'fewer people around, especially at this time of year.'

Anna called Magnus back and he said he'd get the train the day before the search.

Chapter 21

Over the next two days Anna went over the entire thing again. She couldn't see any flaw in their logic and decided to concentrate on her date with Anula. In New York she'd enacted a mutual role play that was huge fun, as well as being sexually exciting, but she had only played a part of herself, not the whole Anna Carr. For Wednesday she wanted both to be herself and tell her friend who she was. She planned her look carefully, and even deliberately turned up a few minutes late to make an entrance. As she walked into the restaurant several people stopped talking to look at her and Anula's heart missed a beat.

Anna had dyed her hair jet black. It was gelled and slicked back. She'd applied black eyeliner and darkened her eyebrows, something she very rarely did. Her black leather jacket was another purchase from New York. The sleeves were covered with dozens of sharp silver studs. The lapels were held back by other studs and there were several zipped pockets set off by a studded belt. The main fastening was diagonal which Anna unzipped to reveal her top. This was cropped above the naval and had lacing that traced out a pentagram. Her trousers were dull black leather with a prominent studded zip at the cotch. On each thigh, cross-strapping came together in silver pentagram fastenings, which were finished by studded knee pads. Finally, her knee length boots had four-inch platforms, each with six side buckles, cross lacing, and another silver pentagram at the top. Anula was, in comparison, very demurely dressed in a pale green silk dress slashed across the shoulder and black suede heel boots.

'Wow!' said Anula. 'You look absolutely amazing!'

Anna said nothing, gave Anula a quick peck and sat down. Anula asked her how her trip to New York had been. Anna was noncommittal but thought she'd be honest about her encounter with Tina if the opportunity arose. They chatted superficially for a while before ordering. They decided to share hummus and olives as a starter, which Anula followed with Moroccan vegetable tagine with jewelled couscous while Anna opted for wild rice, puy lentils, butternut squash, celeriac, cepes, tarragon and red wine ragu. Anula had a glass of pinot grigio while Anna stuck to Diet Coke. After they'd finished their main courses and ordered some ice cream Anula asked: 'Do you really believe in that stuff?'

'What stuff?'

'Satan and that. Last time we met you had a tee shirt that said, "Satan is a Woman", and now there's all these,' she indicated the pentagrams. 'Or is it just to annoy people?'

Anna laughed. 'A bit of both I guess. It's not that I believe in Satan, I'm an out-and-out atheist, but of the two, you know, God and Satan, I know who I'd pick.'

'How do you mean?'

'Well, the Bible is supposed to be the book of God, right? It's written by His supporters so it should show Him in the very best light. But just look at what God does. In the Book of Kings, he sends bears to kill kids. He destroys everyone, including innocent children, in Sodom and Gomorrah, and he kills off the first born in Egypt and that's before the whole "women as the root of sin" stuff. And what does Satan do? He's a bit nasty to Job and does a lot of tempting but that's about it. So, if God's propaganda depicts him as a killer of children and Satan as nothing worse than a bit dodgy, I know whose side I'm on.'

Anula laughed and Anna added, 'And it does piss off some people too. It's like when I have a good argument with fundamentalists or Jehovah's Witnesses. They say they believe every word in the Bible is the literal truth, so I always ask them how well they read Ancient Greek and Aramaic. Because, unless they can, all they're doing is reading some bloke's translation.'

'You really don't like formal religion, do you?'

'Actually, I think religions all have their good side,' Anna replied. 'But those that proselytise, mainly Christianity and Islam, have serious drawbacks, like any faith that tells you what to think rather than you working it out for yourself. How do you feel? Were you brought up a Buddhist?'

Anula said that both her parents were secular Buddhists and

hadn't pushed her in any direction. She was agnostic but agreed religion could be an easy answer to complex issues and had been the cause of great violence. 'Mind you if all religion disappeared, I expect people would still find reasons to fight.'

'Well men would at any rate,' Anna replied.

They paid their bill and headed back to the Cross Keys for a drink. Anula said she'd call a cab to take her back to Woodbridge, so she had another glass of wine and Anna was really enjoying her evening, so she indulged in a pint of Adnams Broadside. They sat in a corner and Anula asked a question she'd wanted to for a while. 'Have you always known you were attracted to women?'

'Pretty much. As soon as I started thinking about it, I realised I fancied women far more than men. And, even when I was very young, I kinduv thought I wasn't normal, whatever that means. You?'

'I've always liked both men and women, or perhaps *some* men and *some* women. I've had relationships with both.' Anna thought of asking about her most recent relationships and preferences but decided against it. Instead, Anula asked, 'But you've slept with men?'

'Oh yes. I thought they were a bit like oysters.'

'Oysters? You mean hard on the outside but squishy in the middle?'

Anna laughed. 'No, I mean that I never thought I'd enjoy oysters, but I gave them a try to check if I was right. I was, I don't like them. Same with men. I picked two when I was a teenager. They were perfectly nice boys, and really quite considerate in bed, but they're definitely not for me.'

It was Anula's turn to laugh. 'I like the idea of "selection". Did they know they'd been singled out for your experiment?'

'Of course not,' Anna replied. 'But generally, men jump at the chance of sex, and they were no exception when I asked them if they fancied a shag.'

Anula laughed again. 'And you haven't slept with men since?'

'No. I've been asked a few times.'

'And how do you respond?'

'It depends on how they ask. Some of them get a kick in the balls but if they're nice I'm polite. There was a boy in my third year who got infatuated. One day he told me that he was in love with me but respected my sexuality.'

'And what did you do. Never speak to him again?'

'No, he was being honest, and he *did* respect me, so we remained friends. Anyway,' Anna continued, 'even if I fancied men equally, it's just more logical to be a dyke.'

'Why's that?'

'You should know, you're the doctor. Lesbians report higher levels of sexual satisfaction than straight women. I read one study that said lesbians reported coming eighty-six percent of the time during sex, as opposed to sixty-five percent for straight women. We're at a huge advantage when it comes to knowing how to make other women feel good. We've done it before to ourselves, lots of times.'

'And I suppose there's simple biology,' Anula added. 'Women can orgasm in waves, which men can't, they need a breather. Your clitoris has eight thousand nerve endings, double that of the penis glans, and women's orgasms last for an average of twenty seconds, while men's last eight.'

'Exactly. We know what a clit is and have realistic expectations about how quickly we can orgasm.'

'Do you know the most orgasms recorded in an hour for a woman is a hundred and thirty-four but only sixteen for a man?' asked Anula.

'I didn't. But did *you* know that Virginia Woolf and Vita Sackville-West once made each other come seventy-three times in one afternoon in the Rose Garden at Sissinghurst?'

'No really?' Anula said with astonishment. She couldn't recall reading this about the pair. Then she looked at Anna, whose mouth was forming a little smile.

'You scoundrel!' Anula exclaimed and Anna burst out laughing.

'I had you with that one, didn't I?' She couldn't remember feeling quite this relaxed with someone before.

'Anyway,' she went on, 'women have better sex with women because we understand each other's bodies, we communicate better and focus more on our partner's pleasure than our own.'

'Do you think that means we're better at keeping our sexual partners then?' Anula asked.

Anna considered for a short time. 'No, I think that's down to different things. The key things in any relationship, serious or casual, are honesty and consent.'

'I agree they're important but what about compatibility or shared interests?'

'Probably some but not everything. People need their own space too,' said Anna, who was starting to worry that Anula might be going to ask about her feelings towards her. Fortunately, Anula realised Anna didn't want the conversation to go there, and instead asked: 'You used the word dyke. Is that what you'd call yourself? What about lesbian or queer?'

'Language is really important. People have reclaimed terms like black and gay and we're some way to doing the same with queer and dyke. But those terms can still be used as abuse as well.'

'And there are other words that people outside that actual group really can't, or shouldn't, use,' Anula added. 'Listen to a black rap artist or a Spike Lee film and black people, especially young males, call each other the "n" word rather a lot. But if you or me, even as a woman of colour, used that word it would immediately mean something else.'

'And cunt?' said Anna.

'Excuse me?'

'It's a word that needs reclaiming. It comes from kunta in Old Norse and was simply descriptive. It's gained a lot of baggage over the centuries, but I prefer it to vagina and definitely to pussy, which is too associated with porn. And the word vagina is Latin for a sword sheathe, which suggests it's simply a holster for the penis.'

'You're probably right,' said Anula. 'Technically speaking, vagina refers only to the genital tract. Vulva is a more correct word for the external genitalia.'

'And so is cunt. It describes the whole shebang, external and internal. So, it takes account of female sexual pleasure. To reclaim the power of our sex, we should take back the word that best describes our sex organ.'

They got another drink as the barman had just called last orders. Anula phoned for her cab. 'This was fun,' said Anula. 'Would you like to come over to my place for a meal sometime next week? I'll be flying back to Sri Lanka for Christmas but could fit something in.'

Anna said she'd love to, and they kissed goodbye. In the taxi home Anula thought Anna Carr was the most amazing women she'd ever met.

*

Back at Summerland, Oliver and Gordon enjoyed a relaxing evening. Gordon cooked a delicious meal and Cloote selected a bottle of 1978 Domaine Marquis d'Angerville Caillerets, a top red Burgundy, to accompany their steaks. They'd agreed not to cook red meat when Anna was around. After the meal they enjoyed an evening of intimacy and passion they hadn't experienced since the whole business with Westley had begun.

Lying in bed later they talked about the case and especially about Anna Carr. 'You were certainly right about her, Oliver. She *is* extraordinary and I doubt we'd have made the same progress.'

Cloote concurred. 'What about her friend? What do you make of her?'

'I like her. And so do her friends and colleagues from what I found out. She's a hugely respected surgeon, one of the youngest in her field, and she's got a strong social conscience. Volunteers whenever she can at the women's refuge in Ipswich.'

'But what does Anna think about her? I'm assuming Anula is bi?'

'Yes, she seems to have had both girl and boyfriends, though not very many. I'm not sure. I think she's trying to make up her own mind. She isn't decisive in everything you know.'

'No, I agree.'

'What about your other idea about Anna?'

'I'm still not certain. But nothing I've seen makes it *less* likely.'

'But you're not going to say anything to her about it?'

'Definitely not. She'd say I was mad and probably run a mile. Now come here. I think we've got a little unfinished business to attend to!'

When Anna got back, she tried to get to sleep but found she couldn't. She was thinking about their treasure hunt and the possible dangers but mainly about her evening with Anula. In the end she got up and put on her running gear. It was virtually a full moon so she could see her way clearly as she ran past the hospital and turned onto the path to the marshes and the sea wall. As she ran along the river, she noticed a smart motor yacht. *Must have cost a packet. Some rich tycoon I suppose*, she thought.

Back at the house she went into the gym to do some exercises. She didn't bother with a shower but instead stripped off her clothes and put them in the washing machine in the garage block before going to the kitchen and fixing a herb tea that would help her sleep. Gordon heard her return, or at least he hoped it was her. Cloote was fast asleep, and he thought he'd better just check. He put on a black silk dressing gown Oliver had bought him and went downstairs. He found Anna sitting on a stool sipping her tea. She wasn't in the slightest embarrassed at his seeing her naked, but he did notice how ultra-fit she was from the look of her abdominal muscles.

'Hi, can't sleep?'

'No. I went for a run.'

'Did you have a good time?'

'Yeh. I did.'

'You really like your doctor friend?'

Anna gave him a slightly fierce look but said, 'Yes. I think I do.'

'You know, Anna, if you ever want to chat about anything, I'm happy to. You know. Well, just if you wanted to.'

Anna realised he was being honest and really wanted to help, so she smiled. 'Thanks, Gordon. I know I've got to work things out for myself. But thanks for the offer.' It was the first time she'd used his name. He went back upstairs and when she'd finished the tea so did Anna. She was finally able to drop off, but her dreams returned.

She was lying on her back looking up into a night sky with thousands of stars. She could smell and hear the sea close by. As she turned her head, she saw a beautiful woman with flowing hair walking towards her. The woman was dressed in a brilliant blue cloak and a headpiece made from black wool trimmed with ermine. She was carrying a distinctive staff which was black and shaped like a sword, except that about halfway up four basket-like strands bulged out for a short way. Beneath this the woman was grasping the staff by a gold covering. The handle or pommel was also covered with gold and seemed to have precious stones inlayed. In the other hand the woman carried a long, thin knife but Anna wasn't afraid. She felt the woman was keeping her safe. When she reached Anna, she stretched out her hand and placed it on Anna's stomach. But then there was a sudden flash of lightning, and the woman disappeared. In her place was a cloaked and hooded figure whose cold hand was on Anna's body. It raised the dagger, readying to strike her, and she woke up panting for breath.

Chapter 22

On Friday a blue van with 'Archaeological Electronics Ltd' on the side drew up at the gates of Summerland. Anna helped Rees unload the equipment. That afternoon they tested it out. Cloote had supervised digs before and Anna had spent one summer at the World Heritage Site at Jelling in Denmark, where she had learned how to use the key items. They'd rejected the idea of using aerial surveying techniques, such as LIDAR, as their site would be quite small and could be hidden by other features. Their two main pieces of equipment were therefore a magnetometer and ground-penetrating radar. Rees remarked that he was sure he'd be able to help work them as he'd been an avid fan of the long-running TV programme *Time Team*. Anna told him it wasn't that easy, and she'd need some practice with the latest versions, which she wasn't totally familiar with.

The magnetometer comprised an H-shaped metal frame which hung by straps round the operator's neck. The cross beam supported a computerised operating panel and display. The two side beams, which hung parallel to the operator, sent out and received the signals. 'Every kind of material has unique magnetic properties, even those we don't think of as being magnetic,' she explained to Gordon. 'Things below the ground cause local disturbances in the Earth's magnetic field that are detectable with magnetometers like this. Their main limitation is that archaeological features can be obscured by highly magnetic geology or modern materials nearby. But looking at our site I don't think this should be a problem.' She did a sweep of the back lawn and immediately identified some foundations of old walls which some digging quickly turned up. Then, near the bottom end, she found an area that showed a strong response which indicated it was where the gardeners used to have their bonfire.

They then unpacked and assembled the GPR unit. This comprised a box about two feet square supported on four small wheels. The operator guided the machine with a control column about four feet long, attached to the control panel. It looked like an oversized version of the machines used to paint white lines on sports pitches. Unlike the magnetometer, where the results needed to be downloaded to a computer, the GPR device connected wirelessly. GPR uses high-frequency radio waves to penetrate the ground, which are reflected by buried objects. GPR can detect things that don't have significant differences in their magnetic field. It can therefore 'see' things like underground voids or changes in density that a magnetometer wouldn't pick up. 'In favourable conditions GPR can be a really powerful tool,' Anna said. 'Sandy soils are best, and we used them a lot in Denmark. The main drawback is that soils with high electrical conductivity, like clays and silts, or rocky areas weaken the GPR signal, or increase extraneous noise.' Again, they did a survey of Summerland's garden. The results were nothing remarkable, but Anna was able to show Rees where there were different layers of soil. 'Probably laid down by the river,' she explained.

That evening Anna had a text from Anula that asked if she could make dinner on Thursday. She said she'd probably be okay and would let her know for sure on Monday.

On Saturday the three of them went to pick up Magnus from Ipswich station in the Jaguar. It was the first time he and Gordon had met. Cloote embarrassed Anna on the journey back by singing her praises to her former tutor. They spent the evening looking over the evidence, plus maps and aerial surveys of Swineshead and the Manwar Ings. Magnus had to agree that their conclusions regarding Johannes of Medhamstead's codes were correct and that he was certainly referring to King John's treasure. 'It's quite remarkable, but it's the obvious conclusion. I suppose it might all just be a medieval practical joke but, if so, it's a very elaborate one.'

They set off just before six on Sunday, a good hour and a half before dawn, on what was a cold but clear December morning. In less than two hours they were approaching the village of Swineshead. They turned right at a roundabout and then carried straight on towards Boston rather than turning left to the village. After about a mile Cloote pointed out a line of trees on their right. 'The remains of the abbey are behind there. I suppose if we draw a blank at the castle, we should think about excavating there.' Anna pointed out that the site was sixty or seventy thousand square metres and had several private buildings on it, so that might be more than a little tricky.

Shortly afterwards they saw Manor Farm on their left. Just before it was a minor road called Bay Thorpe which they took. Almost immediately, across the open fields to their left, they could see a low mound with a few straggly trees growing on it. 'Is that it?' asked Gordon, who had been expecting something a little more impressive.

'That's it,' said Magnus. 'Of course, it would have been higher and the surrounding ground lower in the Middle Ages.'

A short distance along the lane they approached a substantial house beyond which some farm buildings, with piles of stacked pallets, was visible. On the left was a dirt track with a green 'Public Footpath' fingerpost. They took the track which, for the first two hundred metres, was easily drivable before it ended at a gate. 'This is as near as we can get with the car,' Gordon told them.

Fortunately, it was dry, if rather cold, and the path continued for the next hundred metres or so to the northern side of the castle mound. Cloote had obtained large-scale ordnance survey maps of the site and explained, 'Originally there was a causeway that linked the abbey to the castle. The entrance to the castle was on the south-east side where the causeway was.'

By nine they had all the equipment on the site. Their first task was to lay out a nylon string along the line of the twenty-third point, west-south-west, from the centre of the castle motte. This crossed the two ditches before reaching cultivated fields which, at this time of year, were bare of crops. They began by surveying along this line. Anna went first with the magnetometer and Magnus, who was the most familiar with the equipment, supervised Rees and Cloote as they manoeuvred the GPR unit. It wasn't easy on the sides of the ditches, and they wouldn't get great results from these areas, but they surmised that anyone burying something was more likely to have done so at the bottom of a ditch rather than on its banks.

After the first sweep, which took them around an hour, they

sat down to look at the results. 'Nothing that looks especially striking,' Magnus said. 'You can see some variations on the magnetometer results, but they all look quite minor. I'll mark up where there might possibly be something and you do the next sweep.' He got some plastic flags and, using GPS location, stuck them in the ground wherever a small variation had been detected. The others commenced additional surveys either side of their original line.

After the third pass they again looked at the results. 'What's that?' asked Anna. It was on the GPR read-out. In the area of the inner ditch there was a distinct 'hump' in the lines.

'It looks to me like disturbed ground,' said Magnus. 'Oliver what do you think?'

'I agree. And it looks rather *too* clear, as if it's been disturbed quite recently.'

They went to the spot the GPR indicated. Gordon stuck a spade in the ground and prised up the turf. It was obvious that someone had indeed been digging there and, though the turf had been very carefully replaced, the soil was less compacted than it should have been. 'Not a good sign for finding any treasure I'm afraid,' Magnus commented.

'Well, we'd better get digging,' Cloote replied, but by 'we' he really meant the two younger and fitter members of the team. Anna and Gordon took off their jackets while Magnus spread out a blue plastic tarpaulin. 'I know we're treasure hunters, but it still doesn't mean we can't be archaeologists too,' he said.

Anna and Gordon shovelled the earth onto the sheet where Cloote and Strachan examined it more carefully using trowels. After about an hour's digging Anna said, 'I think I might have hit the bottom at my end, there's a definite change in compaction here.' She turned towards Gordon to ask him if he'd found the same thing when she saw the look on his face. 'Gordon, what's . . .' she began, but then she saw why his face had frozen. There was no treasure in the trench, but staring up at them were the unmistakable features of a very dead Professor Clinton Westley.

Chapter 23

After they had recovered from the shock, and Gordon had taken a large swig of whisky from a hipflask Cloote had conveniently brought with him, Anna took charge of the situation. 'Right,' she said forcefully, 'we need to make some decisions. First, how much do we tell the police? Second, what does this mean? Did someone else find the treasure?' The others didn't immediately speak, so she continued. 'I think we have to tell them everything. It was okay while we only had vague suspicions about the Bodleian murder, but now we've got two bodies and they must be linked. Did you see the wound, Gordon?' He shook his head. 'Looked like a knife to the chest I'd say. If we try to conceal things, we'd be assisting the killers.' The others agreed.

The police took their time, this was a Sunday in rural Lincolnshire even though they'd stressed that they'd found a body. When someone finally arrived, he clearly thought Magnus was the one in charge, as he didn't look eccentric and wasn't black or female. He told the story as far as they knew it, which seemed to rather overwhelm the intelligence of the officer concerned, who was now feeling distinctly inferior in the presence of a professor and two doctors. When they got to Boston Police Station, what interested the police most was how a group of archaeologists just happened to dig up the body of a colleague. They stressed that none of them had met Westley but knew him from his photograph. The police were still highly suspicious. This wasn't helped by their scepticism regarding a possible link to the Bodleian crime, but at least they agreed to call their colleagues at Thames Valley. Magnus, who was getting a little irritated, remarked, 'Not exactly Inspector Morse and Sergeant Lewis are they?'

'I still don't think they'll take it seriously. I'll call my friend Nikki,' said Anna and in the car on the way back to Aldeburgh, she called her and told her what had happened.

'I see,' Nikki replied. 'So when you met me all you wanted was to ply me with drink to find the latest on the Bodleian murder,' she said, though Anna could tell she wasn't totally serious.

'So, you're never speaking to me again unless it's to arrest me for killing Westley?'

At the other end of the line Nikki gave a snort. 'Unless I'm the worst judge of character ever to grace Thames Valley Police I'd say you're not a murderer. Anyway, Lincs have been on to us. I'll be interested in their PM report. The security guard was killed with a very distinctive blade.'

'I expect you'll need to speak to all of us when you prove the connection?'

'I shouldn't really go into things with a material witness, especially one who already seems to be telling us how to do our job!' Again, there was a smile in her tone. 'Just you take care, Tiger. If these killings are connected there are some very dangerous people about.' Anna agreed that she would.

'There's two possible explanations,' Cloote surmised. 'Either Westley or the killers discovered something, and he was killed straight afterwards, or they found nothing.'

'What's the evidence?' asked Anna.

'I've looked at all the data from both the magnetometer and the GPR,' Magnus said. 'It's hard to tell whether there might have been something in the trench before it was disturbed.'

'But surely,' Rees interrupted, 'this would have been the find of the century. Something would have leaked out?'

'Not necessarily,' Cloote replied. 'These people are ruthless killers so keeping it secret wouldn't be an issue. Just look at how many priceless works of art have been stolen to order over the years,' he added. 'Eventually something could turn up, but equally it might not. To be frank we have no idea if the whole thing was real or if Johannes of Medhamstead led us on a wild goose chase.'

'It's extraordinarily frustrating,' Magnus concluded.

*

The unusual circumstances of the discovery of Westley's body meant that the media picked up the story and, very quickly, a group of them were encamped outside Summerland trying to get interviews. On Wednesday morning Cloote received a call from Inspector John Cook of Thames Valley Police, Nikki McDonald's boss, to say he would visit them to ask some further questions. He arrived with Nikki that afternoon. She spoke with Cloote while Inspector Cook talked to Anna. Nikki had prepped him on what to expect and he was careful to treat her with both respect and care. 'You were right about the link, Dr Carr. The post-mortem on Professor Westley suggests that the weapon bears a very close resemblance to that used to kill Cecil Arbuthnot. Could you go through your story again for me?' Anna did so, explaining how she'd been employed by Cloote to help him investigate the Gothic manuscript. She showed him the details of how they had cracked the code used by Johannes of Medhamstead and he seemed to follow her reasoning. 'You should perhaps have reported your suspicions to us earlier,' he suggested, but he didn't overstress the point after Anna had made some remarks about how reporting things to the police didn't always lead to positive results. She was thinking about quoting statistics on rape and domestic violence but decided he'd got the message. 'And you really don't know if there was any, umm, treasure, at the site?'

'No. I'm happy to hand over the data so you can have it independently verified,' she added.

Cook said that would be helpful so she zip-filed it and put everything on a memory stick for him. Finally, he thanked her for her cooperation. 'I probably don't need to add, Dr Carr, that should you find out anything more you should get in touch. These are two brutal crimes that show the perpetrators won't hesitate to kill those who stand in their way.' Anna agreed with his summary but was careful not to promise to share every bit of information. She wasn't sure if he'd noticed or not.

When the police had left Anna called Anula. She hadn't yet heard about the discovery as she'd been on duty the last couple of days. Anna asked if she could see her quickly and rode over to Ipswich hospital on the Harley. The hospital in Heath Road is on the eastern side of the town and Anna parked the bike in the multi-storey car park before making her way to the orthopaedic unit on level 5.

After Anula finished speaking with a patient, they went to the coffee bar. Anna told Anula all about her real work, the finding of Westley's body and its link to the Bodleian murder. 'It's more like a film than real life,' Anula responded. 'I had no idea you were really a female Indiana Jones.'

'Don't worry, I'm not,' Anna replied.

'But you are mixed up in something involving people who will kill to get their hands on whatever it is.'

'Yes, and that's the reason for telling you everything. I don't want to put you in any danger.'

'Anna,' said Anula firmly, 'you're my friend. I stick by my friends. I will stick by you. What time are you coming on Thursday?'

Despite the failure at Swineshead, Anna rode back to Aldeburgh feeling better than she had for several days.

*

She found Oliver and Gordon in the library, but Magnus had returned to Oxford. They were both very quiet and clearly disillusioned about their quest. She suggested going for a run to Gordon, but he made an excuse about the weather, it was drizzling, so she went on her own. This time she followed the old railway line that used to run from Aldeburgh to Saxmundham but fell victim to the Beeching cuts. At Thorpeness she turned towards the sea via the golf course and ran back along the coast road, the wind blowing full in her face. To avoid any lingering reporters, she entered the garden via the back gate. From the boat she'd noticed earlier, a young man was looking through powerful binoculars. Harry Spall was a bright and ambitious boatyard worker who'd met Savile Nesfield when he was looking for new crew members for the *Spirit of Freedom*. The normal crew complement was seven on what was the smallest of Elias Forth's three yachts: the others were the sail powered *Spirit of Destiny* and the superyacht *Weisthor*. While the *Spirit of Freedom* was acting as a convenient lookout post, three men were sharing duties on an eight-hour shift system. After Anna went inside, he used his mobile. 'Hi, Savile. The girl's just been out for a run. Nothing unusual. The police haven't been back... Sure, I'll let you know.'

Anna showered, changed, and went to the kitchen to fix something to eat. At least Cloote and Rees seemed a bit more cheerful. She thought it would be a good time to bring up the issue of her employment. 'I suppose that's the end of it then,' she said. 'You won't need me anymore. When would you like me to move out?'

Cloote was genuinely appalled. 'My dear Anna,' he relapsed into his formal mode, 'there's absolutely no question of you moving out or of our arrangement coming to an end. Unless you are completely fed up with us?' She said she wasn't. 'That's good. Anyway, Gordon and I will be away over Christmas so I'd be most grateful if you could housesit for us.'

'Oliver's co-sponsored a production of *The Ring* with the Dallas Opera,' Rees explained. 'The dress rehearsals of *Rheingold* start on the ninth and the first night is January second, so we'll be flying out on Sunday and coming back on the fourth.'

'I don't even want to *think* about terminating our relationship until after we're back,' Oliver explained. 'I'm sure there are other projects we could work on if you were interested. And, in any case, we've both enjoyed having you here. You, err, add colour to our small abode.' It was another over-elaboration, but he clearly meant it.

'Oh. Okay then,' said Anna, who was rather looking forward to having such a wonderful house all to herself. She had never been someone who felt lonely or bored.

Cloote explained she could have the run of the house and even the wine cellar. 'I know you're not a drinker but there are some very decent half bottles if you're so inclined, I'd highly recommend the Krug Grande Cuvee. But if you're going for whole bottles perhaps it's best to confine yourself to vintages after 1990?'

'Oliver!' admonished Rees. 'You're a total wine snob. Anna isn't a complete idiot!'

Cloote was suitably deflated. 'Do forgive me, that was rather stupid.' Anna assured him that as she'd have trouble telling a Burgundy from a claret his admonition wasn't totally unfounded. She also thought such an apology was somewhat out of character for her, so she must be getting rather fond of Cloote.

Chapter 24

On Thursday evening Anna rode over to Anula's flat in Woodbridge. It was indeed part of the mill complex on the quay that she'd seen on her previous visit. As she didn't need to make a statement she was dressed, for her, rather conservatively. Black polo neck sweater with an inverted silver crescent moon motif at the neck and long sleeves with a slash at the elbows, with black jeans and plain boots.

Anula's flat was quite small: a single bedroom, living room, kitchen, and bathroom. You entered at ground level, but the rooms were up a stairway, and the ceilings were high with beams and the roof of the building above. As Anna expected, it was highly organised and spotlessly clean. In the living room there were several masks on the wall which Anula explained were traditional Sri Lankan ones. 'Some of them are used to perform Raksha dances,' she explained. 'This one is a cobra mask, and this the mask of the Demon of Death. Then there's this one which impersonates Garuda, the solar bird who is the vehicle of Vishnu.' Anna especially liked the Garuda mask. 'It's used in the Demon Dance to frighten away the Cobra Demon,' Anula said, 'hence the snakes. But the dance is also practical to warn of the real danger that snakebites pose. The other masks are ones used in healing rituals, Sanni Yakuma, and then these,' she indicated a row that were more human, 'are Kolam masks used in traditional folk plays.'

'I've seen some of these before,' Anna said, 'but the colours were much more garish.'

'They'd be commercially produced ones for tourists,' Anula explained. 'These are painted using traditional methods from plant dyes rather than chemical ones.'

'I've been finding out some more about your country,' Anna said. 'Did your parents name you after Queen Anula?'

'Yes,' Anula chuckled, 'even though she murdered her husband and four other partners.'

'She sounds a bit like Elizabeth Bathory,' Anna added. 'If so, she was probably unfairly maligned so that men could steal her wealth.'

'You could be right, after all her enemies finally had her burned to death.'

They both thought they should get less morbid, so the conversation switched to their exercise routines. Anna wanted to know more about maya angam and how you train for it and Anula explained that it was kept extremely secret, as it's misuse would be deadly in the wrong hands. She also said that its practitioners often handed down its secrets through generations of the same family. 'In that way it's like other magical practices throughout the world,' Anula concluded.

What she was careful not to say, and Anna didn't ask, was whether she herself had any skill in its practice. Instead, Anna suggested: 'I don't think I've got any magical powers, but I do have party tricks. I can show you one if you like?'

Anula said she'd love to, and Anna asked her to clear the objects off her mantelpiece. The shelf was nearly two metres off the ground and perhaps ten centimetres wide. Anna stood with her back to it and squatted down. She then sprang upright pulling her knees up to her chin and flipped slightly backwards so that she was now standing on the mantlepiece. Anula clapped the performance. 'That's quite something. Where did you learn how to do it?'

'I read about it,' Anna said. 'It was a party trick that the great sportsman CB Fry used to perform, and I thought I'd train myself to do it.'

'Oh, the cricketer who was offered the throne of Albania?'

'Well, they didn't quite ask to be become king, but he did take part in the 1919 peace talks,' Anna added.

Anna could smell the food cooking. 'I hope you're hungry,' Anula asked.

'I am if it tastes as good as it smells,' she responded.

Anula got Anna to sit down and told her not to interfere. 'I've done some traditional Sri Lankan dishes, though you wouldn't usually have them all at the same time. And we tend to eat the biggest meal at lunchtime.' She said this while bringing out a stream of dishes. Anna was right in thinking that she wanted to impress her guest. 'This is malu ambul thiyal, sour fish curry. This is Ala Hodi, potato curry. The salad is mallung, the main ingredient I've used is kale, with shredded coconut and onion. This is a parippu, dhal curry. These,' she indicated some things that looked like pancakes, 'are hoppers made from rice flour, coconut milk, and palm toddy.'

'Oh, I've heard of them,' said Anna, 'but I thought they were noodles.'

'Those ones are called string hoppers,' replied Anula. 'Then you've got wambatu moju, aubergine pickle and a pol sambol, shredded coconut, lime juice, red onions, chilli and spices.' Steamed rice in coconut milk completed the impressive feast. 'I've got beer but there's also a lime juice cordial because I thought you . . .' She tailed off because she was nervous of saying Anna would be biking home. She wasn't entirely sure what might happen. 'And there's this drink too.' She poured out a thick, brown liquid that looked a bit like a chocolate milkshake. Anna smelt it and then sipped it. It had a slight smell of raisins and a sour and sweet flavour; unlike anything she'd tried before.

'That's rather nice. Whatever is it?'

'Wood apple juice,' Anula said. 'It's a fruit about the size of a coconut. You blend it with sugar and water to smooth it out. If you want to make friends with a Sri Lankan, tell them you love wood apple juice!'

For dessert there was watalappam, a pudding made of coconut milk, jaggery, cashew nuts, eggs, cardamom, cloves, and nutmeg. All of it was totally delicious and Anna ate far more than she'd done for a long time. Afterwards they settled back on Anula's sofa, and she put some music on. Anna told her to pick what to play; she thought Anula probably wouldn't appreciate Slayer or Dimmu Borgir after a heavy meal. Anula played some tracks by the New Zealand singer-songwriter Aldous Harding who, Anna thought, was a bit weird, which was good, but it was still rather folksy for her. She also played some Sri Lankan music, traditional and pop, and even included some tracks by Stigmata, a Sri Lankan metal band. 'Don't you think I'd like any of your music?' Anula asked.

'I suppose there's some you might think is okay,' Anna replied. She went to the console and searched Anula's streaming provider. 'I just got introduced to this great Latina rapper called Princess Nokia,' said Anna. 'There's a song of hers called "Goth Kid" that pretty much sums up my childhood.'

Anula listened and asked, 'You were a goth then?'

'Yeh, I guess.' But that was the limit of Anna's revelations about her past. The two of them talked well into the night and Anna even raised the subject of BDSM when Anula asked about her choker and pendant.

'It's not something I've ever tried but I do think people should be allowed to explore their full sexuality,' Anula said, a bit unsure of whether she wanted to go further into the subject.

'I met up with this woman while I was in New York,' Anna said, 'and we tried out a role play with me as her sub.'

'You mean she beat you? Do you enjoy that?' Anula had a wealth of questions.

'Absolutely. I like playing both roles at times, it depends on my mood.'

'But where do you draw the line? Can't it just become sadistic?'

'Sadism is just an erotic exchange of power. Abusing a victim is a million miles away from safe and consensual BDSM where either person can withdraw their consent at any time.' Anula wasn't sure about her own feelings on the topic and whether to ask more. 'I'm sorry, have I shocked you?' Anna said.

'No, no. I'm pleased you can be so open about it,' Anula replied and looked at Anna. They both hesitated, not quite knowing what might happen next, but the moment passed and instead Anna asked Anula to pick some more music. She tried Amanda Palmer, whose songs were very direct, personal statements on issues such as abortion, death, and motherhood. Anna liked the ideas more than the style of her music. She then put on the latest album by Sharon von Etten which was rockier and more to Anna's taste. Both liked St Vincent and, as Anna grew rather sleepy, Anula slipped in some quieter singer songwriters like Joni Mitchell and Suzanne Vega. Eventually at 3 a.m. Anna fell asleep on the sofa. Anula spread a blanket over her and slipped into her own bed for a few hours' sleep.

Chapter 25

Anula's flight wasn't until eight-forty on Friday evening, so she had plenty of time before she needed to catch her train. 'It's not every day that I have a Viking expert with me, so why don't we go to Sutton Hoo, and you can impart some of your knowledge? I've been once but I'd love to know more about it.'

They drove the couple of miles over the River Deben to what is possibly Britain's greatest archaeological site. In 1939 Basil Brown, a self-taught Suffolk archaeologist, found an undisturbed ship burial which included a trove of Anglo-Saxon artefacts of extraordinary importance. Most of these, including the famous helmet, are now in the British Museum where Anula had been to see them. She also knew that the person buried in the ship is most likely to have been Rædwald, a king of East Anglia who died in about 624. As they walked round Anula got a crash course in early British history. Anna explained that Rædwald was the son of Tytila, a member of the Wuffingas dynasty, who were the first kings of the East Angles. He reigned from about 599, originally as a vassal of King Æthelberht of Kent. In 616, at the Battle of the River Idle, Rædwald defeated Æthelfrith of Northumbria and both Æthelfrith and Rædwald's son, Rægenhere, were killed. Anula was getting rather lost in all the Old English names. 'Is it right to call them Anglo-Saxons?' asked Anula. 'I read that some people think it's a racist term.'

'I think most of them are Americans,' Anna responded. 'There it's usually tied to "white" and "Protestant". Many Anglo-Saxons in the Middle Ages weren't white and obviously none of them were Protestant. I don't think there's any problem using it in a historical context. What we usually don't call Anglo-Saxon these days is the language they spoke. That's better referred to as Old English.'

'Why did you get interested in this period?' Anula asked.

'Two things. First because it's at that fascinating margin between myth, legend, and historical documentation. You never quite know where the division lies and, in fact, the people at the time didn't make any distinction between them, they were all equally valid in helping people with their lives.'

'And the other?'

'There was someone I knew when I was young who encouraged me.'

'One of your parents?'

Anna shook her head and obviously didn't want to say any more about whoever it was, so Anula asked instead, 'So what's the difference between the Anglo-Saxons and the Vikings?'

'A bit is history, the Anglo-Saxons came to Britain first; a bit is geography, the Vikings came from further north, though their languages were very similar, and a bit is religion, the Saxons became Christian much earlier. But mainly it was about territory, what they held and what the other wanted.'

'And the Vikings turned up here to try to take over the country?'

'That's too simplistic and there's a real difficulty if we think of the ancient and medieval world as made up of nations. The concept of a nation is incredibly recent. They would never have thought that way. The term Viking has nothing much to do with geography. In Old Norse it probably means something close to "pirate". Viking was an identity, or a profession, sometimes just a temporary one, and they could come from anywhere around the North Sea or Baltic. Viking culture was remarkable eclectic, with influences from as far away as the Middle East, and warriors were never entirely Scandinavian.'

'Really, I didn't know that. I thought they were all big, blonde, blue-eyed men.'

'It's a myth that's hard to dispel,' Anna replied, 'and there's also been a great deal of distortion perpetrated by far-right fanatics. The white supremacist who killed fifty people in New Zealand left a rambling so-called manifesto which had Nordic references, and the alt-right is always attempting to co-opt Viking imagery. It's all garbage and their grasp of the subject is nil; the Vikings would have no concept of nationalism and probably very little of ethnicity, but it doesn't stop these ignorant people.'

'Where do these people get their ideas from?'

'It began in the nineteenth century with German nationalists who were trying to build a case for unification. It includes the folk tales of the Grimm brothers and Wagner's operas. But we forget they were trying to forge a new German national identity rather than being white supremacists, whatever people say about Wagner's antisemitism. It was later that the real distortions were perpetrated by the Nazis and the academics who supported them. People like Bernhard Kummer and Otto Höfler, both members of the Nazi Party even though they violently disagreed with each other. Then there was Karl Maria Wiligut, the man called Himmler's "Lord of the Runes."'

'Who was he?'

'Well, he wasn't an academic. There's no historical analysis in his beliefs. He was an early member of the SS and rose to the rank of brigadeführer on Himmler's personal staff. He headed the Department of Pre and Early History in the SS Race and Settlement Office, the most fanatical section of the entire Nazi state. His "theory", if you're generous enough to call it that, was that the ancestral religion of Germans was based on a deity called Irmin. Irminism is less factually based than Scientology: it distorts or misinterprets pretty much every source it uses. Wiligut was the main guy behind the making of Wewelsburg, the castle that was the ceremonial centre of SS pseudo-religious practice.'

'So, what were the Vikings religious beliefs?'

'It's a bit misleading to call Norse supernatural belief religion. It wasn't like Christianity or Buddhism or Roman religion, with a defined set of beliefs, religious buildings, and priests. It was much more integrated into everyday life. For Vikings there was no connection either to a moral code, divine law, or authority. They didn't really worship their gods, felt no requirement to obey them and the gods themselves were as flawed as humans. In fact, one strange aspect is that the Norse gods also worshipped something, though we don't know exactly what it was.'

'I never knew it was that complex.'

'It's probably better to call it something like a "belief system". And it wasn't static. In that sense it was more like Roman religion that assimilated beliefs from other cultures as the empire expanded. A lot of what we now know is totally antithetical to the white supremacist version. For one thing, the role of women. Women were both warriors and key practitioners of magic.'

'I think I read something about female Viking warriors quite recently, but you'll have to remind me.'

'It was probably the Birka burial,' Anna replied. 'The Birka grave was first excavated at the end of the nineteenth century but it's only recently that modern osteological analysis, confirmed by DNA testing, identified the remains as female.'

'That's it. It's because it's connected to my work.'

'Of course, some people have tried to dispute the conclusion that she was a warrior. They say there must have been a male body that's gone entirely missing but the evidence is overwhelming. And once people started admitting the possibility of women playing a role in Viking military life many other things fell into place. There are tapestries and figurines that show women holding spears and swords, and there are quite a few references in literature. And now some previously discovered burials of warriors are turning out to be female. Not huge numbers but significant none the less.'

'And you also said something about magic?'

'Yes seiðr,' Anna pronounced the word 'sayth-r'. 'It was the Viking version of magic. But it was a specific kind of magic and not to be confused with siðr, which is a more general term. Seiðr involved a series of rites and rituals that included divination and attracting spirits to carry out tasks such as conjuring storms, making enemies vulnerable, or your friends invulnerable.'

'And it was carried out by women?'

'Not entirely. Though seiðr practitioners were of both sexes the majority were female. They were called völva. It was a complex system linked to the two most important gods, Odin and Freyja, and involved foreseeing the future. One thing that's now clear about Norse practices, and especially the role women played, is that it's very similar to the shamanism of the circumpolar region. Remnants of these have persisted until very recently, in Siberia, the Sami in Finland, and the First Nation peoples of Northern Canada, and even as far afield as the machi of South America. Their shamans, especially female ones, are simultaneously feared and respected. They live on the fringes of society, and have their own specialisms, but they're fundamental to the cohesion of their societies.'

'It does sound quite like other supernatural beliefs, like those in Sri Lanka. And it hasn't really died out then?'

'Perhaps not and there are also modern revivals of seiðr. Some of them are carefully based on historical knowledge, others a bit bonkers. There's still a lot we don't know, and Nordic beliefs also changed over time, especially after Christianity came along.'

'And that changed things a lot?'

'Yes. It brought the problem of proselytising. Christianity is the worst offender in forcefully converting people. And women had a wider role in pagan society. It wasn't feminism by any means. Women suffered from gruelling work, childbirth, sexual violence, and slavery in Viking society. But, perhaps, it was still better than what followed, where women were considered responsible for sin and sex became unclean.'

'Aren't there still lots of remnants of Viking culture in England? I thought many place names are Viking.'

'That's right, there are hundreds of them. Anything with "thwaite", which means a woodland clearing; "toft", a house or building or "by", a farmstead or settlement for example. And then there's the days of the week, with four named after Norse gods.'

By now they'd got back to the visitor centre and went to the café for a quick bite to eat before driving back to Anula's flat. She fetched her luggage and came out clutching a small parcel. 'Here, Anna. I got you this. Happy Christmas.'

She was a little disappointed that Anna didn't seem to have got her anything but brightened up when she said, 'I'm not doing anything so do you mind if I come with you to the airport?'

'Of course not. It'd be lovely if you came, but are you sure?' Anula got a mild glare in response. She then added, 'Would you mind if I gave you the spare keys to the flat? You can leave your present here rather than carry it to Heathrow and back and perhaps you could pop in and water the plants? I'm not back until the eighth and I'd be really grateful.' Anna was happy to agree.

Woodbridge station was only a couple of minutes' walk and Anna bought a return ticket. On the train Anula was keen to find out how long Anna would be staying in Suffolk. 'I'm not sure, but Oliver wants me to do more work with him, so could be a while I guess.'

'That's good,' said Anula. 'Perhaps when I get back you can give me some more lessons in British history and I can give you some in angampora?'

'Sounds good.'

'Then we've got a deal!'

In London they went to Paddington to take the Heathrow Express to the airport. Anula's flight had just come up for check-in, so they went for a quick drink before she went through security. Just before they got to the barrier Anna pulled something out of her jacket. It was a small box wrapped in black paper with gold pentagrams on it. 'Here,' she said. 'I got you something. Hope have you a good flight.' Before Anula could reply, Anna had turned and was walking quickly away.

As her plane began its ascent out of London, Anula got out the box. When she unwrapped it, she was so overcome the man sitting next to her asked if she was okay. 'Yes, yes, I'm fine. Thank you.' She smiled. The box said 'Viking Handmade Workshop' on the lid. In it was an exquisite silver chain resembling knotted or woven thread with its tips depicting wolves' heads that clipped together.

*

By Saturday Anna was enjoying delving into Cloote's library and had assembled a pile of books. There were obscure histories of the early medieval period she'd only read about second-hand, beautiful editions of the eddas and sagas, and she even picked out a couple of interesting volumes from his occult and magic collection. 'That should keep me busy,' she remarked to Gordon who'd sought refuge in the library.

'Oliver is clucking round and worrying if he's packed everything, as usual. He always does this. And always takes far too much as well.'

As Heathrow was a nightmare to leave a car, they'd arranged

for one to pick them up. Before it arrived Cloote gave Anna some last-minute instructions. 'Do be careful with security. You don't know what the people we err, know about, might do. The police have said they'll let us know if there's any threat, but I doubt that's much good, so I've arranged for the security company to come by twice a day. All you have to do is reply to their text.' Anna frowned but didn't say anything. 'Gordon's stocked up the kitchen so you should be fine for food. And this is for you.' He handed her an envelope. 'Don't open it until Christmas Day but I hope it will keep you amused over the holiday.'

'Thank you,' Anna replied. 'I've got something for you as well.' She went to her room and brought back a large, flat parcel for Cloote and a smaller one for Rees, both wrapped in the same paper she'd used for Anula's present. 'You can open them now if you like. That one's a bit big to take to Dallas and back.'

Gordon's present was a copy of *Ghostland* and a black cashmere sweater she'd picked up in New York. 'Thank you, Anna, they're lovely. I'll take the book to read on the plane and wear the sweater for the opera.'

Cloote was struggling to open his but finally got the wrapping off. 'Anna!' he exclaimed, 'This is magnificent. How did you know?'

'I checked your book collection and couldn't see it, so I got it online and had it delivered to the post office.'

The book was a copy of Hermann Hendrich's illustrations for *Der Ring des Nibelungen* published by JJ Weber verlag in 1910. The original paintings are displayed in the 'Nibelungenhalle' at the Drachenfels, and the book was a limited edition produced before the opening of the hall.

Anna saw them off, promising again to take care and, no, she wouldn't be lonely. She was quite glad to be alone.

Chapter 26

Morten was enjoying hearing Elias Forth berate Savile Nesfield. They were meeting in the dining room at Satterthwaite Hall which ran half the length of the rear of the building, with large leaded windows giving vitas over the landscaped park.

'What exactly possessed you to bury the body in the hole? What was wrong with using the plane?'

'If you remember, sir, the plane wasn't available. You were on your way to Russia.' Forth wasn't especially concerned that Westley's body had turned up. He was dismissive of the police's ability to solve the murders and entirely confident in his own to evade justice. Nesfield tried to add to his defence. 'I did also think there was a certain irony in Professor Westley ending up in the excavation he thought would make his fortune.'

This was too much for Forth. 'Irony! What the fuck are you talking about? If I want irony, I'll employ a fucking poet. You're meant to fucking hurt people.' Morten couldn't suppress a thin smile. Forth turned to him. 'Good God, preserve me from fucking idiots. Where are we with Penhaligon? Has he got any ideas on what to do next?'

'Not exactly, sir,' Morten replied. 'He may be a man of international repute, but he is also of somewhat limited imagination. That's why I was so clear that we must keep a close watch on Oliver Cloote. He has the imagination Penhaligon lacks, even if he is not as corruptible.'

'But he can be intimidated,' Forth replied, 'and we might break him if he feared for his life.'

'Possibly,' Morten responded, 'but a frightened man will say virtually anything. At present we are not under time pressure. We can wait and see.'

'Well, for now he's in the States and it's possible they will simply give up.'

'I very much doubt it, sir. Given our information, it is extremely unlikely the manuscript was intended as a joke.'

'At least Penhaligon was useful in proving that.'

'Yes, his research was helpful but frustratingly limited. I still believe Cloote and his friends will provide the most fruitful insights.'

'I hope you're right. This enterprise has already cost a great deal and failure would not go down well with Oleg.'

'No indeed, sir. Mr Zinchenko does not take well to failure.'

Forth turned back to Nesfield. 'You're keeping watch at Aldeburgh still?'

'Yes sir. It's another reason for thinking that Cloote hasn't given up. He's still employing the girl and she appears to be intending to stay there while he's away. I have the *Spirit of Freedom* moored on the river. There's someone on watch twenty-four seven.'

'I really don't understand what Cloote was thinking of in hiring a girl student,' Forth added.

'She is considered a rather brilliant, if somewhat unconventional, student,' Morten added. 'After all you place a great deal of faith in Miss Clifford.'

'Gabriella is entirely different. She is excellent at legitimate business. I would never trust her with any of my other ... activities.'

'And Miss Prentiss is the opposite?' Morten added. He also made a note not to take Anna Carr quite as lightly as his boss.

'Humpf,' was Forth's response, which meant he agreed. 'We're certain Cloote's trip to the US is purely for the opera?'

'Yes sir,' Nesfield responded, 'but just in case we have someone reporting back from the opera house.'

'I assume they don't know who they're working for? After the Westley business I'm not sure your confidence is reassuring.' Nesfield looked suitably contrite but assured him the contact was entirely in the dark as to his real employer. 'Good. That's how I prefer it.' He saw Gabriella Clifford standing discreetly at the other end of the room. 'Now I need to meet with Gabriella about the hunt.' The two men left, and Gabriella edged around Morten as she replaced them. 'Is everything ready for Boxing Day, Gabriella?'

‘I think so, sir,’ she replied. ‘The catering is confirmed. I’ve stressed to Mr Gripper that Mr Zinchenko must have a sturdy and placid mount and he’s assured me he will.’ Terrence Gripper was the huntsman of the Danbury. Oleg Zinchenko was not renowned as a horseman. When he had gone riding with the Russian president, he famously fell off in front of the entire press corps. Zinchenko had to swallow his pride on that occasion but the same would not be true if this happened when his host was merely Elias Forth.

‘And Gripper has everything else arranged?’ Gabriella again assured him that was the case. She hadn’t been told the details of ‘everything else’ and would have been disgusted if she’d known that one of the arrangements was that several foxes had been trapped and caged and would be released during the hunt so that they could be ‘accidentally’ killed. ‘Good. When will Oleg arrive?’

‘His plane gets into Heathrow at three. Vladimir is meeting him.’

‘Thank you, Gabriella. I can always rely on your efficiency.’

Chapter 27

Oleg Zinchenko was a large man, perhaps six feet three tall and three hundred pounds. He had a bullet-like head with a short grey fuzz of hair and little in the way of a neck. He intimidated people in a far more direct way than Elias Forth. He had had to. To make his fortune in the aftermath of the fall of the Soviet Union he utilised every tool at his disposal, from clever financial deals to murder. He was not a man to be messed with, especially as he had continued to maintain his influence in Russia when so many others had fallen out of favour, or worse. At present he was content, though not exactly happy, to back Elias Forth. After all, the man had made him many hundreds of millions of pounds over the years.

'My dear Elias, but of course I have faith in your approach. When you first suggested that we might discover the greatest treasure of the last century I was a cynic. But you reassured me and even after the ah, disappointment last month, I remain committed to assisting in whatever way I can.'

'Thank you, Oleg. You said you would like Miss Prentiss to be here for your stay and I'm pleased that she is about to join us.'

'Ah, Elias, I did indeed.'

Carrie Prentiss had made her feelings regarding Zinchenko clear to Forth. She was repulsed by him and would not, under any circumstances, sleep with him. Forth had been forced to accede to her wishes. However, what he had done was supply Zinchenko with copies of certain videos depicting Carrie's sexual activities with other men. This served two functions. The first was to placate Zinchenko. The second was to provide him with a potential blackmail weapon should he wish to utilise it. Zinchenko had been highly approving and asked Forth to arrange a live performance.

Carrie had spent an enjoyable few days in the English countryside with a newspaper editor. He had been physically much more to her taste. She hadn't told Forth about her escapade and, after four days, the man had been flagging under Carrie's exacting demands, but he should now be extremely compliant in support of the anti-abortion legislation she had come in Britain to promote.

She greeted Zinchenko politely and he spent rather longer than required kissing her hand. Forth rang for tea to be served. Zinchenko was seduced by English tradition and formality. Forth's greatest coup with him had been two years previously when he had persuaded a member of the royal family to join him on holiday aboard Zinchenko's superyacht for a cruise in the Black Sea. Forth rose in Zinchenko's esteem, which was confirmed by the fact that the yacht now sported many photographs of the Russian and the royal. Forth and Carrie had also collaborated with Zinchenko in persuading Russian politicians not to support changing the country's controversial domestic violence laws. Russia is the only country in the Council of Europe that has no criminal statute on domestic violence, and even blatant examples are often punished by no more than a fine. In the last ten years over forty attempts have been made to pass legislation criminalising domestic violence, but all have fallen at the first hurdle, thanks in no small part to Zinchenko's behind the scenes manipulation. Carrie filled them in on her political, though not her wider, activities and both men expressed their satisfaction.

'And our other enterprise, Elias? Are you any further forward?'

'It's likely to take some time, Oleg. After all a find such as the one we are seeking has lain undiscovered for centuries.'

'Just so, but I am not prepared to wait forever. You know about Smolevski?'

Forth did know about Smolevski. Seven years ago, Dimitri Smolevski, an antiques dealer from Minsk, contacted Zinchenko saying he had discovered the whereabouts of the original Amber Room. Dubbed the eighth wonder of the world, the Amber Room was looted by the Nazis from the Catherine Palace near St Petersburg and, despite many attempts, has never been found. Smolevski extorted a significant sum from Zinchenko before his discovery was revealed to be yet another deception. His fate was said to have entailed a combination of several of the most gruesome forms of execution practised through history. What was certain was that pieces of Smolevski's body were sent to his friends and family to ensure they were fully cooperative in the future.

'We wouldn't want another failure by any of your colleagues,' Zinchenko added.

'Or, indeed by those who are not colleagues,' added Forth.

Zinchenko laughed and Carrie attempted a smile that failed. 'Come,' Zinchenko said, 'I wish to see your famous collection of paintings before dinner.'

Chapter 28

In Aldeburgh Anna strolled down the high street to the post office. A couple of days before she'd received a call from the porter at Merton College. 'A package has arrived here for you, Dr Carr. I thought it was unlikely you'd be calling in and Professor Strachan tells me you're away from Oxford.'

'Does it say where it's from?' Anna asked.

'New York, I think, there's a customs declaration on the front saying it contains a present, so I expect you'd like it for Christmas.'

'Thank you, Sims. Could you possibly forward it to the post office in Aldeburgh, Suffolk?'

Anna showed her ID and the postmistress handed over the package which was about forty centimetres square and quite light. She thought she knew what it might be, and this was confirmed when she got back to Summerland. It was a Share double dildo, but in purple. There was also a Christmas card from Tina. The card featured a bare-breasted woman wearing a Christmas hat and brandishing a small whip standing behind a second woman who was wearing reindeer antlers and bending over. Outside it said, 'This Christmas' and inside, 'Spank Me' with a message from Tina, '(don't) be good, have fun!' She wasn't sure she'd have that kind of fun over the holiday, but she was determined to enjoy it.

*

Christmas Day dawned bright and clear, and Anna was alone. She felt content. After a run, exercises, and a light breakfast she checked her messages. There were Christmas greetings from Anula, who said it was thirty degrees in Colombo, and thanked her again for her beautiful chain. Cloote and Rees sent theirs from Dallas and included pictures of the opera. The production was based on the famous Patrice Chereau version at Bayreuth in

1976 which set the action in the nineteenth century, concentrating on Wagner's critique of capitalism. It was subject to huge criticism from conservative critics but has since become regarded as one of the greatest opera productions of all time. Cloote said he hoped the Dallas version, whose director was the young African American Lottie Enderby, would prove equally controversial, especially for those who think the drama's essential meaning is fixed and hate re-interpretations of the 'master's' work.

She then got a call from Magnus who was overjoyed about his present. He was calling from Scotland where he'd gone to stay with an old friend who'd been a rock musician in the early seventies but was now a deputy lord lieutenant and lived in a rather grand, though smallish, castle. 'It's not exactly portable but it is wonderful,' was his comment on the massive Taschen volume, *The Ingmar Bergman Archives*, Anna had selected. He added that it was snowing there.

While he was on the phone Anna opened his present to her. It was a copy of *A Writer of Our Time: The Life and Work of John Berger* by Joshua Sperling. It was recently published, and she hadn't read it, even though she was a huge admirer of Berger. She thanked Magnus, who responded by saying, 'I'm glad you don't think he was just a "posh white bloke" anymore.' This was a reference to when he had introduced her to Berger during discussions on representation in early English art in a first-year tutorial. Anna had only vaguely heard of him and thought his TV series was akin to Kenneth Clark's *Civilisation*. Magnus said she couldn't be more wrong and that Berger's *Ways of Seeing* was the most influential TV series he'd ever seen. After watching it she had to agree, especially regarding the 'assumed male viewer' in Western art and Berger's argument that power, for men, is extrinsic whereas women are born into a confined space and the keeping of men.

'I'm still thinking about Johannes,' he said, 'and whether there was something in the manuscript we may have missed.'

'Me too,' Anna agreed, 'but I think that if we did, we won't discover it by over-thinking. I'm going to enjoy Oliver's library. I think he's set me some kind of test.'

'Sounds fun. Hope I'll see you in the new year.'

He rang off and Anna opened Anula's box. The first thing she found was a tee-shirt with the motto:

You think I'm weird because I'm different,
I think you're weird because you're all the same

Underneath was a box. The box contained a beautiful Garuda mask painted in natural colours, like the one she'd seen in Anula's flat. The huge eyes of the bird were split by a squirming cobra and adorned by a series of crowns, and two wings spread out from the face. Anna immediately texted Anula. She apologised for disappearing so quickly at the airport and said she thought her presents were wonderful. She hoped she was enjoying her holiday and promised to get in touch after Christmas. It was early evening in Colombo and Anula replied quickly saying she was at a party with her parents at the hospital where her father was a paediatrician. He had insisted on dressing up as Santa Claus to give out presents, which had confused some of the children.

Anna then opened the card Oliver had left. He said he and Gordon had two presents for her. The first was easier to find than the second and the clue to it was on the front of the card. Once she found this, it would contain a clue to the second 'present'.

Anna looked at the picture. The *Très Riches Heures du Duc de Berry* is probably the most famous example of French Gothic manuscript illumination. It is exactly contemporaneous with Henry V's Agincourt campaign and comprises over one hundred and thirty magnificent illustrations. The card was the picture for September featuring the Château de Saumur. There was no other clue, so Anna wondered if the answer was the month itself. On the second floor, Summerland had four bedrooms themed on the seasons. Taking the card with her she went to the 'Autumn' bedroom. Part of the wall decoration included a solar chariot very similar to the one depicted by the Limbourg brothers, the artists of the *Très Riches Heures.* The charioteer held a staff in his hand surmounted by a brilliant, golden sun. Anna followed the line of the staff which pointed to a cornice. Climbing onto a chair she thought she could make out a small gap between the moulding. She tried pulling it. Then pushed it. Finally, she tried twisting it. The corner piece turned easily, there was a click, and below her a panel popped open, revealing a hidden cupboard. It contained a large box and a folded paper.

The paper was in Oliver's handwriting:

> *I won't congratulate you on your find because I'm sure it didn't take you long. Here is your main present but I also want to show you that I have total trust in you. The other gift is one of access. To find it you need to solve my riddle, which has two parts.*
>
> *'I may be black but can't be red.'*
>
> *'You need my song and Ugolino's response.'*

She opened the box. Inside was another note, this time from Gordon:

> *If you're going to play that goddam music, then you better do it properly!*

The box contained a Naim Uniti Star, the Rolls Royce of all-in-one music systems. It would enable her to stream music in high-resolution, play or rip CDs and access radio stations across the world. *While they're away*, thought Anna, *I'll set it up in the library and turn it up to eleven.*

She then started thinking about Cloote's riddle. What kinds of things might be black or red? Paintings obviously, but then there was the clue in the second line. Who was Ugolino? It was an Italian name and the only one she could immediately think of was Ugolino della Gherardesca, a thirteenth-century Italian nobleman who features prominently in Dante's *Divine Comedy*. In that case was it a reference to Dante? *Which means 'red' is really 'read'?* she thought, and the library seemed the logical site for Cloote to have set his riddle.

She carried her Naim downstairs and spent some time setting it up and making the Wi-Fi connections. She thought she'd start with something loud and cheerful and chose 'Battle Metal' by the Finnish band Turisas. With the music blasting out, Anna found it easier to concentrate. She looked to see if there was a copy of the *Divine Comedy* in the library. There were three. Two were relatively modern translations but the third, in Cloote's locked rare books section, was an illustrated Italian edition from the sixteenth century. He had given Anna the key and access code for the rare books but after examining all three she couldn't see any link with the riddle, especially the 'I may be black' bit. *What else can be black? Sheep? Chess pieces? Magic? Yes, magic.* With Cloote's extensive collection of magical works that seemed a strong possibility and, if it was black magic, why couldn't it be read? *Because it's a book that doesn't really exist*, and Anna immediately thought she knew which book it was. She scanned the section and sure enough there were five copies on a high shelf that she needed the library steps to reach. The *Necronomicon* is a fictional grimoire, a book of magic, invented by the American horror writer HP Lovecraft. He refers to it in a number of his stories and it is supposed to contain an account of the 'Old Ones', ancient, all-powerful deities. The purported author of the *Necronomicon* was the 'Mad Arab' Abdul Alhazred.

Lovecraft never wrote an actual version of the book, though he did compose a brief pseudo-history, but, since his time, there have been several writers who have produced their own versions. These were the ones in Cloote's library: the 1973 Owlswick Press version, the *Simon Necronomicon*, which is the best known; George Hay's 1978 'translation' from a copy supposedly owned by the Elizabethan philosopher-scientist John Dee, and the 2004 version by Donald Tyson. The fifth copy was, though, the most interesting. It was in a black calf binding with *Necronomicon per Abdul Alhazred* in gold lettering down the spine. She tried to pull the book down but instead of sliding from the shelf it tilted forward in her hand and she heard a low swoosh. When she looked down, the panel she thought was hiding a radiator – there were similar grills all round the house – had slid into the wall to reveal what appeared to be the door of a large safe about a metre high and a metre and a half wide.

Anna got down to examine it. There was a blank glass panel to the left with a digital keypad on the right. *Do you need both for it to open I wonder? If Oliver really wanted me to get inside, I must be able to do it.* She held her right hand against the panel. Sure enough there was a small buzz, and a green light went on underneath. *That was easy,* thought Anna, *but the combination must be in the second clue.*

What song refers to the Necronomicon? She didn't know, and it was a long time since she'd read Lovecraft's works, though they had been among her favourites when she was at school. A quick look online gave her the answers. In his supposed history Lovecraft says the book was originally called *Al Azif* in Arabic, which Lovecraft said was a 'nocturnal sound (made by insects) supposed to be the howling of demons.' This, in turn, linked to the Gothic novel *Vathek* which alludes to Biblical references to Beelzebub, the 'Lord of the Flies', and to Psalm 91:5. Though modern translations render the key phrase of this verse as 'terror by night' earlier versions, such as Myles Coverdale's 1535 translation, use the words 'bugges by night'.

Thank you, Wikipedia, thought Anna. *So, we possibly have a 9, a 1 and a 5. In that case Ugolino must refer to Pope Gregory IX, born Ugolino di Conti. He supposedly banned the Necronomicon in 1232.'* She tried keying in 9, 1, 5, 1, 2. There was a buzz, and a red light came one. *Too many numbers,* she thought. *It's probably just a PIN so four numbers. What if you add 915 and 1,232?* She punched 2147 into the keypad and there was another buzz and a second green light. The door swung open and a light inside the safe came on. The shelves were full of objects, most of them with a magical connotation. There were goblets, amulets and even two human skulls, one of them on a silver mount. She looked at the inscription. It was in French, which translated as:

> *Skull captured from the royal palace of Abomey by Alfred Amédée Dodds, 17 November 1892. The head is said to be that of a prisoner beheaded by Nansica in 1889.*

Anna had heard about the warrior women of Dahomey. They had been a formidable military force and had fought to the last against the immensely better armed French. Nansica was among the most famous of them. Her story comes from the diary of Jean Bayol, a French naval officer who saw the teenage Nansica behead a young prisoner. Bayol recounted how she:

Walked jauntily up to the prisoner, swung her sword three times with both hands, then calmly cut the last flesh that attached the head to the trunk ... She then squeezed the blood off her weapon and swallowed it.

Anna was rather daunted to be holding such a gruesome trophy. There was also a small, black bladed knife about seven inches long with a handle carved in green stone. She recognised this as a tecpatl, the knife used for human sacrifice by the Aztecs.

By far the largest object in the cupboard was a kind of staff nearly two metres long. It was made partly from metal and partly from wood. At the top was an elaborate gold coloured knob decorated with coloured glass or, perhaps, precious stones. This was surmounted by a clear crystal globe about ten centimetres in diameter. Slightly below halfway was another gold band which could be used to hold the staff and, just above this, a basket-like structure where a few strands bent outwards from the main staff and then came together again fifteen centimetres nearer the top where they were bound by another gold band. Anna immediately knew this was a seiðrstafr that would have been used by a Norse völva or sorceress and played a central role in their rituals. There are even suggestions that the vǫlur rode their staffs, like the witches of popular literature, or employed them in symbolic masturbatory rituals. Whether true or not, it is clear from Norse writings that the vǫlur were regarded as sexually dangerous.

Anna took a closer look at the staff. She'd seen seiðrstafr in museums before and had even been allowed to handle one when she was in Denmark. From what she could see, this was a genuine Viking-Age object. It had, however, some curious elements. The wooden parts must have been restored at some point, but from the look of them they were still very old. Then there was the crystal globe at the top. She had never heard that Viking staffs ever had this addition. The other was, that when she looked very closely at the gold band above the basket, she could make out a glyph.

It was not a Viking-Age rune. It comprised a combination of symbols. There was the symbol for Venus, the universal sign for women, with a dot in the centre of the circle. The circle was cut at the top by a crescent moon and, at the bottom, either side of the stem, were two upward curving semi-circles. Anna's heart skipped a beat. This was the 'Monas Hieroglphica', the esoteric symbol invented by John Dee. In his book on the topic, Dee explained that the glyph embodied his vision of the unity of the Cosmos, combining the symbols for the moon, the sun, the elements, and fire. Today, Dee is thought of as a magician or occultist but he, and his fellow Tudors, wouldn't have recognised the difference between this and what we would think of as science. The two were inextricably interlinked and Dee's attempts to commune with angels would not have seemed at odds with his advanced concepts on mathematics. The connection to Dee also explained the ball. *It must be a scrying stone*, thought Anna, a means of detecting messages or visions and foretelling the future or, indeed, attempting to communicate with angels.

Anna wondered if the glyph, and indeed the staff itself, was authentic but knew how seriously Cloote took all of this. She had a very open mind about the use of sorcery and magic, especially in a historical context. It was certain that Vikings would have thought along similar lines to John Dee but would have conceived the division of the world into the 'physical' and the 'spiritual' as even less distinct than the Elizabethans. They would have believed in the existence of their gods in the same way that they 'believed' in the mountains or the sea.

She put all the objects back in the safe and re-secured it. She'd have to do some more research and thinking on the genuineness of John Dee's seiðrstafr.

*

That evening Anna was feeling in party mood. She turned her new Naim up to an impressive volume; it really was an advantage having no close neighbours. A varied selection of thrash, progressive, and folk metal blasted the walls of Cloote's library. She treated herself to a half bottle of his champagne as she grazed on her own buffet. She even felt like dancing, Anna was much more at ease dancing on her own than in company. She stripped off to her underwear and as the music played cavorted round the library.

On the *Spirit of Freedom* Harry Spall was keeping watch on the house. Anna hadn't drawn the curtains and so was clearly visible. Her antics kept him glued to his binoculars even though he was disappointed that she didn't strip entirely. He wondered if this should form part of his report to Nesfield, decided it didn't, and so finished his evening watching porn. He searched for 'small, hairy, goth' and masturbated.

After wearing herself out, Anna settled down to watch some television. She found that *Night of the Demon*, Jacques Tourneur's 1957 version of the MR James story 'Casting the Runes', was on. Despite a rather 'clunky' demon that appeared near the end, against Tourneur's wishes, she thought the film captured James's ominous sense of impending dread rather well.

That night her vivid dreams returned. She was standing on a cliff top dressed in just a light shift. The blue-cloaked woman who had appeared before returned. She was again carrying a seiðrstafr like the one she had just seen in Cloote's safe, but this had an elongated and rounded top. The woman drove the staff into the ground at an angle in front of Anna who took off her shift and allowed herself to be penetrated by it. She felt warm and was reaching a climax when suddenly she was on her back on the ground being penetrated by a man. She couldn't see his face, which was hooded. As he raped her, she felt colder and colder until he ejaculated, and her entire body froze. She awoke in a sweat, gasping for breath. She switched on the light and found she'd upset a glass of water over herself which partially, but not entirely, explained her nightmare.

Chapter 29

The hunt was assembling outside Satterthwaite Park at the Danbury Arms, for its Boxing Day meet, one of around two hundred that still occur that day, despite hunting foxes with dogs having been illegal since 2004. The Danbury was one of the best-known packs in the country and, since Forth became master, had gained a reputation for less than scrupulous adherence to the law which ensured it attracted the attention of many hunt saboteurs. Despite Forth's attempts to remove rights of way across his land, using both legal and illegal means, he had been frustrated, and public footpaths crossed the park in several places. Forth was employing additional 'security' personnel to keep the saboteurs in check, and Nesfield had been issued with instructions to ensure any who strayed onto private land were to be harshly dealt with.

An aspect of the Danbury that Forth prided himself on was their hunt livery. Forth favoured traditional hunting 'pink', purple facings and 'EF' monogrammed buttons, to emphasise the Danbury was his personal property. This garish attire was being sported by the members of the hunt, most of whom were Forth's wealthy acquaintances and clients from London and abroad. Neither the huntsman nor the field master, farmer Nigel Crewes, one of Forth's neighbours, welcomed this arrangement. 'Can't bloody ride, can't bloody jump, can't bloody do anything,' was Gripper's summary of their abilities. Crewes agreed and said he'd mentioned to Forth that several of them would do better to follow the hunt on foot, but he'd been rebuffed.

'Keep those bloody dogs away!' Forth shouted and Gripper manoeuvred the hounds away from the master. Despite being a keen huntsman Elias Forth had a morbid fear of canines which went back to his childhood. He hated animals of all kinds, believing they were for humans to inflict pain and suffering on. But it was dogs he loathed most of all. It was something about their naïve loyalty. His parents had tried to cure him of his phobia by buying him a puppy when he was seven. Forth hated the animal even though the puppy wanted to make friends with him. One day his parents let him take it for a walk. When he got back, he told them it had run away when he'd let it off its lead. They were suspicious enough not to buy him a replacement and their suspicions were justified. Forth had taken the puppy into the woods, strangled it and buried the body.

The hunt followers were also gathering while 'security' tried to keep the saboteurs, who included Nora Greenwood and Nils Aaronson, at a distance. Nils had flown back to England just before Christmas, when a new crew took over the *Esperanza.* Despite being British, Nora knew nothing about hunting. The fact that they killed foxes in a horrific way was enough to make her oppose it. Nils was far more knowledgeable, and he explained the various groups to her. He pointed out the master, the huntsman, and the field master.

'Who's dem mans?' she asked.

'They're the followers, the supporters who follow the hunt. And those ones,' he pointed at a group who seemed all to be men in flat caps, 'are the foot followers. They're mainly locals and are easily the most knowledgeable about the hunt country and the habits of foxes, much more so than any of the huntsmen. But they're too poor to be part of the hunt. The others are the car supporters who will be from further away.' The hunt began to move off to the first 'covert' to be 'drawn', huntsman and hounds leading, followed by the master and the field, that included a very awkward looking Oleg Zinchenko sitting precariously on a horse that looked several sizes too small for him.

Nora and Nils followed the others. The saboteurs had already scouted out several likely coverts where they found many blocked earths to stop the foxes escaping if terriers were put in to flush them out.

Forth planned the hunt like a military campaign, complete with false trails and ruses to confuse the opposition. He even had a second pack of hounds concealed in a wood that, he hoped, would lead the saboteurs away from the actual foxes his huntsman had deliberately released. This worked to some extent. Many of the saboteurs followed the false trail but others, including Nora and Nils, spotted the main field emerging from the wood and heading towards their pre-prepared covert. At this point Forth's second plan swung into action. A group of Nesfield's men arrived in Range Rovers. They were dressed identically, combat fatigues with black balaclavas and face masks, making identification virtually impossible. As the saboteurs tried to force their way towards the hunt their path was blocked. One of them attempted to reason with the guards, 'It's a public footpath and anyone is at liberty to use it!' There was no response other than for the line of security men to draw short heavy coshes.

'Get the cameras on them!' someone shouted. He was immediately coshed.

'Bastards!' yelled Nora, but they had turned their attention to a man with a video camera and a girl using her camera phone. The first was punched in the face and had his arm smashed by a cosh. The girl was grabbed by the hair and dragged into a field. As others tried to reach her, they were prevented.

'God knows what they're doing,' Nils cried. He got out his phone to call the police but found there was no signal. Forth's men were using blocking devices. The remaining saboteurs were totally outnumbered and were helpless if the guards attacked them.

Nesfield barked out orders and his men formed a line. They started walking towards the small remaining group of saboteurs, slapping their truncheons onto their hands. The saboteurs backed away. They were forced into a narrow lane which ran in a cutting and whose banks were surmounted by thick hedges. They turned a corner, but their escape was blocked. Several huge, round straw bales had been deposited in the road. There was no escape. Nesfield's men were well trained, so it meant no one was killed. Two broken arms, two broken collar bones and a broken ankle were the worst injuries but every one of the saboteurs got a beating. Nora and Nils were among the luckier ones, and both helped more badly injured friends. Finally, Nesfield got a call on his field radio, and he ordered the men to return to their cars.

The bleeding and battered group of saboteurs limped their way back towards the village. At no point did they see any police, despite the Hunt Saboteurs Association having informed them that trouble was likely from privately hired security. This was because the regional police and crime commissioner was a friend of Elias Forth and received preferential investment rates in Elias Capital Investment's products.

Back in the pre-prepared covert the incompetence of the hunters themselves didn't prevent three of the four foxes being ripped to pieces. Of course, when the participants discussed this later, they didn't use such a vulgar word as 'killed'. The foxes had been 'bowled' or 'rolled over', 'accounted for', 'brought to book', or 'broken up'.

Forth was pleased with the outcome. Both 'Charlie', the hunter's name for the fox after the Whig politician Charles James Fox, and the 'antis', the saboteurs, had got what was coming to them. Oleg Zinchenko had been 'blooded' and seemed happy as he'd only fallen off his horse once.

They trotted back towards the Hall as the followers dispersed and the terrier men retrieved their dogs. Their leader, Kevin Tippler, was especially pleased with himself. He'd been singled out for praise by Forth and received a fat wadge of banknotes from him. Tippler doffed his cap and Forth told him to report to Nesfield at the Hall as he might have a job for him. As Tippler found it hard to hold down a permanent job, he usually got into an argument and often a fight, this sounded too good to be true. His good mood continued through his evening's drinking which came as a relief to his wife, Maureen, as it meant he didn't beat her that night.

*

Back at Satterthwaite Hall, Morten was thinking about their quest for King John's treasure. Forth tried to recruit Clinton Westley to their side immediately after Gervase Penhaligon had alerted them to his discovery of the Gothic manuscript. Westley, however, had proved far more problematic than Penhaligon, whose weakness for gambling had placed him at Forth's mercy. Westley had gone missing for over two weeks, and they had only tracked him down at the last minute. If cooperation was impossible then silencing him was the only option.

The security guard had been simple bad luck. A few more

seconds and Morten would have been out of the building. He'd timed Arbuthnot's visits to Duke Humfrey's Library and that was the first time he'd gone there at that point in the evening.

Morten was also not confident in Penhaligon's abilities. True, he came with impeccable academic credentials as the foremost authority on English manuscripts of the twelfth and thirteenth centuries, but Morten's own research suggested he was better at finding well-written obscure theses and papers by junior academics, adapting them, and passing them off as his own work. Morten wasn't even sure that their quest lay in the thirteenth century at all. There were tantalising glimpses that it could lead much further back in time.

If so, Morten felt more than assured by his own knowledge. Though some of the stories about his past were pure fantasy, a few hinted at the truth. In the 1980s he had studied pre-Germanic paganism. More than anyone, he had been influenced by the work of Otto Höfler, with whom he had studied privately in Vienna. Höfler's thesis, 'Kultische Geheimbünde der Germanen', 'Secret Cultic Societies of the Germanic Peoples', became a favourite of Heinrich Himmler's and Höfler became a very active collaborator in Himmler's *Ahnenerbe*. This was an SS think tank devoted to promoting Hitler's racial doctrines, specifically by supporting the idea that modern Germans were descended from an ancient, biologically superior Aryan race. After 1933, the Nazis created eight new professorships in Germanic pre-history and their funding for archaeology was the highest in the world. This included the study of seiðr under the auspices of Höfler. In 1937 Höfler joined the Nazi Party and, in 1943, was appointed head of the Wissenschaftliche Institut in Copenhagen, following the German conquest of Denmark. After the war Höfler escaped serious charges but, as an ex-Nazi, his ideas disappeared from the academic map, despite many of them being based on sound research. Regarding Nordic sorcery, he demonstrated how it formed part of the total social context, an idea scholars didn't return to for another forty years. For this reason, Morten also recognised that Anna Carr may be as dangerous as her patron Cloote, possibly more so. Forth may be sceptical, but he would be keeping an open mind. His visit to the Morgan Library still convinced him that there were unsolved clues in the bestiary of Johannes of Medhamstead.

He could hear the hunters coming up the driveway. It was clear that many of them were already the worse for drink. Morten had no wish to meet any of them and he never drank alcohol. His comrades in the army had always made fun of him, behind his back, never to his face. Because of this, and the fact he never joined their visits to local prostitutes, they called him 'the monk'.

As he got up to go to his room Carrie Prentiss came in. She refused to take part in the hunt, not through any opposition to slaughtering wild animals, but because it could be cold and wet and might be detrimental to her appearance. The two of them exchanged polite but terse greetings. Morten mused on how very different Elias Forth's underlings were, though he did not include himself in that category. He was no one's underling. If Forth had realised quite how independent Morten really was, he would have been extremely disturbed. Morten smiled to himself as he climbed the rear, servant's, staircase.

Chapter 30

Anna spent the next week exploring the library, ignoring the new year, which was never one of her favourite events. She paid special attention to the books on magic to discover more about Cloote's fascination with the subject, and the objects in his secret safe. She looked at early texts including Richard Boulton's *A Compleat History of Magick, Sorcery, and Witchcraft*, from 1715, and John Campbell Colquhoun's 1851 publication *An History of Magic, Witchcraft, and Animal Magnetism*. She also consulted more recent authorities such as Hans Sebald, Jeffrey Russell, and Ronald Hutton as well as several of the publications in the Palgrave *Historical Studies in Witchcraft and Magic* series. This updated her knowledge of a topic she already had more than a passing acquaintance with. She smiled that she didn't need to re-read Melissa Winn's *Golems and Anthropomorphism in the Middle Ages*. She'd received a personally dedicated copy after their encounter at the New York conference. Nowhere, either in the literature or in detailed online searches, could she find a reference to John Dee ever having owned a seiðrstafr. She became more convinced it was a fake.

She let Cloote know she'd found her way into his safe with a cryptic message:

Love has been crafted and D was as easy as A, B, C.

He replied that he thought it would be, that Gordon was getting fed up with wall-to-wall Wagner but brightened up on opening night when a fight nearly broke out in the audience between the traditionalists, who hated the production, and the progressives who loved it. 'It was *Tannhäuser* all over again!' he purred, referring to the performances of that opera in Paris in 1861, which were accompanied by rioting in the audience. Anula also let Anna know that she would be coming back to England the day after Oliver and Gordon. She sent a picture of herself with her parents. She was wearing the Viking chain.

The weather had been foul over the past few days, with strong winds and heavy rain, which restricted Anna's outdoor training and runs. Finally, on the Thursday, the weather changed for the better. There was still a stiff breeze, but the rain had relented. In mid-morning Anna went for the longest run she'd been on since before the holiday. She thought she'd avoid the muddier spots along the river and so headed along the coast to Thorpeness and back via the old railway line. She turned up Leiston Road and left past the 'Red House', where Benjamin Britten and Peter Pears had lived, and which is now a museum and study centre.

As she was jogging back along Linden Road towards the end of the run, she spotted a large tabby cat sitting on the path in front of her. In the way that cats often do, it entirely ignored the human running towards it and instead stuck a leg in the air and began to lick its privates. Anna could only smile but then she stopped dead in her tracks. The cat licking its balls had reminded her of something.

Johannes's text depicted several beavers, but they didn't appear to form part of the code. Beavers' testicles were much valued in the Middle Ages for medicine and their Latin name is castor, due to the unusual way in which the animal supposedly avoided being caught. When she got back to the house she hurried to the library. In *The Journey Through Wales*, by the twelfth-century chronicler Giraldus Cambrensis, she found the description she'd remembered:

> *When the beaver finds he cannot save himself from the pursuit of the dogs who follow him he throws away that, which by natural instinct he knows to be the object sought for, and in the sight of the hunter castrates himself, from which circumstance he has gained the name of Castor; and if by chance the dogs should chase an animal which had been previously castrated, he has the sagacity to run to an elevated spot, and there lifting up his leg, shews the hunter that the object of his pursuit is gone.*

The moral this, entirely fictitious, behaviour demonstrates is that if a man wishes to live chastely then he must cut off his vices and throw them into the face of the devil.

As she thought more about the depictions of the beaver, she also remembered other animals they had previously disregarded. She looked at Inkpen's digitised images and sure enough next to each beaver portrait was one of a partridge. Medieval scholars explained that the partridge stole the eggs of other birds but, as soon as the young birds heard the voice of their true mother, they flew to her. Both male and female partridges were also considered sexually promiscuous. Males were sometimes supposed to have intercourse with each other, whereas females were so lustful that wind blowing from a male could impregnate them. The allegory here was that the partridge's actions were like the devil, who steals souls. But when sinners recognise God as their true parent, they return to Him.

The depiction of both animals was surely an indication that the 'King John' trail was a false one, but the full meaning, especially of the partridge, was still unclear to her. What she also now saw in the Bodleian manuscript was that each time the beaver and partridge appeared so did the boar. They had taken the boar's appearance as proof of the link between the Gothic text, Hildisvíni and Swineshead. But what if it had another meaning? As it appeared after the code for what now seemed to be 'this trail is fake' was it an indication that there was another trail to follow, linked to the boar Hildisvíni, that was a real one?

Anna looked at her phone. Even if she'd wanted to, and felt it was safe, it was now too late to contact Cloote and Rees. She checked their flight information and sure enough it had taken off about half an hour ago. Instead, she sent a text to Magnus. He had just got back to Oxford. His reply surprised her:

Thought the same. Never liked King John idea much. Your geography was wrong too. Let's talk on WhatsApp.

She did and immediately felt a complete idiot. 'How do you mean my geography?'

'What did the Gothic manuscript say? It identified a church of the East Angles. Where is Swineshead?'

'Oh God, how could we have been so thick!'

'Exactly. Throughout the period it was in Mercia. I didn't say anything at the time as you were so certain all the other clues fitted.'

'And what about there being another set of clues?'

'I'd say it's highly possible. But I'm sure they won't be as straightforward as the first.'

'Where do we start?'

'Not sure. You and I need to compare notes, but speak to Cloote first, he might have more ideas than us.'

A few minutes after she'd spoken to Magnus, Anna got another call, this time from Rasmus Kask. 'Anna? Hi. I've only just got back from Tallinn and seen what happened at the abbey. Are you all okay?' Anna assured him they were but also warned him that he too should take care, just in case Penhaligon was linked with what they were doing. 'But that's why I'm calling,' Rasmus replied. 'He definitely is. It was when I saw the photograph of the American professor. I saw Penhaligon speaking with him in Cambridge back in the summer.'

'You're sure it was him?'

'Absolutely positive. Do you think I should tell the police?'

'That's up to you, Rasmus. You don't know what they were talking about I suppose? Where did you see them?'

'It was in the Eagle. I didn't think anything of it at the time, but now I think back, when Penhaligon saw me, he did look apprehensive.'

'If he saw you that's even more reason to be careful,' said Anna, thinking that Penhaligon's failure to mention his meeting with Westley was deeply suspicious.

'Don't worry, my father taught me a lot about how to evade surveillance,' he replied. Anna remembered Rasmus's father had been a prominent member of the opposition to the Soviet Union.

'Well, be careful. And thank you.'

Rasmus glowed a little as he couldn't remember Anna ever thanking anyone.

*

That evening Cloote and Rees got back to Aldeburgh. Despite jet lag both wanted to talk as soon as Anna updated them on her discussions with Magnus and Rasmus. 'Do you think we're missing something?' Anna asked.

'After the East Angles debacle anything's possible,' Cloote replied.

'What if there really is something missing?' Gordon mused. The others looked at him. 'I mean how do we know that Inkpen's photographs cover all of the missing pages of the Bodleian manuscript?'

'That's a very good point,' Cloote said. 'We don't. If our adversaries have more, they could be several steps ahead of us.'

'The only way we'd be able to find out would be to talk to Inkpen himself,' said Anna.

'Assuming he's still alive,' said Cloote.

'Which Penhaligon didn't think likely,' added Rees.

Anna agreed that her best bet was to return to Oxford to see if she could find out anything about where Inkpen might be. She tried a different line of thinking. 'How important do you think the Hildisvini reference is?'

'It looks like it's more important than we first thought, but not for the original reason,' said Cloote.

'If it's not connected to a place what else could it be?' asked Rees.

'Well, Hildisvini was a shape shifter so it might be connected to that,' Anna suggested.

'Which could just be another reference to things not being what they seem,' added Cloote.

After a couple more hours circling the problem Cloote and Rees were too tired to think any more and went to bed. Anna looked up what she could find on Roger Inkpen online, which wasn't much. At least she hadn't found an obituary, which was something.

*

At Satterthwaite Hall Elias Forth was looking back on a highly successful holiday. Oleg Zinchenko had returned to Russia, satisfied at what was being done on the Bodleian trail and more than satisfied with the 'entertainment' Forth had laid on for him. The same could not be said for the young women who had provided it. He was just preparing to turn in when an excited Nesfield burst into the study. 'Don't do that again,' Forth barked. 'Knock.'

'Very sorry, sir, but I've just had Professor Penhaligon on the line.' Penhaligon didn't have Forth's direct number. 'He says he's made a breakthrough.' Nesfield glanced at his phone and played back the recording:

'You see it was a colleague of mine. He's an expert on the famous fourteenth century theologian Meister Eckhart von Hochheim. He's discovered an early paper in the Vatican secret archive where Eckhart talks about an old man he once knew in Paris. He calls him Johannes of Sorø, but I think it might be *our* Johannes. Anyway, I must go to Rome to find out. I'll be in touch when I know more.'

Forth consulted *Wikipedia*, having no idea who Meister Eckhart was. It told him that since the nineteenth century he has acquired a status as a great mystic in popular spirituality within the medieval scholastic and philosophical tradition. 'We'll see if it leads to anything,' Forth concluded, thinking that Penhaligon might just be about to be worth the considerable amount of money he'd provided to clear his gambling debts. If he proved a dud, he could always get his former creditors to do him a favour.

Chapter 31

On Tuesday when Anula got back from Sri Lanka, she texted Anna. She said she wasn't due at the hospital until Friday, and, allowing a day for the jet lag to wear off, would she like a day in the countryside on Thursday? Anna did and they arranged for Anula to pick her up from Summerland at ten. Anna thought a break from thinking about the Bodleian text would do her good.

Her visit gave Cloote the chance to give Anula the full tour of the house. 'I don't think I've ever seen a house in this country that's so wonderful,' was her verdict. They also told her that the trail they'd been on might not be quite as dead as Westley was.

'But if the clues aren't linked to King John, what do they mean?' she asked.

'A very good question,' replied Cloote. 'We don't know unless there's another hidden code in Johannes's text.'

The day was crisp and clear, and they drove to Rendlesham forest and went for a long run and a more leisurely stroll taking in the 'UFO trail' that referenced the UK's most famous sighting of extra-terrestrials, in December 1980. Anula was strongly in the 'sceptical' camp explaining that, as a scientist, she doubted the Earth had ever been visited by creatures from another world. 'If you think about it, our planet is four and a half billion years old and we're still nowhere near developing inter-planetary travel. Even though the universe is about fourteen billion years old, I doubt even the most advanced civilisations that exist have done so either. Perhaps in a few more billion years?'

After their hike they went back to Anula's flat for something to eat and Anna checked her phone, the reception in Rendlesham was very poor. 'Probably the alien influence,' she joked. There were messages from Rasmus and then from Magnus. Anna called Rasmus first. He was eager to tell her what had happened, but Anna quickly stopped him and said they should speak over WhatsApp rather than on the phone. When she finally got him to calm down, he explained.

'I kept an eye on the professor like you said. It wasn't hard, my desk is outside his office. I noticed he's been studying a medieval manuscript a lot. It looks very much like the one Magnus described to me.' Anna frowned. She wasn't sure it was a good idea for Magnus to have told him about Johannes's papers. 'Anyway, I told Magnus what I'd seen, and he got quite excited when I mentioned Penhaligon had been studying some pages that had musical notation on them.' This really was important news. If these pages were from the Bodleian manuscript, they were ones they'd not seen, perhaps Inkpen hadn't photographed them all.

'Go on,' said Anna. 'What else could you see on the pages?'

'Not much more I'm afraid. I didn't have time to copy anything. But there are two other bits of news. The first is what he's been looking at in the library. I've got a friend there and asked him if he'd mind letting me know what Penhaligon had been reading. He's been looking at a lot of stuff from the ninth century, which isn't his usual period at all. My friend also said Penhaligon had mentioned Sorø Abbey to him.'

'Interesting,' replied Anna, who was thinking the potential new lead could take things back to the 800s. Though whether the abbey was a lead or not she wasn't so sure, as it hadn't been founded until the 1140s.

'And now he's gone to Rome,' Rasmus added.

'Do you know where and what for?'

'Not entirely. I know he's gone to research in the Vatican Library and Archives. But I don't know what for.'

'That's pretty good,' said Anna. 'Thanks for everything. If you can find out more let us know.' She then got on to Magnus. 'Well, what do you think?' she asked.

'I'd say he has an additional lead from pages of the Bodleian text we've not seen, and he's gone to Rome to check them out.'

'And it could have some connection with the ninth century?'

'Yes,' Magnus sounded a little doubtful, 'but there's not much about that period in the Vatican, especially about England. But the music could explain something else.'

'What's that?'

‘The swan and the nightingale,’ Magnus replied. ‘You remember they were drawn especially carefully. It might indicate that music is important.’

Anna agreed but said they had better wait and see if Rasmus could find out anything more. ‘In the meantime, I’ll talk to Cloote and think about what Penhaligon could be on to.’ She rang off.

‘It’s all rather exciting,’ Anula said, but then realised that was a poor choice of words as two people were dead. ‘Well, maybe, not exactly exciting,’ but she couldn’t think of another word for it.

‘That’s okay,’ Anna said. ‘Please just be careful. Keep an eye open for anything unusual and tell me straight away. I *really* don’t want anything to happen to you.’ Anula could see that she was deadly serious and promised to do just that.

They drove back to Aldeburgh and Anna brought Gordon and Oliver up to speed with Rasmus’s story. ‘I agree with Magnus,’ said Cloote after careful consideration. He thought about the possibility of one of them going to Rome to try to see what Penhaligon was up to, but quickly dismissed the idea as having too little chance of success. Instead, he said, ‘There’s a tentative link but we don’t have enough to go on yet. Annoying as it is, we just have to sit tight for a while.’

*

Two days later Gervase Penhaligon contacted Elias Forth. As Forth had little historical knowledge it was Morten who spoke with the Cambridge don. ‘So, my dear professor, what exactly have you discovered?’

‘I was right,’ Penhaligon was bubbling with enthusiasm, he was sure his reward from Forth would be substantial. ‘There *is* a link between Johannes of Medhamstead and Meister Eckert!’

‘And it is?’ Morten was unctuously solicitous.

‘It’s in these newly discovered papers. There’s no doubt they were written by Eckhart of Hochheim. He met Johannes when Eckhart was a young man at the University of Paris in the early 1280s. Johannes was very old by then, but a highly respected scholar. Eckhart tells of his background and his previous life; he calls him Johannes of Sorø. Now Sorø was, at that time, the richest and most important monastery in Denmark, so it looks as if Johannes was originally from Denmark. The real clincher is that Eckhart hints, though doesn't say outright, that one thing Johannes told him was that he had laid a false trail to deflect discovery of a major treasure.'

'And he definitely says that?' barked Morten, all trace of unction gone. 'He says the false trail was to divert attention from a real trail?'

'Yes, he says exactly that, "deflectere operam".' replied Penhaligon. 'The unfortunate thing is that Eckhart was not the slightest bit interested in whatever this "treasure" was. He was concerned with their theological discussion.'

'So, there's nothing to help us identify the nature of this alternative treasure?'

'No. Other than the fact that in their debate on religion Eckhart refers more than once to Johannes having some heretical opinions on the old religion of the North. Perhaps a reference to his Viking origins.'

Morten was already mulling over the implications of Penhaligon's revelations. 'Will you be staying in Rome much longer?' he asked.

'A few more days just to be sure there's nothing else to find in the papers.'

'And you don't think anyone else has picked up on this?'

'No, no. no. The only other person who's looked at these papers is Lemaître, the Parisian chap who found them. Of course, they'll soon have Eckhart scholars crawling all over them, but I doubt if they'll be interested in the Johannes connection.'

'Listen carefully, Penhaligon,' Morten said slowly. 'You will ensure that they do not. Make a full transcription and obtain photographs. Then you must have an accident.'

'An accident? I don't understand.'

'Yes, something that will destroy those pages.'

'But, but that's impossible. It's the Vatican Apostolic Archive! They watch you like hawks and besides ...'

'Penhaligon,' interrupted Morten, 'you *will* ensure they are destroyed. If you do not Mr Forth will be most displeased, and *I* will be even more displeased.' Gervase Penhaligon shivered. He was afraid of Forth, but Morten gave him nightmares. Hesitatingly he answered that he would ensure the pages were destroyed.

*

Almost simultaneously Rasmus and Magnus phoned Anna. 'Have you heard what happened in Rome yesterday?' asked Magnus, who got through to her first.

She was sitting in the library with Cloote when the call came through so put him on speaker. 'Sorry no. What?'

'Rasmus sent me the link to the Rome newspaper. I'll try to translate it. The heading is: "Fire in Vatican Archive". It goes on to explain that an English professor, they call him Pelligan, had stupidly left a box of vesta matches in his pocket when he visited the archive. He fell against a table and the matches set fire to his pocket which then caught two pages of a manuscript alight.'

'It sounds ridiculous,' Cloote responded. 'Who uses vestas these days?'

'I agree,' said Magnus, 'and Rasmus told me that Penhaligon has never smoked in his life.'

'He's destroying the evidence,' Anna concluded, with which the others immediately agreed. 'It means we'll never find out what he looked at unless Rasmus can find a way.'

She then spoke to Rasmus, who said Penhaligon was expected back tomorrow. 'The department's abuzz with the story and can't believe how stupid Penhaligon has been. Obviously, the police and Vatican officials have questioned him extensively. He's been incredibly apologetic, offered compensation and everything and it seems they've got no option but to accept it as an unlikely accident. They've no reason to think that an eminent scholar would deliberately burn a manuscript.'

We can though, thought Anna.

A few more days passed before she spoke with Rasmus again. 'I've kept a close eye on Penhaligon since his return. He seems remarkably cheerful for a man who's just caused an international incident and destroyed part of a unique manuscript. He's even been whistling in his study, which he hadn't done for a long time.' Rasmus also told Anna that Penhaligon had redoubled his interest in the period of the ninth century.

'Anything else?' Anna enquired.

'Only the music stuff I told Magnus.'

'What music?'

'He had those pages up again on his screen and I got a quick photo on my phone. I'll send it to you. I'm afraid it's not terribly clear but Magnus thought it could be important.'

As Rasmus had said, the screenshot wasn't very clear. Anna's knowledge of medieval musical notation was not great, but Cloote was more knowledgeable. 'Yes, they certainly look like twelfth or thirteenth century neumes.' He explained that neumes were the basic element of Western musical notation prior to the invention of the five-line staff. By the thirteenth century, the neumes were usually written in square notation, with four lines and three spaces, and a clef marker, which is what these seemed to be.

'Do they have anything to do with the codes though?' asked Rees. Neither of them could tell. The new pages might have no connection whatsoever. The *Codex Johannem Regem* was a long document that covered many subjects. It was just another clue they'd have to park for now.

Chapter 32

Two weeks passed with nothing of consequence reported by Rasmus. Penhaligon was spending a lot of time in various libraries in Cambridge and Rasmus also thought he was getting more anxious again. 'When he got back from Rome he seemed exhilarated, but now he looks quite depressed,' was his summary. 'He also seems to be going back more to his usual line of study too,' Rasmus added. 'Looking at stuff about the German theologian Meister Eckhart.'

Anna and Anula continued to go for runs and train together whenever they could, though Anula had a busy new year schedule of operations to perform. It did mean that she had more convalescent patients at Aldeburgh Cottage Hospital, and she popped into Summerland quite frequently. Cloote was getting rather fond of her and suggested to Anna that he thought her friend was a 'very intelligent young woman'.

Her response was not quite what he was expecting. 'You patronising shit. Of course she's intelligent, she's a fucking orthopaedic surgeon!' she emphasised, stormed off to her room and didn't calm down until Oliver went up to apologise.

Partly to make up for his faux pas Cloote suggested the four of them go out for Sunday lunch, as Anula had a rare day off. He booked a table at the Unruly Pig, a gastropub just outside Woodbridge and close to Sutton Hoo. Anna, Cloote, and Rees drove over in the Jag and Anula joined them at the sixteenth-century country inn. They had a good vegetarian selection – Anula particularly liked their smoked potato gnocchi – as well as more traditional British meats, which Oliver tucked into with relish. They talked about Cloote's Wagner production and the state of the NHS and kept off treasure hunting and the Middle Ages. Just after finishing some rather delicious desserts, Anna's phone buzzed. 'Sorry, it's Magnus. I'd better take it,' she said and popped outside.

'Anna, Anna!' it was the most animated she'd ever heard him. 'I've got it, well part of it. I think . . .'

Anna cut him off abruptly. 'Magnus just be careful what you say.'

'Yes, yes I know. Look you must come and see it for yourself. How quickly could you get here?'

'We're out at lunch now. I could be back in Aldeburgh in half an hour, and I suppose I could do it in two-and-half or three hours. I could be there between five and six.'

'Okay. I'll be in college. In the meantime, think about what animals came *after* the beaver and the partridge.' He abruptly ended the call. Anna went back and told the others what Magnus had said. They paid the bill and, while Anula went home, Rees drove rather more quickly than usual back to Aldeburgh.

Anna took the direct route; as it was Sunday even the M25 wasn't too awful. As she approached Oxford the sun was setting. For once she wished she'd been in a car, even though the weather was fine. She felt a tightening in her stomach that told her something wasn't right. In a car she'd have been able to call Magnus to reassure herself. She parked the bike opposite the college gates and hurried past the hall into Fellows Quad.

Three things immediately struck her. As she glanced up towards the window of Magnus's study, she could see that the curtains hadn't been drawn and there was no light showing, even though it was now quite dark. The second was the sound of music playing in a room on the far side of the quad. It was St Vincent's album *Masseduction.* The third made her trepidation increase dramatically. As she looked to see where the music was coming from, she saw a figure moving quickly but stealthily along the far wall of the quad towards Mob. It was a large man and Anna caught a glimpse of his face as he passed a lighted window.

For an instant she thought about following the man but rejected the idea and instead sprang up the stairs two at a time towards Magnus's room. The door was shut but not locked. She opened it and took in the entire scene in a split second. Magnus's chair had been knocked over. His PC was turned round, and there was a hole in the back where the hard drive had been. The biscuit tin on the desk that usually contained his mobile phone was empty. And on the floor Magnus lay on his back.

Even in the dim light Anna could see there was a dark stain spreading over his light-coloured sweater. For another instant Anna's heart seemed to stop but she quickly gathered her thoughts, as the adrenalin kicked in, and started thinking clearly. She knelt next to Magnus to search for a pulse. He wasn't dead but was clearly fading fast. She rapidly dialled 999 and gave them the details, 'Yes I'm sure he's been shot and is dying. You need to get here quickly.' Though basic first aid was part of her training, she knew there was nothing she could do to save him, the main bleeding must be internal. She felt useless. All she could do was wait. 'Where's the fucking ambulance!'

Magnus seemed to revive a little and looked up at her. 'Anna ... Didn't ... tell.' A smile flickered across his lips as he whispered 'Anna ... my child.'

'Magnus, I know.' It was the first time she had ever called him by his first name. She kissed his forehead, and he was gone.

At that instant all of Anna's senses seemed to be enhanced. She could hear the clock on the mantelpiece ticking. In the distance, she could hear the siren and lifted her head to the window. She looked out and could see every star in the sky. She didn't cry, instead, she knew she must concentrate. Very soon the room would be full of paramedics and police.

It was then that she saw the piece of paper. It had obviously blown under the table when she opened the door. She pulled it towards her. Magnus must have taken it from the wastepaper basket as it had a shopping list on one side. But on the other Magnus had traced some words with his finger using the only thing he could, his own blood.

Not a sequence. A Sequence.

The second 'sequence' had a capital and was underlined.

The sirens were now very close, and she heard one stop. Across the quad she could hear Annie Clark singing the last lines of 'Slow Disco.'

Chapter 33

The paramedics quickly established that Magnus was indeed dead. Anna sat on the stairs outside the room and waited for the police. Her entire body felt numb. She had involved Magnus in this and now he was dead. She looked at her phone. There was a message from Magnus that had been sent about an hour earlier. It read 'It's not a code it's a sequence.' She thought their adversaries must have this message but not the final one on the paper, even though they seemed almost identical.

Soon enough Inspector Cook and Nikki arrived, shortly followed by the SOCOs. Cook quickly got Anna's basic statement, including the description of the man she'd seen in the quad. 'As it's the second time you've stumbled onto a murder, Dr Carr, I will need to speak to you in greater detail. Where will you stay tonight?'

Anna considered. 'I'll stay at Magnus's house if that's okay. His dog will need to be looked after.' Cook was initially doubtful. Anna explained about Garm and said she'd need to tell Nora what had happened. She described Nora as Magnus's 'ward' thinking that was the nearest description a policeman would understand. In the end it was decided that she could stay at the house provided it was after they had done a search for evidence. Anna said she'd come to Thames Valley headquarters in Kidlington in the morning.

She now had the worst tasks. She sent a text message to Cloote giving the basic facts and telling him not to reply, she would call him tomorrow. Next, she phoned Skylight to check if Nora was there. She was. By the time Anna arrived she was pleased to find that Nils was there too. They were planning an evening out.

'Anna, wicked!' Nora exclaimed, but her expression quickly changed as she could tell something was wrong. 'What's up, babe?'

'I've got some really bad news. Magnus is dead.'

'What!' Nils exclaimed. Nora said nothing but the blood drained from her face, and she sat down abruptly on a chair.

Anna explained as quickly as she could what had happened and why. Nora and Nils listened intently. Nora was tightly gripping Nils's hand. When Anna finished, Nora asked, 'What are you going to do?'

'Tonight, I'll stay at Magnus's, with Garm. Tomorrow I'll start finding the bastards that did this.'

'And then?'

'I'll kill them.' She said it in a calm, matter of fact tone, but her eyes shone coldly. Neither Nora nor Nils doubted her.

They said they'd stay the night with her, and Nils said they'd also look after Garm. 'I've got another two weeks leave and after that Nora can have him. He doesn't need much exercise.'

Anna got to Woodstock Road first. There was a policeman outside who told her the forensic team had done their search, and that the dog had been quite friendly with them. She opened the door and Garm came trotting up to her. She fussed him as he looked round expectantly, thinking Magnus must be with her. The dog then looked up at Anna. It was too much for her. She hugged Garm to her chest and sat on the hall floor as floods of tears wracked her body.

Nora and Nils soon arrived and together they sat quietly in the kitchen sipping tea before turning in. They slept in two of the spare bedrooms, none of them wanted to go into Magnus's bedroom or his study downstairs. When Anna finally fell asleep, she had another dream.

She was about twelve years old. She was standing in a deep woodland dell wearing a white shift. There was a large fire in the centre of the clearing close to her. She was dimly aware that many people were standing at the edges of the dell. The woman who'd appeared in her previous dream was standing beside her, as well as a much older woman. The old woman made her drink from a cup. It tasted bitter. She took Anna's hands and studied them intently. Then she looked into her eyes. Anna suddenly felt her entire body had divided and that she was now suspended over the clearing looking down on herself. The younger woman came forward, holding a black staff. She touched Anna on the shoulders and then on the head. Then together both women said 'þat er hana', 'it is her'. When Anna woke, she knew she'd had this same dream before when she was young.

*

Around the same time, Savile Nesfield arrived at Satterthwaite Hall. 'Well?' demanded Elias Forth.

'He's not going to be telling anyone a thing. I've got the hard drive and the phone.'

'Good. We don't have time to wait for that fool Penhaligon. Even without his information they're several steps ahead of him. Give those to Machin and see what he can extract.'

Nesfield phoned Machin, Forth's head of IT, to let him know he'd be bringing some equipment to him in London tomorrow. The death of Magnus Strachan was the last thing on his mind.

Chapter 34

Anna spent several hours at Kidlington. She told the police everything she knew and handed over the bloodied note which she'd entirely forgotten when they'd spoken before. 'And what do you think it means, Dr Carr?' Cook asked.

'I really don't know,' she answered truthfully. She didn't add, 'But I'll damned well find out.'

Cook broke off the interview so that Anna could get something to eat in the canteen, she suddenly realised she hadn't had a thing since yesterday's lunch at the Unruly Pig. It seemed a lifetime ago. In the canteen Nikki joined her. 'The good news is that the autopsy suggests you couldn't be the killer. Magnus was shot before you arrived. We've got a witness who heard the shot, even though the killer used a silencer.'

'That's a relief,' was Anna's reply.

'The other is just advice.' Anna looked at her quizzically. 'These are very dangerous people, and I don't want to see *you* end up like Magnus. So, you ought to tell us everything.'

Anna thought that was an interesting way for her to have phrased the advice. 'Don't you mean "must"?' she asked.

'I know what I said,' replied Nikki. 'You're pretty much the cleverest person I've ever known, Anna Carr. Personally, you're a hell of a lot more intelligent than most of us lot, so, as I say, I know what I said.' Anna gave Nikki a hug and thanked her.

Before she left Oxford, Anna had one more call to make. Allan McLeod was Magnus's closest friend in the city and his solicitor. She went round to his office and broke the news. They'd only met on a couple of occasions and their conversation was rather formal. Allan tried to get over his shock by being intensely businesslike and explained in detail what the procedure was after a violent death regarding the deceased's estate. Anna rather lost his train of thought but did pick up that any funeral would be postponed for some time as investigations proceeded. 'I am also his executor. Did you know?' Anna said she didn't, she and Magnus never discussed such things. 'You know Magnus didn't have any close relatives though?' She agreed that she did. 'So, err, we will need to speak again about, err, things. Ms Greenwood too.' Anna wasn't entirely sure what he was trying to tell her but agreed that she would want to help organise the funeral and gave Allan her contact details.

For the trip back to Aldeburgh Anna decided to meander across country. She didn't feel like riding fast and wanted to think. In the early afternoon she found herself approaching the village of Coggeshall in Essex. She remembered that it was the site of Coggeshall Abbey, founded in 1140 by King Stephen. Now only the abbey gate survives, restored as St Nicholas's Chapel. It was a quiet and peaceful spot by the side of the River Blackwater yet would have been a bustling place in the Middle Ages. Anna sat by the river imagining the monks chanting the mass in the abbey church. She mused as to why she'd thought of that and decided it must be because of the musical notation Rasmus had seen Penhaligon consulting. She got out her phone to listen to some of her music. But as she was sorting through the tracks she suddenly stopped. 'Not a sequence. A *Sequence*.'

What were the meanings of 'sequence' other than a progression? What if Magnus meant a *musical* sequence? It would fit with the missing pages of the manuscript. Anna knew that, in music, sequence could refer to two things. The most common is a harmonic sequence, a restatement of a motif at a higher or lower pitch to elaborate a melody. An obvious example is the British national anthem with the line 'happy and glorious' following 'send her victorious'. But it was the second usage Anna thought Magnus must have meant. This refers to medieval music where the sequence was a Latin text sung in the mass between the Alleluia and the reading of the Gospel. Anna got back on the bike and sped towards Aldeburgh.

Oliver, Gordon, and Anula were waiting for her. Gordon and Anula hugged Anna but said nothing. Cloote remained slightly aloof but was clearly equally upset. He was playing with his glasses and trying to pick the right words. Finally, he said, 'Magnus was a good man, Anna. He was also a great scholar. We'll miss him so much.'

'You really cared for him?' Anula asked.

Anna said nothing for a few seconds and then nodded. 'He was the nearest to a father I ever had,' she said. Gordon looked at Cloote, this was the most personal comment Anna had ever made. He was about to say something more when he noticed her expression harden. 'We're going to avenge his death, work out the puzzle, and finish it.' A fierce determination burned in her eyes. The other three looked at each other, Rees and Anula in some trepidation, but Cloote's expression was different. A flicker of a smile passed across his face as if something he'd been thinking for a long time had been confirmed.

Anna quickly became calmer and practical. 'The manuscript may contain a musical sequence that acts as a code,' she said and explained her thinking, and Magnus's final note.

'And then there's the ant, the crab, and the snail,' added Cloote when she'd finished. 'Come and look.'

They went to the library and again Cloote brought up Inkpen's photographs. 'If you look at the beaver and the partridge in each case there is an ant, a crab, or a snail closely beside them,' he said.

'What do you think that means?' asked Anna.

'Oliver, well the three of us, think it could be a clue as to the nature of the real Brisingamen,' Gordon said. Obviously, they now regarded Anula as a full member of their team.

'I see. And have you got any idea what they might be referring to?'

Cloote smiled. 'I have, though you might think it's even more fanciful than the King John connection.'

'Well?' Anna and Gordon said virtually in tandem.

'What have ants, snails, and crabs got in common?'

Anula was the first to suggest the connection. 'They're all invertebrates, creatures without a backbone,' she said.

'Exactly!' said Cloote triumphally. Gordon and Anula looked mystified, but Anna was beginning to see a connection.

'You think this is connected to Penhaligon's sudden interest in the ninth century, don't you?'

'I believe so,' answered Cloote. 'In which case what would you say was the most likely treasure of that period?'

'You don't mean ...' Anna began.

Cloote raised an eyebrow, 'Go on.'

'You have to mean the treasure of Ivar the Boneless.'

'Indeed, I do.'

'Who's Ivar the Boneless?' asked Anula, to which Gordon added, 'I thought he was just a made-up character in that TV series.'

'Not at all,' said Cloote and he went on to tell the tale.

'Most of the information about Ivar hinn beinlausi – Ivar the Boneless – comes from the Scandinavian sagas recounting the exploits of his father, King Ragnar Lothbrok, who led the sack of Paris in 845.'

'Yes,' Anna added, 'though Ragnar may well be an amalgam of various historical figures and the sagas mix fact with legend and folklore, the existence of Ivar isn't in doubt. His deeds are recorded in contemporary documents, and it's possible to trace his movements with relative certainty. Ivar is well attested in the *Chronicon Roskildense* for example.'

'What's that?' asked Anula.

'One of the earliest accounts of Danish history,' Anna explained, 'written in the later 1130s. I wrote a couple of papers on comparisons between it and other early accounts of the same events, such as Saxo Grammaticus's *Gesta Danorum* and Sven Aggesen's *Brevis Historia Regum Dacie*.'

'You'll have to tell me more about them sometime,' said Anula, 'but go on with the story of Ivar, Oliver.'

'In 865 the greatest invasion of Britain in history took place,' Cloote said. 'The *Anglo-Saxon Chronicle* said a "mycel hæþen here" – "a great heathen army" – came to England. It was led by four of the sons of Ragnar Lothbrok: Hvitserk, Bjorn Ironside, Ubba, and Ivar. In 866, the Danes took advantage of a civil war between Ælla and his rival Osbert and captured York, the Northumbrian capital. The Northumbrians put aside their differences to unite against the common enemy and attempted to retake the city. But they were heavily defeated. Osbert was killed and Ælla was captured and put to death.'

'In a particularly gruesome way,' Anna added.

'Yes, the manner of Ælla's death has generated furious debate among scholars,' Cloote continued. 'His execution is described in detail in Scandinavian sources, and Ivar's personal involvement is stressed. You'll remember the quote better than me Anna.'

'The most graphic description appears in the *þáttr af Ragnars sonum,*' said Anna and quoted: '"They caused the bloody eagle to be carved on the back of Ælla, and they cut away all of the ribs from the spine, and then they ripped out his lungs."'

'This was a form of Viking ritual killing known as the "blood-eagle".' Oliver explained.

'Nice,' said Gordon and Anula grimaced.

Oliver continued the story. 'In 869 and 870, Ivar and the Danes conquered the kingdom of East Anglia, defeating them at Thetford and killed their king, Edmund. They ravaged the land and pillaged the abbey at Medhamstead, carrying away its treasures. After a series of battles with King Æthelred of Wessex and his brother, who became Alfred the Great after Æthelred's death, they made peace with Wessex but went on to sack London, which was part of Mercia.'

'So that might be a reason for Johannes's interest in the tale,' mused Anna. 'It was his abbey.'

'What happened to Ivar?' asked Anula.

'There are various stories about his death,' said Anna. 'One of the poems that recalls Ivar's deeds is *Hauk Ragnarsson's Saga.* Hauk, which means Hawk, was one of Ivar's less than effective sons. The poem tells of Ivar's death in battle.'

'But this is where it gets really interesting,' Cloote interrupted, getting more agitated. 'Because on his deathbed Ivar supposedly revealed where he'd hidden the treasure he'd taken from Medhamstead. His map was torn into three parts, one each was given to the Holmbyggjar, Oestvikingae, and Westmen.'

He went to a shelf and selected a copy of the Skaldic Poems and started reading: '"The Oestvikingae went east to find it. On the way they clashed with other Vikings who stole their fragment of the map. However, the Oestvikingae were wise, and had memorised their fragment, chanting its words and drawing its shapes on the ground. When they met the Holmbyggjar they shared the details which they remembered and together they rebuilt the map in their minds. With the help of some Englisc."

'That's the local Anglo-Saxons,' he explained somewhat unnecessarily: '"The Oestvikingae then followed other treasure hunters to the place where Ivar's gold lay. The keen eyes of Thorhelm quickly spotted the glint of monastic relics. Some of their treasure was stolen by the Holmbyggjar, once again reneging on earlier friendship, so Guðrún and Fritha buried the rest. Later they managed to rescue another piece of treasure from Englisc hands, and Fritha buried it so well that no man could find it, though several saw the area she had hidden it, and searched it long and hard. They then had to get the treasure out of the area, beyond the grasping hands of the Englisc. They dug up their first hoard and entrusted it to Thorhelm's swift legs while the rest of the warband held up the Englisc attempting to pursue him. Then Fritha sneaked out to her buried stash and managed to return it all on her own while the other searchers were distracted."

'What the sagas suggest is that Ivar's treasure was recovered,' Cloote said excitedly, 'and that it was then reburied.'

'But isn't this all just legend?' asked Anula.

'Of course it is,' said Cloote. 'But until quite recently many people doubted that Ivar or his father had existed. Now we may even know where he's buried. Professor Martin Biddle thinks the skeleton of a man discovered during excavations at Repton in Derbyshire is, in fact, that of Ivar the Boneless. I believe you supported Professor Biddle's views, Anna?'

'Yes, I did, he's a brilliant archaeologist. Repton was where the army over-wintered. For me the two hundred and fifty other bodies there suggest the burial must have been of exceptionally high importance and Ivar is the best fit. I suppose it's possible the animals could be a reference to Ivar, but it's pretty flimsy evidence.'

'I know,' said Cloote. 'We need much more and, of course, there's absolutely no clue as to where the treasure might be.'

'Unless it's hidden in the musical sequence,' added Anna.

'What do we do then?' asked Gordon. 'Steal Penhaligon's copy?'

'Far too dangerous,' said Cloote. 'If he really is working with Magnus's killers it would put Rasmus in terrible danger. We must think of another way.'

'It's obvious,' said Anna. The others looked at her, it wasn't obvious to them. 'Inkpen,' she said firmly. 'We have no evidence the man is dead. If he isn't, and he's not senile, he might remember something of the *Codex* and Johannes's illustrations.'

'But won't Penhaligon and his friends think the same?' asked Gordon.

'I'm not sure they will,' said Anna. 'They have the entire manuscript, and Penhaligon has a deep prejudice against his old teacher and would reject Inkpen as a source of information.'

'But how do we find him?' asked Anula.

'Yes,' Cloote added, 'we've tried the obvious leads, but so far there's no trace of him.'

'I've been thinking about that,' Anna said. 'The one clue is that Magnus told me he had retired to somewhere remote.'

'Could be anywhere,' said Rees, 'from the Amazon Rainforest to the Gobi Desert.'

'Again, I don't think so,' Anna continued. 'He was a scholar of Britain and Northern Europe. I think he'd have gone somewhere nearer home.'

'And how can you find him?' Anula asked.

'I've got some ideas,' was Anna's conclusion.

Chapter 35

A couple of hours later, a discreet black van and car drew up outside Summerland. Gordon went to let the guests in. The man in charge bore a distinct resemblance to Will Smith in *Men in Black*. 'Great to see you again, Gordon,' he said. Gordon introduced him as Scott Rimes. He was the founder of the security and countersurveillance company 'Rimes Inc.' and was a friend of Gordon's from his MIT days.

'What have you been working on recently?' Gordon asked. 'You weren't in the States when we spoke.'

'No, I was doing some work in India.'

'Haven't you got a place out there?'

'Yeh, in Kerala. And I was doing some more study of Ayurveda.' Gordon explained Scott was a student of Ayurveda, the Hindu system of medicine, and had been to the sub-continent several times. Scott and Anula got into a discussion on the efficacy of Ayurvedic medicine while his team went over every inch of the house and grounds.

They reinstalled or updated software for the security systems, phones, and computers. Then they turned their attention to the garage and vehicles. Soon afterwards a young woman reported to Scott and handed him a small black box with a wire protruding. Scott found Anna and showed her the device. 'It's a mini-tracker,' he explained. 'A simple GPS device and transmitter that will tell someone exactly where your bike is. It was inside your gas tank.'

Anna took it from him. 'Any idea how long it's been there?'

'Difficult to say, but several weeks from the way the gas has stained the plastic.'

Anna wondered if it had been there since she bought the bike. 'Presumably it's still working?'

'Yeh. It is for now. It's up to you what you do with it.'

'Have you found anything else?' asked Cloote, who now joined them.

'No, but come with me,' Scott replied. They all went into the library where Scott went over their security precautions in detail. 'You're pretty secure here or, at least, as secure as you can be. What you couldn't do easily is fight off a sustained attack.'

'You mean a physical attack?' asked Anna.

'Yes. But no security device could help you there. Do you want me to arrange more physical protection? I could have a permanent guard.' Cloote said he thought it would be a sensible precaution and they agreed that one of the Rimes PPT – Physical Protection Team – would be stationed either in a van on the road or a boat on the river twenty-four hours a day from now on. The vehicle and boats would change frequently to make them as discreet as possible, explained Scott. 'We've also put two zoom cameras focused on the river,' Scott explained. 'If you wanted to surveil the house it would be the best place to do it. You can see the top end of the garden and back windows from anywhere between the yacht club and the bend upstream.'

They agreed they'd not thought sufficiently about their vulnerability from the river before and Anna recalled the boat she'd seen. 'I'm afraid it's a pretty vague description,' she concluded.

'I'll run a check on all the boats I can,' Scott added. 'Might take a while though.'

After Scott and his team had left, a somewhat bemused Anula said, 'I didn't quite understand how serious all of this is, even after Magnus. It's like being in a Dan Brown thriller.'

'God, I hope not!' replied Gordon.

*

'Not a code a sequence,' said Elias Forth. 'What does it mean?'

'Well,' replied Gervase Penhaligon who had been summoned to Forth's apartment, 'it's clear what he meant is that the animals don't just represent a straightforward code, it's the sequence they are in that's important.'

'And you agree?'

'It's a definite possibility.'

'So why didn't you think of it?'

Forth's question discombobulated Penhaligon who, up to

that point, had been rather pleased with his interpretation. 'Well, I, err, I ... '

'Yes?'

'I'm sure I *would* have thought of it.'

Morten, who had been standing silently behind Penhaligon for some time, let out a guffaw which made the professor almost jump out of his skin. 'What is important now,' Morten explained, 'is that we discover what this sequence is.'

'Indeed,' said Penhaligon, hoping to recover some respect. 'I intend to look closely into the possibility of a connection with Ivar's treasure, which means a close study of the Danish sources.'

'Well bloody well get on with it,' Forth responded. 'I have very important people waiting for results from all of this, as I shouldn't need to explain.'

'No, no, of course, of course,' Penhaligon was feeling distinctly uneasy.

'I will also be reviewing your findings whilst pursuing my own enquiries,' Morten added. Penhaligon realised he was overstaying his welcome and hurriedly said his goodbyes.

'Fuck!' said Forth when he'd gone. 'How can we rely on such an imbecile? We need extra care keeping our eye on Cloote.'

'Ahem,' Morten exclaimed. 'That will be trickier than before. They've had security experts in and there's round-the-clock protection on the house.'

'I told Nesfield it was a mistake to move the boat.'

'I think he was actually correct,' said Morten, unusually supporting his colleague. 'The boat was too obvious. I'm surprised they hadn't spotted it earlier,' he added. But his solidarity didn't extend to Penhaligon, 'I expect they'll work out the trail before our friend the professor.'

'Look,' concluded Forth, 'if we're getting nowhere, we'll need direct measures. I think the girl will be the weak link.'

Morten thought Forth was completely mistaken.

Chapter 36

The police wanted to ask Anna some further questions and, as this fitted her plans, she returned to Oxford a few days later. Merton's CCTV had picked up some hazy shots of the man Anna had seen in Fellows Quad. He had slipped past the Porter's Lodge and left the college by climbing the rear fence, dropping into Deadman's Walk, and crossing Merton Field, well away from any cameras.

Following the interview in Kidlington, Anna rode into the centre of the city and dropped her bike off close to her bedsit. She had deliberately kept the tracking device with her, and now left in on the bike. In her flat she changed into inconspicuous jeans and a denim jacket before catching a number 5 bus to Cowley. She got off by The Original Swan pub and walked round the corner to the Oxfordshire History Centre, based in a former church in Temple Road.

Inkpen was a well-known figure before his retirement, which she'd pinned down to 1998. Coverage of university life in the local press was extensive and she thought there might be some clue to his whereabouts in the local archives. These hadn't been digitised and there was no index, so she would have to trawl through hundreds of pages on microfilm to find anything. For this reason, she'd called on the help of Nora and Nils. When the three of them walked through the doors of St Luke's they looked an unlikely trio of researchers. A small angry goth and two scruffy looking hippies with dreadlocks. The receptionist's fears were partially allayed when the goth turned out to know what she was talking about and rapidly requested items from the printed catalogue.

Anna showed Nora and Nils how to use the microfilm readers. She had planned their search with precision. They would concentrate first on the *Oxford Mail*, the City's daily paper since the 1920s, and the most likely source of information about Roger Inkpen. From what she'd already learned, Inkpen had been born in 1926. He'd been a pupil at the Royal Grammar School Worcester and, at eighteen, became a translator for the Allied forces following the D-Day landings. In 1945 and '46 he'd attended the Nuremberg war trials before coming up to Oxford in October to study German. His interests switched to more ancient languages under the tutelage of JRR Tolkien who, in 1945, had become the Merton professor of English language and literature. Inkpen's thesis on early Scandinavian languages was completed in 1952, after which he joined the university staff as a junior fellow, gaining a full professorship shortly after Tolkien's retirement in 1959.

Anna decided to start a few weeks after Inkpen's retirement and work her way back. Nora, who was the least experienced researcher, would begin in 1946 and Nils in 1959. It was not exactly inspiring work and, for the less experienced, easy to get distracted. Nora kept getting excited by how different the world of the late 1940s was. She'd had no idea that there was rationing or how extremely racist comments could be. Each time they found a reference to Inkpen they printed a hard copy of the article. After the first day they had collected half a dozen about the former don.

By Wednesday, Anna thought she could see some pattern and where her search might lead next. It had been Nils who made the key findings. In the 1960s the *Mail* often printed gossip about notable Oxonians. Where they went during the Long Vac, summer holidays to most people, was of particular interest and Inkpen's trips were no exception. He had spent time in most of the Scandinavian countries and Germany, as well as different parts of Britain, but the place he visited most was the island of Colonsay in the Inner Hebrides. Inkpen had been drawn there to look for remains of the famous Viking ship grave. This had been discovered at Kiloran Bay in 1882 by Malcolm McNeill with a full excavation in 1884, when William Galloway discovered the grave of a man with a horse, along with a selection of grave goods, including weapons. The grave had once been covered by an upturned boat about eight metres long and dated to sometime just after 850. Though Inkpen had found no further traces of Viking remains, the island appeared to have captured his imagination and he returned there at least four times during the 1960s and early 70s. He had mapped dozens of archaeological sites and investigated the remains of the Augustinian priory on the smaller island of Oronsay, which was supposed to have originated as a Celtic monastery founded by St Columba.

If Inkpen had an attachment to a remote location this was surely it. On Thursday and Friday Anna left Nora and Nils to continue looking for references to Inkpen, while she researched the island. Even with increases in recent years the population was only a hundred and twenty-five, so an aging Oxford professor should be easy to find. Or so she thought. She turned to the electoral roll. Nothing. No one of that age or with a name remotely connected to Inkpen. Then she tried the local press for the Western Isles, but these were only held on microfilm in Stornaway Library.

She considered a phone call or two at random but that seemed unlikely to be much help and might even hinder her finding out more. Her conclusion was that she would have to go to the island and make discreet enquiries herself. But was it worth it on such flimsy evidence? On Friday two things persuaded her it was. First Nils found another article. It was an interview with Roger Inkpen on the fiftieth anniversary of his coming up to Oxford. There was nothing in it of especial interest, but Anna recognised the reporter's name, Pete Railton. Railton had been one of the journalists who had covered the Bodleian murder and was still on the staff at the *Mail.* Anna rang the paper and asked if she could speak with him. He was out, so she left a message, knowing he would immediately know her name from her connection with Magnus Strachan.

While she was waiting for the journalist to return her call, she also found a clue. It was in a 2012 report entitled *Bheinn Bheag Colonsay*, about the investigation of prehistoric hut circles on the island. The excavation was undertaken by Kilmartin Museum as part of Integrating Archaeology and Sustainable Communities – IAASC – a network of universities, museums, and government institutions working with communities to help them research their heritage. It was a long report but hidden in the acknowledgements was a reference to a local antiquarian,

Professor Roger, who had assisted with their work. Could this be Inkpen? It was certainly the closest she'd got.

At that point Railton phoned back. As she'd expected, he was keen to speak to the main witness to a murder that was all over the local, and national, press. Even though the police hadn't revealed any connection to the deaths of Westley and Arbuthnot, there had been much speculation. Yes, he said, he'd be happy to talk to her straight away. They agreed to meet at The Bear in Alfred Street in an hour.

Pete Railton looked a little like an aging rock singer, Anna thought. He was in his late fifties, wore a battered brown leather jacket, jeans, and cowboy boots. He had an unruly mop of greying hair and was entirely unfazed by Anna. She rather liked him, even though he was extremely cynical about what had happened to his profession over the years.

She said she'd answer his questions about Magnus as far as she could and talked a lot about him, and as little about his death, as possible. On the murder she stuck firmly to the story the police had issued, a possible burglary unconnected with Magnus's life. Pete was also cynical about this. He was a good enough journalist to spot a cover up when he saw one, but he wasn't sure if Anna knew more than she was letting on. In exchange Anna asked him if he remembered meeting Roger Inkpen back in the mid-nineties. She said, quite honestly, that she was trying to track him down, if he was still alive, because her research was dovetailing with some of his work. Railton didn't have any trouble remembering Inkpen as one of the many people who had known the great Tolkien. 'At times you'd think the university hadn't had any other famous dons,' Railton said. 'Especially in the early 2000s it was Tolkien this and Tolkien that, memorial editions of the paper on every bloody thing he wrote.' Clearly Railton was no fan of the man's work. Anna asked if he remembered any more about the interview than what was in the paper and handed him a copy to refresh his memory. 'Can't say I do,' was the disappointing reply, 'but I did keep most of my interviews from that period. Might still have it.'

Anna tried not to sound too enthusiastic when she asked how easy it would be to dig them out. 'Oh, not too hard. They're all on cassettes in boxes in the loft. Do you want to pop round over the weekend some time?' Anna said she did, and Railton gave her his address in Jericho. She said she'd be there at ten the following day.

*

That evening Anna thought Nora and Nils deserved a treat, they hadn't been out since Magnus died. Nora's favourite food was Indian, so they went to eat at Delhish Vegetarian Kitchen, which had recently relocated to St Clement's Street from their original place in Bicester. Afterwards they went for a quiet drink at a nearby pub before getting a taxi back to Magnus's house where Garm greeted them enthusiastically. Nils would be re-joining the *Esperanza* the following week and had arranged a regular dog-walker to call in. Fortunately, Garm seemed to like the dog-walker. Anna drifted off to sleep on the sofa in the living room after Nora and Nils went up to bed.

The same dream she'd had a few nights before returned, only this time it was longer. A man now approached them. He was blond and dressed in a leather skirt. He was stripped to the waist and every inch of skin, including his face, was covered in tattoos. As the man spoke, Anna removed her shift. She lay face down on a raised wooden platform, as many people gathered round. The man took a bowl and a finely sharpened needle and began to tattoo Anna's back. When he'd finished, the old woman brought a polished bronze mirror and Anna could see the design. When she awoke, she knew what she must do next.

Chapter 37

Before she left to meet Railton, she phoned a friend. He asked her to send over a picture and that he'd fit her in at twelve o'clock. Anna walked to Railton's house, a pleasant Victorian terrace in Cranham Street. He greeted her with a mug of coffee, which she didn't refuse, and a stack of plastic boxes. 'I haven't had time to look through them yet, but the Inkpen interview should be there.' Sure enough a few minutes search brought up an aging C90 cassette with 'Roger Inkpen, 20/4/95' on the label. 'Bring it through here,' said Railton and they went into the living room. He had an impressive stereo system that included an old TEAC double-cassette player. Anna slotted the tape in and settled down with a notepad.

Almost inevitably Railton spent most of his time asking Inkpen for his recollections of Tolkien, something he must have been asked hundreds of times before, even though this was six years before the Peter Jackson film trilogy commenced. Inkpen answered these courteously and finally the discussion got round to the professor's hobbies, which hadn't made it into print. He said he enjoyed walking and bird watching and often fitted these into holidays where he did more academic study. He said he was especially fond of trips to the Scottish islands, and Colonsay in particular. He concluded the interview by saying, 'I think if I could choose where to spend the rest of my days, I'd have to pick Colonsay.' This was decisive.

She asked Railton if she could have a copy of the tape which he said was no problem. He linked the cassette player through to a digital recording device and downloaded a copy of the interview onto a memory stick while they chatted about their, rather different, musical tastes. Anna wasn't surprised to hear Railton was a big prog rock fan. Anna thanked him for his help and said if there was more on the Strachan murder story, she would call him first.

She went back to collect her bike, there was no problem

about their adversaries tracking her next movements. She rode to Cowley and got to the shop just as Henry was finishing with his previous customer. 'Hi Henry, did you get the pic okay?'

'Hey, Anna. Yeh, no problem. It's fairly straightforward. Shouldn't take more than a couple of hours. What colours were you thinking of?'

'Maybe red or orange lettering?'

'Yeh, it could match the sunburst if you like.'

Anna went inside the tattoo shop and said hi to Henry's wife, Polly, who asked if she'd like a herb tea while Henry was working on her. She said yes before taking off her top and lying on the couch. The tattoo consisted of a design and a line of text. The text ran at the base of her neck with the design immediately below. This was the Ægishjálmr, the Helm of Awe, one of the most mysterious and powerful symbols in Norse mythology. It has eight arms that look like spiked tridents radiating out from a central point, as if going on the offensive against hostile forces surrounding it. Henry said he'd done the design a few times before and it was one of the most popular ones based on Norse mythology, but that it was the first time he'd executed it on a real Norse scholar. The line of text read:

Ægishjalm bar ek of alda sonum.

'It means: "The awe-helm I wore, to make men afraid."' Anna explained it was taken from the *Fáfnismál*, one of the poems in the *Poetic Edda*, in which the dragon Fáfnir attributes much of his apparent invincibility to the Helm of Awe. As Henry showed an interest, she recited some stanzas from the *Fáfnismál*, first in Old Norse and then English. 'The helm of awe was originally intended to strike fear into the enemy,' she told him. 'It was associated with the power of serpents to paralyze their prey, hence the connection with Fáfnir. The "arms" of the Helm could be Z-runes, runes of protection and prevailing over your enemies. The "spikes" could be Isa runes. Since Isa means ice, they're probably linked with the spirits of winter's cold and darkness, which is even more likely because Fáfnir occupies a role in the tales of the human hero Sigurd like that of the giants in the tales of the gods.'

'Wow! that's great stuff,' said Henry, and a couple of other customers looked equally impressed. 'Can you do some more of that Norse stuff,' one of them asked.

'Sure,' said Anna. 'The *Fáfnismál* is probably the best known of all the Eddic poems, mainly because Wagner used it, with very few changes, as the basis for his opera *Siegfried* and then there are many similarities between Tolkien's Smaug and Fáfnir.' She recited the rest of the *Fáfnismál* telling how Sigurd slays the dragon, drinks its blood, and gains the ability to understand the birds who tell him of his future wife, Guðrún, and of an imprisoned Valkyrie named Brynhildr.

By the end of the tale a small audience of customers, and just passer's by, had assembled in Henry's shop all staring at a topless girl lying on a tattoo couch. They passed favourable comments on both the tattoo and her storytelling, and one suggested she should do this with a proper audience. Anna politely said she didn't think that would be a great idea. She looked at the tattoo in the mirror and was impressed by Henry's work. He covered it with Vaseline and applied a gauze. Despite having done Anna's two earlier tattoos, he carefully went through the aftercare programme and how to spot any problems. Anna thanked him and Polly and went back to her bike. She texted Cloote and Anula to say she was on her way back to Aldeburgh. A couple of the bystanders turned to each other. 'Fucking cool lady,' said one as Anna roared away on the Harley. 'Too true, bro,' agreed the other.

*

Back at Summerland Anna brought the others up to speed about Roger Inkpen. Cloote agreed that going to Colonsay was the best idea. Rees then said, 'Yeh, I agree but I don't think it should be Anna that goes.' Anna glared rather sharply at him. 'No, I don't mean that you shouldn't be the person who *physically* goes. I think you should go as someone else.' He looked at Oliver in a meaningful way.

'Ah yes,' Cloote went on, 'it's something we put together with a little help from Scott and his colleagues.'

'Wait here,' said Gordon and left the room, returning a minute or two later with a box file. 'Take a look at these.'

'I hope you'll forgive our presumption,' said Cloote. 'We thought there might be a need for us to travel more discreetly, so we took precautions. These are your options.' Inside the folder were a selection of passports. There were UK ones, US ones, and European ones. Anna saw a German one which she opened. Staring back at her was her own photograph.

'So, you see, Anna,' continued Rees, 'you could go to Scotland as someone else.'

'Who do you suggest?'

They agreed on an English alias. Anna would be Alexandra Dakin, born in London in 1996. There was a driving licence to go with the passport plus a credit card. They said she'd be free to make up a cover story to match the documents. 'If I'm looking for a professor with an interest in archaeology then I'd better have an interest in it too. But not a professional one that they could check. I'll just be a keen amateur.'

Anna looked up the ferry service to Colonsay. They were on their winter timetable and the ferry left Oban on Mondays, Wednesdays, and Fridays. She booked for the 12.15 sailing the following Wednesday. Then she emailed the Colonsay Hotel and booked a room from Wednesday for three nights, saying she might stay a day or two longer. She also booked stopovers for the Monday and Tuesday, close to her route, and arranged to pick up a hire car in Norwich on Monday. All these transactions were, of course, done by Alex Dakin.

That would be the actual trip. What they discussed next would be their false trail. 'What Scott also said,' Gordon went on, 'is that he can't be sure how closely we're being watched. We know there aren't any more tracking devices, but direct surveillance is almost certainly happening. After all there aren't that many routes out of Aldeburgh.'

'And your vehicles are pretty distinctive,' added Anula.

'What we need is something to confuse them, even if it's only for a short while, because they obviously have significant resources,' Rees continued.

'Yes,' Anna was thinking, 'it needs to be something that fits the information we know they have. So, we have to factor in the new possibilities around Ivar.'

'I suggest we take the rest of the evening to give it some

thought and then pool our ideas tomorrow? How does that sound?' suggested Cloote.

The others agreed and Anula said she could stay for dinner, which Gordon was happy to cook. 'How about a vegetable tagine?' he said.

Anula hadn't had a chance to speak to Anna alone at any length since Magnus's murder and they went upstairs to the Children's Room to talk. This had originally been the nursery and was decorated with scenes from well-known children's literature including a set of wall panels devoted to Lewis Carroll's works. Anna told Anula more about Magnus than she'd previously divulged and explained the meaning of his last words. 'I know he ended up thinking about me as the daughter he never had. He never mentioned his wife, but I found out that when he was an undergraduate in the 1980s, he'd been married for a short time. She became pregnant but then suffered from something called an amniotic fluid embolism and both she and the baby died.'

Anula said this can occur when the amniotic fluid surrounding the baby contaminates the mother's bloodstream. 'We don't fully understand how it happens and it's not easy to diagnose even now, so it must have been even harder back then.'

'It must have hurt Magnus so much, though he never ever mentioned it. Instead, what happened was that, as he got to know me, he started thinking of me as his daughter.'

'And you never talked to him about it?'

'No. Neither of us are, were, much good at that sort of thing. I just knew.'

'How do you feel about it now?'

'I wish I'd said something. I would have been proud to have had him as a dad, even a surrogate one. I don't think there's anyone I've cared for more. And now he's dead and I didn't …' Anula put her arm over Anna's shoulder. She didn't cry, just rested her head there for a minute or two. Then she sat up straight and wiped her hand across her eyes. 'At least I know what I must do. Make myself worthy of his trust … and love.'

Anula thought that being practical would be a good diversion. 'We need to turn you into Alex,' she said. 'So come on, who is she? What's she like?'

'Okay,' replied Anna, who was now entirely focused. 'She's got a sensible job. Perhaps an estate agent?' The passport, which had supposedly been issued four years ago, listed Dakin as a student.

'Oh no, too unlikeable.'

'Accountant?'

'Too boring.'

'Teacher then?'

'Hmm, not sure you could act that one. What about a designer? Something you do at home, so you don't have to talk about work mates and things like that.'

'But what if someone asked me to show them my work?'

'Unlikely but I see your point. How about a translator? You've got the skills, and if it was for academic books rather than novels no one would ask you much about it I think.'

'Perfect,' said Anna. 'Alex Dakin, translator of academic textbooks into German, Danish, and Swedish.'

'What would you look like and wear?'

'Ordinary stuff, I guess. Jeans rather than dresses and skirts and that would suit me. Could I do something with my hair?' She'd kept it black for the past month, which was close to her natural colour.

'You could just get it cut and possibly curled?'

Anna thought about Margot the law student. 'Yeh, that sounds good. I might even wear glasses.'

'Great idea,' agreed Anula. They went online, and Anna selected a pair with a heavy black frame. The clincher was the comment that, 'If you like the nerd look these glasses are pretty unbeatable.'

Anula wasn't on duty until later on Monday, so they decided they'd both go to Norwich. Anna booked an appointment at a hairdresser for 9 a.m. so they could spend a couple of hours buying Alex's wardrobe before Anna picked up the car. They were enjoying planning Anna's transformation.

Oliver asked Anula if she was staying the night. She glanced at Anna, who looked down at the floor. 'Well, I need to check on some patients at the cottage hospital tomorrow, so I could if that's okay?' Oliver said he'd be happier if she did stay rather than driving back to Woodbridge alone, and Gordon made up one of the spare bedrooms for her.

*

In the morning Anna and Anula went for a run and exercised at the outdoor gym as the day was mild, though rather dull. As they showered Anula saw the new tattoo. 'What is it and what does it mean?' Anna explained. 'And will it help protect you? I didn't think you were that superstitious.'

'I'm not . . . usually. But I'm beginning to wonder.'

They gathered for a conference in the library at eleven. 'The easy bit will be to make them think I'm somewhere else,' Anna began. 'If someone takes the tracker and the bike, they could lay a false trail.'

'I can ride a bike,' said Anula. 'Rode them all the time back home. Pretty much everyone in Sri Lanka does.'

'And with leathers and a helmet on it'd be hard to tell us apart. That means I need to get to Norwich carefully.'

'After I've done my visit to Aldeburgh Hospital on Tuesday, I can collect the bike. Where could you be going for a few days?'

'Oxford's the obvious place don't you think?' Anna replied. 'Why don't you take the bike to Magnus's house. Then get a train back the next day?' They agreed it was as good a plan as any and Anna said she'd alert Nora. 'Well, that's the easy bit,' she added. 'What about something a bit longer term, and flexible if we need to use it.'

'I wondered if we should go back to the beginning,' said Cloote. 'Westley contacted me because of my Gothic expertise. What if there's another bit of Gothic text?'

'Go on,' said Anna.

'I could have found another lead. There are several places an additional manuscript might be, and we could write our own text and translation.'

'So, you'll follow up forging identities with forging documents?' Anula said facetiously. 'What paragons of virtue you are. Should I let the police know what you're up to?' But then she laughed.

They spent the rest of the day hatching their plot and polishing the details, which Cloote said he'd complete while Anna was in Scotland.

Chapter 38

Early on Monday, while it was still dark, an inconspicuous figure slipped out of the back gate of Summerland. She was dressed all in black. *If they are watching*, thought Anna, *they'll have to have incredibly good night vision equipment.* She followed the footpath to her right for a few hundred yards. She then slipped up by the town's tennis courts and back into Cloote's road but turned immediately into the car park of the cottage hospital. As she reached the rear entrance the door opened.

Inside Anula showed Anna an old suitcase. 'We're about the same size so there's a pair of walking boots, some waterproofs, a couple of sweaters, some well-used jeans and thick shirts. Just the sort of thing Alex would take with her on a hiking trip to Scotland in winter.'

They climbed into Anula's car and Anna kept well down in the back seat in case anyone was spying. Though Nesfield had removed the surveillance from the river, he still had all routes out of Aldeburgh covered. There was a continuous lookout by the roundabout, cameras relaying pictures from the Thorpeness road and, in case of a movement by boat, by the yacht club. As Anula's car traversed the roundabout into Saxmundham Road this was noted by the team in the red-brick house on the corner. They crossed the Orwell Bridge and Anula dropped Anna off in the car park of the Station Hotel. Alex Dakin caught the seven forty-four train from Ipswich to Norwich.

Anula drove to the hospital where she checked in with her team before getting a taxi back to the station to catch the 9.08. She turned left out of Norwich station down to the River Wensum, which she crossed by the Lady Julian footbridge. Anna was waiting for her in a small café in one of the back streets. Anula admired the new hairstyle. 'It makes you look like someone from a French film of the 1960s,' was her conclusion.

They spent a couple of hours visiting clothes shops, both new and vintage, to complete Alex's wardrobe. They ended their expedition at a well-known outdoor equipment store that was on the way to the car hire depot. The only things that remained of Anna Carr's possessions were her necklace, her phone, and her laptop.

'You keep safe,' Anula told her.

'You too,' Anna replied. She was about to add 'Take care of the bike,' but didn't. Anula might not be as sensitive to comments that belittled her abilities as Anna was, but it would still be putting her down. They gave each other a quick hug and Anna strode off. Anula spent the rest of the day looking round the city, especially the beautiful cathedral which she'd never visited before.

'Ah yes, Ms Dakin,' the man in the car hire depot greeted her. 'Everything's ready. And you expect to be back next Monday?'

'I think so,' said Anna, 'but it might be a little longer. I may also need to drop the car off at a different branch.'

'Not a problem,' he replied. 'Now if you'd like to follow me to your vehicle.'

Anna had chosen a Volkswagen Golf, the kind of solid, practical car Alex Dakin would favour. She was pleased to see it was a silver one, pretty much the commonest colour on the road. A few checks and a signature, as close to that on her new documents as possible, and she was away. It was now gone 3 p.m. and Anna left Norwich to the west past Swaffham and King's Lynn. Her route took her back on the same road they'd followed when they went to Swineshead, and she passed the village with mixed feelings. Perhaps if she'd not agreed to Magnus joining them, he would still be alive. She tried to supress her regrets. *After all* she told herself, *you can never change the past*.

Just north of Newark she joined the A1, the ancient Great North Road, though mostly unrecognisable today with its long stretches of dual carriageway and motorway. Soon afterwards she stopped for petrol and to collect the glasses she'd had delivered to the pickup point there. She went to the toilets and was pleased with the result. She looked like the rather demure, nerdish person she'd been aiming for.

Back on the road she made good progress as the traffic was thinning out. At Scotch Corner she turned west on the A66. The road now promotes itself as the UK's answer to the famous US route, and it does go through some outstanding areas of natural beauty. After fifteen miles she reached the village of Bowes in Teesdale, on the edge of the Pennines. She'd booked a night at The Ancient Unicorn, a sixteenth-century inn where Charles Dickens stayed when he toured the area in the 1830s. He'd immortalised the village academy as the loathsome Dotheboys Hall in *Nicholas Nickleby*. It is also rumoured that the building is haunted by two young lovers whose graves are in the village churchyard.

As she got out of the car the wind was getting strong, the forecast was for gales the following day and Anna was worried this could interfere with the ferry service. The inn was a three-storey stone building with a cosy bar and open fires. She was greeted warmly under her new name and asked if she'd want dinner, as it was now nearly nine o'clock. Dinner was hearty and pleasant and the bedroom comfortable, though the wind made sleep trickier.

The morning was wet and windy. *Not a day for a run*, thought Anna, *and anyway Alex is more the type for a brisk walk*. She had plenty of time and took a leisurely breakfast before setting off again through the Pennines, joining the M6 at Penrith. This stretch of motorway was one Anna didn't mind travelling on. It was rural, less frequented, and went through some gorgeous scenery. As she travelled further north the rain began to clear. By the time she was skirting Glasgow the wind was also beginning to relent. She stopped for lunch at the Drover's Inn, just north of Loch Lomond, which offered a good vegan choice.

A few miles later, at Tyndrum, she turned west which took her through Glen Lochy past the northern tip of Loch Awe then to the shores of Loch Etive and the Firth of Lorn. In little more than an hour after her lunch stop, she saw a cluster of boats on the Firth just ahead of her, then some low buildings and a car park with a sign that said 'Dunstaffnage Marina'. She was about three miles north of Oban and her accommodation was booked at the Wide Mouthed Frog Hotel and Restaurant. She parked the car and checked in. She was pleased to find that her room overlooked Dunstaffnage Bay and the partially ruined thirteenth-century castle. As it was still light and the weather was improving, she took a walk round the bay to the castle and the equally historic chapel.

She didn't need an early start in the morning so thought she'd practise her social skills as Alex Dakin. After dinner she went to the bar and sat at a table idly reading the latest Ian Rankin she'd picked up on the motorway. If she'd been Anna Carr, she'd have stuck her head in the book and scowled if anyone, especially male, spoke to her. As Alex she adopted a more open posture and glanced up at other people. Sure enough, after a short while, a man approached her. He looked to be in his thirties and was casually dressed. 'Is it good? I've not read his latest.'

'I've not got that far into yet, so I'm not sure. You a Rankin fan?'

'Yeh, I've read most of them. Are you staying here or local?'

'No, I'm just here for tonight. On my way to the islands for a short holiday. Alex Dakin by the way.' She shook his hand.

'Lee Mackay. I'm an architect. We're working on some changes to the marina. Could I buy you a drink?' Anna said yes and asked for a white wine. She and Lee chatted amicably about detective novels and architecture. She told him she was a translator and interested in Scottish history. Eventually she said she was off to bed, and he didn't try to come on to her. She wished him luck with his project and congratulated herself at how well she could do 'normal'.

*

After her rounds at the cottage hospital that afternoon Anula slipped out of the back entrance and traced Anna's route in reverse. When she got to the back gate of Summerland Gordon Rees opened it for her. She spoke with Cloote, who said he was working on the distraction scenario but hadn't got the full details worked out yet. She changed into a set of Anna's leathers and rode the bike up and down the driveway a couple of times. It was much more powerful than anything she'd ridden before, but she was confident she'd be able to handle it.

In the early evening she left Aldeburgh and headed for the A12. Nesfield's spies reported that 'the girl' had left the town and the tracker showed her taking her usual route in the direction of Oxford. Three hours later it recorded her arrival at Woodstock Road.

Chapter 39

Anna got up later than usual and after breakfast drove into Oban, following the unexpectedly labyrinthine route through the town down to the ferry terminal, and finally joining the queue for boarding, next to the railway line. It was a good thing she'd not booked on Monday as the storm had caused the ferry to be cancelled. This meant hers was more crowded than usual at this time of year. It included some islanders who had spent an extra couple of days in Oban, though from speaking to them she found this was something regular travellers were used to.

The sea was still choppy and a backpacking couple, who were the only other tourists on board, looked queasy and disappeared in the direction of the toilets. Anna never had a problem with sea sickness and was delighted that the day was clear, so the views were spectacular. They passed the small island of Kerrera before reaching open sea with the Isle of Mull to starboard. Many smaller islands were visible from the port side before the Paps of Jura came into view. The Paps are three mountains on the western side of the island with distinctive conical shapes, pap being a word derived from Old Norse meaning breast.

After two-and-a-half hours the ferry pulled into the quay at Scalasaig, the main settlement on Colonsay. If Anna had been expecting a town or even a village, she'd have been disappointed. Scalasaig is just a scattering of buildings over a wide area containing the island's shop and post office (in the same building), the church, a microbrewery, the doctor's surgery, the village hall, and the island's only hotel. This was a group of whitewashed buildings a short drive from the pier. Her room was named after Ardkenish, one of the island's beauty spots, much favoured by seals, and had outstanding sea views towards Jura. Anna chatted with the receptionist, who asked what brought her to the island in the winter. They had a couple of hill climbers staying, but no one whose main interest was the island's history. She told Anna she should speak to the members of the Colonsay and Oronsay Heritage Trust. Anna asked how she could contact them and was told all she'd need to do was join the hotel's bar quiz that evening in which the trust always put out a team.

Once she'd settled in, Anna went for a walk and climbed to the summit of Beinn nan Gudairean, the hill immediately behind the hotel, whose name reminded her of the famous World War Two panzer commander. Though the hill wasn't very high, just a hundred and thirty-six metres, the views were magnificent, both towards Jura and over the rest of the island. She could see virtually the full extent of Colonsay's eight by three miles, which was surprisingly well wooded for the Hebrides.

Anna took a bath and dressed for the evening. She had picked out a sensible frock in a Laura Ashley print on her shopping trip with Anula. She couldn't remember the last time she'd worn one, probably when she was about twelve. Though it was now dark she could tell that even the restaurant had gorgeous views. She selected locally caught salmon for her main course and made a note to try their other fish dishes in the next few days.

After dinner a few more people straggled into the bar area. The receptionist was still on duty and Anna saw her talking to a youngish man with a tangled mop of ginger hair and a similar beard. He came over to her. 'Ms Dakin? Hello, I'm Niall MacNeil, secretary of the Heritage Trust. Moira tells me you're here to look at our historical sites?'

Anna asked about his local connections as the McNeils had been the owners of the island in the eighteenth century. Niall confirmed that his family had lived here for at least two hundred and fifty years and that his father had a croft, as well as having been the local schoolteacher. He himself went to University in Edinburgh and now only spent some of his time on the island as he worked for Heritage Environment Scotland, the public body that cares for and promotes the country's historic sites. Niall introduced Anna to his fellow trust members Ewan and Caitriona, who were there to play the quiz. A few minutes chat and they were quite impressed with Anna's knowledge of early Scottish history. She played down its full extent but wanted them to think of her as a serious amateur historian. They soon asked if she'd join their team and she was happy to accept. Niall said he was going to Oronsay Priory the following day to do some assessment of the masonry and see if anything needed urgent repair. He asked if Anna would be interested in joining him, which she also accepted.

The quiz covered the usual topics, which meant that on reality TV programmes and the lives of celebrities Anna was totally clueless. However, they then had a round on Celtic mythology where she got two questions the trust members didn't know. One was on the great Welsh tale, the *Mabinogion*, which was: 'What bird does Branwen train to send a letter to her brother Bendigeidfran?' The other was: 'In Gallic mythology who was the goddess of horses?' Her answers of 'a starling' and 'Epona' helped them win the quiz by a single point.

Niall said he'd pick up Anna from the hotel in the morning and she retired to bed reasonably satisfied. She didn't want to ask any intrusive questions about 'Professor Roger' too soon. She'd thoroughly liked the trust members and decided that if everything worked itself out, she'd return to the island to apologise for her deception.

Anna was waiting at 9 a.m. sharp, having consumed a Scottish breakfast far larger than her usual meal. Niall's HES Land Rover pulled into the car park a couple of minutes later. Oronsay is Colonsay's smaller southern neighbour and is joined to the larger island by a tidal causeway. The Augustinian priory was active from the mid-fourteenth to the mid-sixteenth century, and replaced an earlier structure said to have been founded by St Oran in 563. Restoration work took place in the 1880s and 1920s and the remains are substantial. Anna soon convinced Niall that she was entirely capable of assessing the state of medieval masonry and so she covered some of the later parts of the structure, making notes as she went. Niall utilised an inclinometer, taking readings he compared to previous ones, to assess if any walls were increasing their potential for collapse. He had brought bread, cheese, and scones plus flasks of tea for lunch. The day was cold, and he said there could be some snow that night.

'How come you know so much about history and buildings when you're a translator?'

'I chose some electives in those fields,' Anna replied. 'Plus I went on a couple of digs in my long vacs. I've often thought about turning to historical translation, but my current work suits me as I'm pretty much my own boss and it's good money when publishers know you, especially when you always get the work back before the deadline.'

Niall seemed happy with her explanation, so she asked more about the island and, especially, the Viking ship burial. Niall said he wasn't an expert on that as, of course, all the physical traces on site were long gone.

'Is there anyone who knows more about it? All the people who were around when the excavations took place are long dead.'

'Well, there's Professor Roger.' Anna's ears pricked up. 'He's an old guy that lives near to the site and he was a scholar of the period. I think he's still with us. He must be well over ninety but if he'd died, I'd certainly have heard.'

Anna tried to conceal her excitement. 'You say he lives near the site?'

'Yes, it's one of the cottages at Uragaig I think, just beyond Kiloran Bay where the ship was found.'

'Do you think he'd mind me calling on him?'

'Shouldn't think so. I don't think he has any family and he's been here about thirty years, so he doesn't have many visitors.'

'Thanks. Can I mention that you suggested I look him up?'

'Sure. Let me know how he is. I haven't seen him for a year or two, though a friend of my mother's does his housework.'

As it was getting dark, they finished their work and Niall thanked Anna for her help. 'It's saved me at least half a day, thanks a lot. You don't want a job, do you?' Anna politely declined, saying she only had a few days to spare but would like to come back to Colonsay some time. Niall was returning to the mainland the following day and wished her luck when he dropped her back at the hotel.

Anna spent a quiet evening planning how best to explain things if 'Professor Roger' did indeed turn out to be Roger Inkpen.

Chapter 40

The morning was bright and clear but overnight there had been a dusting of snow. Anna set off just before ten to drive the few miles to the north of the island. She passed Colonsay House, the property of the island's owners, the Barons Strathcona. The narrow road continued through pine and birch woods before emerging into open countryside, with low hills ahead. In less than a mile Anna saw the broad sweep of sand of Kiloran Bay on her right. The road narrowed to a track, twisting and climbing the hill behind the bay. She passed a homemade sign that advised: 'Please drive slowly. Ducks and hens', followed by a less friendly one saying, 'All dogs on leads or may be shot', before reaching a scattering of buildings. Anna stopped the car and saw a man looking out of his window. 'Hi,' she greeted him. 'I'm here to see Professor Roger. Could I leave my car here?'

'Aye. Just keep the driveway clear and you'll be fine,' he said.

Niall had told her the professor lived in the last cottage. She knocked on the green door. There was some shuffling and the door opened. A small man with a few wisps of sandy hair peered out. 'Yes?'

'Excuse me but are you Professor Roger?'

'I am.'

'My name is Alex Dakin. Niall McNeil suggested I speak with you. I've got a great interest in the history of the island and the Viking ship burial. I wondered if you could spare a few minutes?'

The professor considered her request for a few seconds as he looked her up and down. Finally, he said, 'Well, in that case you'd better come in, young lady.' The cottage was comfortably furnished and full of bookcases. There was an open peat fire burning in the hearth and it was warm and cosy. 'Please sit down, Miss?'

'Dakin.'

'Yes indeed. Would you care for a cup of tea?'

Anna said she would, and the professor went to the kitchen. She looked carefully round the room, studying the books. They seemed to match the collection of a former professor of early medieval history. Just before he came back with a tray, which included oat cakes in addition to tea, Anna spotted the clinching detail. In a glass fronted case beside the window were a group of works by Tolkien, including the three volumes of *The Lord of the Rings* in their first edition dust covers.

Anna gave the Professor Alex Dakin's background and told him she'd spent yesterday assisting Niall survey Oronsay Priory. They talked about the ship burial, and he fetched a couple of books on the topic including a scarce edition of Malcolm McNeill's 1882 drawings. He talked about other medieval remains on the island, which has one of Scotland's greatest concentrations of Viking graves. He was impressed with her knowledge of the subject and eventually Anna decided it was time to come clean. 'Professor,' she began, 'can I ask you something?'

'Of course, my dear.'

'Is your name Roger Inkpen?'

He briefly scowled but then his face relaxed. 'I haven't been called that for years,' he said. 'Everybody here always knew me by my first name and so, when I moved here permanently, I just adopted it. Why do you ask? I have a feeling your visit is not as spontaneous as it seems.'

Anna admitted it wasn't. She apologised for not using her real name and told Inkpen the whole story. When she reached the explanation of Magnus's murder the professor's hands gripped the arms of his chair tightly. He held up his hand to pause her. He took off his glasses and dabbed his eyes with a handkerchief. 'You cared for Magnus?' he asked.

'Yes,' said Anna, lowering her eyes.

'As did I,' he said. 'He was one of the very best students at Oxford. I didn't have much direct contact with him, but his work was both original and exemplary. He's a great loss. A very great loss.' They talked about Magnus for some time before Anna brought the subject back to the *Codex Johannem Regem*. It was at this point that Inkpen surprised her. 'If only you had found me earlier. I might have saved you a lot of fruitless work.'

'How do you mean?'

'Your pursuit of King John's treasure. Such an obvious red herring. I'd worked that out in about 1965.' Inkpen explained that his interest in the *Codex* began in the late forties, but he hadn't looked at it in more detail until ten years later when he had become an academic. 'I was most interested in the changes and continuities between the reign of John and his son. But the drawings intrigued me. With the blatantly obvious beaver joke I simply thought it was a bored monk playing a practical joke. I'm sorry I misidentified the writer.'

'Did you think the joke could be a cover for something else?'

'Not for a while. But then, yes, I did think there could be more to it. Especially after I looked at the slides.' Anna explained Cloote's idea that there could be a link to Ivar the Boneless. 'Well, that would be quite a coup if there were a connection. Given what you've told me about Johannes I think my "bored monk" thesis is entirely wrong. It looks like there's far more to the animal pictures and other illustrations.'

'Other illustrations?' Anna was immediately listening more intently. She got out her laptop and showed Inkpen the slides she and Magnus had found in Merton library. 'Were there more pages than this?'

'Yes, there were. There were two pages with musical notation. They always seemed more important than the others, but I never found out why that might be. I suppose I became distracted by other topics and never got round to following them up.'

'You wouldn't have copies of those pages I suppose.'

'Oh yes, I certainly do. As I said I thought they were more interesting than the others, so I took them with me when I retired rather than leaving them with the other stuff at Merton.'

'Do you have them here?'

'Hmm. Now let me think,' he paused for a while. 'Come with me,' he said finally. Inkpen put on his coat and Anna followed him to a small outbuilding that had probably housed livestock. Inside were stacks of boxes, a few old items of furniture and some aged fishing tackle. Inkpen rummaged through, eventually pulling out a box. 'I think this is it. Let's get back inside, it's rather cold.'

In the cottage Inkpen extracted a sketchbook as well as some Kodak slides. Anna held the slides up to the window and could see that they were indeed manuscript pages. The sketchbook had Inkpen's excellent drawings of some of the animals Johannes had inserted in the *Codex* as well as some four-line neumes from the missing pages. 'You're welcome to take them, Dr Carr,' Inkpen said. 'If Magnus thought so highly of you so do I.' He smiled. 'And by the way, do be careful of Gervase Penhaligon.'

They hadn't really mentioned him up to now. 'He was another of your students I believe?'

'He was. And he is a weasel and a rat, if that is possible and isn't being unkind to those animals. I still believe his thesis was significantly plagiarised though I could never prove it.'

Their conversation drifted away from the *Codex,* and Inkpen told Anna more about his life at Oxford. Anna mentioned the Tolkien books in his case. 'He got rather irritated about his fans,' Inkpen said. 'He'd have got even more annoyed if he'd lived longer. I believe the films were quite successful.' He revealed that he'd never seen them and didn't own a television. He got the three books out of the cabinet to show Anna. In each there was a personal, handwritten dedication from the author in his flowing Elvish script, that Anna had seen reproduced but never in the original. The one in *The Fellowship of the Ring* was longer than the others and Inkpen translated it for her. As she wasn't a huge fan, Elvish was one language she didn't know. What she did say was that he ought to take more care of the books. 'The set must be worth at least a quarter of a million' she told him, 'maybe more as they're probably unique.'

Inkpen was surprised but not worried. 'I don't think theft is likely. We did have a crime on the island in 2013 when the policewoman's boyfriend had his car vandalised but nothing since.' He then asked Anna more about her research and Cloote's ideas about Ivar's treasure. Inkpen then took out one of his drawings. 'I read one of Oliver Cloote's books a while ago. He has some rather fantastical notions based on slightly flimsy evidence, but I must admit he has insights I've not read elsewhere. So, I'll assume his idea to be correct for now.' Anna was beginning to marvel at the nimbleness of Inkpen's thought processes. This was a man of ninety-four; what must he have been like in his prime? 'Might there be something in the pages that you've not seen before? Let me see your excellent animal code.' Anna found it on the laptop. 'Remarkable devices aren't they? I don't use one, but they work so quickly, and the screen is so clear. Really marvellous.' After studying for a while, he said, 'Take a look at these,' pointing out some rows of animal illustrations just above the musical notation. 'Why don't you try your code and substitution grid on them?'

Anna did as he suggested while Inkpen went to make some more tea. He also asked Anna if she'd like some leek and potato broth, cheese, and bread. 'The broth and bread are homemade by my housekeeper Eileen. I think you'll enjoy them.' He was right, all three were delicious.

By the time she'd finished her lunch she had a result. Inkpen had been right, Johannes was sending another message:

In quo sunt divitiae suae
Taxo sagittam ligneam
Scriptum litteris lapis
Praetorium concilio superiors
Terra Suiones

Which roughly translates as:

Where the wealth of
Yew-wood arrows
Written in letters of stone
Upper council halls
Land of the Swedes

'Can you make any sense of it?' he asked her.

'Some of it I think,' said Anna. But before she could start telling him Inkpen stopped her.

'No, Dr Carr, *don't* tell me. If the people who killed Magnus are that ruthless it's best if I don't know. If I don't know, I can't tell.' Anna had a sinking feeling in her stomach and hoped she hadn't put Inkpen in danger. But she refrained from saying any more.

She spent the rest of the afternoon with Roger Inkpen talking about a wide range of subjects. She wondered if he got lonely or lacked intellectual stimulation, but he said no. 'When you have these beautiful surroundings and wonderful people, how can you be lonely?' he asked.

Before it got dark, they went for a short walk down to the bay. Inkpen pointed out exactly where the Viking burial had been discovered a hundred and forty years before and they looked out across the sea to the Ross of Mull about fifteen miles to the north. They sat on a rock and watched the sun go down in a spectacular burst of red, emphasised by thin cloud that stood out in bands of purple. 'My only regret these days is that I can't walk far,' Inkpen said, 'but it's still the best place in the world.'

Anna said her goodbyes, promising to tell him the outcome of their quest. 'You can always get a message to me through Niall,' he said, 'though I won't tell him anything about the real reason for your visit.'

She took the box back to the car and drove to the hotel. There she planned her trip back. The first ferry to Oban would be on Monday but there was one on Saturday afternoon that went via Port Askaig, on Islay, to Kennacraig on the Kintyre peninsula. She decided this would save her at least a day and booked the other ferries she'd need to take, as well as an overnight stop.

There was live music at the hotel at eight from a local folk duo who sang some traditional Gaelic songs of the Hebrides. Niall's colleague Caitriona was there, and she was able to tell Anna more about them. She was a native of the Isle of Lewis and spoke Gaelic fluently. She explained Scottish Gaelic to Anna, whose knowledge of Celtic languages was less extensive than those of the Scandinavian countries. 'It's a Goidelic language, like Modern Irish and Manx, developed out of Old Irish. Scots Gaelic became a separate language in the thirteenth century. Nowadays just over one percent, maybe sixty thousand people, in Scotland speak it.'

'It existed alongside Norse I believe,' Anna said.

'That's right. The Norse influence was huge among the Norse–Gaels, the people who dominated the Irish Sea and Scottish islands from the ninth to the twelfth centuries.'

'And there are many survivals of the language?'

'Sure, Old Norse words have influenced modern Scots English and Scottish Gaelic. One of the most obvious is "bairn" for a child which comes from the Norse "barn".'

'Of course. I'd never thought of that connection before.'

Anna was pleased to have found a fellow language enthusiast but kept her exceptional scholarship in check. She told Caitriona that she'd met with Professor Roger and would she thank Niall for the introduction. Caitriona moved the conversation on to more personal issues asking Anna about partners or boyfriends. She thought she'd not try to invent anything so told her she was gay but didn't have a partner at present. Caitriona said she was currently in the same position but that she and Niall had had a brief affair a couple of years back.

The music finished around eleven but, as no one seemed to be going home, Anna stayed on. They were joined by the musicians who Caitriona introduced. The singer was Flòraidh, Flora, and the fiddler was Cathal. They talked about music for over an hour before they headed off and Anna went to bed.

*

The following day Anna had time to kill before the ferry departed, so she contacted Anula to check how things had gone. 'No idea if I was being watched but the bike is at Magnus's house. Nora's quite a character isn't she?'

Anna said she would be coming back to Suffolk via Oxford and would pick up the bike. Anula told her she'd dropped in on Oliver and Gordon and they were working on what she called 'the plan'.

Next, Anna called Cloote and asked him what he thought about Johannes's new clue. 'I've got some ideas,' he said, 'but we can put our minds together when you're back.'

Anna looked out of her window. Steady snow was falling, and she checked the forecast. Fortunately, it didn't look too bad, and the roads would probably be clear. The ferry left promptly at four-thirty, heading south to the narrow channel of the Sound of Islay that runs between that island and its neighbour, Jura. Anna stared out at the latter thinking of the time George Orwell lived at a farmhouse there while completing the novel *Nineteen*

Eighty-Four. The ferry docked for half an hour at the tiny Port Askaig. She just had time to purchase a bottle of Port Askaig one-hundred-percent proof malt, that she thought would make a suitable gift for Cloote, before re-embarking. The ship continued south across the Sound of Jura, skirting the small island of Gigha to starboard, before heading up West Loch Tarbert to the terminal at Kennacraig, which is little more than a landing stage. The drive to Tarbert was only about five miles, so she reached The Anchor overlooking the picturesque harbour, in time for a late dinner.

Her ferry, a small vessel that only took a dozen or so vehicles, left at nine the following morning for the short hop across East Loch Tarbert to another tiny port, Portavadie. An hour's drive brought her to the main resort on the Cowal Peninsula, Dunoon, from where it was another twenty-five-minute trip on an open ferry across the Firth of Clyde to Gourock. By eleven-thirty she was on the road heading south. Though it was boring, Anna stuck to the quickest route via the motorways all the way to Oxford. Here she'd booked a night at the dull, but anonymous, Holiday Inn, where the hire company said they could pick up her car. When she checked in, she asked if there was anything for Alex Dakin and the receptionist fetched the bag Nora had left.

She got an early night and rose before six. When she dropped the key card into the slot at reception it was Anna Carr who did so, Alex Dakin had disappeared. She caught the park and ride bus opposite the hotel, which went down Woodstock Road and stopped close to Magnus's house. She retrieved her bike and set straight off to Aldeburgh. As she passed the roundabout Forth's lookouts dutifully reported that 'the girl had returned'.

Chapter 41

Anna held a conference with Oliver and Gordon. She showed them the new slides and documents she had borrowed from Professor Inkpen. Gordon had a convertor that was able to digitise the slides so they could be looked at in more detail. 'As I see it,' Anna began, 'we have an easier part and a harder one. The easier is the new coded message: "*Where the wealth of Yew-wood arrows Written in letters of stone Upper council halls Land of the Swedes.*"

'And the harder is working out what, if anything, the music means.'

'I suggest we tackle the easier bit first,' Cloote said. 'What does Johannes's message mean?'

'Okay. He's saying that a great wealth is held by a person associated with archery. That's consistent with your idea about Ivar the Boneless. The name Ivar is derived from "yŕ", meaning yew or bow, and "herr", warrior or army. So, the treasure *is* linked to Ivar. Written in letters of stone could be a reference to Viking runic inscriptions and the last two lines where the runes are to be found. A place that means "upper council halls" in Sweden, so Uppsala. Correct?'

'My own view entirely. There is something about this search that gets stranger the more we discover. Increasingly it seems to be touching things that we're close to. The latest is this. It's telling us to go back to my old university.'

'Which is also famous for its runestones,' Anna added.

Gordon asked if they could tell him about these, so Cloote explained. 'They became fashionable after the Danish king, Harold Bluetooth, raised the Jelling Stone to commemorate his parents, sometime between 960 and 985. The Jelling Stone set off a craze that lasted through the eleventh century, and into the twelfth. Today, there are about three thousand runestones in Scandinavia and the British Isles, and new ones keep being discovered.'

'Presumably they're called runestones because they're covered in runes?'

'Correct. Most are carved with the sixteen-letter script of the Younger Futhark, in curving bands that sometimes end with the heads of serpents or other creatures. They usually record the name of the person the stone's dedicated to and who did the raising and carving. Their main purposes were to mark territory, explain inheritance, commemorate dead kinsmen, or tell of important events. But the Vikings also believed that runes had magical powers. That they could predict the future or counteract harmful forces, so they were used in incantations, curses, and magic spells.'

'What kinds of spells?' asked Gordon.

'Well, the Glavendrup stone on Funen is an absolute cracker. It has a warning to anyone who dares to damage or move the stone.' As he said this Cloote pulled down a book. 'The inscription reads: "Ragnhildr placed this stone in memory of Alli the Pale, priest of the sanctuary, honourable þegn of the retinue. Alli's sons made this monument in memory of their father, and his wife in memory of her husband. And Sóti carved these runes in memory of his lord. Þórr hallow these runes. A warlock be he who damages this stone or drags it to stand in memory of another."'

'But Oliver,' said Rees, 'you've said there are literally hundreds of these runestones. How do we know which one Johannes is referring to?'

'Yes, in Sweden alone there are over two thousand. I can't think of any I've studied that refer to Ivar's treasure, though I'm not familiar with them all.'

'The only stone I know of that mentions Ivar is the Steine or Long Stone in Dublin,' said Anna.

'What's that?' asked Gordon.

'It's a re-creation of a pillar originally erected by the River Liffey, in the tenth or eleventh century, by the inhabitants of Viking-Age Dublin. It disappeared around 1750 but there's a replica just outside Trinity College.'

'And nothing else that's relevant?'

'Not that I can think of,' said Oliver. 'But there could be indirect references. Though the language and information of runic inscriptions are well researched, we know little about how Viking-Age people read them. Perhaps we should compare runestones to newspapers or a web page, where the reader is attracted by headings and pictures. There could be a hidden meaning somewhere. I'll need to do some digging online.'

'They're well documented then?' asked Gordon.

'Yes indeed. We won't need to go to Sweden to search for clues,' he concluded.

They turned their attention to the musical notation on the new slides. 'It's not my specialism,' began Cloote, 'but I've been looking into musical notation of the twelfth and thirteenth centuries. The earliest medieval music didn't have any kind of notational system, it was just a memory aid for singers who already knew the melody. Single notes were drawn as dots or lines, called punctus, and several notes on one syllable were drawn as a connected group known as a neume. Several neumes one after another was a melisma. After about 900, notation became more complex with "heighted neumes", neumes placed at different heights in relation to each other. Then lines, representing a particular note, started being drawn. Originally, they were scratched on the parchment but later were drawn in colours. Usually red for F, and yellow or green for C. By about 1200 the notes themselves were changed from dots and lines to the square shape of the Gothic style. What we have here looks like part of an early thirteenth-century setting of the mass.'

Anna and Gordon looked more carefully. The staff lines were inked in red with mainly black notes on them. 'Is this a Sequence then?' Anna asked.

'I'd say so. I've compared it to others, and it follows the form, but it also seems quite distinctive,' Cloote replied. 'For one thing there are no words.'

'Just explain again what a sequence is,' asked Rees.

'The sequence is part of the mass,' Cloote continued. 'A Latin text associated with a specific chant melody, sung between the Alleluia and the reading of the Gospel. It developed in the ninth century from the trope to the jubilus, the florid ending of the last syllable of the Alleluia. By the eleventh century the sequence developed a common poetic form that reflected the musical structure: typically, an introductory followed by a series of rhymed, metrical couplets of varying lengths. Each syllable was set to a single note of music.'

'But how could Magnus know it was a musical sequence when he hadn't seen the missing pages?' Gordon asked.

'A very interesting question,' replied Cloote. 'I don't know. He must have seen something that we've missed.'

'I think it was the more detailed animals,' said Anna. 'Magnus mentioned the nightingale and the swan and then there were the dolphin and the cricket too. I never had a chance to ask him more about them.'

'Do you think those creatures are a way of interpreting the music then?' Gordon asked.

'I honestly don't know and it's not something we're going to crack by staring at the bloody thing,' said Anna.

'Indeed,' Cloote said. 'In the meantime, Anna, I have an idea for throwing our, ahem, friends off our trail.' Oliver outlined his plan.

When he'd finished Anna said, 'Okay, it's as good as anything I could think of. When do you leave?'

'I've already taken the liberty, so I'm flying to Hannover, via Amsterdam, tomorrow afternoon. What I *haven't* worked out is how we get this information to them without them suspecting it's all a ruse? I suppose Penhaligon could be our conduit?'

'Yes, he must be,' said Anna. 'Don't worry. I know *exactly* how we can do it. All I need is a bit of help from your security friend,' she said to Gordon, and then explained her idea.

'Anna. That is brilliant, mad, and quite immoral. Will he do it?' Gordon asked.

'Oh yes,' she said matter-of-factly. 'He trusts me, and I think we can ensure that he's blameless, in case they find out it's a fake. I'll go to Cambridge to get the ball rolling.'

With the plan agreed, Anna contacted Rasmus. She asked whether Penhaligon was around and was pleased when told that he was. 'I'll explain everything when I see you tomorrow,' she said before ringing off.

*

Elias Forth had returned to his London flat, partly to keep abreast of his business and partly to keep a close eye on Carrie Prentiss' lobbying. She was sitting in Forth's spacious living room overlooking the Thames. He was pleased when she reported that she'd secured an interview with both a Sunday newspaper and BBC News and that the social media campaign, spreading false information on the harmful effects of abortion, was gaining momentum. 'We're stepping up the picketing of abortion clinics as you'll have seen from the cuttings,' she said. 'The woke press is going apoplectic about it, trying to lobby the government to ban them.'

'And we're confident they won't cave in?'

'Fairly. But if they do, we have the campaign on suppression of free speech ready. You've seen our successes in that direction too? The statement by the education minister on academic freedom being denied. It's all going better than we'd hoped. It does help to have a pliant print media. It's far harder back home with the lying *New York Times* and *Washington Post*.'

'But TV is trickier?' Forth added.

'You never know,' Carrie replied. 'If the campaign to remove funding from the BBC succeeds then a Fox News equivalent could fill the void.' Forth laughed. A few years ago, even he wouldn't have expected things to have worked out so well. He thought Carrie deserved a little present and so did she.

'Who was the boy who brought those documents from Nesfield this morning?'

'He's called Harry Spall, works on the boats.'

'He's delicious,' Carrie said. 'Have you seen him naked?'

'Not completely,' Forth replied as if it was the most obvious question in the world.

'Well, *I'd* like to. He'd make a pleasant change from Vladimir and those wimpish politicians. Do you know that Meads broke down sobbing last night?' Clarence Meads was a newly elected MP who had made a name for himself during the Brexit campaign and been promoted to junior ministerial level.

'He was feeling guilty about cheating on his wife, much as she'd care. And he was pathetic in bed. Needed two Viagra just to get it up long enough. Jesus Christ, what I go through.' She took a long gulp from a glass of bourbon by her side.

'I'll give Spall a job in London,' Forth agreed. 'You can report back to me on his physical attributes.' His phone buzzed. 'Nesfield. What's up?'

'There's activity in Aldeburgh, sir. The girl has been in Oxford the past few days but she's back and Cloote is at Stanstead.'

'Where's he going?'

'Amsterdam and then Hannover.'

'Can we track him there?'

'Yes, sir. I've got our German agents in place. They'll let us know where he's headed.'

'Good. Still nothing from Penhaligon?'

'No.'

'I think you should pay him a visit. He needs a little encouragement.'

'Of course, sir, it would be a pleasure.'

Chapter 42

Before she left for Cambridge Anna called Rasmus again. Penhaligon was in his office. 'Where does he usually go for lunch? Does he have a routine?'

'Yeh, he usually goes to the Riverside in the university centre.'

'I know where it is. Look. When he goes out follow him to check that's where he's going. I'll meet you there.'

Anna parked at Darwin College – the tracker was still on the bike – then phoned Rasmus again. Penhaligon had just left the building. 'He's walking along Silver Street and crossing the river,' Rasmus reported. 'Now along the river, yes into Granta Place.'

Anna was watching from outside the Doubletree Hotel and saw the tubby figure enter the university centre. Rasmus was fifty yards behind. 'Hi. Look Rasmus I need to ask you again. Are you sure about helping us? There are things I can't tell you, but the people Penhaligon is working for are murdering swine who will stop at nothing.'

'I know, and they're the people who killed Magnus. He was my friend. I really want to help.' For a second, he looked her directly in the eye before looking down.

'Okay. Then this is what we'll do.' They found Penhaligon in the main dining hall, a large open-plan restaurant, rather than the more exclusive Riverside. He'd obviously decided on a cheaper option, or perhaps he was in a hurry, as it was self-service. Anna and Rasmus got their food and, though they sat well away from him, she was confident he'd spot them. Sure enough, though he finished his food first, he remained in his seat pretending to look at his phone. They finished their meal and strolled out. Penhaligon followed. He now thought he was tracking them.

Anna and Rasmus went into the Mill, the pub next door to the centre, ordered drinks and sat at a small corner table. Sure enough Penhaligon slipped into the building after them. He sat a few tables behind them. Anna moved next to Rasmus on the bench. She put her arm round his neck and kissed him passionately on the lips. He responded and his hands felt for one of her breasts as the kiss lingered. After a few minutes Penhaligon was in no doubt that they were romantically involved. He needed to get instructions so moved to the back bar and called Nesfield.

'Ah, professor. You've saved me a call. I was going to pay you a visit.'

'Listen,' said Penhaligon excitedly, 'that girl of Cloote's is here. She's with one our research assistants, the one who was Strachan's pupil. They're all over each other in the bar.'

'Thought she was a dyke,' Nesfield replied sceptically.

'Obviously bisexual,' Penhaligon replied. 'Anyway, those bastards must have been spying on me all along.'

Nesfield considered. 'Do you have access to his computer?'

'Yes, easily. His desk is in the open plan area of the office.'

'In that case I *will* come to see you. I can be there by four. Okay?'

*

Anna and Rasmus headed off for his room in Pembroke College, which was only minutes away, with Penhaligon following them at a distance. 'If he wasn't convinced we're fucking each other this should do the trick,' Anna told Rasmus. He blushed and said nothing. In his room Anna brought out a hard drive that she connected to Rasmus's phone. 'This will download the texts I told you about.'

'And the photos and videos?'

'Yes, those too. It's okay you can look at them. In fact, you'd better just in case.' Rasmus blushed again.

'Now,' Anna said, 'you should continue using your old phone to tell me how sexy I am and for all the usual stuff. But if you need to contact us about anything else use *this* instead.' She produced a new phone from her bag. 'And keep it hidden. We don't want Penhaligon to know you have two. We've already connected with your PC by the way.' Rasmus didn't ask how they'd done that, and Anna didn't want to explain Scott's tricks.

'It will show some email activity between us, but nothing too intimate. It'll just add to the idea that we've been together for a while. When we're sure Penhaligon has made a move, I'll be sending you some files.' She thanked Rasmus again, gave him a quick peck on the cheek, and headed back to Darwin.

*

When Nesfield met Penhaligon at his college, Trinity Hall, he was far more pleasant than he'd planned to be a few hours earlier. It looked as if the professor might have his uses after all as a way into Cloote's little coterie. He explained to Penhaligon what he needed to do.

At five-thirty Rasmus received a call from Penhaligon asking if he was in the department. He replied that he wasn't, which the latter knew already. 'A pity. I wanted to show you some new photos of the fine rolls I've been working on. I'd value your opinion.' Fine rolls are financial records of the English Chancery in the Middle Ages that were first used during the reign of Henry III. It was the first time Penhaligon had said he valued Rasmus's opinion on anything. However, Anna had indicated something like this would occur, though he was surprised at how quickly it had happened. Rasmus said he'd be happy to look at the documents and a few minutes later three photos turned up. One of these contained the spyware Nesfield had prepared and when Rasmus opened the photo it downloaded to his phone. It was well-designed to run with minimal impact on the speed of apps and would be undetectable other than to an expert.

Back at ASNC Penhaligon switched on Rasmus's PC and plugged a USB drive into one of the ports. A minute or two later he took it out. He went to his own office and switched on his personal laptop. Following Nesfield's instructions he was now able to open an app that gave him direct access to both Rasmus's PC and his phone. Penhaligon checked the documents on the PC. From a first scan there was nothing that looked unusual for a post-grad researcher. He then went to the emails which he sorted by sender and quickly found a small group from Anna. These came from both a Merton College account and a personal one. Most of them were arrangements to meet or exchanged comments on historical topics, but a few included personal terms of endearment and remarks only lovers would make.

He then turned his attention to the phone. There were numerous calls to and from 'A' going back about fifteen months. Then he looked at the texts. Again, there were lots from 'A', several of a sexually explicit nature. Hers to him were far more explicit than his to her. *Yes, that fits with the little weasel's personality. Timid and submissive. Can't see what she'd see in him, even given that she's a freak herself,* thought Penhaligon. He then went to the photos. *What have we got here? Fuck! She certainly doesn't leave much to the imagination does she!* The existence of the video had been indicated in one of the texts when she talked about missing his 'fantastic cock' and though Penhaligon tried to tell himself she was a hairy goth dyke, viewing it aroused him significantly.

He re-contacted Nesfield and described what he'd found. Then, using a secure cloud storage facility, uploaded the emails, texts, photos, and video. By eight, both men were convinced that Rasmus had been Anna's lover since their Oxford days.

Chapter 43

Forth's agents in Germany had been personally selected from among supporters of the German identitarian movement which emerged in the early 2000s as opponents of multiculturalism and immigration. Identitarians try to make racism modern and fashionable while denying they are racist. Their adherents are sharp-suited, clean-cut young white men who smile and look presentable on TV. Klaus and Werner were two such. They were employed by one of Forth's subsidiary companies and had undergone extensive surveillance and countersurveillance training in both Germany and the US. In other circumstances Forth used them for industrial espionage, gaining information to make short-selling decisions before his competitors. They were waiting in the arrivals hall at Hannover airport when Cloote's flight disembarked. He took a cab which Klaus and Werner followed. In an hour they saw him being dropped off at the Parkhotel Altes Kaffeehaus in Wolfenbüttel.

The following morning Cloote walked a few minutes across the old town to the Herzog-August-Bibliothek, the ducal library, which hosts one of the best collections of ancient books in the world, and from which Westley had pilfered the Gothic manuscript that had started the whole saga. Cloote had visited several times and was well-known to the staff.

'Herr Doctor, how pleasant to see you again,' the director greeted him personally. 'How may we be of assistance on this visit?'

Cloote explained that he was there to study possible links between scholars in the early thirteenth century who had connections between Germany, France, and England and, at the director's insistence, was given priority over several other readers who were waiting for their selections to be delivered.

Cloote didn't expect to find anything new. He knew the library's collection very well but was hoping his movements were being studied, as indeed they were. Klaus came into the library and asked some questions about doing some research there. While the archivist's attention was distracted, Werner attached a tiny camera to the bottom of a shelf that overlooked Cloote's desk.

*

Anna and Anula met up, first for a run and more training, then for a drink at the Cross Keys, after which they decided to eat fish and chips at the Golden Galleon. 'You should definitely take up angampora more seriously you know,' said Anula, as she tucked into incredibly fresh haddock. 'Those last moves I taught you took me two years to get right and here you are perfecting them in a few weeks.'

'I'm still nowhere near your level of skill though.'

'Maybe, but it's getting to the point where I can't really teach you more.'

They chatted for a while before Anula said, 'Do you mind if I ask you something?'

'Depends on what it is.'

'Well, you're incredibly good at concentration and focusing your mind when we practise and yet you're a really hard person to get to know.' She waited to see if Anna would say anything. She didn't. 'And when we work out you seem to trust me. But, you know, you don't want to trust me emotionally. There I've said it.'

'You're right. I trust you as a teacher. You know more than me. But trusting people. Really trusting them. I don't do it.'

'Is it something that happened? In the past?'

Anna didn't answer directly instead she explained: 'When you put your trust in someone you give them power over you. I won't do that. No one will have power over me unless I decide it's going to happen. And it's nothing personal. If I was going to trust anyone, you'd be the most likely.'

'Thanks for being honest, Anna.'

'I'm nearly always honest. At least I am with people I like.' She smiled.

'Have you always been like this? What were you like as a girl?'

'Angry.'

Chapter 44

Anna continued to learn as much as she could about runestones. She'd not studied them in depth before and wanted to be sure that she could match Cloote's understanding. He was certainly right about the online information. The Rundata.net website provides a database of runic inscriptions that covers most of the known runestones of Northern Europe. Its excellent search facility allowed Anna to check a wide variety of terms. She spent what, for her, was a fascinating afternoon and evening looking through the database and testing out all the combinations that could link to Johannes's message. Cloote seemed to be right, there were no stones having a connection to Ivar, East Anglia, or the Great Heathen Army. The nearest were a group of about thirty stones in Sweden that refer to Viking-Age voyages to Britain, known collectively as the England runestones. But these were much later than the period they were interested in, referring to payments of so-called Danegeld in the late tenth and early eleventh centuries.

Drawing a blank, Anna started idly looking through other information about runestones. One that kept coming up was the so-called Kensington runestone. In 1898 a Swedish immigrant to the USA, Olof Ohman, reported he'd discovered an inscribed stone near the town of Kensington, Minnesota. The inscription purported to be a record left by Scandinavian explorers in the fourteenth century and, though scholars have since dismissed it as a fake, there's a devoted group who maintain its authenticity. On the pages that discussed the Kensington stone one of these adherents mentioned another stone: 'There are other runestones that so-called experts have dismissed as fakes. There are, for example, those discovered in the River Fyris by Viggo Lund in 2013.' Intrigued, Anna looked this up and found some references in the Swedish press. Viggo Lund was a diver with the University of Uppsala sub-aqua club who had been working with the local police following a stabbing. He was searching the river, Fyrisån in

Swedish, looking for the knife when he found two stones. When taken out of the river they appeared to be runestones from the ninth or tenth centuries but, after examination by academics at the university, had been declared to be forgeries, probably perpetrated by a group of students trying to fool their professors. Lund had been accused of being in on the deception, though he had forcefully denied the accusation.

Anna tried to find Viggo Lund. There were three people of that name on Facebook and eight on LinkedIn. Sure enough one of the LinkedIn ones had been to Uppsala University. Anna messaged him saying she'd like to ask him about the runestones he'd found in 2013. She couldn't find anything more about the fake stones or any inscriptions, so she texted Cloote about them.

*

The following day Werner reported to Savile Nesfield. 'Your professor appears to have found something. Our camera picked him up getting very excited about one of the papers he was examining this afternoon. I can't tell you what it was, but he immediately started texting someone about it.'

'And what did he do after that?'

'He went straight back to the hotel, paid his bill, and he's now waiting for a taxi. He's probably on his way back to England.'

'Keep me informed about what he does. Have you cleaned up?'

'Yes, I've retrieved the camera in the library and the one outside his room. The listening device is still in place just in case, but he seems to use text all the time.'

'Okay. Confirm if he does go back to the airport.'

Werner was correct. Cloote returned to Hannover airport where he took an evening flight to Amsterdam. He stayed overnight in a hotel by the airport before getting the nine thirty-five to Stanstead where Rees picked him up.

That afternoon, Anna composed a long email to Rasmus, attaching some documents. Within a few minutes Penhaligon had forwarded these to Nesfield. In the evening Forth sat down with Nesfield and Morten at his London flat. 'What do you make of them then?' he asked.

'They are certainly intriguing and consistent with what we know,' Morten began. 'And they confirm the link with Meister Eckhart that Penhaligon found.'

'Okay explain it to me,' Forth demanded.

'What the girl has told the Estonian is that Cloote has found a link between the Gothic manuscript Westley stole and Meister Eckhart via a monk called Meister Ruthard. This Ruthard was a colleague of Johannes of Medhamstead in England and was, at this time, a monk at the Priory of Eye in Suffolk. Ruthard says that he knows the secret to Johannes's "callidus codice", clever codes. He claims that he has written all this down in a document he has concealed within one of the priory's most treasured books, the so-called *Red Book of Eye*.'

'The what?' Morten explained that the *Red Book of Eye* was a version of the gospels thought to have been used by St Felix, the seventh century missionary who established a bishopric at Dunwich on the Suffolk coast. The book, so-called because it was bound in red, was preserved at the Priory at Eye to save it from destruction by the sea. The subsequent fate of the *Red Book* was a mystery because it disappeared sometime after 1536. Various sources have suggested its fate, the most notable being MR James, who, though being best remembered as a writer of chilling ghost stories, was also an outstanding scholar of medieval literature and palaeography. In his 1899 book, *The Sources of Archbishop Parker's Collection of Manuscripts*, James says the *Red Book* had been cut up for game-labels.

'Fucking great help!' exclaimed Forth. 'So, it's in a book that doesn't exist!'

'That's where it gets more intriguing,' said Morten. 'The girl is asking for Kask's help in tracking it down. She's going to meet him to give him more information.'

'I see. We could force the boy to give us the information?'

'No, that's not an option. There's no evidence he's been told about the connection to any treasure. As far as he's concerned it's just a piece of academic research.'

'Then our best option would be the girl, unless we can get everything from her correspondence with Kask?'

Nesfield intervened, 'She wouldn't last long if I was interrogating her,' he was thinking about the photographs and video he'd received from Penhaligon and imagining what he might do to Anna.

'I agree,' said Forth, who had also viewed the images. 'We keep a close watch but if nothing emerges in a week or two, we put Nesfield's plan into action.'

Morten didn't agree but said nothing.

Chapter 45

'You've been busy,' was Cloote's assessment when he looked at Anna's research. 'I remember seeing something about these new stones a few years ago but didn't pay them much attention. Do we know who it was at the university that declared them fakes?'

'No, I haven't found that out. No specific name is mentioned in the Swedish reports and there's next to nothing in the international press. I thought you'd be able to do that through your connections there.'

'It shouldn't be a problem. I'll email Thyra, Thyra Nyström, she was a PhD student with me. Now she's professor of early-modern history there.'

Anna had tried other ways to find Viggo Lund but had drawn a blank. She was about to try LinkedIn again when she saw there was a message waiting for her. It was a reply from Viggo. It was cautious but asked her to ring a mobile number.

'Hallå. Vem är det?'

'Det är Anna Carr. Är det Viggo Lund?'

He said it was. She explained that together with Dr Oliver Cloote they were researching runestones missed by the compilers of the Rundata website. She asked where he was and was surprised when he said England, working for the Swedish construction company Skanska. She asked if he would speak with her and Cloote. Lund replied that he'd be in London for the rest of the week if they wanted to meet one evening.

'Vänta. Jag behöver bara fråga Dr Cloote.' Cloote had just come back from trying to contact Thyra. She said she had Viggo Lund on the line and could they meet in London one evening.

'We certainly can. Monday evening? At my club perhaps? The Royal Overseas League.'

'Hallå. I morgon kväll? Klockan sex på kvällen? På Royal Overseas League. Det är nära Green Park tunnelbanestation.'

*

Gordon drove them to London and parked in the Park Lane underground car park that Anna always associated with her favourite vintage TV programme. It was where the opening credits for *The Prisoner* had been shot. They ate a late lunch at the Chinese restaurant Hakkasan, before walking to the Royal Overseas League which occupies an imposing building at the end of a short cul-de-sac off St James's Street. This is the heart of London's clubland, though the league is a far from a typical example. Founded in 1910 to encourage international understanding, the club has always admitted women and people of every race and creed. They met with Viggo in the members' drawing room overlooking Green Park. Despite both Anna and Cloote speaking fluent Swedish he said he'd prefer to speak English in such surroundings.

'It was after a man stabbed a female student,' Viggo explained. 'One theory was that he had thrown the weapon in the river and police divers were searching for it. I was studying engineering and was a member of the university sub-aqua club and we offered to help. Most of the search was concentrated near the city centre where the attack happened, but there was one report of a man acting suspiciously by the river at Gamla Uppsala. So, I went to Storvad, you know the little beach? There were three of us. Visibility was bad and we were searching with our fingertips, without gloves. I felt a large stone which wasn't unusual, but then my fingers felt what had to be carvings on it. When I got back to the university, I went to see a friend who was doing history and told him about it. It took them a few weeks to get round to finding the stone and, in the end, they brought out two. After that, one of the professors studied them and said they were fakes.'

'I hope they caught the attacker?' said Anna.

'No, I'm afraid they didn't. Two other girls were attacked by the same person, but they never caught him.'

'Do you know why the professor thought they were fake?' asked Cloote. 'Can you remember his name?'

'Sorry I don't know on either of those,' Viggo said, 'but I do have some pictures of the stones. I took them after they'd got them onto the bank.'

Anna and Cloote crowded round his tablet. It was hard to make out much. 'Could you send me those?' asked Anna.

'Sure,' he said and quickly mailed them.

'What did you and your friend think about the find?'

'Well Hans thought they'd been dismissed too quickly. And I wondered, if they were a hoax, why put them in the river? Surely burying them would have meant they'd be much easier for someone to find.' Anna thought he had a good point. If these were attempts to copy the Kensington stone, then it was essential they *were* found. The photos weren't much help. You could see there were runes carved on the stones, but they were indistinct, as the photos were taken to show the people rather than the stones themselves. They went downstairs to the bar. After a quick drink Viggo said he had to go. He needed to be up early to get onsite at the major drainage project he was supervising.

Shortly after Viggo left Cloote got a call. 'Thyra. Hur bra att höra från dig ... Ja. Ja. Du är säker?... Tack så mycket. Var är de nu?... Kommer du kolla? Ja, vi kan se varandra mycket snart ... Förresten, kan du inte nämna att vi har talat. Tack Thyra. Adjö. Well, well, that's interesting. Thyra says it was none other than Mattias Söderberg who studied the stones.'

'And he is?' Gordon asked.

'An idiot,' said Anna.

'Now, now, Anna, that would not be doing him justice. I would say he is a complete imbecile.'

'That good! I guess you both know him?'

'I've heard him speak,' said Anna.

'And I had the misfortune of hearing him many times. He was a junior lecturer at Uppsala when I was a student. His views on religion bordered on the fanatical. It was no surprise when he got a very well-paid job at some obscure private university in the US.'

'So, you'd say his judgement that the stones were forgeries could be wrong?'

'I think there's a very good chance he was wrong, especially if the inscriptions refer to pagan gods or practices.'

'And where did Thyra say the stones were?' asked Anna.

'She thinks they're still locked away somewhere in university storage, but she's going to check for us. I was wrong. We do need to go to Sweden.'

*

Elias Forth was at Satterthwaite Hall for the weekend. Carrie Prentiss was telling him the latest on their anti-abortion campaign. 'And thank you by the way,' she added. 'Young Harry is splendid. He was a bit timid to start with, but he has amazing stamina and is very obedient.'

'I hope you have the evidence for me?' Forth said. Before she could reply his phone went. It was Nesfield and his mood changed violently. 'What the fuck do you mean they've disappeared! With the resources I've given you. What happened?'

Nesfield said that after a trip to Cloote's London club all three had been ensconced at Summerland for a few days. He had used heat sensitive detectors from a safe distance which indicated three people in the house. Then two days ago everything had gone quiet. No people detected. No one leaving. 'The girl hasn't been going for her run and we think they've left.'

'But how?'

'It can only have been by boat, unless they were smuggled out in vehicles we don't know about. I can't see how else it could have been done.'

'Fucking hell. You had better come up with something, Nesfield. Let me know *immediately* you find out anything.'

'Shit.' He slammed the phone down on the table. 'Why am I surrounded by crettins? You, of course, excepted, my dear. Now, I believe you have some film to show me.'

Chapter 46

Two days earlier.

Just after midnight three figures slipped out of the back gate of Summerland. They headed along the path towards the town, carrying packs and rods, equipped for a night fishing expedition. They walked down to the seashore alongside Fort Green Mill. The beach between here and the Martello Tower is a popular spot for night fishing and there were a number out that evening, each with their own shelter and light. Another group attracted little attention as they set up, well away from the others. Half an hour later a small rigid inflatable boat was rowed to the shore. After carefully checking no one was near, the three figures collected their gear and climbed into the boat. When it was well away from shore the boatman started a powerful outboard motor, the craft turned and headed north.

Less than an hour later the boat reached the port of Lowestoft. After passing the main town, it cut its engine and the boatman rowed toward the North Beach car park. There the three people got out, leaving the fishing equipment behind. A discreet BWM X3 was waiting. Scott was driving. 'Everything okay with you guys?' Gordon said it was. 'I've pre-cleared you, there should be minimal formalities.'

They headed north, bypassing Great Yarmouth, before turning due west. When they reached the Norwich ring road, they turned north again to arrive at Norwich International Airport by 3 a.m. The passports of the people who checked in claimed they were Anthony S Hiebert, a restaurant owner from Columbus, Ohio; Thomas Byrne, a businessman from Portkellis in Cornwall; and Daisy Herbert, a nurse, who lived in Shipton-Under-Wychwood in Oxfordshire. 'Daisy!' Anna had exclaimed. 'Do I really look like a Daisy?'

'It was that or Gladys,' joked Rees. 'Anyway, your name doesn't match you, it's the other way round. It will probably transform what people think about Daisys.'

Their private plane was a Bombardier Challenger 605 painted bright red. Cloote and Rees took advantage of the fully reclinable seats, converting them into beds for the flight. Anna had never travelled by private jet before and never slept well while travelling. She decided Daisy was the sociable type, given her profession, so she chatted to the flight attendant about the plane, asking lots of questions about load, speed, and range.

By 7 a.m. local time the plane was on the ground at Arlanda Airport where their hire car, a Volvo XC90, was waiting. Arlanda is nearer to Uppsala than it is to Stockholm so before eight they were at their hotel, the small and discreet Villa Anna. 'It seemed appropriate, and it's got the best restaurant,' was Cloote's reason for choosing it. 'Also, they don't know me there so there shouldn't be any problem over identities.'

That afternoon Thyra Nyström called to say she had located the stones Viggo had found. They were in the basement store of the archaeology faculty, and she'd arranged for them to have access the following morning. The weather was not pleasant and Cloote and Anna spent time brushing up on their runes. Designed to be inscribed rather than written, runes were used by Germanic-speaking peoples from about the second to the eleventh centuries, before the adoption of the Latin alphabet. They are made up of vertical lines with branches, or twigs, jutting out diagonally. They can be written from left to right, or vice versa, and each rune has a major and minor version. The rune represents a phoneme – a distinct unit of sound – and has a name, made up of a noun that includes the sound the rune is associated with.

The alphabets used in Scandinavia are known as futhark, derived from the first six letters of their alphabet: F, U, Þ, A, R, and K. The Elder Futhark was used until the eighth century when it was replaced by the Younger Futhark, utilised during the Viking Age. This version dropped eight of the original twenty-four characters and simplified or changed the shape of the remainder. This makes interpretation of Younger Futhark runes more complex, as they have more than one possible sound attached to them as well as having many regional variations. The Younger Futhark is further divided into long-branch and short-twig runes, the former used in present-day Denmark, the latter in Sweden and Norway. In the tenth century, the climax of the simplification process was reached with the development of staveless runes.

Uppsala is a major site for Viking-Age runestones. In the park between Domkyrka, Uppsala Cathedral, and the main university building are nine runestones, with another row just outside the cathedral entrance. The main Viking settlement had been at Gamla Uppsala, close to where Viggo's stones had been found. Here the so-called 'Temple of Uppsala' was the site of the ancient Norse religion, though it was also a feasting hall, rather than being used purely for religious purposes.

*

Thyra came to the hotel for dinner. Anna thought she looked like a rather severe schoolteacher, with grey hair and a tweed skirt and jacket, but Cloote obviously trusted her. He'd explained they were using aliases and Thyra said she'd seen that he'd been linked to the discovery of the body of a fellow academic at Swineshead. In conversation Thyra was much less formidable than she appeared, with a frequent and rather loud laugh.

'I was working in Russia at the time the stones were discovered,' she explained, 'so I wasn't involved in their interpretation. Also, my main interest is the fourteenth century, so I accepted they were fakes. Given what you said, Oliver, I've been careful not to say anything to my colleagues in archaeology. I've asked to look at a number of other items as well as the stones which I thought might obscure things a bit.' Cloote agreed that had been a good idea and they arranged to meet up in the morning.

In the night Anna dreamed she was standing in a clearing in a forest of silver birch. It was bright sunlight, and the trees were in full leaf. She was aware of laughter coming towards her and a group of young girls streamed into the clearing. They were wearing light shifts of white and had garlands round their necks. Anna heard herself begin a chant, which the girls repeated as they began circling her. Their dance and the chant got faster and faster until they were in a frenzy. At that moment Anna felt her mind leave her body and she was looking down on herself as she rose into the sky.

Chapter 47

The following day the weather had relented and their walk to the Centre for the Humanities in the Engelska parken was a short one. Cloote was uncharacteristically dressed like a traditional businessman in a dull, grey suit, and he'd swapped his demi lune glasses for larger tinted ones, in case he met someone he knew from his time at Uppsala. Thyra met them in reception and guided them down to the basement. This was where old furniture and equipment was stored, rather than valuable artefacts or records, and so access was quite straightforward.

After a few minutes search Rees pulled a dust sheet off some large objects leaning against a wall. 'Are these our stones?' The others agreed they were. Fortunately, they were only inscribed on one side, and this was the one facing them. Moving the stones would have been impossible without a winch or block and tackle.

A quick perusal told them two things. First, if the stones were authentic, they were from the period that used the Younger Futhark. Second, they would not be simple to interpret as they used a variation none of them was immediately familiar with. 'That might well explain why a fool like Söderberg would think they were fakes. If he didn't recognise the runic alphabet, he would assume it was fake,' Cloote suggested.

Rees had brought a high-quality camera with a flash and photographed the stones from every angle. As he did so he remarked, 'This looks like it's in Morse code.' Anna explained that was because it utilised staveless runes.

'If only they were as easy to understand as Morse,' Cloote sighed.

Cloote, Anna and Thyra spent time examining the stones. They were made of granite and the tooling marks were consistent with their being authentic. After they'd finished, they went over to the history department and brought up Rees's images on a large screen in a lecture theatre. 'I think we should proceed on the assumption that these are genuine,' said Cloote. 'See if we can agree a date, discuss any inconsistencies, and then attempt a translation. Does that sound reasonable?' The others agreed it did.

Their first task was to date the stones, which isn't at all easy. Earlier systems of dating relied on linguistic differences. But it was realised that this failed to consider regional variations in alphabets. More recently Anne-Sofie Gräslund, Isolde Holmberg, and others have placed more reliance on style and ornamentation. 'Gräslund emphasised the way in which the stones depicted animals, which she based on her knowledge of her own dogs,' Thyra explained to Rees. 'She considered things like the shape of the heads and how the eyes were carved, or the type of tail or feet. From this she established a chronology from the late tenth century onwards. I can see there are at least three creatures. Two on this stone and one on the other.'

'I think these two,' Anna indicated the first stone, 'are a boar and a dragon.'

'Yes,' said Cloote, 'that's interesting given our other finds.'

Rees had picked up enough by now to also get a little excited. 'You mean the boar could be Hildisvini and the dragon could be Fáfnir guarding his treasure? And the third figure?'

'I don't think it's an animal,' Thyra added.

'I've not seen it before. How about you, Anna?'

She agreed. 'It looks more like a man than an animal but not like any I've studied.'

'At least the boar and dragon help place the carvings in Holmberg's chronology. They're both in that rather thin, sinewy style,' Cloote concluded.

'So probably no earlier than 900 or later than 950?' Anna added.

'Well, that's the easy bit,' Cloote said. 'I'd suggest some lunch before trying to interpret the runes.'

They walked to a restaurant by the river to eat rather than staying in the university, discussed what they'd seen so far and agreed nothing was inconsistent with the stones being authentic. 'One point we've not mentioned much is, if they're authentic, why were they in the river?' Anna said. 'Why would they have been disposed of like that? They're about one and a half metres high, a metre wide, and half a metre thick. That's about two-and-a-half tonnes, not easy things to move about.' No one had any immediate ideas.

They returned to the university and spent the next few hours trying to read the inscriptions. They did this individually to start with. Their first task was to transcribe the runes into Old Norse, the language of the Vikings from the eighth to the fourteenth century. It was originally written in runic script but started using Latin after Christianisation in the eleventh century.

One stone utilised a version of short-twig Swedish runes, the other staveless runes. After an hour or two Thyra said, 'Both stones use a variant that is found elsewhere in Uppland. There are differences, but I'd say they're like U 344, or the ones credited to runemaster Åsmund Kåresson, though they certainly aren't his work.'

'I tend to agree,' said Cloote. 'Look at the twig of what must be the "fé" and "kaun" runes here. Don't you also see some similarities with the Karlevi Runestone?'

'That's the one that was found on the island of Öland and has the oldest record of skaldic verse, isn't it?' Anna asked.

'That's right,' Thyra confirmed. 'It's associated with the Battle of Fýrisvellir which was in about 984, though that doesn't have any depictions of animals.'

They carried on their examination. Suddenly Anna, who had been working on the staveless runestone, said, 'No. That can't be right. On the other hand ...' The others looked at her enquiringly, but she said, 'No. Carry on. I'll tell you in a bit.'

Sometime later it was Cloote who exclaimed, 'I think I've seen the same thing as you, Anna. And I agree it might answer two other questions.'

'What are they?' said Thyra.

'Why the stones were in the river and why Söderberg rejected them as fakes.'

It wasn't until nearly 6 p.m. that all three reached their conclusions. 'I suggest we adjourn to the hotel for dinner,' said Cloote. 'We can discuss our findings tomorrow morning after we've had a chance to refresh our creative juices.'

Back at Villa Anna Rees had booked a private dining room. Both food and drink were superb. Anna enjoyed an extraordinary main course of Hällestads mushrooms with duck egg yolk and truffles and she even tried a small glass of the ridiculously expensive single vineyard Burgundy Cloote had ordered. ''Spose it's not bad,' was her conclusion. 'But for Christ's sake at that price you could feed the homeless for a month.'

'It is an indulgence, and I will make suitable recompense. But I thought we deserved it.'

'I agree with both of you,' said Thyra, 'especially Anna. But I will make an exception and drink it with pleasure. Perhaps, Oliver you might donate to a suitable organisation as penance?'

'What would you suggest?'

'The National Centre for Knowledge on Men's Violence Against Women is raising funds for a new refuge here in Uppsala.'

'What do they do?' asked Anna.

Thyra explained that NCK is a research and resource centre based at Uppsala University that raises awareness of men's violence against women. They also run a national twenty-four-hour helpline for which Thyra was a volunteer. 'Okay. I think you give them twice the cost of the meal,' said Anna. Cloote agreed and guiltily sipped his wine.

Chapter 48

In the morning they reconvened in Thyra's department. They spent another hour discussing details of interpretation but, finally, agreed about what they said. The first stone began with a standard dedication but referred to someone they were extremely interested in. The runes looked something like this:

[illegible]

In Old Norse this read:

> *Sigvid jörð ór angles farmaðr sveitungr Ivar ræisa stæin þenna.*

Which translates as:

> *Sigvid the England traveller who followed Ivar raised this stone.*

'If we're right about the date then this Sigvid would have been an old man when the stones were carved,' said Anna. 'The events in England were around 870, perhaps forty years earlier?'

'Yes, and it's confirmed by the second inscription,' Cloote said.

The second inscription, with translations was:

[illegible]

> *Ek tökumk fran konungrinn báð hans kollr ok hans krown at var ór finenessr godanaloner Maykonceiver.*

> *I took from the king both his head and his crown that was of a fineness the gods alone may conceive.*

'Wow!' exclaimed Gordon before Cloote added, 'And I think we now have not one but *two* treasure troves. The first is Ivar's treasure that he seized from Medhamstead and the Danes squabbled over.'

'But this is new,' interrupted Anna. 'It can only refer to the crown of King Edmund the Martyr.'

'You mean the guy Bury St Edmund's is named after?' asked Rees.

'That's him,' said Anna. 'None of the sources have ever mentioned the crown before. There's the legend of the English finding his head after being guided by a magical wolf. And the *Anglo-Saxon Chronicle* says: "Ac æthebban ðone lêodgebyrga duguð âhwæðer hê hêafod hêafdes sîn ýr." And from Edmund the king the heathens took both his head and his gold.'

'That dates our stone to after 870 then?' Thyra asked.

'Yup,' said Anna. 'What happened to his crown, none of the chronicles or myths tells us. I can't think of anything in the *Chronicon Roskildense*.'

'No, nor in the accounts of Henry of Huntingdon or Abbo of Fleury, the other key sources of Edmund's martyrdom,' Thyra added.

'So, it's not beyond possibility that Ivar or his henchmen seized the crown when they killed the king,' Cloote said.

'And, if it's to be believed, Sigvid is telling us the Norsemen did take it,' concluded Thyra.

'If this stone tells us there's more treasure, does the other one say where it is?' asked Gordon.

'Sadly not,' replied Cloote, 'but in many ways it's even more intriguing than that.'

There were three separate inscriptions on the second stone. The first, transcribed into standard runes was:

[illegible]

Sindri smithinn hafði Ivar stonesrinn. Hann var taken með myrkálfrr.

Sindri the smith had Ivar's stones. He was taken by a myrkálfar.

'Who's Sindri? And what is a myrkálfar?' Gordon asked, who was getting a bit lost in the mythology.

'I think that's supposed to be a myrkálfar,' said Anna pointing to the creature none of them had been able to identify before. 'And this is where Söderberg would have lost faith,' she added. 'I'll explain. In Old Norse "sindri" means "sparkling" or "the spark sprayer", so he's a blacksmith. He's also a dwarf. He forged the golden boar Gullinborsti, the ring Draupnir, the ship Skíðblaðnir and the hammer Mjǫllnir. His brother and assistant was Brokkr.'

'A different boar to the other one?' said Rees.

'Yes, the Vikings were rather fond of them. And this one was also associated with Freyja. Gullinborsti means "golden bristles" and Freyja rode him to Baldr's funeral. Anyway, in Norse cosmology the myrkálfar or svartálfar are the black or dark elves, beings who dwell in Svartalfheim. The division between these dark elves and the ljósálfar, light elves, is supposed by many to be the result of Christian influence, an importation of the concept of good and evil and angels of light and darkness. There's no confirmed source from as early a date as this. But the second inscription adds more mystery.' She told Rees what it said:

ᚦᚹᛁ ᛅᛏ ᛅᚱ ᚦᛁᛌᛌ ᚹᛁᚱ ᚼᛅᚠᛅ ᚹᛁᚢᚱᚱ ᛏᛁᛚ ᚴᛅᛏᛅ

því at ór þessi vér hafa véurr til gæta.

Because of this we have set a protector to guard it.

'A protector? What of?'

'I'd say the first stone is speaking of Edmund's crown but this one about the treasure from Medhamstead.' Cloote and Thyra agreed that was the interpretation. 'And it's warning people about finding them,' continued Anna. 'Look at this carving.' She pointed to something that looked a little bit like a child's hobby horse. 'I'd say it's a representation of a níðstang, a nithing pole.'

'What's that?' asked Gordon.

'The most spectacular way of cursing an enemy was by the níðstang. They were poles about three metres long on which insults and curses were carved in runes. A ceremony was performed to activate the destructive magic and a horse's skull was fixed to the top of the pole which channelled the forces of Hel, the goddess of death.'

'It isn't any wonder someone as narrow-minded as Söderberg dismissed these stones as fakes,' Cloote said.

'And I agree with Anna's earlier point,' said Thyra. 'When Christianity came, the blatant pagan references might have been a motive for having the stones thrown in the river.'

'So, we're reasonably clear on the first two inscriptions,' said Anna. 'They're saying this treasure is very dangerous and guarded by both light and dark forces. But the last one I find very opaque.'

ᚢᛅᛚᚠᛅᚱ ᛘᚢᚾᚢ ᚱᛁᛋ ᛚᛅᛁᛏᛅ ᛅ ᛋᛁᚴᚱ

'It says: "Volvar munu risa leita á sigr" which means something like "a völva will arise to go on a journey to victory".'

'What's a völva? Presumably nothing to do with the car,' Gordon joked.

'They were the female practitioners of seiðr, Norse magic.' Thyra explained. 'The völva wandered from place to place performing commissioned acts of magic in exchange for room, board, and other gifts. The most detailed account of a völva comes from the *Saga of Erik the Red*. She's called Thorbjǫrg, "Protected by Thor".' She searched online and found the reference. 'Here I'll read it: "Now, when she came in the evening, she had a blue mantle over her, with strings at the neck, and it was inlaid with gems down to the skirt. On her neck she had glass beads. On her head she had a black hood of lambskin, lined with ermine. A staff she had in her hand, with a knob thereon; it was ornamented with brass and inlaid with gems round about the knob. She wore hairy calf-skin shoes on her feet, with long and strong-looking thongs to them. On her hands she had gloves of ermine-skin, and they were white and hairy within."'

'She sounds interesting,' said Gordon, 'I wouldn't mind meeting her.'

Anna remembered her recent dreams. The woman in them could only be a völva. She wondered if they were caused by the quest and the discovery of the seiðrstafr at Summerland. She looked at Cloote. All the time Thyra had been reciting he had been very still. 'We've done a wonderful job,' he said finally.

'Thyra, you've been the most fantastic help, I can't thank you enough.'

'But does it get you any nearer to finding if this treasure still exists?' she asked. 'As I see it, you have some tales of dubious provenance and little to locate anything, other than a vague Gothic fragment and an extremely hard to break code written by a thirteenth-century monk.'

'You're right of course,' Cloote continued, glad that the conversation had moved away from sorceresses. 'We can only take our findings back to England and keep working on Johannes's text.'

'There's one other thing that struck me,' Thyra added. 'You said your manuscript includes music?'

'That's right,' said Anna. 'It may be part of a sequence.'

'Then before you go you should speak to Emil Sigurdsson, in our department of musicology. He's one of the leading experts on early medieval music. He's also a good friend, and very discreet,' she added. 'I'm sure we'll find him in today, it's cake day.'

They set off the short distance to the music department as Thyra explained that Emil was a very keen amateur baker and had even appeared on television in the Swedish version of *Bake Off*. As she'd predicted, they found him explaining his new recipe for lemon drizzle cake to his colleagues. He was a large man with a round, red face and a trimmed black beard and moustache that met together. After sampling the cake, which they all agreed was delicious, they adjourned to Emil's room. Cloote explained that had been studying a manuscript that had musical notation and Anna showed him the document onscreen. 'Hmm. Not a great discovery in the musicological sense I'd say. A bit dreary. Certainly not by one of the known masters such as Perotin or Léonin, and not even a hand I know.'

'Could it contain some kind of message other than the music do you think?' Anna asked directly.

'I don't think so, but then I'm no expert on medieval codes. As the thing makes sense musicologically it would have to be deeply hidden. I don't suppose there was any other musical notation in the document?'

'No,' said Anna, 'these are the other pages though.'

Emil looked at them carefully. He then asked them to come

to a larger room that contained a projector and put the scans up on a big screen. After a while he said, 'You know that sometimes at this period musical notation wasn't just written horizontally. They were still experimenting with different kinds of staffs. Sometimes, and I'm not saying this is one, but sometimes the notation was done vertically. If you look at the alignment of the heads of all these creatures,' they all crowded round the screen, 'Just here,' he pointed, 'and here. I think you can see pinpricks.'

'Fucking hell!' exclaimed Anna, who immediately apologised for her robust language. 'You're right. They aren't the holes done for aligning the text, they're totally separate.'

'Someone wanted to ensure your animals were organised exactly as they wanted them,' said Emil.

This revelation quickly led to Cloote asking Emil if they could buy him lunch and do some more work on the text, to which he readily agreed, 'A free meal at the Anna, with Anna. Ho, ho! How could I refuse?'

*

They took a projector back with them to the hotel and, after lunch, went to Cloote's room where they displayed the pages of Johannes's manuscript for Emil. Rees manipulated them and drew staff lines down the pages that coincided with the pin pricks. They appeared to show four staff lines rather than the five of modern musical notation. 'That's not at all surprising,' said Emil. 'The first use of modern staff lines was by Guido d'Arezzo in the middle of the eleventh century. He used a four-line staff. Five-line staves first appear in Italy in the thirteenth century and up until about 1600 four, five, and six lines were all used before five became the standard.'

What was immediately noticeable was that the heads of the creatures, or at least most of them, now fitted onto or between the staff lines. 'It's as if *they* are the notes,' said Gordon.

Emil agreed. 'But they don't make musical sense, unless this person was a post-modernist, eight hundred years before post-modernism!'

'Then it has to be a code that isn't solely based on music but on the position of the heads on the staff?' Anna suggested.

'Yes,' Cloote agreed, slightly hesitantly, 'but what are we to make of the drawings that don't fit onto the stave?'

'Could they be the key to the code I wonder?' suggested Gordon. 'If so, are they in the same code Anna brought back from New York?' They tested this and immediately decoded a message on the first page of the manuscript:

Ab imo in serie.

Or

From bottom in sequence.

'Does he mean alphabetically?' Thyra asked.

'No, I think there's another interpretation,' said Emil.

Anna started drawing on a pad. 'You mean like this?'

I/R
H/Q/Z
G/P/
F/O/
E/M/W
D/M/V
C/L/U
B/K/
A/J/S

'Yes', said Emil and Gordon added, 'If that's the key how does the text read?'

They began to translate the new code, taking a section each. 'Here's the first bit,' said Anna.

SWOBNWXXIEFSJMHJSSNGGTEBODULMJQXAQBYE ZIZDEQQO

'He's used Latin up until now so we should assume this is also in Latin, right?' said Gordon. 'Let's try substitution codes and see if we get a readable text.'

But after a further four hours they had tried every conceivable approach and got nowhere. No version of a Caesar alphabet or any other known medieval code gave them anything readable. They'd missed dinner and it was now approaching midnight. The only clue was that the message, whatever it was, had a total of four hundred and eighty-nine characters. All five were frustrated but agreed they couldn't go any further.

'What about the final bit that doesn't align with the musical stave?' Emil asked. At the end of the manuscript there was a second group of drawings they found could be interpreted through a Caesar cipher. This time, however, its meaning was far from clear:

> *Pro illis qui adhuc quaerere. Et fecerunt quattuor custodes illum diuina temerantem. In Anglia Gilbertus de Rameseia. In Dania Berenger de Vestervig. In Germania Hugo de Frauenchiemsee. In Gallia Guillelmus de Floriacensis.*
>
> *For those who seek further. Four I have made custodians. In England Gilbertus de Rameseia. In Denmark Berenger de Vestervig. In Germany Hugues Frauenchiemsee. In France Guillaume Floriacensis.*

'Might they be colleagues of Johannes's?' suggested Thyra.

'Yes, but what is it he has made them custodians of?' Cloote added.

'And after eight hundred years what chance is there that we could still find it?' Anna said.

By now it was beginning to get light. 'Thyra, Emil. I don't know how to thank you,' Cloote concluded. 'I should also say again that the others trying to discover this are exceptionally ruthless, so please keep everything completely secret for now. Hopefully someday soon we'll be able to go public on our work.'

They both swore they'd not say a word and headed back to their homes. Anna, Cloote and Rees decided to get a few hours' sleep before driving back to Arlanda.

Chapter 49

'We have a good idea where they've been,' Savile Nesfield reported.

Elias Forth was relaxing at his London flat. Carrie had pulled off another coup, planting a member of the audience on the BBC's *Question Time* TV show. Social media was now buzzing with her 'disgusting views', according to many, or 'brave honesty', according to others. The BBC would never have agreed to Carrie appearing on the *Question Time* panel but, if anything, having a member of the public say the same things had a greater impact.

'It's about time,' Forth finally responded, 'it's taken more than a week!'

'We tracked a number of private flights from the UK the day they disappeared. One of them left Norwich and filed several flight plans, so it wasn't obvious which they'd followed. Yesterday another flight returned to Norwich that we've been able to confirm left Arlanda in Sweden.'

'And what were they up to in Sweden?'

'I'm afraid we don't know that yet.'

Morten had been listening carefully. 'Vikings,' he said. Forth and Nesfield looked at him. 'Cloote and the girl are both Norse experts. We're seeking a trove from that period. Sweden is the centre of the Viking world.'

'Has our esteemed Professor Penhaligon been of any use?' Forth asked him.

'Not greatly. As we suspected he doesn't have the imagination of Oliver Cloote. We have clues but nothing concrete.'

'So Cloote and his friends are closer to solving the riddle than we are?'

'It's certainly possible. Penhaligon is convinced the link with the *Red Book of Eye* will produce results.'

'Are you of the same opinion?'

'I'm not an academic, sir,' Morten concluded.

'But you are a master of reading people's intentions.' Forth's praise produced a slight nod of recognition.

'I have an open mind, sir.'

'We can't allow them to beat us. They'd make the entire thing public and our work with Oleg impossible.'

'Then do I have your agreement to plan the alternative approach?' Nesfield asked.

'What's the situation regarding their security system?'

'We have our man on the inside and he's been helpful.'

'How helpful? And is he reliable?'

'We can rely on him. We have both positive and negative incentives. He's previously sold information to art thieves which, given the evidence we have, would send him to jail for a very long time. And we're paying him handsomely. There are, however, significant issues we can't overcome.'

'Which are?'

'It's impossible to gain access without the physical presence of one of the three.'

'And how do you plan to overcome this difficulty?'

'By waiting for exactly the right moment when only one of them is present. We then make a concerted assault that takes out the physical and electronic security.'

'Then make all the preparations and inform me when you're ready to go,' Forth concluded. 'Now I have things to discuss with Miss Prentiss.'

Nesfield and Morten left. Forth glanced at his phone and saw a missed call from Gabriella Clifford. He listened to the voicemail. She sounded agitated, which was not at all usual for her. 'Gabriella? What seems to be the problem?'

'I don't want to worry you, Mr Forth, but I've just received information from the FCA regarding OZ account number three.'

'Yes?'

'I wasn't aware there was an account number three. I only have two listed.'

'It may be a mistake,' Forth replied. 'I'm sure we can clear this up when I'm next in the office.' Gabriella Clifford didn't sound entirely convinced but she let the matter rest. *What the hell are the FCA playing at?* thought Forth. *It must be a rogue investigator*. He wondered if Gabriella Clifford might prove a trifle too honest. 'If so,' he mused, 'despite her many attributes, she might become surplus to requirements.'

There was a discreet knock. 'Come in. Carrie, my dear. Would you care for some oysters?' Forth indicated a large dish on the table.

'No thank you. I'm not fond of eating things that have been alive recently.'

'Ahh, in that case remind me never to offer you monkey brains. They are a delicacy I tried in China. Excellent news about *Question Time* don't you think?'

'I'm quite satisfied. There are opposition MPs saying the BBC shouldn't give a platform to people with her views, which helps our campaign immensely. We've had to do very little online to stoke the flames, it's happened quite spontaneously.'

'I expect the media are trying to track down Mrs ... what was her name?'

'Honor Stack. She lives in Chesterfield. We've been very careful. She has no idea how we've helped her, shall we say, develop her thinking. It's all been done through the social media she frequents. There's no way the press will think she's in any way been manipulated.'

'Excellent. Now I believe you have something else to show me.'

'Elias, you know I have. Would you like to make yourself more comfortable?' Forth lay back on the sofa as Carrie put a memory stick into the PC and brought up the film on the screen. It was a recording of her encounter with young Harry Spall. As the scenario unfolded, she deftly unzipped Forth's fly and attended to his requirements.

Chapter 50

Anna, Cloote, and Rees returned without incident to Summerland. Once away from the airport they saw no reason to conceal their movements. 'At least identifying the places the four custodians lived isn't complex,' Anna began.

'No,' Cloote continued. 'We've got four monks at well-known religious houses in Europe. In England, Gilbertus de Rameseia, that's Ramsey Abbey near Huntingdon; Berenger de Vestervig, that's Børglum Abbey in Jutland; Hugues de Frauenchiemsee, which is a monastery on an island in the Chiemsee lake in Bavaria and Guillaume de Floriacensis, Fleury Abbey near Orleans.'

'And I've been trying to find out where the various records and archives of those places are now,' said Anna. 'I know it's a long shot that any papers of these monks have survived but it is a possibility.'

'Even if the primary source has disappeared there could be copies that are still accessible,' Cloote added. 'Any luck?'

'Some,' Anna went on. 'Most of the Ramsey records from the thirteenth century are in the British Library, with a few at Peterborough Cathedral. With Børglum it should be clearer. All are deposited in the Royal Library in Copenhagen. The other two are more tentative. As we know countries that suffered greater upheaval have had far more of their historical records lost. In France the biggest problem was the Revolution and many ecclesiastical records, and even entire archives, were destroyed. The surviving records of Fleury are in the Archives Nationales in Paris. For Frauenchiemsee it's even more unlikely anything relevant survives. The library storing most of them, in Nuremberg, was destroyed by Allied bombing in 1945. The remaining ones are in the Bavarian Public Archives in Munich.'

'And what about the monks themselves? Any record of them?'

'Not in any of the online catalogues. We'll have to visit the archives and check the likely documents.'

‘It’s always possible the letters of an ordinary monk might be bundled with other material.’ Cloote agreed. ‘We’ll draw up a schedule.’

‘Okay. How about the far more difficult question of what the code means?’

All this time Gordon had been silent. ‘I may have an idea,’ he said tentatively. They both looked at him. ‘I’ve been checking the incidence of the letters in the sequence. What’s most interesting is the randomness, and the fact that the proportion of each letter is almost identical – so there are as many Zs as Es and Ss.’

‘What does that tell you?’ Anna asked.

‘That Johannes was using a sophisticated system. It may be a Vigenère cipher.’

‘You have to be joking,’ said Anna.

‘I know. The first known description of a Vigenère cipher is in 1553. But I’m with Sherlock Holmes on this. You know, “When you have eliminated the impossible whatever remains, however improbable, must be the truth.” And there’s another reason for thinking he was using a Vigenère cipher or something very similar, otherwise what was it that he sent to his four friends?’

‘I see,’ said Anna. ‘You know you might just be right!’

‘I’m afraid you’ll have to explain this Vigenère thing,’ Cloote said, and Rees complied.

‘The Vigenère cipher is a method of encrypting text using a form of polyalphabetic substitution based on the letters of a keyword or text. In the nineteenth century the method was misattributed to the French diplomat Blaise de Vigenère. For centuries the cipher was considered unbreakable. But in 1854 Charles Babbage managed it, though he didn’t publish. Then, in 1863, Friedrich Kasiski, a Prussian army officer, finally published a method of decryption.’

‘And how does the cipher work?’ Cloote asked.

‘To carry out the encryption you need a table of alphabets, called a tabula recta, Vigenère square, or Vigenère table,’ explained Rees. ‘It has the alphabet written out twenty-six times in rows, each one shifted one letter to the left compared to the previous one. Here, look at this.’ Rees displayed the table on the screen of his tablet.

	PLAIN TEXT																									
KEY	A	B	C	D	E	F	G	H	I	J	K	L	M	N	O	P	Q	R	S	T	U	V	W	X	Y	Z
A	A	B	C	D	E	F	G	H	I	J	K	L	M	N	O	P	Q	R	S	T	U	V	W	X	Y	Z
B	B	C	D	E	F	G	H	I	J	K	L	M	N	O	P	Q	R	S	T	U	V	W	X	Y	Z	A
C	C	D	E	F	G	H	I	J	K	L	M	N	O	P	Q	R	S	T	U	V	W	X	Y	Z	A	B
D	D	E	F	G	H	I	J	K	L	M	N	O	P	Q	R	S	T	U	V	W	X	Y	Z	A	B	C
E	E	F	G	H	I	J	K	L	M	N	O	P	Q	R	S	T	U	V	W	X	Y	Z	A	B	C	D
F	F	G	H	I	J	K	L	M	N	O	P	Q	R	S	T	U	V	W	X	Y	Z	A	B	C	D	E
G	G	H	I	J	K	L	M	N	O	P	Q	R	S	T	U	V	W	X	Y	Z	A	B	C	D	E	F
H	H	I	J	K	L	M	N	O	P	Q	R	S	T	U	V	W	X	Y	Z	A	B	C	D	E	F	G
I	I	J	K	L	M	N	O	P	Q	R	S	T	U	V	W	X	Y	Z	A	B	C	D	E	F	G	H
J	J	K	L	M	N	O	P	Q	R	S	T	U	V	W	X	Y	Z	A	B	C	D	E	F	G	H	I
K	K	L	M	N	O	P	Q	R	S	T	U	V	W	X	Y	Z	A	B	C	D	E	F	G	H	I	J
L	L	M	N	O	P	Q	R	S	T	U	V	W	X	Y	Z	A	B	C	D	E	F	G	H	I	J	K
M	M	N	O	P	Q	R	S	T	U	V	W	X	Y	Z	A	B	C	D	E	F	G	H	I	J	K	L
N	N	O	P	Q	R	S	T	U	V	W	X	Y	Z	A	B	C	D	E	F	G	H	I	J	K	L	M
O	O	P	Q	R	S	T	U	V	W	X	Y	Z	A	B	C	D	E	F	G	H	I	J	K	L	M	N
P	P	Q	R	S	T	U	V	W	X	Y	Z	A	B	C	D	E	F	G	H	I	J	K	L	M	N	O
Q	Q	R	S	T	U	V	W	X	Y	Z	A	B	C	D	E	F	G	H	I	J	K	L	M	N	O	P
R	R	S	T	U	V	W	X	Y	Z	A	B	C	D	E	F	G	H	I	J	K	L	M	N	O	P	Q
S	S	T	U	V	W	X	Y	Z	A	B	C	D	E	F	G	H	I	J	K	L	M	N	O	P	Q	R
T	T	U	V	W	X	Y	Z	A	B	C	D	E	F	G	H	I	J	K	L	M	N	O	P	Q	R	S
U	U	V	W	X	Y	Z	A	B	C	D	E	F	G	H	I	J	K	L	M	N	O	P	Q	R	S	T
V	V	W	X	Y	Z	A	B	C	D	E	F	G	H	I	J	K	L	M	N	O	P	Q	R	S	T	U
W	W	X	Y	Z	A	B	C	D	E	F	G	H	I	J	K	L	M	N	O	P	Q	R	S	T	U	V
X	X	Y	Z	A	B	C	D	E	F	G	H	I	J	K	L	M	N	O	P	Q	R	S	T	U	V	W
Y	Y	Z	A	B	C	D	E	F	G	H	I	J	K	L	M	N	O	P	Q	R	S	T	U	V	W	X
Z	Z	A	B	C	D	E	F	G	H	I	J	K	L	M	N	O	P	Q	R	S	T	U	V	W	X	Y

'At each point in the encryption process, the cipher uses a different alphabet from one of the rows. The reason the cipher is so strong is that the alphabet used at each point depends on a repeating keyword, phrase, or text that you must know to decipher it. For example, suppose that the plaintext to be encrypted is TREASUREISBURIED.

'The person sending the message chooses a keyword or text and repeats it until it matches the length of the plaintext, for example, the keyword "BRISINGAMEN": BRISINGAMENBRISI.

'The rows of the table correspond to the key, the columns to the plaintext. So, in the example the first letter of the plaintext, T, is paired with B, the first letter of the key. Therefore, row B and column T of the Vigenère square is used, namely U. Similarly, for the second letter of the plaintext, the second letter of the key is used. The letter at row R and column R is I. The rest of the plaintext is enciphered in a similar fashion like this.'

Plaintext	T	R	E	A	S	U	R	E	I	S	B	U	R	I	E	D
Key	B	R	I	S	I	N	G	A	M	E	N	B	R	I	S	I
Cipher text	U	I	M	S	A	H	X	E	U	W	O	V	I	Q	W	L

'Decryption is done by going to the row in the table corresponding to the key, finding the position of the ciphertext letter in that row, and then using the column's label as the plaintext. For example, in row B, from BRISINGAMEN, the ciphertext U appears in column T, which is the first plaintext letter. Next, in row R, from BRISINGAMEN, the ciphertext I is located in column R. So, R is the second plaintext letter.'

'Can you break the code then?' asked Cloote. 'You said it can be done.'

'Okay, let me just explain a bit more. The idea behind a Vigenère cipher, like all other polyalphabetic ciphers, is to disguise the plaintext letter frequency to interfere with the application of frequency analysis, as we've already seen. For instance, if P is the most frequent letter in a ciphertext whose plaintext is in English, you would suspect that P corresponds to E, since E is the most frequently used letter in English.

'But if you use the Vigenère cipher, E can be enciphered as *different* ciphertext letters at *different* points in the message, which defeats simple frequency analysis. You can see in the example that repetitions of letters in the key – S for example – is encrypted first as S and then as W. Though this makes cryptanalysis difficult, it's not impossible. The main weakness of the Vigenère cipher is the potential repeating nature of its key. Let's say you use a four-letter keyword then every plaintext letter can be encrypted in four ways. If a cryptanalyst works out the key's length, the cipher text can be treated as interwoven Caesar ciphers, which you can break individually. A good example was in the American Civil War. The Confederate States used Vigenère ciphers, but their messages were regularly cracked because they relied on just three short key phrases: "Manchester Bluff", "Complete Victory" and, as the war ended, "Come Retribution".

'The first step in cracking a Vigenère cipher is to look for sequences of letters that appear more than once in the ciphertext. The most likely reason for the repetition is that the same sequence of letters in the plaintext has been enciphered using the same part of the key. Both Kasiski's method from the nineteenth century and the Friedman test, invented in the 1920s, can determine the key length.'

'So, you can crack it?' Cloote was getting impatient.

'No, I can't.'

'Why not?'

'Because if the key isn't a word or phrase but a text that is as long as the plaintext itself these repetitions don't occur. And that's the case here. I've tried both the Kasiski and Friedman tests and they don't help.'

'So how do we break the code?'

'As I said to Anna, another point in favour of this being a Vigenère cipher is that it must have a key and Johannes may have given it to these four trusted friends. The only way we can break it is to know what the key is.'

'So, it's essential to find it in one of the archives,' said Anna. 'When do we start?'

'I'd suggest I try Germany. Gordon can explore Paris and you, Anna, could cover London. After that we should decide who goes to Copenhagen.' Travel details were arranged. Cloote and Rees would use aliases, but Anna would visit the British Library as herself.

'We also need some additional detail for the *Red Book* scenario,' Anna said. 'I'll work it out and contact Rasmus, then let you know what I've done.'

'Good. We may need additional distractions if we find anything,' Cloote replied.

Anna rang Rasmus using his secure phone. He told her Penhaligon had been looking more than a little harassed in the past few days. 'I think he's at a loss as to what to do next.'

'Not a surprise given the limitations of his intelligence. Let me know if anything changes and, meanwhile, I have some more instructions I'll send you via email, ones that Penhaligon can be given. There'll also be some I'll send you on this phone. These are only to be used if the circumstances they describe occur.'

'Okay,' said Rasmus, 'you can rely on me.'

*

Two days later Gordon headed for the Eurostar as John D Schwartz, from Irvine California, and Cloote flew to Munich, via Schiphol, as Thys van der Straten from Molenweg in the Netherlands. Anna biked to Saxmundham and caught the train to London. She took the tube from Liverpool Street to King's Cross St Pancras and walked the short distance to the British Library. The Manuscripts Reading Room is on the second floor, and she had pre-ordered the documents pertaining to Ramsey Abbey. She spent the night in a hotel close by, continuing her search the following day. But she found nothing, not even a reference to Gilbertus or Johannes of Medhamstead. She wondered if she should stay another night and continue a wider search, but it was so unlikely there would be any clue she decided against it.

Leaving the library shortly after five she checked her phone and found several messages from Anula to add to the ones she'd received the previous night. They hadn't seen each other since before her trip to Uppsala. Anna texted to ask if they could meet, and Anula replied that she'd see her at a pub in Woodbridge that evening before she went on duty.

She'd also got one from both Rees and Cloote. Neither of them had found anything at all in Paris or Munich. They were both on their way back. Gordon said he was going to meet Oliver at Heathrow and they'd stay overnight at the Marriott there before heading back to Aldeburgh in the morning.

Anna and Anula met at the Crown and Anna told her what they'd found in Uppsala. 'You think you're close to solving Johannes's messages then?' Anula asked.

'Only if we can discover the key text,' Anna replied. 'If not, it'll probably be hopeless.'

'You know I'll help in whatever way I can?'

'I know. But I don't want to put you in any more danger. You already know enough for those bastards to want to harm you.'

'Anna, I'm your friend and . . .'

'Fuck it, Anula!' Anna was feeling conflicted, and this was driving her frustration. 'I think I was wrong to have got you mixed up in this. It's best for us not to meet for a while.'

'But Anna . . .'

'No, I've made up my mind.' At that she got up and left the pub. Anula sat staring into her drink wondering when, and if, she'd see her again.

Chapter 51

Anna caught the last train from Woodbridge to Saxmundham and retrieved her bike. It was nearing midnight when she got back to Aldeburgh. In retrospect there were several chances for Anna to have noticed something wasn't right, but she was distracted by her feelings for Anula and storming out on her. She should have noticed that Scott's guard in the van was someone she'd never seen before and that it was very late for the man on the aerial platform to be working on the telegraph pole opposite.

She secured the bike in the garage before walking back to the front of the house. With Summerland unoccupied she had to enter by the main door to disable the security system. The instant she tapped in her code she felt a sharp pain in her neck as if she'd been stung by a wasp. Her hand instinctively shot up to the source of the pain and she felt a cold metal dart. Even before she could pull it out, the tranquilising drug prevented her. Anna was dimly aware of several black-clad figures, wearing night vision goggles, converging on her from over the wall and the side of the house before she fell forwards into the door and blacked out.

When Anna came round her first thought was that she had a bad hangover. But she hadn't been drunk for years. She then remembered what had happened and became aware of her surroundings. She was in the workshop at the back of the garage. Her hands were fastened together by a plastic cable tie, and she was suspended from the lifting gantry. Her jacket and boots had been removed and her feet could only just touch the floor. She was dimly aware of a figure sitting in a chair on the other side of the room. As she began to move, he got up and quickly left. A few minutes later she heard footsteps. Three men entered. One of them she couldn't make out very well. He was tall and thin, and his face was partly covered, though she could see the shape of his long nose. The second was obviously in charge. He was in his fifties and looked familiar, though Anna couldn't immediately recall where she'd seen him. She then remembered his picture being in the papers and on television, the billionaire businessman Elias Forth. But it was the third figure that made her stomach retch. He was unmistakably the man she'd seen crossing Fellows Quad the night of Marcus's murder. Anna was now in no doubt as to who these people were, and her mind was crystal clear.

Even before Forth began speaking she had summed up her situation. *They're making no attempt to hide their identities. That means one of two things. Either they don't care if I identify them later, or they have no intention of ever giving me the opportunity.* She decided to work on the basis that, after finding out what they wanted, these people intended to kill her. *Perseverance, self-control, and indomitable spirit,* Anna told herself. *I must stay focused and distract or disrupt them.*

'Ah, Miss Carr, you are back with us I see,' Forth said in a calm, condescending tone. 'I'm sure you know why we are here?'

There's two ways I can play this, thought Anna. *The frightened little girl to lull them into a false sense of security or as angry as possible and hope they make a mistake.* It only took her a fraction of a second to decide. 'I forgot to pay my subscription to "Dickhead Monthly" and you've come to collect it in person?'

That seemed to work. Forth glared at her. 'I suppose you think that's funny. Well, you won't for long, you little bitch, not when we've finished with you.' He moved slightly closer to Anna as he spoke.

Come on, just another step, she thought.

'What you are going to do is unlock your computer and download all your files,' Forth told her. 'If you don't comply, then my friend here,' he indicated Nesfield, 'will persuade you.'

'I suppose he'll be able to do that because he's got a bigger cock than you?'

This was not the response Forth had expected. He stepped closer to Anna. Even though her feet were barely touching the ground she managed to gain enough traction to swing her right leg into a decent kick. Her foot caught Forth directly between the legs and he collapsed backwards with a grunt. Nesfield sprang forward and smashed his hand into the left side of Anna's face. Fortunately, he didn't use his fist, which would certainly have broken her jaw, but the force was still massive. She felt blood trickling down her chin and her tongue identified that a couple of teeth were distinctly loose.

'Nesfield!' Forth bellowed once he'd regained his breath. 'Secure her feet.' Nesfield found two spare counterweights for the garage doors. Meanwhile Forth had gone to the large tool chest by the workbench just behind him, about three metres from Anna. First, he selected a pair of pliers. He went over to where coils of electrical wire hung on reels. He cut two lengths of thin wire that he handed to Nesfield who used them to fasten the weights to Anna's feet. 'You are about to regret that, bitch,' he said.

Forth then cut a length of thicker wire about two metres long. He took a Stanley knife from the workbench drawer and found a new packet of blades. He placed one in the knife handle, leaving the remainder on the bench. With Anna now unable to resist, Forth came over to her. He stood behind her but just too far for her to jerk her head back into his face as she'd planned. *Anyway, he seems pissed off enough*, she thought, and she began to prepare her mind for what was coming next.

'As it's obvious you're not going to be cooperative, I will use a different approach. I assure you; you will not find it pleasant. And remember, however painful it is, I have the option of making your pain many times worse.'

Forth moved in front of her and unbuckled her belt. He pulled her trousers down to her ankles. Next, he took the Stanley knife. At first Anna thought he was going to cut her face, but instead he cut through the neck of her tee-shirt and sliced it down the side. He glanced at her choker and medallion but left them in place. He then ripped off the remains of the shirt and cut through her pants in the same fashion. He picked up the thicker wire, wrapping one end round his wrist and said, 'You can scream as loudly as you like. No one will hear you.'

The first lash caught her between the shoulder blades and wrapped round her body to her right breast. She felt the wire cut into her flesh, followed immediately by a cold trickle of blood down her back. Forth worked his way down with each strike, first across her back then on the buttocks and thighs. Anna's mind was perfectly focused. She made no sound and Nesfield was amazed that she didn't flinch as the blows fell. Forth was sweating as he finished. Anna stared directly at him not blinking, cold hatred in her eyes.

'Morten,' Forth said, 'her phone.' Anna could now make out the third figure more clearly. He must be the man Nora told her had left the Bodleian on the night of Arbuthnot's murder. She looked at him more closely. *Interesting*, she thought, *there's not the same anger there as the others. He's far more detached and controlled.*

Forth now used her face recognition to open the phone and dialled Cloote's number via WhatsApp video. 'Anna what ...' Cloote's voice trailed off.

'Listen very carefully, Dr Cloote,' Forth said. 'I will show you what I have done to your little friend.'

He circled Anna with the phone. As he got behind her Anna could hear Cloote's voice breaking. 'My God, Anna! You bastards, what have you done to her?'

'Nothing in comparison to what we *will* if you don't do exactly what I tell you,' Forth replied. He was now standing in front of Anna and noticed her eyelids fluttering. He thought she was about to cry. She wasn't.

'Now Dr Cloote. I will give you an email address. You will then send *all* your research notes to it within the next hour. If you do not, or if you don't send everything, then I will kill your friend here, very slowly and very painfully. Do you understand?' Cloote said he did.

Nesfield went to the hoist and lowered Anna's arms. He cut the cable ties but attached another, binding her hands together. He did the same to her feet before removing the weights. As he did, Anna let out a loud moan and collapsed in a fake swoon. She fell towards the workbench and her hands went out to stop her head hitting it. She had precisely calculated the distances and her hands swept the loose Stanley knife blades onto the floor as she fell, face down, next to them. Before Nesfield dragged her to her feet she flicked a blade into her mouth with her tongue.

Nesfield bundled her into the workshop storeroom. She heard the door being locked. At first there was a low buzz of voices but then they stopped. They must have gone into the house to await Cloote's email. She also hoped he had got her message. Thank goodness Cloote had told her he understood Morse code, because the message she'd sent via her flickering eyes was:

_· _ _ _·· _· _· _· _ _·· _·· _ _·· _··· _ _· _···

No Inkpen. Plan B.

She slipped the knife blade from the roof of her mouth to between her teeth and brought her hands up to cut through the cable tie. She then cut the tie on her ankles. There was enough light to see dimly around the store. Tins of paint, some garden furniture, a step ladder, and an old boiler suit covered in paint. She put this on. She didn't check her wounds. There was no point. She couldn't do anything about them yet.

She'd already worked out her escape plan. She couldn't get through the door and, even if she did, there would certainly be a guard in the workshop. The walls were brick and breezeblock, so the only option was the ceiling. She carefully put up the step ladder, found some masking tape and taped the blade to the handle of a paint brush. It wasn't the best implement to cut through plaster board, but it was at least silent. After half an hour she'd cut a hole large enough to get her hand into and started widening it using a combination of cutting and pulling. Ten minutes later and she was in the roof space above the workshop. She crawled to the far side at the back. This would be above the wall between Summerland and the neighbouring property. She had no idea if Forth and his minions were monitoring the CCTV but didn't want to take any chances.

She carefully removed the roof tiles one by one. She put her head out through the hole and looked round. She could see a dim figure in the road outside the house. She looked toward the garden and there was another man there, close to the back wall. She waited a couple of minutes then pulled herself out onto the roof. Moving feet first she slid to the edge of the garage. She was about a metre from the wall which was also a metre below her.

Her back was now really beginning to hurt but Anna refocused her mind and sprang onto the wall.

Hanging by her hands she dropped the final three metres into the garden of the house next door. She hadn't reckoned on there being another of Forth's men stationed there. Kevin Tippler was enjoying his work but, with his lack of experience, had been given what was supposedly the easiest job of the night, ensuring the nearest neighbours were not alerted. Suddenly a figure dropped from the wall as he walked round the end of the house. Anna saw him, and his gun, just in time. Tippler was about to call out when the figure took off into the air. Anna's foot caught him flush on the chin. There was a nasty crunch as he went down. Before he could respond Anna's fist hit him repeatedly in the face. She really didn't care if she'd killed him or not. There was no time to check or disable him further.

She crept to the back of the garden. A high, thick hedge bounded the footpath behind the properties, but there was also a gate, which she climbed over, dropping onto the public path. She moved quickly toward the back of the hospital. She had two thoughts. First, she'd be able to find some medical supplies for her wounds. Second, she knew from when she'd been there with Anula where the staff room was. She was hoping she might be able to find some keys and take a car.

The back door was impossible to open but she found a small window with the fanlight open. Anna climbed on a waste bin and squeezed through. She was in a toilet. She crept out, located the pharmacy, and began looking for antiseptic and gauze. She could already feel congealed blood sticking the boiler suit to her back. Just as she found what she was looking for the light was abruptly switched on. Anna was about to attack the intruder when she heard a familiar voice. 'Anna! What the fuck! Jesus!'

Anna hadn't known Anula would be on duty. 'Anula! You need to help me get away.'

'But your back, what's happened?'

'There's no time. The people who killed Magnus are at Summerland. Soon they'll know I've escaped.'

Anula snapped into action. 'I've got medical supplies in my car. Everything else can wait. Follow me.'

They quickly went to the staff room and Anula handed Anna

a set of medical overalls and some sandals. 'Put these on. No, don't take that off put them over it.' She snatched her keys and they slipped out of a side door into the car park.

'Give me your phone,' Anna said. 'You drive but go slowly and tell me what you see.'

Anna got into the back of the car and sat down on the floor from where she couldn't be seen unless someone came right up to the window. She dialled Cloote. He answered immediately. 'It's me. No, don't say anything. I've got away. Did you get the message? Good.' She told him what to do.

Anula's car was approaching the barrier at the end of the private road. 'Anna, the barrier is down and there's someone in the road. At the end near the library. It's a policeman.'

'It's not a policeman. I can't get you into this further Anula. I'll slip out and try going round them.'

'No Anna. Listen to me. This is what we'll do.' She quickly explained her plan. Anna had her doubts but there wasn't time to argue. The policeman held up his hand for her to stop. She did, but rather than winding down her window she got out of the car.

'What's the problem officer?'

Vladimir tried to mask his accent but didn't entirely succeed. 'I'm sorry, madam. There's been a serious incident in the town, and we've had reports that the offender may try to evade us by stealing or hiding in a vehicle.'

'What does he look like?'

'It's a young woman. Mid-twenties, dyed hair.'

'I'm sorry I haven't seen anyone like that.'

'I just need to check your car.'

'Of course, officer.'

They moved to the back of the car. He opened the tailgate with Anula behind him. At that moment Anna saw her grip his neck with just the thumb and index finger of her right hand. Vladimir collapsed as if he'd been shot. 'One day you'll have to tell me how you do that,' said Anna, failing to mask her admiration. 'I'll drive now,' she said. Anna was a considerably faster, and more reckless, driver than Anula.

'We need somewhere to go,' said Anna. 'It can't be your place. They'll quickly work that out and go there. Any ideas?'

'Yes,' said Anula, 'Devon.'

At first Anna thought the shock had addled her brain. Anula realised she was puzzled. 'No not Dev-*on*, Dev-*Ann*, Devan Patel, my colleague at the hospital. He owns a couple of holiday cottages at Kessingland. They're unoccupied because he's just had them redecorated. Do you know how to get there?'

She said she did. 'Now,' said Anna, 'call the police. Tell them who you are, that you've seen people acting suspiciously round Dr Cloote's house and you know he's away.'

Anna considered the best way to go. How extensive was Forth's network? Could he get the police to find them? Given the power he wielded she thought anything possible, so she took a route through the backroads, avoiding the A12, other than crossing it near Blythburgh and at Kessingland itself. They had no problems reaching Devan's property, which comprised a semi-detached pair of bungalows, at the far end of Beach Road, just before the Holiday Park. Anna pulled into the covered car port at the far side. The key was in a key safe. Anna was about to smash it off the wall when Anula punched in the code. 'I came here for a party in the summer,' she explained. 'We won't need the car jack!'

Inside Anula carefully removed the boiler suit to reveal Anna's wounds. They were deep and messy but looked worse than they were. She gave her a pain-killing injection and cleaned them up. She didn't ask her what had happened, simply listened to the facts Anna told her. 'We're up against one of the most powerful men in the country, if not the world,' she explained. 'There's no point going to the police. Even if they believed us, Forth would have an alibi that he was having dinner with the prime minister. No, we've got to beat him. And I will beat him if it's the last thing I do.'

Anna called Cloote. Gordon answered. He told her they were on the road back to Aldeburgh. He'd been in touch with Scott who said he was certain there must have been a leak in his own organisation and was totally mortified. He too was on his way to Suffolk with two people he trusted absolutely.

Anula made some tea and gave Anna a couple of pills. Soon she was sleeping. Anula didn't sleep. She kept watch, just in case. She swore to herself that she would keep Anna safe and help her get revenge. She sat on the bed and stroked Anna's hair. Perhaps the shock of what had happened had heightened her senses, but Anna's hair felt like steel wool under her touch. A few tears came into her eyes as she bent down to kiss her.

Chapter 52

When Anna woke, Anula redressed her wounds before saying she had better go to the local shop for some food. 'Don't worry, I'll walk,' she said. 'We don't want the car spotted.'

While they were eating breakfast there was a call. It was Scott. He said that he'd soon be with them and a few minutes later a black Mercedes Vito van pulled up outside. The first thing Anna asked was, 'What happened to your guy outside Summerland?' She'd worried that Forth had simply had him killed.

'He's okay,' said Scott. 'Found him unconscious in the boot of his car, thank goodness.'

'You know who we're up against?' Anna asked.

'Yeh, it figures. Pity we couldn't have dug up the information sooner, but I was right about them watching you from the river. One of Elias Forth's boats was moored in the Alde around Christmas and New Year.'

With Scott was a big man with a bald head and a goatee beard. He was wearing a denim waistcoat and had a large tattoo of Dimebag Darrell, the Pantera guitarist murdered on stage by a deranged fan in 2004, on his arm. Scott introduced him as Roly Sharp. They shook hands. 'Great guitarist,' said Anna. Roly grunted.

'Roly was there, you know,' said Scott.

'What when Dimebag and the others were killed?'

'Yeh. I was a roadie for Damageplan. It was after that I decided to stop things like that ever happening. That's why I'll help stop those scumbags who hurt you,' he added.

'You two ever handled a gun?' Scott asked. Anna and Anula both said they hadn't.

'You should,' said Roly, 'something like this.' He reached into his waistband and produced a large handgun. 'It's a Smith and Wesson 500. Whatever you've heard from Clint Eastwood, this motherfucker is the world's most powerful handgun.'

'We'll get Roly to give you some lessons, but perhaps with something smaller,' said Scott.

Roly covered Anula's car with a thick dustsheet and the four of them got into the Vito. 'We should be safe from attack,' he explained. 'The van has armour plating and is built to withstand pretty much anything short of an SSM.'

'SSM?' queried Anula.

'A surface-to-surface missile to you.'

Anula pondered her situation. Not long before she was just a doctor, now she was protecting herself from missiles.

On the drive back to Aldeburgh Scott explained that they'd identified their leak. 'He didn't know everything but enough to give Forth the information about how to attack you. Anyway, I've got Asayo Negishi on her way here.' He explained that she was his leading countersurveillance expert. 'She's flying in from Kansas City. Unfortunately, she was doing a job for some people I thought were in more imminent danger. I'm sorry I was wrong.'

As the van pulled into the drive at Summerland, Cloote rushed out to greet them, tears streaming down his face. 'Anna, my dear, it's all my fault, please forgive me.'

'There's nothing to forgive,' said Anna matter-of-factly. 'I knew what I was getting into. I made the choice. Now we have to show them we don't give up.'

Gordon was standing in the entrance. He stepped forward and gingerly embraced her. 'You're a tough one,' he said. 'I knew they wouldn't break you. I told Oliver you'd find a way.'

'Thanks,' said Anna, 'let's get to work.'

Gordon explained what they'd found when they got back. 'Nothing was out of place except for a couple of books in the library. There was no trace in the workshop. Not a drop of blood on the floor either. The only thing they couldn't cover up was your hole in the ceiling. But they'd taken out two whole plaster board panels to make it look like there were some repairs being done. Even if we'd called the police, they'd find nothing.'

'At least you now know who you're up against,' said Scott. 'Elias Forth is an incredibly dangerous man. The only reason you're all still in one piece is because you must still be useful to him.'

'I guessed that,' said Anna, 'so we need to keep him thinking we're useful.'

There was a buzz on the house's intercom. 'It's Asayo,' said Roly. 'I'll let her in.' Anula summed up Asayo Negishi as a Japanese-American version of Anna Carr, but with IT and surveillance as her specialisms rather than languages and history. She was no more than twenty-five and after a brief greeting asked dozens of questions about their security, their plans, and their adversaries.

'Are you going to involve the police?' she asked. 'They already know a lot and you have a friend there.'

'No,' Anna was quite firm. 'Forth is one of the most powerful men in the country. He'll have a cast-iron alibi and they left no forensic evidence. It just wouldn't work.'

'Okay,' said Asayo. 'I agree.' She then asked more questions about Forth, Nesfield, and Morten.

'Forth is probably a psychopath,' Anna said. 'Deep down he feels sexually inadequate. He hates and underestimates women. He gets angry easily, which is a weakness. Nesfield is less intelligent. Enjoys violence but stays calm in a crisis. The one called Morten is much more difficult to sum up. Clearly a killer but not simply for the sake of it. He's the most dangerous one of the three.'

'Thank you. You should be a detective or a psychologist,' Asayo said. She then outlined her plans. 'We can't totally protect you so, as Anna has said, you need to work out how to make them leave you alone.'

'Yeh, I've thought that through,' said Anna. She then outlined what their next steps should be.

*

'How could you have let that fucking stupid girl get the better of you?' Elias Forth was letting off steam. Nesfield said nothing. Morten thought the blame was Forth's but said nothing either. 'We can't even be certain what Cloote's given us is true!'

'I think we can be fairly certain,' Nesfield contradicted him at his peril. 'The messages we've intercepted between the girl and Kask are consistent with them. And now,' he said with an emphasis he hoped would deflect Forth's anger, 'we have new ones following her, umm, escape.'

Forth calmed down a little. 'And what do they reveal?'

'They say that Cloote found a new lead while he was in Munich,' Morten continued. 'It was another reference to the *Red Book of Eye,* and it links with the Meister Eckhart material too.'

'She says,' Nesfield interrupted, trying to ensure he gained most of the credit, 'they're planning another trip to Europe to find what she calls "the final link".'

'And where in Europe are they going?'

'Ah, that we don't know, but this time we have everything in place to ensure they can't leave the country undetected,' Nesfield concluded.

Chapter 53

'There's one thing I don't understand,' Anula said to Anna as they were making the final preparations for their trip. 'How can you be so certain you'll find the key to the code? You've already said that the chances of any of Johannes's letters to his friends having survived is slim.'

'I don't,' said Anna. 'It's just something I can *feel*. I know we're very close to the end of this. I've never been so certain.'

'I've always known you'd be the key,' Oliver Cloote said. 'I'm convinced you're right. But we must ensure we make the right choices.'

'I'll be keeping everything under close watch,' said Asayo. 'I'll be going on ahead to monitor the situation.'

Before they left, Anula checked Anna's wounds. They were beginning to heal but still looked awful. 'You must keep them clean, get Oliver or Gordon to do it. And change the dressing twice a day.'

'Okay, Mum,' Anna smiled.

'Don't make jokes! I'm your doctor and you were nearly killed. I don't want you killed, you know.' She embraced Anna, who quickly felt uncomfortable.

'I'll see you soon anyway,' Anna said. 'Are you sure you've got everything clear?'

Now it was Anula's turn to be irritated. 'Yes, sir. Of course, sir.' Anna gave her a playful cuff. Anula then strapped some bandages around Anna's head. There was a large bruise where Nesfield had hit her, and her left eye was black. Even so the bandage wasn't medically necessary. It was there for a different purpose.

Soon afterwards Anna, Cloote, and Rees left in Scott's van, driven by Roly. They bypassed Ipswich, crossed the Orwell Bridge, and turned south round the Stour estuary through Manningtree. By eight they were in Harwich. They boarded the 10 p.m. ferry for the Hook of Holland. Among the foot passengers was Harry Spall and another of Forth's operatives. As soon as the ferry left Spall, dressed as a Stena Line crew member, went to the car deck. He fixed a small tracking device to the wheel arch of the Vito. In his cabin Roly Sharp was alerted by a beep on his phone. He checked Asayo's app and smiled.

The ferry docked at six-thirty after they all, except Roly, who kept watch, managed to get some sleep in their cabins. Gordon took the wheel for the next leg of the journey while Roly took a nap. They drove through the Netherlands past Rotterdam, Utrecht, and Arnhem, before crossing the German border. Near Oberhausen they turned east, following the Ruhr Valley, and stopped for something to eat and to change drivers. Roly drove them deeper into Germany. They skirted Dortmund before, at Kassel, turning southeast. They were now travelling through the more remote and picturesque parts of Eastern Hesse before reaching Eisenach, famous as the site of the Wartburg Castle, where they had another stop for refreshments. Cloote was getting more agitated, triggered by the delayed shock of Anna's capture. He was talking too much as he told them that the Wartburg was where Wolfram von Eschenbach wrote part of his *Parzival*, in 1203, and Martin Luther translated the New Testament into German. 'But of course, the castle was also where the legendary Sängerkrieg, or Minstrels' Contest, was held you know. In 1206 the great Minnesängers Walther von der Vogelweide, Wolfram von Eschenbach and Albrecht von Halberstadt took part and…'

Gordon finished his sentence, 'And Wagner used it in *Tannhäuser*. Yes, Oliver, we know!'

Cloote looked aggrieved but then realised, 'I'm sorry, I'm jabbering, aren't I? I'll shut up.' Anna managed a chuckle and Cloote realised they were just pulling his leg.

By early afternoon they were in central Thuringia approaching their destination, the city of Weimar. Famous for giving its name to the republic formed after World War One, Weimar was mythologized by the National Socialist movement. But it's also one of Germany's cultural centres and a world heritage site. In the eighteenth century the city was a focal point of the German Enlightenment, home of both Johann Wolfgang von Goethe and Friedrich Schiller. In the twentieth, Wassily Kandinsky, Paul Klee, Lyonel Feininger, and Walter Gropius came to the city and founded the Bauhaus.

They were booked into the Hotel Elephant in the city centre under their own names. Roly stayed with them overnight before heading back to England. Scott was also staying in the hotel, having travelled by plane to Leipzig via Frankfurt. They took dinner together, though without Scott, who was booked in under an alias. In the morning they walked a short distance to the Duchess Anna Amalia Library, whose main building is the Green Castle built in the 1560s for Anna Amalia, Duchess of Saxe-Weimar-Eisenach. Despite a disastrous fire in 2004, the library houses a major collection of historic documents.

The group's progress was being carefully watched by Klaus and Werner. After a full day in the library, they reported that Anna, Cloote, and Rees went back to the hotel and then for dinner in its Michelin-starred restaurant, aptly called the Restaurant AnnA.

The following day, while Klaus followed Cloote and Rees back to the library, Werner had to make a diversion to keep track of Anna. Rather than visiting the library she caught a taxi from the hotel. She headed north for about ten kilometres, where the taxi dropped her. Werner followed at a discreet distance. She wasn't difficult to spot with her head bandaged.

In July 1937, the SS had the forest here cleared to build the largest concentration camp in the German Reich. From then until 1945 more than fifty-six thousand people died there from torture, medical experiments, and disease. The name Buchenwald became a synonym for the Nazi concentration camp system. Even after the war the horrors of Buchenwald didn't end. The state was part of the Soviet zone of occupation and, from 1945 to 1950, the camp was reused by Soviet occupation forces. As NKVD special camp Nr. 2, twenty-eight thousand prisoners were held there, of whom over seven thousand died. Today the remains of Buchenwald serve as a memorial, permanent exhibition, and museum.

Before the trip, Anula asked Anna if there was a special reason she wanted to visit the site. Anna nodded. After a while she said: 'They were very young. He was twenty-one, she was nineteen, and Jewish. They were both Communists. They'd hidden from the Nazis for months. She had a baby, which a kind couple took. Then someone betrayed them. They were both sent to

Buchenwald. To the prison. After torturing them the Gestapo took them to a room where they made her watch as they garrotted him with wire. They experimented on her, looking for a vaccine for typhus. She died on her twentieth birthday.'

'Who were they?' asked Anula.

'My great-grandparents,' said Anna. It was the only time she'd mentioned any members of her family. Anula realised it was her way of saying sorry for storming out of the pub, and that Anna was trusting her with something she'd never told anyone else.

Werner followed Anna as she walked round the former camp. The buildings are now few, and spread out, as most, mainly those that housed prisoners, have been demolished. She then went into the former prison building. Several cells were furnished as an act of remembrance for inmates killed there. Anna stayed for twenty minutes then headed to the main museum and information centre where she went into the toilet. Werner hung around and then followed her to the car park where she caught a taxi that took her back to the hotel.

A few minutes later a woman with straight blonde hair came out of the toilet. She wore large horn-rimmed glasses, a rust-coloured polo neck sweater, short brown skirt, and thigh length brown boots. She was wheeling a small suitcase and also took a taxi. It dropped her at the train station in Weimar, just north of the city centre. Here she caught a train via Erfurt to Berlin. From the station she took a bus to Tagel airport. She went to check in where the man behind the desk looked at her passport. It identified her as Hildegard Kirchner, twenty-three years old and born in Hamburg. It stated her profession as art historian. 'Guten tag, Fräulein Kirchner. Ihr flug sollte in ungefähr fünfundvierzig minuten an bord sein. Tor nummer zwölf. Sie haben nur handgepäck?'

Anna said, yes, she just had one cabin bag, and thanked the man. He noted her North German accent and gave her more than a lingering glance as she walked towards airport security.

Anna had toyed with the idea of asking Nora to act as her decoy but decided she'd have been too tall. Despite the difference of skin colour Anula was exactly the right height and build and the head bandage effectively hid her face.

An hour later Anna, or Hildegard, was in the air heading north.

Chapter 54

It was late afternoon when Hildegard Kirchner made her way into the arrivals hall at Copenhagen, Kastrup, airport. As she looked round a tall woman, her blonde hair gathered in a ponytail, approached her. She looked like an athlete from her build. 'Fräulein Kirchner? Bin ich Freja Kristensen. Ich hoffe du hattest eine gute reise?'

'Ja dankeschön. Überhaupt keine probleme. Sollen wir Englisch sprechen?'

'Of course. I hope Gordon is well. It's a while since I saw him, but I caught up with Scott in the States a couple of months ago.'

Freja had been at MIT with Gordon Rees and Scott Rimes, though she was a biologist by training. She was now senior researcher at the Nano-Science Centre of the University of Copenhagen. Both men had said Anna could trust her implicitly. She and Anna had spoken before their trip and agreed that Anna would remain 'Hildegard' for her stay in Denmark. They walked the short distance to the car park where Freja's Volvo XC40 was parked. The airport is south of Copenhagen, close to the Øresund bridge linking Denmark to Sweden, but their destination was north of the city.

'You've been to Denmark before?' Freja asked.

'Yes, I spent a summer at Jelling,' Anna replied, 'working on the archaeological site. But I flew to Aarhus, so I've never been to Copenhagen.'

'Oh, then that's something we need to put right,' said Freja. 'As long as your work doesn't take up all your time of course. I'd love to show you something of my city. We can start by taking the route through the centre, it shouldn't take much longer than going via Vesterbro.' They drove close to the sea before going inland and crossing to Christianshavn. 'It used to be a working-class neighbourhood,' Freja explained, 'but became very bohemian in the 1970s, you'll have heard of Christiana of course.' Anna said she certainly had heard about the famous 'hippie commune'.

As they crossed the Knippels Bridge to the city centre Freja pointed to their left. 'That's the Royal Library,' she said. 'We call it the Black Diamond.' Anna could see why. It was an ultra-modern, wedge-shaped building of black glass by the waterfront. 'We're now on the island of Slotsholmen. That's the Børsen, the seventeenth century stock exchange, and beyond is the Christiansborg Palace, the seat of the Danish parliament.' Anna hadn't expected the guided tour but was rather enjoying it. At least it took her mind off the main reason for her visit and her back, which was beginning to sting. After crossing another bridge, they encountered heavier traffic. They circled Kongens Nytorv, King's New Square, and were then on a straight road called Bredgade. 'We're now in Østerbro,' Freja said. 'It's more upmarket and residential.'

'Where do you live?' asked Anna.

'In Vesterbro. I suppose you'd say it was the Hoxton or Williamsburg of Copenhagen. It used to be run-down but now it's very hip. Just like me!' She laughed. Anna thought she would like Freja a lot.

They were now heading out of the city on a wide boulevard with a railway line to their left before the road ran along the Øresund. They turned away from the sea, between some very smart, whitewashed houses, before Freja turned left and right into a car park. 'Welcome to Hvidøre,' Freja said.

They got out of the car and entered a modern extension to a much older building. This was white with a prominent tower capped by a small blue dome. Anna knew it was now a Conference Centre for the Novo Nordisk pharmaceutical company, owned by the Novo Nordisk Foundation, that focuses on medical treatment and research. Freja was a member of the board of the foundation, the largest in Denmark. What Anna didn't know was the history of the house. 'Hvidøre was the home of the Dowager Empress Maria Feodorovna of Russia, daughter of King Christian IX and sister of Queen Alexandra, the wife of Edward VII. She was the mother of the last emperor of Russia, Nicholas II.' Freja explained. 'The sisters bought the house in 1906 and used it as a summer residence until the

Russian Revolution. Maria Feodorovna, Princess Dagmar before her marriage, lived here until her death in 1928. In 1937 Thorvald Pedersen, the founder of the Novo company, had the house adapted into a diabetes sanatorium and Hvidøre was a hospital until 1991, when it was superseded by more modern hospitals funded by the foundation.'

Anna checked into her room and had a quick shower and change. She applied more dressings to her back before re-joining Freja for dinner. The house was magnificent with high ceilings and elegant arched doorways. 'It was originally built in 1871,' said Freja. 'Come and see some more.' She led Anna through the dining room to a comfortable living room that looked out over the sea. This had double doors that opened into the library. On the walls were some small watercolours that didn't look that exciting until Freja explained they had been painted by Nicholas II and his father, Alexander III. 'Dagmar was originally betrothed to Alexander's elder brother, Nicholas, but he died of meningitis before the marriage, so she fulfilled his dying wish by marrying his brother. It was apparently a happy marriage, despite Alexander's reactionary politics. It was one of Russia's great tragedies that his father, Alexander II, was so comparatively liberal but was the one who got assassinated.'

'I suppose as an art historian I should immediately have known who painted them,' Anna said with a smile.

Their dinner in the private dining room was superb. Freja told Anna that the cuisine at Hvidøre was rated the finest in Denmark. Afterwards Anna said she wasn't surprised and was appreciative that the staff had given her a vegan meal. 'The wine cellar too is exceptional, should you ever wish to try it.' Anna said she probably wouldn't and anyway found it hard to tell one wine from another.

They took coffee in the library and Anna asked Freja about her work. 'Well nano means one billionth of something. You can ascribe it to any unit of measurement. For example, you can express a very small mass in nanograms or the amount of liquid in a single cell in terms of nanolitres.'

'So, what is nanoscience?'

'It's the study of structures and materials on the scale of nanometres. I'll give you an idea' and Freja took a book off one of the shelves. 'This page is about seventy-five thousand nanometres thick. When structures are made small enough, in the nanometre size range, they take on interesting and potentially very useful properties.'

'So has it all come about very recently?'

'In a way no. Nanoscale structures existed in nature long before scientists began studying them. A single strand of DNA is about three nanometres wide. The scales on a butterfly's wings contain nanostructures that change the way light waves interact, giving the wings their brilliant metallic hues. Peacock feathers and soap bubbles get their iridescence from similar structures just tens of nanometres thick and we've now created materials in the laboratory that mimic some of the amazing nanostructures in nature.'

'I can see the attraction. It all sounds fascinating. How can you work on things this small?'

'We can use beams of electrons or ions to etch features as small as twenty-five nanometres into various materials. And nanostructures can be created by the reaction of chemicals, generating nanofibers, nanocrystals, and quantum dots, some as small as one nanometre wide. We're now learning how to build three-dimensional structures at the nanoscale, called nano-electro-mechanical systems, or NEMS. That's my specialism and one day they might be used like microscopic robots. NEMS could carry out surgery on a single cell or act as mechanical actuators to move around individual molecules.'

'It all sounds like science fiction,' Anna said. 'But that's the future, is your work having an impact now?'

'Yes, indeed. Nanoscience has already produced innovations like stain-resistant fabrics, inspired by nanoscale features found on lotus plants. Working across disciplines we're using nanoscience for applications in energy, medicine, information storage, and computing. You must come and visit the centre and I'll show you what we're doing.'

Anna agreed that she'd be fascinated and delighted to do so. 'Is it a large centre?'

'We have around a hundred and fifty scientists, nine-and-a-half thousand employees and eighteen thousand students. We're one of the biggest in the world.'

They moved on to more personal issues though, as usual, Anna said little about herself. Freja was more forthcoming. She was divorced, amicably, and had two daughters aged twenty and eighteen. Inevitably Anna said, 'You don't look old enough,' though she knew she must be about the same age as Gordon and Scott.

Freja laughed. 'I'm forty-four, but I do like to keep fit. Gordon says you're something of a martial arts expert.'

'I wouldn't say that,' replied Anna. 'What's your sport?'

'It used to be handball but now I'm more of a runner and a swimmer. If you have time we could go for a run? Will you be staying through the weekend?' Anna said she wasn't sure but said if she was still here on Sunday they could go. It was now getting late. Freja said she'd check in with Anna on Friday to see how her research was getting on and they said goodbye.

Back in her very comfortable room in the new extension, Anna messaged Cloote. His reply said that 'Anna Carr' was enjoying her stay in Weimar and wishing her luck. Another dream interrupted Anna's sleep.

She was kneeling near a cliff top. A storm was sweeping around her and yet she wasn't getting wet. Lightning was flashing and she could hear wolves howling. The storm got fiercer and fiercer, but she was very calm and relaxed. She saw a tall woman walking toward her, surrounded by a dazzling blue light so bright it was hard to fully make out her features. Anna only knew she was amazingly beautiful. The woman reached out and touched Anna's upraised hands. As she did so a flash of blue lightning struck Anna. But it wasn't normal lightning. Instead of coming down from the sky to her, it went up from her to the stars.

She'd had the dream when she was a child. Whenever life seemed about to overwhelm her, she had dreamed about the beautiful woman, and had felt better. It was the first time she'd had the dream for many years.

Chapter 55

In the morning she got up early. Unlike libraries in the UK the Royal Library opened at 8 a.m. and didn't close until 9 p.m. A ten-minute walk took her to Klampenborg station where she took a train six stops to Østerport. Here she changed onto the very modern Copenhagen Metro City Circle Line to Gammel Strand. Leaving the station, she walked over Højbro, High Bridge, past the front of the Christiansborg Palace and between it and the Børsen, which Freja had pointed out the day before. She crossed a neat formal garden to the far side of the Royal Library where the main entrance was located. Behind the ultra-modern Black Diamond, the library has an older building, built in 1906. Three bridges connect the two. She made her way to Reading Room West, in the new part of the building, which houses special collections.

She began a systematic search through the Børglum Abbey records, looking for anything connected with a man called Berenger. Børglum Abbey had originally been a royal farm dating back before 1000. In 1086, when the peasants revolted against him, King Canute IV fled Børglum, and the royal residence was burned to the ground. Sometime in the 1130s, Børglum was granted to the Church and became the seat of the bishop of Northern Jutland. A monastery was also established and remained there until the Reformation.

Her first day proved fruitless, as did the second and third. She read several hundred names of monks but not a single Berenger. On Friday evening Freja called and asked if Anna would like to have dinner at her flat on Istedgade. She said her older daughter, Nadja, would be there.

At eight Anna got a taxi to Freja's apartment. Istedgade is the Vesterbro area's main street and exemplifies its diversity. In between porn shops and strip clubs are some of the city's best boutiques, restaurants, and bars. The apartment was in a former factory above a trendy looking clothes boutique and opposite a rather seedier bar and a flower shop. She rang the bell and was buzzed into the entrance hall. The apartment door was open and Nadja was standing there to greet her. She had dark hair in two plaits with steel-rimmed glasses. She was wearing denim dungarees and a checked shirt. 'Hi, you must be Hildegard? Mum said we should speak English. I'm Nadja. Mum's just in the kitchen.' They shook hands and Anna entered an ultra-modern, and very tastefully decorated, flat with stripped wood flooring and some interesting looking modern art on the walls. Nadja took Anna through to the large kitchen, past a living room containing pale blue sofas and a dining table set for three.

'Hi,' Freja greeted her. 'Nadja, fix Hildegard a drink, will you?'

'Beer, wine, or juice?' Nadja asked.

'Could I just have juice thanks.'

Freja explained that both her and her younger daughter were keen cooks. 'I'm not,' said Nadja. 'I just eat.' Anna liked her cheeky grin. 'I'm also the odd one out in the family. Mum, Dad, and Pernille are all scientists, but I study history. Mum says you're an art historian?'

'That's right. I'm over here looking at early Danish art from the Viking period.'

'Oh great. We should talk some more. But I think the food's coming.'

Freja had prepared a vegetarian meal for them. The main course was spicy lentil patties with a Danish potato and cabbage salad and pan-fried courgettes. There was also fresh mayonnaise, thinned with lemon juice as a dipping sauce for the patties. This was followed by Danish-style pancakes with raspberries and cream. 'That was absolutely delicious,' Anna said. 'Thank you so much for a lovely meal.'

They moved over to the sofas and Anna asked Nadja about her sister and father. 'Pernille is the serious one,' she replied. 'She's in Canada studying to be an engineer. She wants to build bridges. Real ones rather than social ones like me. Dad's an architect. He travels all over the place, but we see him when he's in Denmark.'

Anna asked Nadja about her course at Copenhagen University and she confirmed it covered the Viking Age. 'It's the period I'm most interested in. You say that's what you're studying too?' Anna said it was and she thought it was fine to say that she'd been to Denmark before for a summer dig at Jelling. 'For my project this semester I'm looking into the history of Sorø Abbey,' Nadja said. She explained that the abbey was founded by Asser Rig, the son of Skjalm Hvide, Zealand's most powerful noble, in 1142, and she was studying its early years before and after Bishop Absalon replaced the Benedictine monks with Cistercians in 1161.

'Are you going up to the turn of the century when Saxo Grammaticus was writing the *Gesta Danorum* at Sorø?'

'I'm not saying too much about him because he's so well-known' said Nadja, 'but he gets some mentions. You know a lot about the period for an art historian.'

'Well, you have to know about the background,' said Anna hurriedly. 'What are you concentrating on?'

'Mainly everyday monastic life,' said Nadja. 'I'm fascinated by the ways monks and nuns lived, worked, and practised their religion. There were so many differences from place to place, even within the same religious order.'

'Such as?'

'Their names for one thing. You'll know they were usually identified as so-and-so of such-and-such an abbey or priory and if they moved to another, they'd usually change their second name. Well sometimes they changed their first name as well. So, a nun might have a traditional Danish name, like Regnild, a pagan name, that she'd keep for a while and then change it to a Christian one, say Rachel. They'd even swop the other way at times.'

Anna became more attentive. 'I'm not sure I knew that,' she said, 'or if I did, I'd forgotten. How fascinating. Have you found many examples?'

'Oh yes, there were quite a few. Hang on I'll get my notes.' In a minute she was back and sat on the sofa next to Anna. 'Here are the ones I found at Sorø. This list has their names at their previous house and this one has the few that I traced when they moved elsewhere. There's even a couple who went overseas. Anastasius became Adelmo of Milan and Johannes kept his first name and became . . .'

Anna completed her sentence: 'Johannes of Medhamstead. Nadja, you are a brilliant researcher!' Nadja blushed. Anna glanced over at Freja who shrugged. 'Okay, Nadja, I need to tell you something,' Anna continued. 'My name isn't Hildegard and I'm not an art historian.' Nadja was the one who was now listening intently as Anna told her as much as she thought safe about their search, and the people who were opposing them. 'So, you can really help us. Give me everything you have on Johannes and see what else you can find. Hold on I need to make a call.' She called Gordon and explained the situation to him. 'I want you to get a secure phone for Nadja,' she concluded. Gordon said he'd speak to Scott, and one would be delivered by courier by Monday at the latest.

'Wow! I didn't think history was like this! It's more like Indiana Jones than Terry Jones,' Nadja said, and added, '*Monty Python and the Holy Grail* is one of my favourite films by the way.' For the rest of the evening, they talked about other topics, music, art, and life in Copenhagen. 'You'll have to come out tomorrow night,' Nadja said. 'We can go to Vela. You're gay, aren't you? Anyway, even if you're not it's very easy going, even Mum comes sometimes.' Anna's opinion of Nadja, and her mother, went up another notch.

'Nadja!' said Freja.

'It's fine,' said Anna. 'Like I said you're perceptive. Yeh. I'd love to come.'

'Do you play table football?' Nadja asked unexpectedly. Anna said she hadn't played since she was an undergraduate.

''Cause they have a competition at the club tomorrow. You can be my partner.'

'Nadja prides herself on her table football skills,' said Freja. 'Can't get her to do any proper sport, it's another way she's different from the rest of the family.'

In the taxi back to Hvidøre, Anna thought more about the unexpected things Nadja had told her. Not only had she unearthed information about the writer of the Bodleian manuscript, she'd given her an idea for her research the following day.

Chapter 56

On Saturday Anna thought it was great to be in a country that still valued its public services so highly. Many British libraries would have been shut to researchers at the weekend. She ordered a completely new set of papers, this time from Sorø, from the dates before Johannes had left. She also called up the library's holdings of the *Gesta Hammaburgensis ecclesiae pontificum, Deeds of the Bishops of Hamburg.* This treatise was written between 1073 and 1076, by Adam of Bremen. It's one of the most important sources of medieval history, most famous for containing the oldest report of the discovery of North America by the Vikings. No original version exists, but the Royal Library has the best copy, dating from around 1230. Anna knew the book, especially for its description of Norse paganism practised at the temple in Gamla Uppsala. When the manuscript arrived, she re-read this and the accompanying notes, of which the Royal Library held the only copy. At the end was a short piece of music sketched by a hand that could be none other than Johannes of Medhamstead. He must have compiled the copy of Adam's work. She carefully photographed the page.

The Sorø papers were now ready, and she spent the rest of the morning and into the afternoon studying them, fascinated that some contained handwritten notes by Otto Höfler himself. Anna mused that if Nazism hadn't swept him up Höfler would have had a highly distinguished career. *He was weak*, thought Anna. *Like so many who follow fascists, he took the easy course.*

At two o'clock she struck gold. A directive from the abbot was addressed to: 'In ipso optimum fratribus,' 'the very excellent brothers,' 'Johannes amarius. Frater Berenger.' The armarius, or provisioner, was the director of a monastic scriptorium. This had to be their Johannes and his friend Berenger. In a later entry she found another reference to Berenger: 'Venerabilis Frater Noster pro nobis hodie episcopatus Berenger Vendsyssel.' This translated as, 'On this day our esteemed brother Berenger left us for the bishopric of Vendsyssel.' Vendsyssel was another name for Vestervig or Børglum. It was the same man. But when he reached Børglum he had changed his name. Anna returned to her notes made in the previous days. 'Of course. What an idiot!' It had been staring her in the face. Some of the first documents she'd dismissed were a group collected by a monk named Quirinus. In Augustan Rome, Quirinus was an epithet of Janus, as Janus Quirinus, but in earlier times his name had been derived from the Sabine word 'quiris', meaning 'wielder of the spear'. Berenger is a Germanic name meaning 'bear' or 'spear'. They had to be the same person and when Berenger moved to Børglum he had dropped his alternative name and called himself Quirinus.

Anna quickly called up Quirinus's documents. She was just in time as the last order was about to go. There were only a small number. Quirinus too had been the amarius of the scriptorium at Børglum. The documents contained lists of books, inventories of writing materials, and other supplies for the scriptorium and some notes probably for work that Quirinus/ Berenger was planning. Then she saw it. It was just a few scribblings at the end of a list of manuscripts to be copied:

Johannes de tempore in Anglia delitescunt. Genesis 1: 20.

From Johannes now in England. Genesis 1: 20.

The clincher was that Berenger had also used a third language. It was just a brief phrase, but it contained the words 'qiman', meaning to come (from) and 'andwairþs', something happening in the present. *Gothic!* Anna exulted. *It was Berenger who wrote the paper Westley stole from the Herzog August Library.*

She got out her laptop and searched for the Vulgate Bible, St Jerome's Latin translation that he completed around 405. She turned to Genesis, chapter 1, verse 20, where she read:

Dixit etiam Deus producant aquae reptile animae viventis et volatile super terram sub firmamento caeli.

In the English King James version this reads:

> *God also said: Let the waters bring forth the creeping creature having life, and the fowl that may fly over the earth under the firmament of heaven.*

What more fitting text could Johannes have chosen for his key?

For a few seconds Anna sat absolutely still, despite the urge to scream and shout, this was, after all, a library. She collected her papers and laptop. As she left, she thanked the archivist. 'Min meget taknemmelige tak, du har været så hjælpsom.'

She stayed calm, checked carefully for any sign of being followed, and then returned to the metro station. Back in her room at Hvidøre she told herself to be systematic. *First check the music for a code*, she told herself. Sure enough the same version Johannes had used in the Bodleian manuscript was in use here. It turned out to be more corroboration, rather than revealing new information:

> *Et adferent gloriam et coronam Regneri Sancti Edmundi qui dixit non amisit. Ego Johannes scitote esse falsum.*

Which translates as:

> *The treasure of Ragnar and the crown of Saint Edmund are said to be lost. I, Johannes, know this to be false.*

She then turned her attention to the key text. She knew the encrypted version was four hundred and eighty-nine characters long. First, she copied the Latin version of Genesis, chapter 1 starting at verse 20. By the end of verse 25 there were five hundred and ninety-one characters. She typed the key text into the middle line of three in an Excel spreadsheet. Below each cell of the key, she copied the encrypted text they had deciphered from Johannes's 'sequence'.

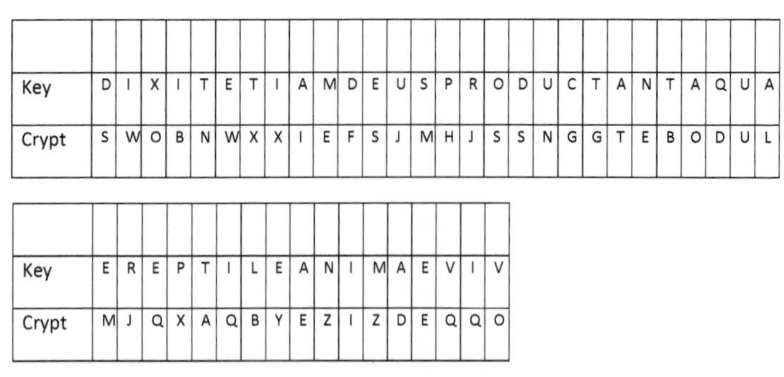

Key	D	I	X	I	T	E	T	I	A	M	D	E	U	S	P	R	O	D	U	C	T	A	N	T	A	Q	U	A
Crypt	S	W	O	B	N	W	X	X	I	E	F	S	J	M	H	J	S	S	N	G	G	T	E	B	O	D	U	L

Key	E	R	E	P	T	I	L	E	A	N	I	M	A	E	V	I	V
Crypt	M	J	Q	X	A	Q	B	Y	E	Z	I	Z	D	E	Q	Q	O

Then, using the Vigenère square, she began cross-referencing the key and crypt letters to find the plaintext letters to which they corresponded. The first key letter was D. She followed the D row until she came to the crypt letter S, which is in column P. So, P was the first plaintext letter. Likewise, the second key letter was in row I, its crypt was W, which is in column O. The second plain letter was O. The first few words were as follows:

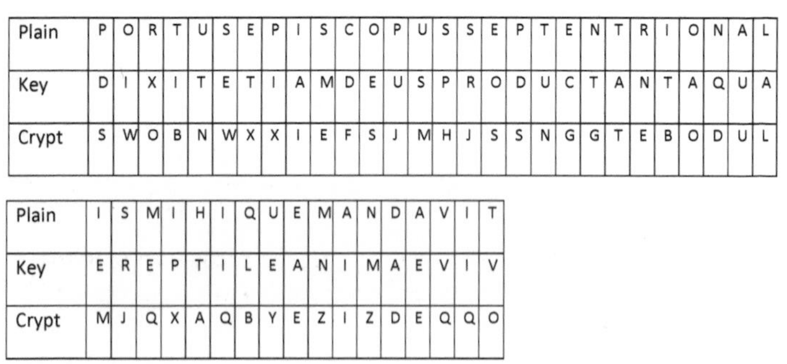

Plain	P	O	R	T	U	S	E	P	I	S	C	O	P	U	S	S	E	P	T	E	N	T	R	I	O	N	A	L
Key	D	I	X	I	T	E	T	I	A	M	D	E	U	S	P	R	O	D	U	C	T	A	N	T	A	Q	U	A
Crypt	S	W	O	B	N	W	X	X	I	E	F	S	J	M	H	J	S	S	N	G	G	T	E	B	O	D	U	L

Plain	I	S	M	I	H	I	Q	U	E	M	A	N	D	A	V	I	T
Key	E	R	E	P	T	I	L	E	A	N	I	M	A	E	V	I	V
Crypt	M	J	Q	X	A	Q	B	Y	E	Z	I	Z	D	E	Q	Q	O

Or, crypt: SWOBNWXXIEFSJMHJSSNGGTEBODULMJQX AQBYEZIZDEQQO

Plain: Portus episcopus Septentrionalis mihique mandavit.

Eventually she had translated the entire code, which she christened 'The Bodleian Sequence', in memory of Magnus. In Latin the first part read:

> *Portus episcopus Septentrionalis mihique mandavit in Brisingamen ad removendum Ivari interitus. Cum autem*

in Praeceptoris Templar scriptor et abstuli eas. In aeternum non periit ut apponam. Centum cubitos Via Rex a porta media. Septentrionis quinquaginta cubitos. Hic Magnce murus erat. Et foderunt murum. Et facti sumus despectio converte nos custodire sanctus custos et evenit nobis prospere.

This translates as:

The Bishop of North Port commanded me remove the Brisingamen of Ivar. With the Preceptor of the Templar's, I removed them. I set this down to ensure they are not forever lost. One hundred yards King's Street from the Middle Gate. Fifty yards to north. The wall of Friary was being made here. We dug beneath the wall. We prayed to the saint to protect us from the Guardian and the saint answered our prayers.

The second part was:

Quod gentes coronam de quo sanctus permanet in sinistra est. Et sub ecclesia S. Botulphi de contingentibus. Viginti cubitis inde altare. Supra prefatum lapidem illius.

The crown of the saint remains where the heathens left it. Beneath the church of Saint Botolph's Abbey. Twenty yards from the altar. Beneath the stone.

Anna jammed in her ear buds and put on Slayer's album *Reign in Blood* at top volume. She messaged Cloote. 'Got it! Coming back Monday. Will encrypt and send in chunks.'

She then phoned Freja. 'Tell Nadja I'd love to go out on the town tonight. Will you come too?' Freja said she would.

Fuck Hildegard, thought Anna. *Tonight, I'll dress like Anna Carr.* She pulled on a pair of black jeans and a bright red tee-shirt, the 'Don't Fuck With My Energy' shirt Tina had given her.

Chapter 57

Anna met Freja and Nadja at the apartment. They had booked dinner at the nearby Restaurant Cofoco, which offered a modern Danish menu including vegetarian options. It was in Abel Catherines Gade, just a few metres from the Vela Club in Viktoriagade. The club was friendly and welcoming, with a mainly lesbian clientele, but also a few men, both queer and straight. Looking round Anna thought Danish dykes liked short skirts and lipstick much more than Brits.

Freja introduced her to a couple from her department, Kristiina Rautakorpi, from Finland, and Yejide Adeyemi, who was Nigerian. They'd been among the first same sex couples in Denmark to get married in 2012. Kristiina said that Finland hadn't passed a similar law until 2017 and Yejide explained that Nigeria had even passed a Same Gender Marriage Prohibition law in 2013. 'If we went there, we wouldn't be welcomed. When I attended my mother's funeral two years ago, I received death threats from militant Islamists who knew who I was.'

'Hey, we're on!' Nadja came over and said to Anna. The table football competition was beginning. Nadja and Anna were entered as 'FC Valhalla'. Neither were the most skilful players but through a combination of Nadja's passionate competitiveness and Anna's quick reflexes, they managed to win a couple of games before getting beaten by two of Nadja's friends, Julie and Louise, who went on to win the trophy.

Anna saw a small group gathered round a woman in an electric wheelchair. 'Come on, I'll introduce you to Sarah Glerup,' said Nadja. Anna thought she'd seen the woman before and when Nadja introduced them, almost forgetting to call her Hildegard, she remembered. Despite having muscular dystrophy she'd had a stellar academic career. As a cartoonist she'd won the Ping Prize in the 'Best Comic Book' category in 2014 for her blog *The Sarah Kastiske Corner*. Then, in 2016,

Glerup became the first member of the Folketing, the Danish parliament, who was a wheelchair user.

'Didn't you also take part in the Danish edition of *X Factor*?' Anna asked.

Glerup said she had. 'I managed to get to the second show.'

'What did you sing?'

'Goldfrapp's "Strict Machine" and Tom Waits' "Time".'

'Well, that was the problem wasn't it?' said Anna. 'If you'd sung some death metal, you'd probably have won.'

Glerup laughed. She said that Nadja was a prominent member of her party, the Unity List, also known as the Red Greens. 'We're the furthest left party in the Danish parliament,' she explained.

'Where do you stand between the red and the green then?' asked Anna.

'Well, our objective is a society based on democratic socialism, equality, and ecology. We've currently got thirteen of the hundred and seventy-nine seats in the Folketing. Here in Vesterbro, we were the strongest party in the last election. Nadja is one of our most active members. What do you make of her?'

'Fierce. Passionate. Committed. Idealistic,' suggested Anna.

'That's about right,' Glerup replied. 'She's our redder version of Greta Thunberg, I guess. Could be a future MP. She speaks her mind and doesn't care about challenging people she disagrees with, including me.'

Nadja was now dancing with some her friends and Freja had joined Glerup's group. She and Sarah knew each other well. 'You'll be making her ears burn saying that,' she said.

'She's a really great girl, Freja,' Glerup replied.

'Yes, I'm very proud of her.'

Anna and Freja moved off to sit in a quieter corner as lots of other people wanted to talk with Sarah. 'God, I wish we had a few people like that in our parliament,' said Anna.

'German or British?' joked Freja, but knew which she meant.

Freja talked more about herself, saying she'd got married when she was a post-grad. She'd always wanted a family and Frederik was nice guy. 'I know it's a cliché, but we just grew apart,' she said. 'It was no one's fault and I'm glad we both recognised it. I think the divorce came as a relief to us both. Of course, it had an impact on the girls, but much less than if we'd stayed together and argued the whole time.'

Anna asked her when they realised Nadja was gay. 'Really quite early. When she was small, she wouldn't wear a dress. Once she ripped her dress off in the street and walked down the road in her pants glaring at people! We tried not to judge and let her find her own way. But when she brought home her first girlfriend I almost cried with joy. Frederik felt much the same.'

'She was lucky to have parents like you,' said Anna, thinking of her own childhood. 'And her politics?'

'Started real young too. She was organising eco protests when she was twelve and, a year or so later, ran her own campaign in folkeskole. It was called "Hyld dine kønshår", "celebrate your pubic hair". She was mad that so many young girls thought body hair was unhealthy and repulsive, so she organised an opposition. She got doctors to talk about how it was healthy to have hair and did protests with her friends. They got arrested for taking their clothes off at one of them. They'd been inspired by Femen, painted slogans on their bodies and wore pubic wigs. What do you call them in English?'

'Merkins,' said Anna.

'Ah yes, merkins. Such a lovely name. Anyway, they were let off because they were under fifteen and the protest was political. It was quite a famous case.'

'I can imagine,' said Anna.

Nadja came over and asked Anna to dance. Unusually she said yes, and Freja said she'd head home. 'How about we go for a run tomorrow? You can stay at our place tonight.'

Anna said that would be great and then enjoyed herself so much she lost track of the time. At about 3 a.m. they decided to head back to Istedgade. Nadja looped her arm through Anna's as they walked back. 'Do you have a girlfriend back home?' she asked.

'No, not, no,' Anna replied.

Nadja grinned, 'Oh! There *is* someone isn't there?' Anna didn't reply. 'We could still sleep together, you know. Mum won't mind.' Anna didn't reply. 'Okay, it's cool. But we are friends, aren't we?'

'Nadja we are definitely friends. And you can really help me with your research. You're a pretty remarkable girl you know, and thanks for introducing me to Sarah, she's amazing.'

'She is, isn't she?'

'Do you want to become a politician?'

'I don't know. If I can get more done outside parliament then maybe not.'

'Sometimes that's certainly true,' said Anna. 'I think you'll be a success whatever you decide.' Nadja gave Anna a kiss on the cheek, and they were now back at the apartment.

Chapter 58

The morning was unusually warm for early April. After a late breakfast Anna, Freja, and Nadja drove to Hvidøre where Anna changed into her running gear. Freja left the car in the car park. 'You're not coming too?' Anna asked Nadja.

'No way!' she replied. 'Table football is energetic enough. Oh, and fucking of course,' she added with a grin. 'I'll meet you at the beach in an hour or so.'

Anna and Freja ran up the hill past the railway station, where they entered the huge Jægersborg Deer Park. The park had miles of paths across open spaces and through forest and, at one point, they passed the Hermitage Hunting Lodge, built in the 1730s to host banquets during royal hunts. It reminded Anna of Richmond Park in London, where she'd been a few times, and which had also been created as a royal deer park by Charles I. Eventually they headed back to the sea and the village of Taarbæk, which Anna knew meant 'Thor's Stream'. Freja said the village had an important spa in the nineteenth century. 'Now it's most famous because their priest was Thorkild Grosbøll. In the early 2000s he became famous for publicly announcing his disbelief in a creator God.'

'Pretty radical. A priest who doesn't believe in God. What happened?'

'The church tried to sack him, but his parishioners supported him. Eventually he retired, but he still lives here.'

They passed the pretty harbour of Taarbæk and followed the coast road for a while, until turning off down a track to a beautiful beach of white sand. 'Bellevue Beach,' announced Freja. 'It's one of the most famous beaches in Denmark.' There was a smattering of people on the beach. Several were clearly gay couples and many of them were nude. 'We're pretty relaxed about nudity here,' said Freja. 'Hope you are because I'm going for a swim.'

She threw down the small backpack she'd been carrying,

removed her clothes and ran towards the water. Anna wasn't bothered about the nudity but was wary of the water; at this time of year it would be absolutely freezing. As she tentatively entered Freja was already swimming strongly. 'Just think of it as an ice bath,' she called out to Anna. 'Athletes swear by them!'

Anna wasn't a bad swimmer but in comparison to Freja was a novice, so she stayed safely near the shore. She saw Nadja arrive, so she got out of the water. Nadja saw the wounds on Anna's back. Though they were healing they still looked bad. 'My God, Anna. What happened to you?'

'It was some very bad people. Don't worry, I'm fine, but they won't be.' Freja asked the same question when she joined them. 'You do need to take care though,' Anna said. 'It's why I'm here as Hildegard. They've killed at least three people including one of my best friends.'

'I don't mind fighting,' said Nadja as she undressed. 'I had a big fight with some Nazis outside the Folketing last year.'

'Who won?'

'Well, we were going to, but the police rescued them.'

'Nadja, you got a black eye and were hit on the head with a cosh!' said her mother.

'You should have seen the guy that did it though. I had him on the ground when the cop pulled me off!'

The sun was out, and, after the sea, Anna felt pleasantly warm. She admired Freja's body that looked every bit as athletic as she'd thought. 'She's pretty sexy, my mum?' said Nadja.

Freja smiled and Anna said, 'Everyone is beautiful in their own way.'

'And by seeing the beauty in others we make ourselves more beautiful. Carole King,' Freja added.

'Who?' said Nadja.

After a while, during which Anna even found herself drifting to sleep, Nadja asked, 'When are you leaving?'

'Tomorrow,' Anna said. 'We're not taking any chances so I'm flying home from Malmo via Stockholm.'

'I'll come and see you off then,' Nadja said emphatically.

*

That evening they had dinner together at Hvidøre and Anna got an early night. The flight was at one thirty and the drive to Malmo was just over an hour, so she and Freja had time for another run before they left at ten. They picked up Nadja from the apartment and drove back towards Kastrup before heading into the Drogden Tunnel, which forms the first part of the crossing from Denmark to Sweden. The tunnel crosses the artificial island of Peberholm before reaching the Øresund Bridge, the longest combined road and rail bridge in Europe. The relatively small Malmo airport, which used to be called Sturup, is nearly thirty kilometres east of the city but, being a Sunday, traffic was light, and they made it in plenty of time for Anna's flight. Nadja hugged her tightly and her eyes blazed as she said, 'I'm so pleased I met you, Anna. You must keep safe and come back here soon.'

'Thanks. It was a pleasure to meet you too and I'll definitely come back.'

Anna and Freja exchanged slightly more formal goodbyes. 'Say hello to Gordon and Scott and tell Gordon he owes me a visit too.'

Anna said she would, and Hildegard Kirchner checked in for her departure.

*

Anna only had a short gap between flights and was back at Heathrow at 5 p.m. Anula, Cloote and Rees had got back to England the previous day. They hadn't wanted to risk Anula's impersonation of Anna at an airport's security checks so Scott had driven them to the Calais ferry. Scott was there to meet her in his Mercedes van together with Asayo Negishi, but Anna was surprised to find the other three there as well.

'It couldn't wait,' said Cloote. 'As usual you were right, the key *was* there after all.'

Asayo filled them in on her findings. 'I travelled separately to Weimar, as I told you. You were all under surveillance while you were there, however, when Anna left, as far as I can tell, you weren't being tracked.'

'And if Asayo says you weren't being tracked; you really weren't being tracked,' added Scott.

'Their surveillance techniques are not exactly sophisticated,' Asayo continued. 'Their first resort is blackmail or intimidation. That was how they turned our guy. My concern is that though you might outsmart them for a while, eventually they'll again resort to something cruder.'

'What you're saying is we'll never get rid of them?' asked Cloote looking intently at Asayo.

'Not unless you do something to permanently deal with them, no.'

On the drive back they began discussing the meaning of the Bodleian Sequence. 'Johannes begins by saying it was the "Bishop of North Port" who gave instructions to hide Ivar's treasure. That's Norwich, right?' Anna said.

'Why would they do this?' asked Gordon. 'Why hide the treasure?'

'I'd say there are three possibilities,' Cloote replied. 'First would be as protection. Was there something going on, unrest, civil war, that made them fearful?'

'We're talking about the 1230s,' Anna said. 'Things were much more peaceful then than earlier in Henry's reign, or indeed later. There might have been local problems, but it's not a likely reason.'

'Second. They were stealing it,' said Cloote.

'No, I don't buy that either,' said Anna. 'We've started to get an idea of Johannes's personality and he doesn't strike me as someone who would help a bishop steal a fortune. I think there has to be another explanation.'

'Which is?' Gordon looked at her and Cloote enquiringly.

'They were genuinely frightened it was cursed,' Cloote replied. 'After all, Johannes says, "We prayed to the saint to protect us from the Guardian and the saint answered our prayers."'

'My thoughts exactly,' said Anna. 'Then we have the runes from Uppsala,' she added. '"Sindri the smith had Ivar's stones. He was taken by a myrkálfar." The dark elf could be another description of the so-called guardian.'

Cloote looked thoughtful as if considering this further, but said instead, 'The most important thing is to identify where they concealed the treasure. It's a place that had a Templar church and a friary with a street called King's and a Middle Gate.'

'So pretty much any city in England,' said Anna. 'Sorry, I'm being a bit facetious. We can narrow it down by the involvement of the bishop of Norwich. Could it be Norwich itself?'

'It had a King Street but not, I think, a Middle Gate. Nor did Bury or King's Lynn. I think there's only one place that meets all four criteria.'

'And that is?' enquired Gordon.

'Dunwich,' Cloote said.

Chapter 59

When they got back to Aldeburgh, Cloote got out some maps that showed the medieval and modern versions of Dunwich together with its progressive losses to the sea. 'Okay, Oliver. You're telling us that we've trekked all over Northern Europe only to find the treasure is a couple of miles up the road!'

'Come, come, Gordon, you're exaggerating. Dunwich is at least six miles away.'

Sometimes dubbed 'Britain's Atlantis', Dunwich today a small village, but it was once the early medieval capital of East Anglia. A town called Dommoc is recorded in Bede's *Historia Ecclesiastica*, completed around 731, and it served as the seat of St Felix, the first bishop of East Anglia. In the Saxon period a 'wic', or trading centre, was established, which subsequently became the medieval town of Dunwich. In 1086 the Domesday Book put its population at over three thousand, making Dunwich one of the ten largest settlements in England. By 1225 the town extended approximately a mile from north to south, an area similar in size to London. But then, in the thirteenth and fourteenth centuries, Dunwich was hit by destructive storms which were followed by eight hundred years of coastal erosion. By 1587, half the town had gone, and the last of the medieval parish churches, All Saints, fell into the sea between 1904 and 1919. Now most of the original town is beneath the sea. Since 2008, historians, local divers, scientists and, in 2011, the television archaeology programme *Time Team*, have utilised every modern archaeological technique to trace the ruins of what has become the world's largest underwater medieval town site. Cloote told them more as they looked at the maps. 'In the Middle Ages, Dunwich had eight churches, three chapels, five houses of religious orders, including Franciscan and Dominican monasteries, and a preceptory of the Knights Templar, two hospitals, and probably a mint and a guildhall. It's thought that the Templars' church was a round structure, like the one in London.'

'So, all the pieces of Johannes's description fit?' asked Anula.

'Indeed they do, Anula. But if, as we suspect, Johannes was securing the treasure around 1240 this was when Dunwich was at its height,' Cloote explained. 'The two great storms that began the destruction of the town were in 1286 and 1347.'

'So, there's a good chance it's now at the bottom of the sea?' Gordon added.

Cloote got out the archaeological report on Dunwich from 2012. They studied the map of the reconstruction of the town, looking especially at the position of King Street and Middle Gate. 'I have a feeling Johannes was a man who understood history and planned ahead,' he said. 'Look. King Street is the one that runs northwest from Middle Gate, and he mentions a friary that was being built. Greyfriars was constructed in the thirteenth century and, though the remaining walls are fourteenth, they may well be on earlier foundations. I think there's a good chance his site is still on dry land.'

'In that case we have to decide how we go about looking where he told us,' Anna replied.

'Johannes says he placed it under a wall,' said Cloote. 'If that wall is still standing that could explain why nothing has been found. All the surveys and digs would have been looking for buried walls not digging under ones that are still standing.'

'We need a preliminary survey to pin down the location,' Anna continued. 'If it looks promising, we decide how best to proceed.'

'We'll need a legitimate permit then, like at Swineshead?' queried Rees.

'Yes, we'll need to see who currently has permission to work there, and if they're on site now,' Cloote concluded.

It didn't take long to find out that Oxford University School of Archaeology held permits for further investigation of the work carried out by the University of Southampton. There was no indication of current activity, and a quick phone call to the department, supposedly from the *East Anglian Daily Times*, established there wouldn't be any work going on in what was now the Easter vacation. 'As Southampton are involved, could you get permission again from your friend?' asked Anna.

'Bernard might be rather wary after Swineshead,' Cloote replied. 'I think the best idea is to dig over Easter and send him an email just before. So, we've asked, but he hasn't had time to say no.'

'How do we go about a preliminary survey?' asked Rees.

'I could do that,' Anula intervened. 'I could take Leo Houghton.'

'Who?' asked Anna.

'He's one of my patients who's in recovery. He needs to do exercise and he's very interested in the history of the Suffolk Coast. He's a musician, and he once did a song about Dunwich. Don't worry, I won't tell him why we're there.'

They moved on to consider the second part of Johannes's message, after which Anna said: 'If we're going to be searching at Dunwich we'll need to throw Forth and his friends off the trail. I'll work something out and get it to them through Rasmus.'

Cloote had been looking pensive for some time. 'Just a second, Anna. I've been thinking. Elias Forth has extraordinary resources, eventually he's going to work out what we're doing. I think we need another approach.' He outlined his idea to the others.

'Crazy,' said Gordon.

'It's so dangerous,' Anula added. 'All sorts of things could go wrong. And what about Scott?'

'I'm sure he will go along with what we decide,' said Cloote. 'And what's the alternative? We can't keep a man like Forth at bay forever. Even if our search is successful, he'd come after us.'

'I think Oliver is absolutely right. Even if there are bits I don't understand.' It was Anna who convinced the others, though she wasn't sure if this was a rational choice, or one influenced by her desire for revenge. 'Finding a solution to Forth is the most important thing of all. We've agreed we can't go to the police.'

Over the next hour Anula and Gordon were gradually convinced that Cloote's plan, despite the risks, was the only option.

Chapter 60

Anula drove into Dunwich with Leo and his wife Isobel. They were still running the band they started in the early 1970s and, though never hitting the big time, their recordings had achieved cult status with lovers of what has become known as 'acid folk'. 'We'd never heard of the term until a few years ago,' Isobel said, 'and it's rather ironic as I've not even been drunk and certainly never took drugs.' Anula hadn't listened to their music before and asked Leo to put it on the car stereo. She found it haunting and enchanting, especially their song about the fate of the medieval town. *Anna would probably hate it*, she thought.

They were travelling along a quiet tree-lined road until suddenly, on their right, a high stone wall and then the two large archways that form the friary's entrance appeared. There are a number of walls and other arches that survive from the old buildings, thought to be from the refectory and kitchens but, after 1538, when the friary was dissolved, the rest was demolished. Later, the site passed into private ownership, and, in the eighteenth century, the perimeter walls were rebuilt. They passed the friary, on what is now called Monastery Road, before heading to the car park at the end of Beach Road. They walked up St James's Street, past the Ship Inn and the church, before heading across the fields to Broom Hill. Leo was recovering from hip surgery, which Anula had performed some weeks before, and walking was part of his rehab. They turned back to the road at Sandy Lane Farm and continued onto what is called the high street but is more like a rural lane with a few houses.

Turning off the main path through Greyfriars Wood and then back towards the sea, they reached the southern boundary wall of the friary on their left. They were now looking towards where most of the lost town once stood. Here the friary walls were in serious disrepair, having suffered the ravages of erosion. Anula checked the GPS on her phone. They had been talking about the history of the town and Anula got out a printed version of the medieval map of the town. 'I think we're about here,' she said.

'Yes, Middle Gate would have been about fifty yards out to sea,' Leo replied. 'We're walking along what would have been King Street.'

Anula retraced her steps to get a better view the friary site. She was calculating where the spot indicated by Johannes would be: 'One hundred yards from the Middle Gate' and 'fifty yards to the north.' This wasn't an exact science, as a yard wasn't a precise measurement at the time. Originally the length of a man's belt or girdle, in the twelfth century, Henry I decreed the yard to be the distance from his nose to the thumb of his out-stretched arm. She could see there was a low, ruined wall about the right distance away. Beyond it were the more substantial remains of the monastic refectory. After the dissolution these had been converted into a house then, in 1710, Sir George Downing incorporated them in a remodelled dwelling. By the late eighteenth century this too had been abandoned and, in the 1800s, most of the additions were demolished. By the 1880s, except for some scattered walls, the refectory ruin was the only building remaining. She took photos of the site and then strolled back to the café in the car park with Leo and Isobel.

*

Easter Saturday was unusually hot for the time of year, almost oppressive. A dark blue van, with the University of Oxford logo and 'School of Archaeology' on its side, pulled up outside Greyfriars. Anna, Cloote, and Rees got out and unloaded their equipment. Anna had paid a visit to the hairdresser and was slightly surprised that no one had made a facetious remark along the lines of, 'What's she doing having her hair done at a time like this.' Instead Cloote simply said it was a 'valuable addition' to their work. Anna's hair was now a striking shade of electric blue with one side of her head shaved far more closely than the other.

When they were sure no one was around, Gordon cut the chain on the gates with a bolt cutter. They knew the approximate area for their search. Given the date of Johannes's concealment of the treasure, the walls mentioned in his message would be the earliest on the site, almost certainly built upon over the following centuries. The fact the location had escaped detection for eight hundred years meant that finding it would not be straightforward. Use of the magnetometer would be limited by the profusion of other magnetic sources among the friary remains. GPR might be more successful, especially at locating voids beneath the walls, if they weren't too deep.

Over the next couple of hours, they pegged out and surveyed an area of approximately a hundred square metres, as near as possible to the place they thought Johannes had meant. When they stopped for lunch, they looked over the results and identified the most likely places to begin digging. As this could be beneath later structures, their equipment included boxes with adjustable struts to shore up any larger trenches.

In the afternoon they began digging. They were as careful as possible given the protected nature of the site, but also aware that what they were doing was illegal. 'If we find nothing no one will find out,' Cloote had reasoned. 'If we do, they probably won't care.' It was good as a justification, but not one that would stand up in court. They discovered nothing for the next five hours. The most promising trace on the GPR turned out to be an old latrine, connecting to a culvert, that ran towards where the medieval refectory once stood. As dusk was fast approaching, they decided to make one more test pit nearer to the friary's infirmary. This proved to be the opposite end of the culvert they'd discovered earlier. There was no need for their trench supports, as the sides of the culvert were made from roughly hewn stone. Anna decided to use a handheld GPR unit, a StructureScan Mini XT, which could reach depths of up to sixty centimetres. It was now quite dark, and Gordon rigged up mobile lights powered by a diesel generator.

Anna climbed out and she and Cloote looked at the printout. 'What's that there?' said Anna.

'It looks like some kind of void,' Cloote replied, 'with a less dense object within.'

Anna and Gordon climbed back into the trench. 'Here,' said Anna. 'The space is behind this block.'

Gordon tested the stone block with his hands. 'The mortar's

quite loose,' he said. 'Hello what's that?' He was pointing to the bottom right-hand corner of the block. Anna took a closer look.

'It's a jeran!' she exclaimed.

'A what?'

'A J rune from the Elder Futhark.'

'And J stands for . . .'

'Johannes!'

Together they carefully removed the mortar from around the block. After a few minutes they got either side of it and pulled. The block slid out quite easily and they laid it at the bottom of the trench. 'Just a second, Anna,' they heard Cloote say. He had now got down beside them in the trench. 'I need to do something before you go further.' In a low voice they heard him say, 'Invoco te custos. Nos autem venerunt fures non, ut protectores eius.' It meant, 'I invoke thee, guardian. We come not as thieves but as protectors.' He had also brought something with him. It was the seiðrstafr Anna had found in the library safe.

'Now,' said Cloote to Anna.

Though they had the lights trained on the hole she couldn't see exactly what was within. Her fingers touched something. 'It's a box,' she said. She felt around it. The box was about forty centimetres by thirty and around twenty high. She carefully pulled the box out from the hiding place where it had rested for eight hundred years. It was exceptionally heavy.

'It's incredibly well preserved,' said Gordon. 'What's it made from?'

'I'm not sure,' said Anna. 'I think it might be bone.'

Cloote took the casket from her. 'I agree. It looks something like the Franks Casket.' The Franks or Auzon Casket is a chest from the early eighth century, now in the British Museum. 'This seems to have similar decorations. There are certainly many runes, but the decorative scenes look more pagan than Christian.'

'Aren't you going to open it?' Gordon was getting impatient.

Cloote lifted the lid but just as he did so Anna heard a familiar voice. 'My dear, Dr Cloote,' said Elias Forth, 'thank you so much for all your hard work. Now if you'd all like to come up here. But be careful. Any undue movement and my colleague here will shoot.'

Anna saw Savile Nesfield standing beside Forth. He had a gun in his hand that she recognised as a Smith and Wesson 500. Forth too had a gun, a smaller automatic. The three of them climbed out of the trench. As they did, Anna saw Cloote take a folded paper from his pocket and slip it into the casket. He also placed the seiðrstafr on the ground near the top of the trench. When they were back on the surface, Anna saw they were accompanied by the man called Morten and there was a large, dark coloured pickup truck, with searchlights attached, pointed toward the trench. Another man was standing there directing the lights. They wouldn't have heard the vehicle's engine approaching above the noise of their own generator. Nesfield shut the generator down and they heard a rumble of thunder in the distance. Out to sea a flash of lightning lit up the water. 'Good,' said Forth. 'Do exactly as I say, and no one will get hurt.' He paused. 'At least not yet.'

'How did you ...' Cloote's question tailed off.

'You can blame your little girlfriend,' said Forth. 'She is far too indiscreet.'

'Anna!' said Cloote.

'Thank you for doing the work for us. I hate manual labour. Now, Dr Cloote. Walk slowly toward me.' When they were about five metres apart Forth said, 'Put it down there,' indicating a place a couple of metres in front of him. Cloote did as he was instructed then backed away until he was level with Rees and Anna.

The storm was getting closer. It would reach them very soon. Forth bent down to examine the casket and Nesfield too looked down. At that instant all the searchlights on the truck went out. 'What the!' exclaimed Forth. There was a flash of lightning that briefly illuminated them in the act of fleeing. Both Forth and Nesfield fired. Forth's shot hit Gordon behind the knee, and he fell to the ground with a cry of pain. Cloote dodged behind a doorway.

Nesfield's shot caught Anna's left shoulder as she leapt over a low wall. She realised he wasn't using conventional bullets as a large piece of flesh ripped away. There was a lot of blood, but she thought the collar bone itself hadn't been hit as she could still move it. Anna hadn't seen where Morten had gone but knew Nesfield was now in pursuit. She ran through an arch and turned to her left. The storm was now nearly overhead and the lightning flashes more frequent. Torrential rain began to fall, and Anna could feel it on her wounded shoulder. It felt good. She kept her back to the wall, moving slowly away from the door. She could hear Nesfield's breathing close by. As the next flash lit up the scene, she briefly caught sight of him moving further into the ruined friary away from her.

She turned a corner and Morten was immediately in front of her. He was holding a long, thin knife. There was no time to turn and flee so Anna drew on her taekwondo experience. She employed the jump spin hook kick, but Morten was incredibly quick. He dodged to avoid the blow and, at the same time, thrust at her with the knife. Just in time Anna managed a further spin turn so the blade, instead of striking her in the side, hit the sole of her boot. Though the boot had a thick rubber sole the knife penetrated it. Anna gave a sharp cry of pain and surprise. With a monumental effort she twisted her foot sideways and away and the knife came out of Morten's hand. As she did so the next lightning flash revealed a small figure behind him. It reached out and grasped his neck in a pressure hold and he fell to the ground.

'Anula!'

'Anna! Where's the other one?'

'I don't know.'

Anula looked at Anna's foot. 'Pull the fucker out!' Anna said.

'It isn't the best idea; it depends on the wound.'

'Just do it!' Anula pulled out the knife and they edged back towards the doorway Anna had come through.

'Which way? Back to Oliver or the way he went?' Anula asked.

'You go to Oliver,' said Anna, 'I'll deal with him.'

Moving away from the door in the direction she'd seen Nesfield take she could see the main gateway ahead. She was about to go through a doorway that stood between two ruined walls when she heard a sound behind her. As she turned Nesfield came round the side of the wall. Despite her wounds Anna had the element of surprise. She aimed a flying kick at his solar plexus, and he went down, dropping the gun, which slid a few metres away. Nesfield was winded but not for long. Anna was about to move toward the gun when he produced another from his jacket. He fired at Anna. But she wasn't there. She'd had her back to a wall about a metre and a half high and employed her CB Fry trick. From the top of the wall Anna executed a perfect somersault. Nesfield fired and missed again. Landing next to the discarded gun her hand reached for it. Nesfield screamed something she couldn't hear and at the instant he fired again so did Anna. His shot grazed her cheek. For a second Anna couldn't see whether hers had been better aimed. She prepared to shoot again, just as another lightning flash illuminated Nesfield slumped against a low ruined wall. She moved over to the body. From the front there was no obvious wound. She grasped his shoulder and he slid away from the wall. The bullet had struck him through the roof of his open mouth. She was right about him using expanding bullets. The shot had blown a huge hole in the back of his skull and blood and brains were cascading down the stonework.

Anna moved as quickly as she could back towards where she had left Oliver. The good news was that both he and Anula were still unharmed. Gordon was on the ground with a crude bandage Anula had improvised, wrapped round his knee. The bad news was that Forth still had his gun and had been joined by Morten. As Anna arrived clutching Nesfield's gun, Forth placed Morten between himself and her. 'Perhaps I did underestimate you, Mizz Carr,' he said. 'But I don't think you are an expert shot. By the time you have tried to shoot me at least one of your friends will certainly be dead.'

'I don't understand how he can have recovered so quickly,' whispered Anula, meaning Morten. 'With that maya angam hold he should have been out for hours.'

'Where the fuck are the others?' Forth demanded.

'It would appear they've been held up,' replied Morten.

The storm had increased its ferocity. The thunder and lightning were virtually continuous. Anna and Anula were slightly apart from Cloote. He had retrieved the seiðrstafr. Anula now heard Anna saying softly under her breath: *'Let þar munu þoka Ok let þar munu kvikindi Ok let allr þessi undur Hinder þinn umsækjendur.'*

Keeping a close eye on both Anna and Cloote, Forth picked up the casket. He lifted the lid, and his face was lit up by the gleam of many coloured jewels. A thin smile came over his lips. He took out the piece of paper Anna had seen Cloote insert. As he looked at it, and then the contents of the box, Cloote lifted his staff and in a clear voice said, *'Et precor, o custos. Venite ad me et projiciamus meus inimicos in abyssum irent.' ('I invoke thee oh guardian. Come to me now and cast mine enemies into the abyss.')*

At the same time Anna moved slightly away from Anula and she too lifted her arms toward the storm: *'Geyr nú Garmr mjök fyr Gnipahelli, festr mun slitna, en freki renna. fjölð veit ek fræða fram sé ek lengra um ragna rök römm sigtíva.'*

As Cloote spoke, Anula saw a strange blue glow start to appear round his body. It was like the blue flame from a gas jet encircling him. Then another, larger, blue flame appeared in the distance. It crossed the boundary wall of the site. At first it wasn't easy to see what it was but, as it got nearer, the outline of a huge wolf was revealed, it's eyes burning with an even greater intensity than the flames surrounding it. Forth was too intent on the contents of the box to see the approaching apparition but Morten wasn't. He moved away from Forth, making the latter glance up. A look of abject terror came over him. As he dropped the casket, there was a last deafening clap of thunder and a flash so bright their eyes were temporarily blinded, but not before they saw the monstrous wolf leap at Forth's throat.

'Því at ór þessi vér hafa véurr til gæta.' Because of this we have set a protector to guard it, thought Anula.

They now heard a different roar from that of the thunder. A deeper, rumbling sound that went on for a long time, gaining in intensity. When their eyes readjusted neither Forth, Morten, nor the ghostly wolf could be seen. Instead, where they had been standing had disappeared. Anula was the first to move, Anna limping behind. The entire cliff, for perhaps fifty metres, had crashed into the sea below. They gingerly looked over the edge but could see no sign of Forth or Morten.

For a few minutes no one said a word. The storm had miraculously vanished, and the night was suddenly still and quiet but, from out to sea, they heard the muffled sound of a bell tolling. Anula couldn't help recalling the song Leo and Isobel had played just the day before, which ends with the suggestion that the sunken bells of Dunwich will ring again.

As she was the least injured, Anula was the first to snap out of the reverie. 'Okay. Now leave it to me. Their driver is unconscious in the Land Rover and Scott and Roly have got the others.' She got out her mobile and dialled 999. 'Yes, Dr Anula Hathurusingha. We are at Greyfriars in Dunwich. One man dead, two others possible. I have a male with a gunshot wound to the knee and a female with gunshot and knife wounds. Yes, I have immediate first aid available. Good. And the police? Yes, I understand.' She turned to the others. 'The ambulance is on its way from Ipswich. The police from Leiston. So, we need to decide what to tell them.'

'Let's get in our strike first,' said Anna. Despite her pain she was thinking very clearly. 'I'll call Nikki and get it taken out of the hands of the locals.'

She did. Nikki was very quiet during the call and ended with a businesslike, 'I'll get things in motion here. Anna Carr, you're a total . . .' But Anna had rung off.

While they waited for the ambulance, Anula went to her car, that was parked a few hundred yards down the road, and retrieved her medical bag. She attended to Gordon first, as his was the more serious injury. 'It's a good thing Forth was the one who shot you. I'd say it was ordinary nine millimetre ammunition. It's made a neat hole but with a bit of surgery you should be fine in a few weeks. If the other guy, what's his name?'

'Nesfield,' said Anna.

'Yes, the dead one, had shot you with an expanding bullet you'd need an artificial knee. That is if you hadn't already bled to death.' She then turned to Anna. She'd lost a fair bit of blood from the shoulder wound but as she'd suspected the bone was intact. Taking off her boot and blood-soaked sock the knife wound was quite clean and should quickly heal. 'How are you feeling?' Anula asked.

'Oh great,' Anna replied. 'I'm recovering from being flogged, have had my shoulder ripped apart and my foot impaled. I've never felt better!'

'If you can be that flippant, you're fine.'

The police, a sergeant, and a constable, arrived soon after. Anula took them in hand. She explained they had been there on a legitimate archaeological dig when these people attacked them. One of them had been shot with his own gun when he had tried to kill Dr Carr. One was unconscious in their vehicle, after banging his head in a fall, and two were missing following the collapse of the cliff in the storm. The policemen seemed out of their depth and were very relieved when they got a call to say that a team from the Met and Thames Valley would be taking charge of the case as soon as they arrived the following morning. They at least managed to alert the coastguard and fire brigade, who would assist in the search for the bodies of Forth and Morten. The ambulance crew were known to Anula and were far more efficient. Nesfield's body was left where it was until police forensics arrived. Gordon was put in the ambulance and Cloote accompanied him.

Anula took Anna in her own car. They began to talk about what they'd seen and make sense of it. What Anula didn't tell Anna was that she had seen something else on the cliff top. In addition to the blue flame that had encircled Cloote there had been a similar, but even brighter one, around Anna's body, capped with a thinner flame that extended into the clouds.

Chapter 61

Twenty-four hours earlier.
Before they executed their plans at Dunwich, Anna, Cloote, Rees, and Anula had interpreted the second part of Johannes's message in the sequence:

> *Quod gentes coronam de quo sanctus permanet in sinistra est. Et sub ecclesia S. Botulphi de contingentibus. Viginti cubitis inde altare. Supra prefatum lapidem illius.*
>
> *The crown of the saint remains where the heathens left it. Beneath the church of Saint Botolph's Abbey. Twenty yards from the altar. Beneath the stone.*

'He's telling us that St Edmund's crown is secreted in a different place from the rest of the treasure,' said Anna.

'Why wouldn't they have put them together in the same place?' Anula asked.

'For the same reason they decided to bury Ivar's treasure,' said Cloote. 'The treasure was cursed but not the crown, and it was an important Christian symbol.'

'So why bury it at all?' Rees added.

'That is not immediately clear,' said Cloote. 'What I think *is* clear is where it is!' he added.

'Who was St Botolph then?' Anula asked. 'Isn't there a St Botolph's church at Aldgate in London?'

'That's right,' said Cloote. 'St Botolph, or to give him his full title, St Botolph of Thorney, was an English abbot who died around the year 680. We don't know much about him, other than what's in in the *Anglo-Saxon Chronicle*: "Botulf ongan thoet mynster timbrian oet Yceanho", "Botolph founded an abbey at Icanhoe", which means Ox-island. Now some claim this abbey was in Lincolnshire, where Boston is a contraction of "Botolph's town". But most of the evidence points to another spot. We also have the fact that in 970 King Edgar had Botolph's remains moved from the abbey to Burgh, near Woodbridge. He did this because, as Johannes suggests, in 870 the same Viking army who killed King Edmund, raised Botolph's Abbey to the ground, killed its monks and looted the monastery. So Icanhoe should be somewhere near Woodbridge. Then, in 1977, excavations discovered a Saxon cross incorporated into the fabric of a church that stands on this alternative site.'

'But Oliver,' said an exasperated Gordon, 'where the heck is it?'

'Iken,' replied Cloote. All of them knew where he meant. Iken is a tiny village situated on a headland, at a bend in the Alde River, between Snape and Orford.

'So, it's even nearer than Dunwich!' Rees exclaimed. It was after this exchange that Cloote outlined his plans. What they agreed was that they would first attempt to recover the crown from Iken, which they would do in the utmost secrecy, in order not to alert Forth and his friends. For the Dunwich expedition Anna would be 'indiscreet' in a message to Rasmus.

'If I say straight out, "We're off to Dunwich to recover Ivar the Boneless's treasure," Forth is bound to smell a rat. It'll need to be more subtle. A hint about where we're going and when.' They settled for her telling Rasmus they would be going to: 'Where, over the grave of a city, the ghost of it stands,' lines from the Victorian poet Algernon Swinburne's *By the North Sea*, that was inspired by the bleakness of Dunwich. It also said that they would be there on: *'ⲚⲒ ⲠⲒⲤⲀⲂⲂⲀⲦⲞⲚ ⲞⲨⲞⲈⲒⲚ.'*

'It means "the Saturday of Light" in the Coptic language,' said Anna, 'and it's the name Coptic Christians give to the Saturday between Good Friday and Easter Sunday.'

'That should strike the right balance between obvious and obscure,' Cloote suggested. They explained their plans to Scott, who didn't like it but finally agreed after Asayo supported their idea.

For the Iken expedition, he and Roly would remain at Summerland, staying in touch via secure radio link. At Dunwich all three would take up position near the site, intervening if things got critical. 'Are you sure you're okay handling the boat?' Scott asked Gordon.

'Yeh, no problem,' he replied.

'There's one other thing we'd like you to do,' Anna said to Scott. 'We need you to reconnoitre Iken church for us,' and she gave him precise instructions what to look for and photograph.

'Okay, I can do that tomorrow but, as for the rest, it's the darndest, foolhardiest thing I've ever heard,' Scott concluded. 'But I guess you know best,' he said to Cloote.

While trying to look as confident as he could, Oliver realised there were a host of things that could go horribly wrong.

*

Two days later Anna, Anula, Cloote and Rees prepared for their short journey to Iken. All four were dressed in dark clothing, with their faces covered in camouflage makeup. 'If we get caught dressed like this, we certainly won't get away with claiming we're innocent archaeologists,' was Anula's conclusion.

It was nearly midnight when Scott and Roly arrived. 'We've done a thorough sweep,' Scott told them. 'There's no sign of surveillance. We found a TV camera mounted near the yacht club, but its night vision is very limited. They also have an observation point as you leave the town, but you won't be in sight of the camera and there's nothing on the river.'

'All the gear's in the boat,' Roly told them. 'Battery powered lights. A small hoist. The GPR unit. Crowbars and picks. If anything goes wrong or you need something else, just use the radio.'

'Okay,' said Anna. 'Thanks. We're off.'

They left by the back gate, turned right down the path, then took a track to the left that led to the sewage works by the river. Skirting the works, they climbed the bank. About a hundred metres to their right was a small landing stage, erected to bring in materials for the reconstruction of the flood defences. Moored to it was the amphibious RIB they'd used to take them up the coast. When they were on board Gordon started the motor, which would be safe to use for the first part of the trip where they were well away from habitation.

They moved upstream, passing West Row Point and Cob Island. Here, Gordon cut the motor for a while as there were houses close to the bank. Starting it up again, they passed Collier's Hole, Barber's Point, and entered the stretch called Long Reach. They could now see the lights of the village of Snape in front of them while, to the left, was the shadowy outline of their destination, St Botolph's church. Rees cut the motor completely and took out the oars, steering them into Church Reach as the river bent sharply southward. They had timed their trip to be at the highest point of the tide, given the time constraints. But, despite the shallow draft of the RIB they grounded a few metres short of the shore.

'Right,' said Anna, taking charge, 'everyone out and haul the boat.' That was relatively straightforward, even though Cloote wasn't happy having to get up to his knees in estuarine mud. 'First make up all over my face and now this!' He got no sympathy from the others.

There was a short stretch of turf, beyond which was the high boundary wall of the churchyard. In this a wooden gate was secured with a padlock and chain. Gordon opened the padlock with a pick and between them they carried the equipment through a short band of trees. They were on the north side of the church, so the tower was closest to them. This contained a door they had decided to use, rather than entering by the main west door, where they might be visible from one of the small number of houses nearby. The lock was easily opened with a skeleton key, and they entered the church, which today is in three parts. The oldest is the nave, which dates from before 1200. The tower was constructed in the mid-fifteenth century. The chancel, like most others in England, fell into disuse after the Reformation so that, by the eighteenth century, it was a ruin. It was then demolished before being rebuilt in 1853.

Gordon and Anna returned to the boat to fetch the battery pack for the lights, their heaviest piece of equipment, which needed two people to carry. The lights had barn doors to direct the illumination down and away from the windows. They took time to examine the Saxon cross, which was in the nave, resting on a wooden cradle. As they had seen from Scott's photographs, it was carved with the heads of dogs and wolves, the symbols of St Botolph.

Twenty yards took them to the centre of the nave, which was

covered in floor tiles, dating from the nineteenth-century restoration. These had to be prised up as quietly and carefully as possible, which took the best part of an hour. Beneath them were much more ancient flagstones, each of them perhaps two metres square. 'They certainly look thirteenth century,' Cloote said after a close inspection.

They brushed and cleaned the stones. As well as tungsten lights, Anna also had a portable ultraviolet light to show up any hard-to-see markings. Sure enough, on one stone there were faint carvings. 'They match the wolves' heads on the cross,' she declared. They began the delicate task of removing the mortar, and centuries of dirt, from round the stone until they could just get two crowbars under one edge. The stone was far too heavy for even four people to lift, which was why they'd brought the folding crane, equipped with a hand pump, for lifting. By manoeuvring the stone with the crowbars, they were able to get fabric slings under it. They attached these to the crane and, using the pump, the stone came away from the floor and swung to one side. A draught of cold air came from the darkness below. They adjusted the lights to reveal a flight of roughly carved stone steps. 'This must have been the original crypt,' Cloote explained. 'From when the church was first constructed.'

'I think there's a very good chance that was during the lifetime of Johannes of Medhamstead,' added Anna. 'It would have provided a perfect hiding place.'

They descended into the crypt, which was quite small, perhaps five metres in length, and narrower than the nave. The floor was simple beaten earth, but perfectly dry, even though they must now have been at the level of the river. It was stone lined and in the walls were sixteen alcoves, each containing some human remains. There was no obvious treasure. 'Look here,' said Cloote, pointing low down at the walls. 'Do you see? There's a narrow band of charcoal. It must be the burned layer from the Norse destruction of Botolph's Abbey.'

Each of them had a powerful torch in addition to Anna's ultraviolet light and they began a careful survey for potential hiding places. It was Anula who struck lucky. 'Here,' she said, 'it looks like more of Johannes's animals.' Sure enough, on a stone on the side of the steps, at about eye level, was a carving of a boar.

'Hildisvíni!' Cloote exclaimed. 'You can see it's Freyja riding him. Westley's original find was true after all! *"Airknastains Brisingamen bairgan Hildisvíni aikklesjo austra Aggils." "The jewel Brisingamen is kept by Hildisvíni at the church of the East Angles."'*

There seemed no way for the stone to move, but then Anna had an idea. She pressed one thumb onto the wolf and the other onto the boar. Immediately they moved slightly into the stone block, and she could grasp it with her hands. Incredibly, even after eight hundred years, the stone slid away from the steps. It was extremely heavy, and she nearly dropped it, but she handed it to Rees and peered into the hole.

At first, she thought there was nothing there. Then she made out a dull looking box. She reached into the hole and carefully got it out. It was clearly made of lead. Cloote slowly raised the lid. Inside was a thick, vellum manuscript. He unrolled it on the block Rees had placed on the floor. 'It's definitely by Johannes,' he said. 'The letters are unmistakable and there are new animal drawings. But the text is in plain Latin.'

Anna was staring back into the hole. 'I … think … you … need … to … see … this!'

'Anna, don't touch it!' Cloote said quickly. They looked into the space. In the light of Anna's torch, they could see the gleam of gold and jewels. 'Wait. I need to read more of the text first,' he said forcefully. They waited as he quickly read the document. When he'd finished there was a look of amazement on his face. 'Okay. I've read the key part. What we must do is this, even though I can't quite believe it myself.'

'What do you mean?' asked Anna.

'Well, the text begins in Latin and is addressed to the: "Duxi adfectatoris de corona s. Eum martyris". That is, "The esteemed seekers of the crown of St Edmund the Martyr". It then says that, to escape damnation, the seekers must be true of heart and purpose and have: "Nulla turpis vel malum cogitationes in corda eorum". "No foul or evil thought in their hearts". That seems reasonable. Johannes goes on to explain why he secreted the crown here: *"Ego visionem. Quibus revelatum est mihi corona martyris debet esse occulta, nostra tueri populus. In futuro tempore erit, inventum ab iis, qui intelligunt, et usus eius potentia.*" "I had a vision. It was revealed to me that the crown of the martyr must be hidden to protect our people. In a future time, it will be discovered by those who will understand and use its power."'

'Wow!' Anula exclaimed. 'Does that mean us? It sounds a bit of a burden.'

'Wait there's more,' said Cloote. 'He tells us that each of the finders must swear an oath to use the crown only for good but before that is the most remarkable bit. He suddenly goes into Greek and begins a story that was becoming well-known in the thirteenth century. Here's the piece.' He indicated the Greek text.

'And what the heck does that mean?' said Gordon.

'It means: "Lying far beyond Egypt the country of the Indians, as it is called, is vast and populous. It is washed by seas and navigable gulphs, but on the mainland it marcheth with the borders of Persia. A land formerly darkened with the gloom of idolatry, barbarous to the last degree, and wholly given up to unlawful practices."

'It's the opening of a story we know from a Sanskrit tale of third-century origin. It passed through different versions before being translated into Latin in 1048 when it became well-known in Western Europe as the story of Barlaam and Josaphat.' It was obvious to the others that Cloote was getting excited, so they let him continue the story. 'Josaphat was an Indian prince who was kept confined to the palace by his father who was afraid his son would be exposed to the temptations of the world. When Josaphat did leave, he met a blind man and a beggar and, eventually, a hermit named Barlaam who converted him to Christianity.'

'That sounds a familiar story,' interrupted Anula. 'It's just like the path of the Buddha towards Nirvana.'

'And so it should,' said Cloote. 'Because that's exactly what it is. A Christianised version of the life of the Buddha, with Josaphat as the Buddha. Numerous events in Josaphat's story mirror those of the Buddha. Even the protagonist's name, Josaphat, derives from the Sanskrit Budhasaf or Bodhisattva, an enlightened being, who helps others reach Nirvana.'

'And would Johannes have known this?' asked Anula.

'He certainly did, because of the reason he gives for inserting the tale. He goes on in Latin: *"Qui invenit coronam necesse est habere reverentiam antiqui Deos Aquilonis. Illa, qui primo tangit coronam oportet esse discipulum de Josaphat."* "Those who find the crown must have respect for the ancient Gods of the North. She who first touches the crown must be a follower of Josaphat."'

'You're kidding!' Gordon looked incredulous and Anna and Anula were equally stunned.

'You're certain that's the only interpretation?' Anna asked.

'Absolutely no doubt,' said Cloote. He glanced at his watch. 'It will be getting light soon and there's one more thing we must do before Anula removes the crown.'

'And that is?' Anna asked.

'To swear the oath, of course. Listen carefully. Each of us must recite these words in Latin.'

The words they spoke were four lines:

'Luro numquam uti coronam, quia lucrum vel Gloria.
Luro restituere coronam ad populum Angliae.
Luro tueri coronam a latronibus, et pessimorum.
Luro uti virtute coronam ad bonum commune, et populus contra tyrannidem.'

'I swear never to use the crown for gain or glory.
I swear to restore the crown to the people of England.
I swear to protect the crown from thieves and evildoers.
I swear to use the power of the crown for the good of the common people and against tyranny.'

Anna couldn't be sure but, after she finished reciting the oath, the light in the crypt seemed to become brighter, though where its source was, she couldn't tell. Cloote then said, 'Now, Anula, take out the crown.' Anula stepped forward and hesitated. Then she reached inside and grasped the crown. It was very cold, and she nearly let go. But as she drew it towards her it seemed to warm up incredibly quickly. 'Here. Put it in this,' said Cloote and he produced a bag of what looked like velvet from an inside pocket. Anula placed the crown carefully inside.

They replaced the stone and, when they were back in the

nave, the flagstone and then the floor tiles. Gordon had a bag of ready mixed grouting with which he was able to secure the tiles, and they scattered dust and dirt on top. 'It won't stand up to close inspection' he said, 'but hopefully, as tomorrow is Good Friday, no one will be looking too much at the tiles or cleaning up until after Easter weekend.'

Oliver and Anula gathered the equipment, while Gordon and Anna lugged the battery packs back to the boat. Finally, they relocked the tower door and replaced the padlock on the gate.

It was past 5 a.m. and the first rays of sun were appearing behind the church. The tide had gone down, so Anna steered while Gordon pushed the boat off the mud. Once they were out into the river, he started the engine. They called Scott on the radio. 'I thought you'd all drowned,' he said with a chuckle. 'Everything go okay?' Anna replied that things couldn't have gone better. He said to leave all the equipment in the boat and that he and Roly would deal with it.

As the four of them trudged along the track towards the house the sun had risen and was casting a bright orange glow on the marshes. It was going to be a glorious day, even though they knew they now had to prepare for an even more challenging task. Inside the house they went to the library. Cloote took the crown out of the bag and placed it on a table. It was truly magnificent. From a broad gold band four trefoils extended. The edges of the band and trefoils were studded with small pearls. The band itself was set with many precious and semi-precious stones, quite roughly cut. At the front was the largest stone, a perfect blue sapphire. 'It's not dissimilar to the Essen Crown,' Cloote said. 'That dates from around 1000, but this isn't as ornate, so an earlier date in the ninth century seems reasonable.'

They were too exhausted to do anything further. Cloote secured the crown in the library safe. He again wondered if his plan to confront Forth was the right one but consoled himself with the thought that everything he'd so far believed about Anna Carr had been vindicated. If so, his final and most audacious theory about her would be their ultimate weapon.

Chapter 62

On the morning of Easter Monday, Anna, Anula, and Cloote assembled in Gordon's room at the hospital. Anula had operated on Gordon's knee, which she had saved from complete replacement, though it would be some weeks before he was walking without support. Anna's foot wound was superficial, but her shoulder was strapped up and would require physiotherapy to restore full movement.

Anula had insisted that any police interviews with Anna and Gordon would have to wait at least another day. 'It seems to have worked with the detectives we saw before,' said Anula, referring to Nikki and Cook, 'and with the chief superintendent the Met have sent. They said something about it being taken out of their hands, but I don't know what that means. We've had a lucky escape, Oliver, so I think you need to explain exactly what went on back there.'

'Oh no, Anula,' Cloote replied, 'there was no luck involved. It was all carefully planned even though everything didn't *quite* go as smoothly as it might have.'

'You can say that again!' Gordon intervened. 'If that bastard had fired higher, I'd be dead!'

'But he couldn't, Gordon, the spell prevented him.'

'Spell? Look, you need to tell us more,' replied Rees. 'Before this happened, I agreed we'd follow your plan, but you didn't go into the details, except about Anna.'

'What about me?'

'Just that I knew from the minute we met that you had a gift,' said Cloote. 'You remember I said there were *several* reasons I chose you?'

'I thought you needed me to recite the lines you gave me because it had to be from a woman. I don't dismiss the idea of magic having played a part but what *exactly* was my role?'

'You, Anna, are undoubtedly a völva. It's well-known among shamans that the gift for it runs through families. My guess is that it has run through *your* family for many generations, though often with the women involved never knowing it. Vikings also believed that everyone had a fylgjur, a follower. They were protective spirits who were always female, even for men, and they too were inherited within families.'

'A bit like Philip Pullman's dæmons in *His Dark Materials*?' Anula asked.

'Yes, very similar. You'll also know that one aspect of seiðr about female sorceresses, völva, is their act of riding. This had two meanings. The first is the physical act, similar to how witches were supposed to ride broomsticks. In the Old Norse poem *Hyndluljóð* the goddess Freyja meets the völva Hyndla and they ride together to Valhalla, Freyja on Hildisvíni and Hyndla on a wolf. The other meaning refers to a supernatural attack on an enemy so that the sorceress "rides" the victim, being able to inflict anything from bad dreams to death itself. That was your role in the destruction of Elias Forth. I, of course, had the seiðrstafr, or perhaps I should say, John Dee's seiðrstafr, but my role was secondary.'

'You're saying Anna is a witch?' Anula asked.

'Not exactly a witch, but certainly someone with the *potential* to exercise magical power. You're sceptical?'

'Not entirely. You know a little of maya angam and whether that involves supernatural powers I wouldn't like to speculate.'

Anna had remained quiet throughout Cloote's explanation. One part of her, the objective academic, wanted to dismiss his idea out of hand. But another part, of which she had been aware since she was a child and was reinforced in her dreams, led her to agree with him. Finally, she simply said, 'Go on. Tell us more.'

'Perhaps I should start with an explanation of the two spells I asked you to recite? The first one was: "*Let þar munu þoka ok let þar munu kvikindi ok let allr þessi undur hinder þinn umsækjendur.*" This means: "Let there be fog and let there be creatures and let all these wonders hinder your seekers."

'I adapted it from *Njals Saga*, a thirteenth-century Icelandic tale that describes a blood feud. It explains how the requirements of honour lead to minor slights that then spiral into prolonged bloodshed. I thought it appropriate that something that began with an innocent scrap of paper had led to so many deaths. The second spell comes from the *Völuspá*, the prophecy of the Völva, which is the first and best-known poem of the *Poetic Edda*. It's about the creation of the world and its coming destruction, related to the audience by a völva addressing Odin. There's a repeated refrain which goes: *"Geyr nú Garmr mjök fyr Gnipahelli, festr mun slitna, en freki renna. Fjölð veit ek fræða fram sé ek lengra um ragna rök römm sigtíva."* "Now Garm howls loud before Gnipahellir, the fetters will burst, and the wolf run free. Much do I know, and more can see of the fate of the gods, the mighty in fight."

'Of course, Garm is the dog who guards the gates of Hel's kingdom. This links to the other key player, the guardian, who turned out to be the wolf Fenrir. Indeed, some scholars have suggested that Garm and Fenrir were originally identical. However, Fenrir is specifically identified as a sibling of Hel and the prophesy is that, at Ragnarök, Fenrir will run wild through the world devouring everything in his path.'

Anna finally interjected. 'Wolves were the animals most closely connected with seiðr, weren't they? In summoning gandir, sprits, it was most often a wolf that was summoned. Sometimes the vǫlur even rode the animals. And wasn't weather magic another form of attack in seiðr?'

'Quite so, Anna,' Cloote replied.

'But was it real? Did it actually happen or was it an illusion?' Gordon implored.

'What is real depends on how you define reality in the first place,' Cloote replied enigmatically. 'What is vital in using any form of spell is that those you use it on must believe in it.'

'And Elias Forth did?' Anula asked.

'Undoubtedly. It was something he'd mentioned more than once in interviews, which is why I used the final element of our attack.'

'Which was?' asked Anula.

'The curse in the casket?' Anna suggested.

'Yes indeed.'

'What did it say then?' asked Anula.

'I'm afraid I can't reveal that,' said Cloote. 'The spell is the most powerful I know. Repeating it can have dire consequences. The key element is that the adversary accepts it willingly which, of course, Forth did by asking for the contents of the casket. The exact nature of the attack is determined by your foe's greatest fear. The incarnation of Fenrir that appeared wasn't entirely our doing, it was also conjured from Forth's own subconscious.'

'But you said it didn't all go to plan, which is why Anna and I got shot?' asked Gordon.

'There's always uncertainty with ancient magic,' Cloote replied. 'I also hadn't anticipated they would have such a skilled exponent of the art. I used a spell that should have rendered their guns useless, but Morten intercepted and counteracted it. Fortunately, you, Anula, disabled Morten long enough for me to initiate the spell and summon the guardian. By the time he recovered it was too late for him to stop me. Though I expect magic may have had some role in his survival.'

'What!' exclaimed the others in unison.

'Oh, didn't I tell you? You were all so busy. I spoke with your friend Nikki, Anna. Morten seems to have disappeared. They found Forth's body all right, though are somewhat puzzled by his injuries.'

'In what way?' asked Gordon.

'He appears to have had his genitals ripped off, which seems hard to have been the result of the cliff fall. In addition, the pathologist found wounds on his neck that looked like huge teeth marks. I didn't enlighten them, by the way. It's best to let sleeping wolves lie. Sorry, Gordon, you asked about the unfortunate gun shots.'

'The Vikings believed spells could be laid directly on weapons,' said Anna, 'either to make them more potent or to render them useless. However, opposing sorcerers could lay other spells to counteract them. Isn't that right?' she asked.

'Quite so,' said Cloote, 'as I said, they can be counteracted.'

'It all sounds very reminiscent of *Gongu-Hrolfs Saga*,' said Anna, 'in which there's a battle between the dwarf wizard Mondull and the evil sorcerer Grimr Aegir. It also describes the use of runes as a spell, which is turned back on the sorcerer, driving him insane and making him jump off a cliff to his death in the sea.'

'Ah Anna, there you go again. You see things everyone else misses,' Cloote added.

*

A short time later Nikki gave them an update. Her suspicion about the case being taken out of the hands of the police was correct. 'The security services have taken over I'm afraid. They're treating it as a matter of national security and we're pretty much out of the picture.'

'Great,' said Anna. 'So, we can expect some form of cover up?'

'I couldn't possibly comment,' replied Nikki, 'but I can fill you in some more before they arrive and fuck up, I mean, clarify the situation. As you know we found the body of Elias Forth and the man you shot, Anna. His name was Savile Nesfield, a South African former game hunter and personal assistant to Forth. The other man is called Morten. We don't yet know his surname nor very much about him. He may be a Russian national, but the strange thing is we haven't found his body. The debris from the cliff fall has been searched and all we've come up with is his mobile phone. Of him there's no trace at all.'

'Why do you think he could be Russian?' asked Anula.

'The knife. There's no doubt it was the weapon that killed both Arbuthnot and Westley by the way. It's called a Rys and was used by a spetsnaz unit of the Russian National Guard called the SOBR, special rapid response unit. They carried out special operations under the MVD, the Russian Interior Ministry, as well as taking part in more conventional warfare in Chechnya.'

'And what about the treasure?' Gordon asked.

'We've found two opals and the remains of the casket but nothing else. Of course, later that night, the storm returned and battered the shoreline so it's possible much of it, and even Morten's body, could have been washed out to sea. At least you managed to hold onto the crown.'

They agreed this was a bit of luck. Scott had retrieved the crown from Cloote's safe and put it in Anula's car, so their story was that it had been found with the rest of Ivar's treasure, but they hadn't handed it over to Forth.

*

Two anonymously dressed men arrived at the hospital. They introduced themselves as Jonathan Humphreys, from MI5, and Robert Nicholson, from MI6. They checked the statements each of them had already made to the police. They were most intrigued by Anna. 'You've admitted killing a man and yet seem unconcerned, Ms Carr. Don't you have some feelings on the matter?' asked Nicholson.

'It's *Doctor* Carr. Well, I have regrets. I regret that he died so quickly. He deserved to suffer far more.' Nicholson quietly made a note.

Finally, the agents got all four together. 'We need you to understand the situation very clearly,' began Humphreys. 'Elias Forth was an important cog in this country's financial economy. It is essential for national security that those markets remain stable. For this reason, his role in this affair will remain undisclosed.' Anula, Cloote and Rees looked at each other. Anna stared directly at Humphreys. 'The story we will release to the press, and the one you will *all* support,' he looked at Anna, 'is that Forth was funding the search for' he looked at his notes, 'King Edmund's crown. After it was discovered, three of his associates, Savile Nesfield, Vladimir Krylov, and the man called Morten, attempted to steal the crown. Forth and yourselves managed to overcome them but, unfortunately, Forth fell to his death when the cliff collapsed. Nesfield and Morten are also deceased and Krylov has been deported. Is that entirely clear?'

'I should add,' said Nicholson, 'that should any of you stray from this version of events it will be treated as a breach of the Official Secrets Act and you will be dealt with accordingly.' No one said anything and the agents appeared satisfied.

'Fuck them,' Anna was the first to speak after they'd gone. 'Or rather, I'll fuck them. I don't want any of you getting mixed up in this but I'm not going to let that bastard Forth rest in peace.'

'Anna, please don't do anything rash,' Cloote urged.

'Don't worry, I think I'm intelligent enough to know how to do it,' said Anna.

'Be careful, but I'm with you,' said Anula.

'Me too,' Gordon agreed.

Chapter 63

With the identity of Magnus's killer established, his body was released. Anna confirmed he wanted to be cremated, with his ashes scattered on Merton Field. The ceremony was packed with friends and colleagues. These included Marc, whose house he'd stayed at over Christmas, and who read a tribute which included reference to Magnus's wife. Anna read a passage from *The Battle of Maldon*, and Nora and Nils an old Monty Python sketch originally performed by Michael Palin and Terry Jones. It made people laugh, as much because of the incongruity as the original humour. As the curtains closed on the coffin a lone piper played 'The Flowers of the Forest'.

The guests assembled back at the college for the wake. Rasmus Kask was there, as were Anula, Cloote, and, in a wheelchair, Gordon Rees. It was the first chance they'd had to thank Rasmus for his help. 'Honestly, we couldn't have done it without you,' Anna said. Rasmus blushed. 'Any sign of our friend Penhaligon?'

'No, he's not been about since this all happened,' Rasmus replied. 'Apparently he's on indefinite sick leave.'

'I expect those security, ba— people have been to see him,' said Anna. 'He's bloody lucky they've decided not to prosecute him as an accessory to murder.'

'I'm sorry to interrupt, Dr Carr,' it was Magnus's solicitor, Allan McLeod, 'but might I have a word with you and Ms Greenwood? Perhaps we could use the room there?'

Once out of earshot McLeod said, 'I'm not sure how much you knew about Magnus's will but, after some charitable legacies, he bequeathed his estate equally to the two of you. He left you this note.' He handed an envelope to Anna. She and Nora read:

> My dear Anna and Nora. I have no idea what circumstances will have led to your reading this, but I wanted to

> explain my instructions. I know neither of you give much credence to possessions but that's a good thing. I dwell too much on the past and should really have done more with my money, but I think the two of you will make better use of it than I could. You mean more to me than I ever said, perhaps I was a fool for not saying more, but at least I was a fool who chose his beneficiaries well! With my love and respect. Magnus.

Anna was not surprised. Though they'd never discussed anything like this, she understood that he felt as if she and Nora were his surrogate daughters. However, what McLeod said next was a surprise. 'I don't know how much you knew about Magnus's affairs, but his estate is not, errm, inconsiderable.'

'I thought it was just the house and his university pension,' said Anna.

'Not quite. He also had inherited land holdings in Scotland, plus a major investment fund. The income from that is paid to medical charities researching health disorders in pregnancy. If you include the house and pension, it comes to around ten million.'

'Nah way! For reals?' Nora was stunned.

'Absolutely for real, Ms Greenwood. You are now officially a millionaire.'

Though true, this status, as Magnus had predicted, did not last very long. Anna and Nora quickly agreed what would happen with Magnus's money. The investments would be gifted outright to the medical research he had so passionately supported. One aspect would be the creation of two PhD fellowships in the name of Imogen Strachan, Magnus's wife. The land in Scotland was given to the Scottish Wildlife Trust and Magnus's house, together with enough money to run it, was to be turned into a hostel for the homeless. Nora kept enough to buy her small flat and a new studio in which to paint. Anna also kept some to enable her to buy somewhere to live, and then gave the remaining money to charities combating domestic violence.

Anna was pleased she didn't find the funeral and wake at all depressing. Instead, they were uplifting and celebratory. The day after, she and Nora went to Merton Field to scatter the ashes. 'Goodbye, Magnus. I hope I live up to your expectations,' Anna said. Nora put her arm round her and together they shed some tears for their lost friend.

*

The next day was a more joyful affair. It was the opening of Nora's graduation show. Her work had impressed the director of the Contemporary Art Space and he'd asked for it to take place at their gallery. This attracted the attention of several London dealers and gallery owners, and, throughout the afternoon, Nora was in deep conversation.

Anula had stayed on, though Oliver and Rees had returned to Suffolk. While they were talking, a girl Anna recognised came up to them. 'Margot, hey. How are you doing?'

'I'm doing great, Anna. I'd like you to meet my girlfriend, Thema.' She was joined by a tall, exceptionally beautiful girl.

'Very pleased to meet you,' said Thema. 'Is this your girlfriend?' she asked indicating Anula.

'She . . .' said Anna.

'I'm . . .' said Anula.

Thema giggled. 'Oh! I see.' Margot cuddled up to her.

'I've told Thema you were instrumental in my education,' added Margot.

After they'd moved on Anula said, 'By "education" did she mean what I'm thinking?'

'I really don't know what you mean.' Anna smiled.

*

When they returned to Aldeburgh, Anula was pleased with Gordon's progress. They convened at Summerland for a meal which he insisted on cooking. After they'd eaten Cloote said, 'I told you when you first came here, Anna, that the dining room was a place for telling stories. So, if you're all sitting comfortably . . .'

'I'm not,' said Gordon, 'and I won't be for some time!'

'Well, if we're *nearly* all sitting comfortably, I wanted to read you Johannes's story. It was in the document we found with the crown. "I, Johannes of Medhamstead, also called Johannes of

Sorø, set this down in the twenty-seventh year of the reign of our sovereign lord, Henry, son of John."

'He means 1243,' Cloote added. '"To you, the finder of this document, greetings. As you have both the knowledge and the pureness of spirit to have succeeded in the task, I owe to you my story and that of the concealment of two great treasures: the crown of the blessed St Edmund and that of the Dane, called by some Ivar the Boneless.

'"I have no illusion that the discovery of these treasures, and the overcoming of their protectors, may take many centuries. It may be that the gods and our Christian Lord may never allow them to be found, but I trust in the perseverance of the human intellect and believe these words will, one day, be read by those worthy to hear them.

'"I was born in the first year of the reign of King Valdemar Sejr." That's Valdemar II, or Valdemar the Victorious, who came to the throne in Denmark in—'

'1202.'

'Thank you, Anna. "I entered the Abbey of Sorø as a postulant in my twelfth year. As I showed a talent for drawing, I worked in the scriptorium becoming amarius. I gained a fascination for numbers and for the old religion and yearned to travel to other libraries to learn more. Abbott Erik indulged me as his protégé, and I travelled to many lands. I studied the texts of the Romans and those from beyond Constantinople on how to write secret codes that could not be broken. After many years study I devised a code that could only be read if one was in possession of the text upon which the code was based."'

'That's going to upset a few histories of codes and ciphers,' commented Gordon.

'The next part is even more revealing,' said Cloote. '"It was in the Kingdom of the Swedes that I met her. She was called Geirvifa and from her I learned the truth of seiðr." Geirvifa means "Spear-Wife" does it not?'

Anna agreed that it did.

'"Some would call her a sorceress and that her power was granted by Satan, but this is a lie. From her I learned of the old times when seiðr practitioners were of both sexes, though females are more widely attested, with such sorceresses being known as vǫlur, seiðkona, and vísendakona.

'"She it was who taught me how to read the stone writing and I spent many hours recording their meanings. One day I read the stones that told of the treasure of Ivar. For the time I kept this knowledge to myself.

'"In the thirtieth year of King Valdemar Sejr's reign, Abbot Erik told me of a request from England for a learned monk, skilled in illustration, to become the amarius at the Abbey of Medhamstead. The abbey had been the greatest monastery of the Mercian kingdom and its library was the finest in England.

'"Many of the texts had never been catalogued and so I set out to do so. It was here that I found the clues that, together with certain skills taught to me by Geirvifa, led me to the resting place of the martyr's crown."'

'This explains why those original documents don't exist,' said Anna. 'Most of the contents of the library of Peterborough Abbey were destroyed in the 1530s by an exceptionally zealous local commissioner during its dissolution.'

'Yes, it was something I'd wondered,' Cloote said. 'If Johannes had found these things out, where did he get his information? And, what happened to those sources? This explains it. But it's very interesting that he also says that certain "other practices" assisted his quest.'

'What would those have been?' asked Anula.

'I think they would involve divination,' Cloote replied. 'There was a great emphasis on divination in seiðr, and vǫlur would enact elaborate rituals to discover significant information.'

'Johannes was an interesting mixture, wasn't he?' said Anna. 'There's Christian, pagan, and even Buddhist in there.'

'Quite so. And it was a mixture that brought success: "I found the crown at Icanhoe together with the Danes map of the location of the treasure of Ivar which I discovered beneath the church of St Wystan." That's the church in Repton that was the burial place of Mercian kings and where the Great Heathen Army wintered in 873 to 4,' explained Cloote.

'"But I was much troubled by this. The Danes had placed a curse upon it and, though a holy man, and a fellow Dane, the guardian came to haunt my dreams as my greatest personal fear.

I will not tell of its exact form but, through my understanding of seiðr, I was able to keep the guardian at bay. But I knew both treasures should be secreted. The crown to wait until the time it could serve the people, and the treasure of Ivar until such time as the curse was lifted. I consulted my abbot and the bishop of Norwich, and we agreed that the crown must be returned to Icanhoe, and the Dane's treasure reburied.

'"The bishop instructed that only I and a small number of trusted friends should know of the site. In England my closest friend was preceptor of the Knights Templar, Robert Saunforde. With his help we secreted the treasure at Dunwich, well inland, as I knew the sea would claim much of the town. I devised a code for those who come after to follow and sent the key to four trusted friends.

'"But even my knowledge of secret codes might not be enough to keep the two treasures from the hands of those who would wish harm to others. I therefore decided to lay a false trail to distract those of lesser skill and understanding. The treasures must only be refound by those who respect the ancient magic and who wish only good for others.

'"I had been told of the story of the former king and the loss of his crown jewels. I knew the truth of these tales. The king's baggage had indeed been lost forever in the sea, but many would not believe the truth of this. I therefore used a simple code to make fools believe where the jewels of King John were to be found. This, together with the first steps toward the real treasures, I laid out in the manuscripts on which I worked for King Henry.

'"Throughout the years I have told a few of the false trail to test their allegiance, no one has yet searched for it."'

'I hope we're not the fools too,' said Gordon.

'In the end no,' Anna replied. 'But Forth and Penhaligon come into his definition. Is that all of it?'

'Not quite,' replied Cloote. 'There's just one more intriguing titbit. "My final message to you, the true finders of the crown, is this. I may be one of the last who believe in the old magic of the North. I have therefore set down my knowledge in a text. When I die this text will also be secreted by my most trusted friend. The instructions I will give to him I will place with the treasure of Ivar. Now, farewell my friends, and may God, and the gods go with you."'

'So, these instructions were in the casket?' Anna asked.

'It would appear so,' Cloote replied. 'And unless they turn up in the cliff fall, they are probably in pieces at the bottom of the sea.' What neither of them realised was that they were now in the possession of a man who had been their mortal enemy.

Chapter 64

The discovery of the crown of King Edmund, and the death of one of the country's most prominent financiers, brought massive media interest. This increased more when it became clear that the people involved had also been the ones who had found a body on a previous dig, after which one of them had been murdered. The story concocted by the security services appeared to be generally accepted, though one or two journalists, including Caoimhe O'Driscoll in a piece in the *Observer*, were saying there were unanswered questions.

Cloote was the centre of attention, with most of the press calling Anna his 'assistant' and Gordon and Anula described as 'friends'. He fronted a press conference at which he said the details of the deaths were too painful to discuss and could still be the subject of criminal investigation. Instead, he concentrated on the discovery of the crown and how 'his team' had uncovered the secret medieval code that led them to the site. The headlines were revealing. *The Times*'s was, 'Greatest Archaeological Find Since Sutton Hoo,' the *Telegraph*'s, 'A Tale Worthy of Agatha Christie'. The *Sun* was the only paper to mention Anna and Anula prominently with 'Boffin Babes Crack Secret Code', which was greeted by Anna with a dismissive snort and prompted Anula to say it was the first time she'd been described as a 'babe'. Finally, the *Daily Express* led with 'Does Crown Really Belong to the Queen?' a suggestion that was quickly quashed in a joint statement from the British Museum and Buckingham Palace who pointed out that it didn't and would be treated like any other discovery under the Treasure Act of 1996.

The media also reported that the remaining members of the board of Elias Capital Investments had appointed Gabriella Clifford as their new CEO. Anna spent some time researching Ms Clifford's background. She wasn't a fan of her politics but what was apparent was that everyone seemed to think she was honest. While she pondered her next move, she received an email from Caoimhe O'Driscoll. 'Dear Dr Carr,' it began. 'Please forgive me contacting you. I was given your email by Pete Railton of the *Oxford Mail* who, I believe, you know. I am working on a piece about the late Elias Forth and have received some interesting information from the new chief executive of ECI, Ms Clifford. I wanted to ask if you would be willing to meet me and Ms Clifford to discuss these matters?'

Anna phoned Pete Railton. 'Dr Carr, what a pleasant surprise. I hope the information you got about Professor Inkpen was of help? And please forgive me for passing your email to Caoimhe.'

'No problem,' Anna replied. 'And yes, your tape was crucial in tracking him down. Without it we wouldn't have made the breakthrough. I said I'd be back in touch to thank you and I promised to let you have my side of the story first, but should I talk to Ms O'Driscoll instead?'

'Yeh, that's why I put her on to you. This story is out of our league and Caoimhe is one of the best investigative reporters I know. If you say something off the record, she won't print it, but if you want to get to the bottom of it, she's your gal.' Anna wasn't quite sure about the final description, but Railton's words were reassuring. She emailed O'Driscoll and received an invitation to meet at 11 a.m. the following Monday.

*

Anna caught the train to London and then the tube from Liverpool Street to Farringdon. She walked the short distance down Cowcross Street to the discreet, boutique hotel The Rookery. She was shown to the library that Caoimhe O'Driscoll had booked for their meeting. 'Hi, Dr Carr. I'm Caoimhe.'

'Please call me Anna,' she replied. Caoimhe O'Driscoll was in her late thirties, quite well built and with long, auburn hair. *She looks efficient*, thought Anna.

While Anna helped herself to herbal tea Gabriella Clifford arrived. Anna was far warier of her. *Definitely not my type*, she thought. She was tall with immaculately cut, straight blonde hair. Her makeup looked newly applied and her black business suit expensive. Gabriella was equally wary of Anna. Despite having chosen a plain black tee-shirt, the boots and, especially, her bright blue hair marked her as someone with whom Gabriella would not usually socialise. Caoimhe realised her first task was to break the ice between her two informants. She did most of the talking for the first half hour, telling them what she already knew about Forth, what she could back up with evidence and what she suspected. Gabriella sat with her legs firmly crossed, clutching a glass of water. She appeared to be grappling to decide what to say.

Caoimhe glanced at Anna, who made up her mind. 'Everything you've suggested about that bastard is right.' Gabriella looked up at her sharply but without hostility. 'He masterminded the murder of Arbuthnot, Westley, and Magnus Strachan and he did this to me.' With that she turned and pulled up her tee-shirt. Even though some weeks had passed the scars were still vivid. 'If I hadn't escaped, he'd have killed me too.'

Gabriella now looked down. She took a deep breath then opened the briefcase she'd brought with her. She took out a large pile of papers and a memory stick. 'Forgive me if I'm a little hesitant. I still can't understand how I could have been so blind for so long. I can substantiate nearly everything you've said. Elias Forth was a fraudster, a thief, and an abuser of women. I can't prove he actually killed anyone, but I'm not surprised that you've told me he did. God, I can't believe I'm saying this. Two days after he died, we had people from the security services all over the offices at ECI. And they were at his London flat and Satterthwaite Hall, that's his country estate, as well. Before they got to the hall there was a fire. I don't know how it happened, but Carrie Prentiss was staying there, you know her? She was, shall I say, a close friend of Elias.'

Anna and Caoimhe said they knew who Carrie Prentiss was. Gabriella continued. 'The agents took everything, but I had a tip off they were coming, I don't know from whom. I copied everything I could, I knew most of his passwords, but not all, and I insisted we had access to certain files if the company wasn't to go under. I've got evidence of money laundering on a vast scale. There are investments in a huge range of shell companies that reveal Forth was behind all kinds of dubious political campaigns and organisations, including some run by Carrie Prentiss and her friends. There's direct involvement in illegal financial trades, such as armaments in Russia, and then I found these.'

She got out a tablet and showed the recordings to Anna and Caoimhe. 'I'll only show you extracts. They're just too horrible.' They watched recordings of Forth, Nesfield, and Vladimir with several girls. She stopped when she got to the 'St Eulalia' tape. 'I want to do everything I can to atone for what he did and what I,' she looked down again, 'what I aided and abetted.' Tears were now running down her cheeks. After a minute or two Gabriella pulled herself together. 'Here,' she said, handing the documents and memory stick to Caoimhe, 'you can use any of it and you can quote me too.'

Caoimhe stood up and walked over to the drinks. 'Anyone want something stronger?' she asked. Gabriella said she would and Caoimhe poured her a large gin and tonic. Anna stuck to her tea.

'What are you going to do?' Anna asked Gabriella.

'Return as much as I can. Try to track down the girls in these tapes and help them, or their families if...' she hesitated again. 'Go to the FCA and the police.'

'You'll need to be very careful about that,' Caoimhe interrupted. 'The security services won't be pleased when their cover story gets blown sky high. We need to coordinate things.' She began to look through the documents. 'Wow! You do know some of the names here? This might even bring down the government.'

Gabriella nodded. 'Yes,' she said, 'I know exactly what I'm doing. I've never been more certain in my life.' When the meeting broke up, they had worked out the details. Though Anna had been told not to deny the cover story, neither Caoimhe nor Gabriella had made any kind of promise to the security services.

On Friday the story broke. Caoimhe's article appeared on the front page of the *Guardian* simultaneously with Gabriella giving a press conference at ECI's headquarters. Anna arranged for Scott to take over Gabriella, and the company's, security and several of their employees had been fired. For the next week the fallout from what the media was calling 'Forthgate' was spectacular. The cover story devised by MI5 and MI6 collapsed entirely. Three government ministers resigned, just about saving the bacon of the prime minister, but not before he had had to make a TV statement regretting his own 'lack of judgement' regarding Elias Forth. Five other MPs announced they would be 'spending more time with their families', and sixteen individuals, including the police and crime commissioner for a Midlands police district, were arrested, charged with corruption. The Alvin Testerwood Foundation disbanded, and three linked UK charities had their accounts suspended and alternative trustees appointed by the Charity Commission. Finally, the huntsman, and several other individuals connected with the Danbury Hunt, were facing prosecution for persistent and flagrant breaches of the Hunting with Dogs Act.

At the weekend Gabriella, accompanied by Roly Sharp, who seemed a little out of place in her company but for whom she had already gained significant respect, visited Satterthwaite Hall. She was not looking forward to her meeting with Carrie Prentiss but knew it had to be done. 'If there's any problem, I'll be right outside,' Roly said.

Carrie was dressed in black, her form of mourning for her ex-boss. 'Sit down, Carrie. First, I should tell you the fire has been investigated so don't give me any bullshit about electrical faults. The paintings were destroyed but there was enough left to make it quite clear what went on down there.' Carrie looked as if she was about to deny all knowledge so Gabriella quickly continued. 'And don't try to deny it. Scott Rimes' operatives have already tracked down two of the girls. Second, this house is the property of ECI, I want you out by the weekend. And, by the way, the company will be changing its name to Equity Capital Investments. Third, all funding for your little projects has ceased, and you no longer have a job. I hope you've invested the fortune he paid you wisely. If you make *any* kind of protest the information I've gathered will be sent straight to the police.'

Gabriella paused as she collected her thoughts before going onto the most personal aspect of the conversation. 'I've also discovered in Mr ... um, his files, a number of recordings of yourself. I think you'll know what I'm talking about.' Carrie's face reddened and tears started running down her cheeks. 'As long as you are sensible you don't need to worry about what I'll do. All of those with just yourself, him and willing partners have been destroyed.'

Carrie looked up, 'Thank . . .'

'No, don't thank me. I'm afraid these weren't the only copies. Forth sent everything to Oleg Zinchenko and there's no telling what *he'll* do with them.'

'Oh God!' Carrie was now in floods of tears and Gabriella couldn't help feeling some compassion for her.

'Look, Carrie. I can understand something about what you did. After all, Forth fooled me, or rather, I allowed my ambition to stifle any doubts I had about him. I intend to make amends for those mistakes, and you can too.'

'You don't understand!' Carrie blurted out. 'You might have been poor when you were a kid, but you didn't have to go through what I did.' Gabriella was slightly taken aback. On any normal judgement she'd been the one with the tough upbringing. Carrie's parents had indulged her every wish and she'd been a child celebrity. But she could see Carrie needed to say more. 'You didn't have your father fucking you from the age of, God, I can't even say it. And then he moved on to my little sister, letting his friends fuck me. There I've said it.' For an instant Gabriella wasn't sure she was being honest but then berated herself. The look on Carrie's face told her what she'd said was the horrible truth. Gabriella got up and was going to put her arm round Carrie, who was moving from confession to anger. 'The bastard stole my childhood, stole everything. After that working for Elias Forth was easy. I wanted others to suffer like I'd suffered. I can't . . .' Her voice tailed off and for a while neither of them spoke.

'Carrie, you should get help. You need to talk through these things properly, with someone who understands what to do.'

'Yeh. I guess,' she let out an ironic laugh. 'I'll have plenty of time to think about it.' Gabriella looked quizzical. Then Carrie said, 'You might not be going to the police, but I will. I'm going to tell them everything.'

*

At his dacha near St Petersburg, Oleg Zinchenko was trying to keep his anger in check. 'Seven hundred and fifty million dollars, and now that bitch is blabbing to the British police. I always knew Forth was a damned fool but telling her the details of my private affairs. Anyway, I'm arranging to have her dealt with.'

'My dear Oleg, are you sure that is the wisest thing to do?' Morten was the only person who would dare question Zinchenko on such an issue.

'Why? What do you mean?'

'It depends if you ever want to conduct international business affairs again, but if anything happened to Carrie Prentiss it would be too obvious who was behind it.'

Zinchenko let out an exasperated sigh. 'I suppose you're right. And the last time I gave a job to those particular friends of ours what happened? They poisoned the wrong person and left a trail so obvious any idiot could track them. I don't care anymore, you do what you have to. Just remember, someone needs to pay for that pizda Forth's cock-up.'

'Thank you, Oleg. I will do so. I will need to return to England, but I know exactly what to do.'

Chapter 65

As the weeks passed the media frenzy died down, especially as the principle 'treasure finders' refused all offers to print their stories. This didn't stop certain members of the press publishing sensationalised rubbish about them. It wasn't long before Cloote and Gordon's relationship became widely known, but Anna got most attention. She cut out the *Daily Mail* article that described her as an 'unrepentant lesbian', which came with a photo taken by a paparazzo of her getting onto her bike and giving the photographer the finger. She was less pleased with the girl who spoke to the *Sun on Sunday* about 'My Night of Kinky Sex with Lesbian Historian', but then she was a student and really needed the money.

Anna began thinking about her future. She had Magnus's legacy to buy a flat somewhere, though wasn't sure where, or even if she wanted to settle down. Cloote had said they could continue to work together, but she hadn't agreed. Most of all she still hadn't reconciled her feelings about Anula. She hadn't felt this way about anyone before, but, equally, she was reticent to take the relationship to the next level. Despite everything that had happened, even when Forth had her captive, she hadn't felt this scared. She decided to focus on other things and wait.

St Edmund's crown was now in the British Museum, who made an announcement that, in the autumn, a major new exhibition would open. 'Edmund's Crown and The Great Heathen Army' would be curated by Oliver Cloote. Initially Cloote had refused unless Anna was a co-curator, but she'd declined the invitation. Instead, she was thinking about writing a book to provide a distraction from her personal turmoil.

Anna returned to Oxford. She'd not renewed the tenancy on her bedsit and stayed with Nora and Nils at their flat. She also paid another visit to Henry's tattoo parlour.

'Hey, Anna! You're quite the celebrity. Oxford's own Indiana Jones.'

'Henry! Don't. I swear I'll strangle the next person who says that.'

'Okay, no problem. I got your sketches and I've come up with this.' Henry showed her the design he'd done which Anna approved.

'Do you want to do it in one long session or take a break and come back tomorrow?' Anna said she'd like it done in one session and was there for the rest of the morning and through the afternoon as Henry worked on the new tattoo. When he was finished Anna stood up to look at herself in the full-length mirror in the private booth they'd worked in.

'What do you think?' he asked.

'It's terrific, Henry. Just how I imagined it.'

The tattoo started on her right thigh and extended across her buttock to her waist. It was of a leaping, snarling wolf, outlined in blue flames.

*

It was now after six but, as Midsummer was less than a month away, still bright and sunny as she got back to Merton College. It was the first time she'd been back to Magnus's rooms since his death but, now the investigations were over, she needed to clear them out. Nora had offered to help, but Anna said it was something she'd rather do herself. She spent the next couple of hours packing books into boxes that the porters had delivered for the purpose. She had many thoughts about her old friend, remembering volumes she'd borrowed from him at different times. She came across a bound copy of his doctoral thesis, on migration and colonisation in the Anglo-Saxon period, but then opened a drawer that made her heart skip a beat. In Magnus's house they had found nothing that related to his marriage, but here was a box of photographs and letters. They were love letters to Magnus written by his wife, Imogen, when they were undergraduates. She hesitated. Should she read them? Should she just burn them? She spent the next hour reading them and shedding some tears. They were beautiful and tender. Imogen had been an English literature student and a poet of no little talent. Anna determined that not only would she keep the letters, she would get the poems published. She stashed the letters in her jacket as she left the room for the last time.

It was now after eight but, as it was a glorious evening, she decided to take a stroll across Merton Field and Christ Church Meadow. She walked along the river, then back toward the town turning left along the rear wall of the college on Deadman's Walk. She was walking directly into the setting sun which threw an orange glow over the meadows and cast a long shadow behind her. Just before she reached the far end of the walk a figure emerged from around the corner right in front of her. Even though she had trouble seeing clearly with the sun in her eyes there was no mistaking who it was. She had two choices, turn and run or see if she could again be too quick for his knife. But before she made a move Morten held up his hand. 'No, Dr Carr. Please don't make any sudden movement. I intend *you* no harm.' Despite this assurance Anna was poised for action. 'I needed to tell you this in person. I admire you, Dr Carr. I have had many adversaries, but you have proved my most dangerous. I can also assure you that, as long as you do not pursue me, I will not harm you or your friends. If, however, our paths cross again as enemies I will not fail a second time. My only regret is that we could not be allies. I have certain ... projects on which we might have collaborated.'

'Not a fucking chance,' Anna replied.

'A great pity, Dr Carr. Together, we would be ... invincible.' With that he spun round and disappeared round the corner. Anna was there quickly but when she looked up Merton Grove there was no sign of Morten. Either he was an incredibly quick runner, or he'd scaled the wall in record time. Could she believe what he'd said? She certainly couldn't ignore the fact that she'd just met a man wanted for at least two murders.

She then noticed something on the ground. It was a scrap of parchment. On it was written: '*Valkyrie vocatio Walvater*', 'Valkyrie calls Walvater'. It could only have been written by Morten. The Germanenorden Walvater of the Holy Grail was a pre-Nazi secret society of the early twentieth century and Walvater was another name for Wotan.

She phoned Nikki McDonald. 'Thanks, we'll put out an alert immediately. Could you meet me at the Bookies in, say, an hour?' Anna said she could and walked over to The Old Bookbinders Alehouse, a quirky gastropub close to the Oxford Canal in Jericho, that features in the *Inspector Morse* stories.

'Thanks,' said Nikki as she sat down and took a gulp from the Guinness Anna had bought. Anna handed Nikki the parchment. 'What does it mean?' she asked.

'Some kind of parting message perhaps?' said Anna. She had an alternative explanation but decided to keep it to herself.

'Your encounter with our friend Morten wasn't perhaps as unexpected as you thought. Look at these. By the way I hope you haven't eaten recently.' Anna took an A4 sized envelope from her friend. Inside were some colour photographs. They were of a dead body, but not just dead. The body had been dissected in an especially gruesome fashion. The chest was split through the sternum, the ribs hinged back, and the lungs exposed and pulled through the opening to be displayed at the sides. The face was instantly recognisable as that of Gervase Penhaligon.

'You know what this form of killing is called don't you?'

'Yeh, I've learned rather more about your Vikings. It's a "blood eagle" isn't it?'

'Not quite. The ritual killings like the one Ivar the Boneless is supposed to have carried out on king Ælla, were done through the back, not the front. Morten has put his own mark on it. When did it happen and where did they find him?'

'Just yesterday. The press hasn't been informed yet. He was found on the lawn at his home by a terrified neighbour. Apparently Penhaligon took great pride in his lawn.'

'All that blood won't help the grass. I guess this is a warning to anyone who fails to deliver what they promised to Morten or his masters?'

'We assume so. And we're pretty sure who that ultimate master is. Ever heard of Oleg Zinchenko?'

'The Russian oligarch, or is it mafioso?'

'Both. A very powerful and dangerous customer. Our other friends, the ones who tried to save Forth's reputation, have become more cooperative and shared some of their intelligence about Morten and Zinchenko. There's a list of crimes as long as your arm for Zinchenko, everything from extortion to murder, but nothing provable. We even have a possible identity for your man Morten.' Anna was even more attentive. 'We think his real name is Afanasiy Volshevnikov.'

'I think you'll find that's still an alias,' said Anna. 'It means "immortal wizard".'

'Given everything that's happened, nothing would surprise me!' Nikki responded. 'Anyway, this Volshevnikov studied pre-Germanic religion in Vienna in the late eighties. He turns up next as a member of the Russian spetsnaz in the First Chechen war of the mid-1990s. He then disappears for some years before re-surfacing in Russia again, as a special instructor to elite spetsnaz members in Moscow around 2010. A number of informants call him a "prikhvosten", I think that's like a henchman, for Oleg Zinchenko, and he has a terrifying reputation even though he never appears to have used a gun.'

'Quite a CV,' Anna replied. She mused that they had, perhaps, been fortunate that, at Dunwich, Morten had been distracted sufficiently to have his powers minimised, and that he had decided Anna was worth keeping alive when they'd met again. Anna handed the photos back to Nikki. 'How confident are you of catching him?' she asked.

'Well John says his luck's bound to run out. Me, I don't think we'll get him. He seems to have any number of aliases, and, despite his distinctive appearance, he slipped out of the country after Dunwich. Though we know how,' Nikki added. 'We found blood in a house nearby and there was a car missing. And, later that night, a Zinchenko-owned container ship left Felixstowe early. Anyway, I've got some more positive news.'

'Which is?'

'I'll be starting a new job next month. Detective Inspector on one of the Met's MITs, that's the Major Investigation Teams that cover homicides in London.'

'That's great news. I think it even calls for a special celebration. I'll get you another Guinness and I'll have a tequila. You off tonight?' Nikki said she was. 'Why don't we eat,' The Bookies had a great French bistro-style menu, 'then we could pay a visit to Plush.'

Chapter 66

Anna intended getting up early the following day, but overslept after a late night and, for her, a heavy margarita intake. She had a long journey ahead, but it was quicker on the bike than it had been by car. Nevertheless, she decided to break it on the shores of Loch Lomond. The following day she was back on the ferry to Colonsay. She'd arranged to meet Niall McNeil at the Colonsay Hotel.

'Alex, or should I say Anna? It's good to see you again.'

'I'm really sorry for the deception. It was more for your protection than mine, you'll have seen the kind of people we were dealing with.'

'I certainly have, and it also explains your knowledge about history. It's okay, we understood. I've been to see him already by the way. He's far less surprised about all this than me.'

'Is he expecting us?'

'Yeh. Shall we go in the Land Rover? Nice bike by the way.'

They drove the short distance to Roger Inkpen's house and the professor greeted them at the door. 'Anna, Niall, come in, come in.'

Sun was streaming through the windows of the cottage as Anna told them about the hunt for the crown and Ivar's treasure. When she'd finished, she said, 'I suppose you've heard about Gervase Penhaligon?' They had. His death had been reported in the media, though the grisly details had been kept back. Anna explained about the blood eagle.

'Poor man,' said Inkpen. 'He was a fool, but he didn't deserve that. His killer seems both extraordinary and ruthless. I hope you won't see him again.'

'I've also brought you this,' said Anna as she reached into her rucksack and got out a small silver Thor's hammer. 'It belonged to Magnus. He always kept it on his desk. It came from a dig he was on back in the 1980s in Sweden.'

'Yes, I remember,' said Inkpen. 'He worked at Birka on a

number of occasions and was one of the first people to support the idea the Birka warrior was a woman. But I think this,' he indicated the hammer, 'he brought back from the nearby island of Adelsö. Thank you so much. I'll cherish his memory every time I look at it.'

Together they walked to the beach at Kiloran before all driving back to the hotel for dinner. Niall would be staying with his parents and so took Inkpen back to his cottage. Before he left, Inkpen clasped Anna's hand. 'I knew Magnus hadn't been wrong about you, my dear. You certainly have exceptional qualities, some of them ones even he didn't fully realise.' There was a twinkle in the eye of the professor that suggested he knew more than he was telling her.

'Thank you. We certainly couldn't have cracked the code without your help,' and she kissed him on the cheek.

She caught the ferry at lunchtime on Wednesday, deciding not to have an overnight stop, and arrived in Aldeburgh at two o'clock the following morning. She was surprised to find Oliver and Gordon still up, consulting various websites in the library. 'Anna, lovely to have you back,' said Cloote. 'We're going to have a party!'

Chapter 67

Cloote's party was scheduled for Midsummer's Eve. 'Definitely the most appropriate day for a party at Summerland,' was his reasoning. They invited everyone who had helped in their quest, and most replied that they'd come. Roger Inkpen and Niall McNeil sent apologies and Freja Kristensen was at a conference in Japan, but her daughter Nadja would be there.

'There might be some interesting encounters,' was Cloote's summary. In addition to the three of them Anula, Nadja, Nora, Nils, and Rasmus would be staying at Summerland. Nikki, Pete Railton, Caoimhe O'Driscoll, Thyra Nyström, Emil Sigurdsson, plus Scott Rimes, Roly, and Asayo Negishi would stay at the nearby Brudenell Hotel, courtesy of Cloote. Other members of Scott's team, and Anula's colleague Devan Patel, whose cottage they'd 'borrowed' after Anna's escape, were also expected. A large marquee arrived and was erected on the back lawn. Catering was being done by Cloote and Co. from their London store, with Oliver paying special attention to the wine list.

The day before, Anna went to Heathrow on her bike to meet Nadja. She'd cut her hair much shorter and dyed it a vivid orange which made her easy to spot. 'Anna! Great to see you and thank you so much for inviting me. Sarah sends her love by the way and says she'll only forgive you for not telling her what was really going on if you come back to Copenhagen sometime soon.'

'Thanks. I'd love to if I can. What are you going to be doing after your finals?'

'I'm not sure yet. They've asked me if I'd like to do a post-grad, but I might take a year out to do some travelling or something else.'

They reached the bike and Anna strapped Nadja's rucksack to the back. 'Here. You'll need to wear this,' she said, handing her a spare helmet and her retro goggles.

'This is *so* cool,' Nadja replied. 'I thought it's the kind of bike you'd have. My friends were really jealous when they found out I knew you by the way.' Anna didn't reply and felt a bit embarrassed at Nadja's obvious hero worship.

*

By late afternoon on Midsummer's Eve the party goers were arriving. Gordon had set up a PA system which, for the present, was playing soothing classical music. He was now walking quite well with the support of a single cane. 'We'll have something a bit livelier later,' he told Anna, 'but maybe not too much Slayer! By the way we're going to have a long holiday from next month.'

'Where to?'

'We'll start in India and make our way further east. We could be away for some time, though we'll be back for the opening of the exhibition. So, will you stay on here, or do you have other plans?'

'Not really. I guess that's okay. I can always let you know if things change.'

'Thanks, Anna. I hope we'll stay close friends now all this is over.'

'I hope so too, Gordon. You've both been amazing.'

'Oh! Then I hope you won't be annoyed at what Oliver has planned for later.' Without telling her what it was he went to supervise the delivery of some fresh pastries.

When everyone had arrived Cloote called them into the garden. 'Welcome, everybody. We've been part of an unusual and unique experience. Tragically three totally innocent people have lost their lives and so, first, I'd like us to take a moment to remember them.' After the moment's silence he continued. 'As I said all of you have played a part, but I wanted to single out two people who I've come to know and respect in the past few months. I hope they'll forgive me for doing this. Anna, Anula, would you come over here, please.'

They did as Oliver asked. He then called Gordon, Nora, and Nadja forward. The two women had changed into long white gowns and held goblets; Rees was holding a sword. 'I don't in any way suggest this is a re-enactment of an actual Viking ceremony,' continued Cloote. 'I've devised it purely for my own, and hopefully your, enjoyment. The words are my adaptation of the *Hávamál*, which means "sayings of the high one" and is our most important source about Norse philosophy. The verses are attributed to Odin and are an account of how the god won the runes, and the Ljóðatal, a list of magic chants or spells.'

Gordon handed Cloote the seiðrstafr and he chanted his adaptation of the poem. When he'd finished, he said, 'I now call on Frigg and Freyja to witness the rebirth of our sisters here before us. Come forward Anula and come forth the first cup-bearer.' Anula stepped forward and Nora handed her a cup. 'Drink from the cup, dear sister, and accept your re-naming. Henceforth those here present will know you as Sigrun, our Rune of Victory over evil and bigotry.' Anula drank from the cup and handed it back to Nora. 'Now, sister Anna, come forward and come forth the second cup bearer.' Nadja came forward with her cup, from which Anna drank. 'Drink from the cup, dear sister, and accept your re-naming. Henceforth those here present will know you as Herja, the devastator and destroyer of worlds.' Cloote then led everyone in a round of applause. Both women looked rather embarrassed.

'I can see you as a Sigrun,' Anna said to Anula, 'but I'm not sure I'm a devastator!'

'You certainly are for some people,' Anula replied.

The party music changed to something more appropriate, and more to Anna's taste, with tracks by some of the bands who base their music on the early pagan religions of Northern Europe such as Skáld, Danheim and Heilung. 'Fucking weird, man,' Anna heard Roly telling Nikki, with whom he seemed to be striking up a slightly unlikely friendship.

Later Gordon changed the music to more typical party stuff, from the sixties to the present. Copious quantities of food and drink were being consumed, and some people were dancing on the lawn. 'This takes me back a bit,' Pete Railton was telling Thyra and Emil, who were highly impressed that he'd seen bands like the Clash and the Sex Pistols in the seventies.

Nadja was making friends with everyone, especially Nora, and was practising her MLE slang. As the evening wore on, and she consumed more vodka Red Bulls, she started telling anyone who would listen that, 'I'm totes off my tits!'

Anna was pleased to have a much longer talk with Asayo. She found out she was bisexual and had gone to university in Japan at the age of twelve, gaining her doctorate at just eighteen. 'There you go,' said Anna tongue in cheek, 'just proves history is so much superior to maths. No way could a twelve-year-old pass a history entrance.'

Asayo laughed. 'It did have its drawbacks. I wasn't exactly welcomed into most social activities. Mind you, when I did, I was pretty wild. A few people got quite shocked, and I didn't conform to what my parents and professors wanted. After I got my PhD, I travelled the world for a while before meeting Scott. The things others thought unconventional, he welcomed, and the kinds of jobs he found were really interesting, but yours has been the most bizarre of the lot.'

Anna noticed that Rasmus was standing rather shyly next to them. 'Rasmus let me introduce Asayo. She's a mathematical and computer genius. And Rasmus will be very modest and tell you he's just a historian but he's far better than me because he can concentrate, where I'm all over the place.' Anna left Rasmus with Asayo as she could see he was very interested in getting to know her.

The evening warmed up, with Thyra proving a hit with some somewhat unexpected pogoing, before Emil entertained everyone using Oliver's electric keyboard. His repertoire included everything from boogie-woogie, through rock-and-roll to the classics. He also accompanied some less than brilliant karaoke, that Anna avoided, though Nikki's Tina Turner impersonation was a high point.

Around 1 a.m. Anna felt she needed to wake herself up and thought some exercises in the gym might help. Despite her ordeal in the building, she'd overcome her reticence about going back inside. But as she opened the door, she realised the gym was occupied. The unmistakable sound of two people having vigorous sex was clear. She peeped round the door. Asayo had her back to the multi-gym with her arms on the bars. In front of her was Rasmus. Both were naked. Asayo caught sight of Anna but didn't seem embarrassed. Instead, she gave her a big wink and thrust forward even more onto her lover. Anna smiled back and quickly shut the door. 'Oh well, it'd better be a quick jog round the block.'

When she got back and had a shower, it was after three and the sun would soon be rising. Anna went back to the garden where Anula was beginning to doze off in a chair. 'Hey,' said Anna, 'you're flagging.'

'It's the typical doctor's lack of sleep,' said Anula. 'I'm used to being awake at this time though.'

'Well, I'm getting quite hyper. Come on, let's go for a walk and watch the sun come up.'

They went down Crag Path, beside the beach, and then along the road towards Thorpeness. They talked about the various ways Midsummer was celebrated and Anna told Anula that 'For Wiccans, Midsummer is one of the four "Lesser Sabbats" or "Low Holidays". Some of them call the day Litha, the day of the Lord of Light, and many pagans bathe skyclad under the sun while honouring Sol.'

After a short distance they went onto the beach towards the Scallop, the fifteen-foot-high stainless-steel sculpture by Maggi Hambling dedicated to Benjamin Britten. Its two interlocking shells bear the words, 'I hear those voices that will not be drowned', taken from Britten's opera *Peter Grimes*. 'I've got an idea,' said Anna, who was beginning to feel rather manic. 'You know Botticelli's *Birth of Venus*? Get your camera out.' With that Anna took off her clothes and jumped up onto the sculpture. Standing on the lower shell she struck a pose to imitate the painting, right hand across her breasts, left hand demurely covering her crotch. 'I'm afraid my hair doesn't work but it's as near as I can get.'

'Wow, Anna,' said Anula indicating the new tattoo, 'When did you get that!'

'Oh, I'd been planning it for a while. Like it?'

'Yeh, I guess so.'

As she took some photos, she shook her head at her friend's brazenness. Anna changed her pose to something more confrontational. Left hand on her hip and right clenched in a fist above her head. She climbed down from the shell and was thinking about her next step when Anula's phone suddenly rang.

'Yes, what, okay, where? Probably about forty minutes? Okay see you soon. I'm really sorry, Anna, there's been a bad smash on the A12. I'll need to go to Ipswich to operate on a couple of the casualties.'

Perhaps its fate, thought Anna as she put her clothes back on.

They walked quickly back to the house and Anna watched as Anula drove off in her small red car.

Chapter 68

Anna got a few hours' sleep before getting up around midday. Gordon was already busy supervising the party clear up. As she made breakfast, she was joined by a very perky Asayo. 'Rasmus might be a bit quiet normally,' she said, 'but get him in bed and he's an animal!'

Anna laughed. 'I'm glad you enjoyed yourself. You've probably worn him out.'

'Oh, I think I'll manage to get him to spring into life quite soon,' she replied and went back upstairs with a supply of strong coffee and orange juice.

Anna thought she'd better check on Nadja, as she'd been put to bed by Gordon after getting quite drunk. She looked a little pale but was otherwise fine and accepted a tray of toast, coffee, and yoghurt from Anna. As Anna was about to leave, she said, 'You really should tell her you know.'

'Tell who, what?' Anna replied.

'Anula of course. I can see what you feel about her.'

Anna didn't reply.

*

Later that afternoon Anna took a long walk with Nora and Nils out to Snape and back. They'd never visited this part of the country before, and Nils was fascinated by the landscape and artistic connections. ''S'bit school ain't it?' said Nora, who was less than riveted by the countryside.

Nils groaned but still gave her a kiss as Anna cuffed her and called her a philistine. 'There's your boyfriend going all round the world to protect nature and all you can do is say is it's a bit boring!'

Though the walk cheered her up for a while Anna still felt down. Nadja's words were gnawing inside her and she couldn't decide what to do. If Anula hadn't got that call perhaps? But then professing her love on Aldeburgh beach in a state of nudity might not have been a great idea either. 'Fucking, fuck it!' she said out loud. She went up to her room and played her music. This invariably raised her spirits, even if she played the most extreme or depressing songs. She worked her way through Slayer and other metal bands before deciding to change tack to some women artists. By now it was getting dark, and the playlist reached Sharon van Etten's 'Your Love is Killing Me'.

Anna sprung up from the bed. She pulled on a pair of Kevlar jeans and motorcycle boots and grabbed a tee-shirt from her wardrobe. It bore the lines: 'I was born in a storm. I have lightning in my soul, thunder in my heart and chaos in my bones.' She ran downstairs. Several people were around in the hallway and library.

'Anna. Where ...?' but before Gordon could finish his sentence, the door slammed.

Nadja joined Gordon in the hall and slipped her arm through his. 'I think *I* know where she's going,' she said.

*

Anula was in bed, but not asleep, when she heard the familiar sound of Anna's bike approaching. She got up and went downstairs, opening the door just as Anna slammed her helmet down on the bike's seat. Anula was about to say something when Anna grabbed both of her arms by the biceps and pushed her firmly back into the hallway. Just before the staircase Anna's mouth met Anula's in a frenzied and passionate kiss. For an instant Anula's entire body tensed before relaxing into Anna's embrace. She was forced down onto the stairs and Anna's mouth left hers.

'Anna, I thought you'd never ...'

Anna's hands were now inside Anula's shirt, and she responded by unbuttoning Anna's jeans. It wasn't until the jeans were down by her ankles, and Anula was grasping her buttocks, that they realised the door was still wide open. Anula sprang up and slammed it closed with a laugh. Anna kicked off her jeans and they both raced upstairs.

*

Later they were relaxing in each other's arms. 'I really fancy …' Anula began.

'Me?' enquired Anna.

'Yes, you, but also a drink. What would you like?'

'I could murder a margarita if you could manage it.'

'I think that could be arranged. Why don't you put some music on?'

When Anula came back with the drinks, margarita for Anna, G and T for her, plus a large bucket of ice, St Vincent was playing. 'Did I tell you?' Anna said. 'Someone was playing "Slow Disco" when I found Magnus.'

'No, you didn't. You can put something else on you know.'

'No, it's fine. I think it's just that I hear her at really important points in my life.'

They listened to her first album, *Marry Me*. When it got to 'The Apocalypse Song' Anna said, 'Do you think you might be ready for a bit of that?'

'A bit of what?' said Anula warily.

'Little death,' said Anna as her hands slipped down Anula's body. She reached over to the ice bucket and took out a large cube. 'You remember that scene from *Do the Right Thing*?' Anula said she knew exactly what she meant. 'Then close your eyes,' Anna commanded as she touched Anula's neck with the ice cube.

By the time they relaxed again the playlist had reached the *St Vincent* album and the track 'I Prefer Your Love'. 'When are you due back at the hospital?' Anna asked.

'Two. So, we've still got a couple of hours. Would you like something to eat?'

'Hmmm,' said Anna.

'No! I mean food,' said Anula, and then in a mock schoolmistressy voice and wagging her finger, added, 'You're a very naughty girl!'

They shared a buffet of olives, hummus, pitta bread and salad, washed down with juice. 'I like the tee shirt,' said Anula. 'Is it a quote?'

'Nearly,' said Anna. 'It's adapted from the poet Nikita Gill,

have you heard of her?' Anula confessed she hadn't. 'She's really popular on the net, she's often called an Instapoet.'

'She sounds good, got any more quotes?'

Anna thought for a minute and then her face looked more serious. 'Yes. I have. This sums up how I feel. How I *really* feel, I mean. "You are every beautiful thing that has ever happened to me wrapped in a person. You may think you are ordinary, but to me you are as magical as the ocean."'

For a while Anula could say nothing. Then tears started welling up. 'Oh Anna, my love. That's the most beautiful thing anyone has ever said to me.' They embraced again, tears of joy flowing down their cheeks. Finally, Anula had to prepare to go to work.

'Here,' said Anna. 'You take my tee shirt. Give me one of yours.'

Anula gave her a bright blue Sri Lankan cricket team shirt with the gold lion emblazoned on the front.

'Call me?' asked Anula.

'Of course.'

'Come back tomorrow night?'

'Yes.' They kissed and, with that, Anna got back on the Harley.

'Wait!' called Anula. Anna paused as she rushed back inside. 'Okay. Now you can go.'

Anna smiled to herself as she realised what Anula had done. She started the bike; several people were staring at them. As she roared away, 'Rebel Girl' resounded across the quayside.